A Stitch in Time

A DI Murray novel
Book 9

*Hope you enjoy the
adventure with D.I. Murray!*

Best Wishes

Michael Patterson

Cover design and layout by:

JAG Designs

ISBN: 9798396340510

Twitter: @DI_Murraynovels

Instagram: detectivestevemurray

www.detectivestevemurray.co.uk

Since the first Inspector Murray book was released in early 2017 the last few years have been filled with fascinating adventures.

Lots of wonderful characters have come and gone in the series. In the numerous storylines several have retired and others quietly moved away. But let's be perfectly honest...... most met gruesome, grisly deaths.

Ha ha ha... isn't that all part of the lovely art of storytelling. The beauty and magical, mysterious make-believe of entering into the unknown. Though aren't we also truly grateful that we don't live in Steven Murray's Edinburgh? At this rate, only Midsomer has more murders per capita per square mile.

On behalf of DI Murray and his team - thanks to each of you for the loyalty and ever increasing support along the way. I hope that you continue to enjoy the journey and also the new characters in this latest instalment. Out of curiosity, let's see how long they last!

Kind regards and happy reading.

Michael P.

A Stitch in Time

Prologue

"I've been down to Saint Andrew to pay for my sins. Love, come save me. Love, come save me soon"

- Bedouin Soundclash

St. Andrew's Day - 30th of November 2017.

The Athens of the North certainly knows how to capture life's beauty in equal measure. It's a city of passion and of apathy. It hosts both Prince and Pauper. It is exceptionally conservative, yet displays a sombre theatricality. Its aesthetic and political heart still beat in its small historic core comprising of the medieval Old Town and the Georgian New Town, and much of its impressive physical presence is derived from its picturesque setting high amongst crag and hill. On a daily basis its landmark buildings with their towering spires of precious stone, inspire, enthuse and uplift the local spirits. In Edinburgh, people are equally split between admiration and trepidation.

As many of Auld Reekie's residents seek an extra ten cosy minutes in bed, two professional police officers have risen early.

"I didn't mean to wake you," Barbra Furlong said in soft hushed tones as Steven Murray made his way into their en-suite bathroom.

Wearing only his boxer shorts, it was there that the tousled-haired inspector found his partner gently brushing her pearly white teeth. She greeted him with a sunny, playful tap on the nose and an ever increasing frothy smile. Outside a strong, blustery wind gained force as the watery alphabet of clouds drummed down onto the frosted, decorative window.

"I was trying so hard to be quiet," she mumbled, wiping at her mouth. She added thoughtfully... "Did you know, Steven, that your fingers have fingertips, yet your toes don't have toe-tips? So I tiptoed in here because I couldn't tip-finger! Mind boggling, isn't it?"

Her mischievous, infectious grin lit up the low ceilinged room as her pleasing reflection bounced sensually off the glossy wall mounted cabinet mirror.

Murray shook his head at those bewildering words.

"It's okay, you didn't wake me. Memories woke me."

His lips began to tremble with pent-up emotion. That was when he placed his hands delicately on Barbra's flawless bare shoulders and kissed her softly on the cheek.

"Well, I hope they were good ones?"

"Good ones tend not to wake people." He shrugged. "In fact, I think they often do the opposite." He continued to watch over her for a further period of time, before anxiously asking. "Do you ever think about us, Barbra?"

With only a three-quarter length negligée on, Detective Chief Inspector Furlong immediately placed a gentle hand either side of his rough, stubbled, world-weary face and teasingly ran her smooth fingers down from his eyebrows to his lips, before adding...

"US… is all I think about DI Murray."

"And what about memories of years gone by?" He persisted. "Our challenges these past twelve months. Do you ever think about those?"

"Steven," she whispered. "I think about now and I think about tomorrow. I even think about this throbbing abscess that I've woke up to. But I don't give any thought to yesterday."

"Sadly, *yesterday,* is what continually eats away at me."

His lips quivered as she witnessed his genuine concern.

"Yesterday eats away at everybody," she said. Wiping a delicate tear from his cheek. "That's exactly why I don't talk about it." Then attempting a cunning preemptive strike of her very own, the attractive, easygoing woman looked lovingly at him. "This is going to be a GREAT morning," she yelled. "In fact, why don't we go back to bed for a minute or two?"

On hearing those words, Steven Murray's eyes rose in pleasant unexpected surprise.

"Yes, a minute or two sounds about right," he grinned. Offering the daring Barbra Furlong, a cheeky, playful wink into the bargain.

Bilton Lane was a narrow pedestrian passageway. It ran directly off Lothian Rd at its junction with Stow Street. Walk along its cobblestoned footpath and you'd soon be introduced to the untended back courts of its impressive historic tenement buildings. Each one lined up bravely to stand guard and defend the busy thoroughfare. Street lights flickered and danced in the darkness. Whilst at busy junctions, red and amber changed smoothly to green. Thus allowing the early morning traffic to flow freely and remain oblivious to the dark, sinister events that had occurred nearby.

An array of varied storefronts were packed with numerous Christmas displays, yet devoid of paying customers. In fairness, it had only just turned 6.03am and the in-car radio announcer had confirmed to its Police Scotland occupants that it was the coldest day of the year so far. The sky was overcast with cloud and the temperature had fallen as low as minus four overnight.

This morning the lane's solemn, gloomy entrance had been quickly cordoned off and festively decorated. The arctic white tape with the bold, blue lettering warned:

Crime Scene - Do Not Enter and celebrations were muted.

The car radio was switched off and the CSI tape had been hoisted high as Murray and DC Brooks ducked their heads and made their way along the alleyway. There they would be greeted by a multitude of uniformed officers and forensic personnel. On arrival, those individuals were already busy scouring for clues and doing the basics, while the inspector familiarised himself with the so-called crime scene.

"Why all the rubbish?" He'd questioned abruptly, spotting an assortment of debris lying strewn across the ground. He turned around and swiftly discovered the prime suspect.

The highlighted font on the old label was clear: **Please use the blue bins to recycle card packaging, cardboard boxes, magazines, newspapers, comics, office paper, brochures, yellow pages, junk mail, envelopes, drinks cans, food tins, empty aerosol cans and plastic bottles.**

"So how do you mistakenly put a dead body in one?"

A few others looked up to hear Murray add… "It states quite clearly what's deemed appropriate to go in there. Some people just take downright liberties these days," the man hollered at the top of his voice.

Any neighbours not aware of a strong police presence in the area, certainly would be now. Whilst DC Brooks stood rooted to the spot thinking - Was he for real?

"Please ignore him, Constable," echoed the wise words and soothing baritone voice that belonged to the experienced, yet part-time pathologist. The genial man gave both officers a cheery wave.

Andrew Gordon had lost the ring finger on his left hand over three decades ago. As a keen, amateur football referee back then, he'd been hanging up a net on goalposts. But when he proceeded to jump down, it caught on a nail attached to the crossbar and ripped his finger clean off. Nowadays he happily laughed about it. Which matched his general larger than life attitude.

Andy was a naturally friendly and helpful individual. Officially he'd retired a few years previous, but liked to take advantage of the more lucrative money on offer from the emergency call-outs and holiday cover, etc.

"A friggin' naked body at that!" Murray announced.

Brooks was just off the phone and quickly beginning to wisen up to her inspector's showboating. She was gradually taking his remarks with a pinch of salt. Yes, he was indeed quite a character.

"Sure it's dismembered," Murray continued. "Which is helpful. But need I remind the individual responsible, it's still in the wrong bin. You can't have slim, slender, hairy testicles rubbing up alongside the very latest Ian Rankin bestseller. That's sacrilege - plain and simple!"

Everybody instantly grinned, then equally as quickly returned to shivering in the cold.

"So, Doc. What do you have for us?"

"Well as you so eloquently put it, Inspector. He's in the wrong coloured bin for a start. However, as a little side note, I've actually just won forty pounds thanks to you. Because I bet two of your officers that you would begin your opening observation...... with that very rant."

Brooks stiffened and immediately held up her hands to protest her innocence at being one of the named pair. The increasingly wealthy pathologist followed up that statement with a self congratulatory belly laugh. Murray frowned and his latest protégé cheekily added...

"Oh to be so predictable, sir."

A fully fledged smile desperately wanted to make an appearance, but the officer wisely decided against it.

"Yes, quite," the inspector said, slightly crestfallen. "Doctor Gordon this is DC Brooks. We call her..."

"Babbling?" the Doc guessed, seemingly randomly.

"Stuff off!" Murray sighed. "What's happening here?"

Neither Andrew Gordon nor Janice Brooks made Steven Murray any the wiser that they'd met several times before at crime scenes while she was in uniform. It felt right to give the man a taste of the medicine that he so obviously often gave out to others. Was it karma?

"Okay, clever clogs. But what can you tell us about our poor victim?" Murray asked. Trying to do empathy and sincerity - yet failing miserably on both counts. "And what in the name of the wee man is that smell?"

"From first impressions," Gordon began. "He's been ripped, torn and wrenched apart like a Christmas turkey. One that's been bleached and rinsed for good measure."

"I see that you're feeling exceptionally humorous and filled with wisecracks today, Andy. But how about you give us something significant that may be helpful to us."

"Oh, that reminds me, Steven. The man's funny bone was also shattered. But other than that - Nothing!"

The doctor stifled a laugh at his own remark. DI Murray shook his head and the 'merry old pathologist,' offered the affable Janice Brooks, a secretive sly wink.

"So the smell is obviously bleach. Had he been trying to get rid or remove incriminating evidence, Andy?"

"On initial inspection, it wouldn't appear so, Steven. I think they poured it over the body to send a message."

"Isn't that the empty bottle by your feet, sir?" Janice alerted him.

DI Murray read the slogan on the Domestos label aloud. Although it was popular enough that he knew it off by heart... "Kills all known germs! Well it certainly did in this instance," he continued to remark.

Brooks shook her head, trying not to encourage him.

"I suspect it would've been a very painful death, Inspector," the Doc added. "Because what I can tell you is that this individual, whoever they may be. Was definitely alive when their dismemberment began. How long he lasted after that would just be random guesswork I'm afraid. Isn't it fascinating that the killer felt the need to dissect the body into numerous body parts though. Don't you think?"

"I don't know about fascinating, but I certainly think it's personal, very personal indeed," Murray asserted. "Something seems off. I know it's in front of me for sure, but I'm missing it."

Brooks monitored the interaction between both men. What she found fascinating was the mutual respect and camaraderie that so blatantly existed between them.

"Whoever left the bin here obviously didn't realise it was St. Andrew's Day and that all the council refuge workers had a Bank holiday. Which was a bit of good fortune for us," Steven Murray announced.

The man eventually thanked Andy Gordon, mumbled something about this being the third male murder victim in the last two weeks and started to walk away.

Soon afterward, as was often the case, he began to whistle. Janice, although easily three decades younger than her inspector, knew that she recognised the upbeat tune immediately. Though as much as she tried, she couldn't recall its title. She eventually relented and shook her head. Giving Steven Murray the all too familiar look that said... *Okay, I surrender!*

"Sorry to be so predictable once again," he grinned. "But I simply couldn't resist teasing you, Constable."

'Babbling' smiled and continued to shake her head in disbelief. Her new partner soon began to shimmy his broad shoulders and belt out the 1970's classic…

"Oh, yes they call him the Streak (Boogity, boogity). Fastest thing on two feet (Boogity, boogity)."

With a straight face, Janice Brooks suddenly asked…

"Weren't you once a Mormon Bishop?"

"Indeed I was, young lady." Knowing that piece of redundant information was now public knowledge amongst all of the other officers after he their last case.

"But you knew that already, Constable. Didn't you?"

"Yes I did, but I just wanted to double check, sir. Because I'd have been far more impressed if you'd started singing… *Dem bones. Dem bones. Dem dry bones. Dem bones. Dem bones. Dem dry bones. Dem bones. Dem bones. Dem dry bones… Hear the word of the Lord!*"

At that the amiable pairing enjoyed a good laugh and Murray offered up an impromptu, off-key version of…

"Getting to know you, getting to know all about you."

Brooks wasn't entirely sure he was dedicating the classic song to her. Because at the precise moment he began to sing, the devilish Inspector Murray displayed an extra-wide mischievous grin and stood beside the large blue refuse bin. Had this weirdly warped detective just dedicated those lines to the severed corpse inside? It was after all that particular individual that they still had to find out a heck of a lot more about.

That was when Steven Murray received a text from Joe Hanlon to return urgently to the station. As he began to depart the scene, the bold Andrew Gordon simply shook his head, added two crisp twenty pound notes to his wallet and suitably revelled in the moment.

One

"They're just ordinary people fighting all their demons away. Because some heroes don't wear capes."

- Callum Beattie

It was mid-morning when the trio heard the determined voice on the recording not only threaten to smash the woman's elbow with a hammer, but to also crack open her skull. Given the harrowing screams that followed, it could be assumed that the man carried out those particularly violent threats. As they listened intently, another female begged for mercy. Her unrelenting cries went unheeded and after a while, several powerful heavy thuds seemingly pounded down upon her. Those listening could only imagine what was happening. Over time her pleas lessened and eventually all fell silent.

Next up, the officers heard what appeared to be the disturbing rape and strangulation of a terrified woman. The highly aroused male voice grunted, groaned and climaxed. Whilst the frenzied pleading of his victim for her own mother to save her, gave them a clear indication of her age and undoubted vulnerability. Within seconds, the unmistakable explosion of a single gunshot ended the proceedings.

Who had made these vile recordings and how long ago? And why were they marked... 'FAO' DI Murray? Did the inspector have a personal attachment to any of the victims? Who in fact were the victims? It was probably more likely he had history with one of their assailants. Or maybe the whistleblower that sent the audio, simply knew that he was a detective that cared. A man that could be trusted to investigate matters further.

Joseph Hanlon, Janice Brooks and Steven Murray were the only officers to have heard the extremely disturbing and worrying contents on the memory stick.

"I thought that you would want to access it right away, sir. It's not every day that you get a package handed in to you."

"I appreciate that, Sergeant. Thank you."

Steven Murray was fooling no one. Janice Brooks knew that the men were close friends outside work. But it was good to see her inspector keep things professional.

"If these attacks had been carried out on different women and at different times," Murray mentioned. "Lizzie would normally help us check it out. But she's swamped under at present with all these killings in the past couple of weeks."

The small parcel had been delivered into the station's front desk by a motorcycle courier, forty minutes previously. Currently that was all they knew and had to go on. Was the recording of one brutal sadistic thug out there over time? Or a gang of sick individuals?

"Leave it with me, sir." 'Sherlock' nodded. "I'll do it."

Murray said nothing. He knew that if Sgt. Hanlon was willing to run with the ball, he'd come up trumps. What that eventually looks like - who knows! But the inspector had every confidence that Joe would uncover deeds noteworthy and valuable to the case. Assuming that is, that there's even a case to answer. Though based on those limited sound bites, it was surely only a matter of time before something turned up. Murray sincerely hoped that it was *something* and not *somebody*.

Eight months ago an expectant DI Sandra Kerr and DC Andrew Curry had sat terrified on Sandy's settee in her modest Lochgelly home. Both officers had been held captive by a drug dealer named, Habib Abdullah.

Subsequently, Abdullah had been overcome and killed with a knife to the throat by Inspector Steven Murray, though not before the psychotic individual had time to shoot and wound 'Drew Curry. Paramedics at the scene had given the young officer a 50/50 chance of survival.

Today a heavily pregnant Sandra Kerr sat up anxiously in her warm, cosy hospital bed. Her baby was a week overdue and she'd been taken into her local maternity unit to monitor a few concerns that had been raised. Meanwhile across the water back in Edinburgh, Curry had thankfully survived. He too, sat up warm and cosy - though these days, he was now confined to a wheelchair!

Since his shooting back in the springtime, Drew had undergone multiple intense surgeries. Unfortunately the experienced surgeons could do nothing for him. The bullet had severed his spine and left him paralysed from the waist down.

After surviving that attempt on his life, the officer was informed that he would never walk again. It was at that point, in his wisdom, that he chose to exit the Force. So he'd quit and was gradually adjusting to life outside of Police Scotland.

When he had vacated hospital back in July after ten weeks of treatment, including several protracted rounds of physiotherapy and counselling - on his release day, he'd been informed that a certain DI Murray would be picking him up. That was when he reminded staff that he stayed in a grubby, rundown council flat. It was several storeys up, in one of Edinburgh's less salubrious areas. How on earth was this going to work? They repeatedly told him that the inspector had regularly assured them that everything was in hand. Of course, he had! As well he would. What was going on here?

Drew Curry's relationship with his parents had broken down about two years previously. It was when they'd cashed in on their four-bedroomed, detached house in the shadow of Scotland's international rugby stadium.

They had sold up their stunning Murrayfield villa and moved to super cheap Bulgaria. There they instantly began to love life again and selfishly cut themselves off from any remaining family and friends back in Scotland. As they often say... 'Nowt so queer as folk!'

During his hospitalisation, 'Kid' Curry had received regular visits from his colleagues Steven Murray, DCI Furlong and DI Sandra Kerr, who to this very day continued to feel guilty about his shooting.

"You're a hero. He's a hero," she'd continually remind all the wonderful medical staff at the hospital. "He saved my children, my twins," she'd announce at regular intervals between breaking down in tears. Her ability to keep her emotions in check had changed dramatically. She blamed pregnancy and her erratic hormones.

The doctors were all aware of the man's valiant heroics. They'd been well documented in all of Scotland's national newspapers. So much so, Murray's journalist 'friend,' A. L. Lawrie, gave 'Drew a special two page write-up in Edinburgh's very own weekly Gazette.

By mid-July after all the praise, hype and adulation had died down, reality kicked in. All the troubled 'Kid' could now think about was what he'd do for a living and where he would stay? He was at breaking point. Fully depressed and heartbroken, if truth be told.

That day, all those months ago in Sandra Kerr's home - his impulsive actions had changed his life forever and not necessarily for the better. Being a hero was all good and well, but it didn't pay the bills. It didn't provide any financial security moving forward and this young man had high expectations. He dearly hoped that he still had a thirty year working life ahead of him.

At that point the so-called hero had no home. He had no job. No partner. And as he saw it - No future. That was what Andrew Curry had to occupy his worried fragmented mind on a daily basis.

However one of the few things that cheered him up, that made him smile and got him through his darker days were personal visits. Two in particular always seemed to do the trick.

The first was from his newly 'adopted' nieces, Carly and Stephanie Kerr. Their tiny precious smiles were infectious and they'd always visit wearing Superman capes in honour of their 'only' Uncle. A man that they'd always consider *'their hero.'* He had saved one of their precious lives that day. Who knew which one Abdullah would have killed, had he been given the chance.

Drew loved to see the girls. They made him laugh with their crazy high-octane antics and provided great therapy. Either from their various failed attempts at throwing grapes into the tiny fruit bowl by his bedside, or from their much loved attempts at calling him Uncle Andrew... 'Cunc Anoo' and 'El Do Do,' were among his favourite efforts.

Although all his team and several other friends from out-with work had visited regularly at times over the weeks and months. The other STAND-OUT visit which perked him up the most, was also the one that made him regularly blush with embarrassment. Who knew that after her short-lived dalliance with Inspector Murray, that 'Radical' Lizzie would be more than happy to come out and play with a brand new paraplegic?

During their time together, Steven Murray recognised like everyone else, her ability and determined focus with anything electronic or IT related. However what most people wouldn't know about Lizzie was just how much she cared for individuals. They never saw her impressionable, loving and extremely tender side.

Sure, she and Murray had enjoyed numerous sexual romps and hedonistic experiences together, but he'd also recognised how much the woman went out of her way to help others. In her private moments she was a big softie like the inspector himself. She would assist, support and offer guidance to people on so many levels.

In fact, her outlandish make-up, fancy themed outfits and quirky hairstyle and colourings, all appeared to be a well-oiled defence mechanism. A barrier that Murray recognised she'd established for herself to keep out any unwelcome intruders. It allowed her to camouflage her fears and anxieties on a daily basis. Very much in the exact same way that her canny inspector continually hid behind laughter and humour - for invaluable protection.

To relax, the tech-savvy woman regularly secretly read many of DI Murray's good, bad and for the most part, extremely mediocre poems. She never did discover that he actually knew that she read them. The man had been somewhat flattered by her love of his amateur prose.

Now in recent months her caring, sensitive nature had turned dramatically toward Andrew Curry. She'd always flirted with him by teasing him in the past. But her true feelings toward him were definitely growing daily.

During her last hospital visit she'd simply oozed sexuality. She'd quietly sat by his bedside and gently held and stroked his hand for over an hour. On her arrival, 'the Kid' had been lying back resting his eyes. Then when Lizzie took hold of his hand, which was sat on his tummy, Drew decided to keep his eyes closed for the remaining sixty minutes of her visit. Oh the joy.

Ten weeks later and the day of his official hospital release had finally arrived. It was mid-July and DI Murray had appeared on time with two capable private care assistants in tow. They were called Sid and Nancy.

The couple's respective name badges aligned with that fact. They were actually husband and wife, and both children of parents who had obviously embraced the punk revolution of the 1970's. The pairing worked well for the music obsessed inspector, with Steven Murray's jubilant gleaming smile being the first thing that 'the Kid' spotted as the man swaggered positively into Curry's fully occupied, four bedded ward.

"Are you ready, young man?" Murray asked warmly.

Drew desperately wanted to share in his optimism and enthusiasm, but could only muster a half-hearted grin.

"Where are we off to, sir? Have you got me a ground floor flat back in my fancy tower block? Plus you'll have ensured that a concierge is on hand, no doubt?"

A potential smile hesitated at the very thought of that.

"It's all sorted. Don't worry," Murray assured him.

That's exactly what worried him. What had this man planned? What is all sorted? In Murray's world what did that actually look like? How would it manifest itself?

Outside the hospital, Sid got behind the wheel of a specially adapted SUV, whilst Murray pushed Curry's wheelchair up the ramp and straight into the back of the vehicle. It had spacious seating for a further three people, including the front passenger seat. It was there that Nancy and a bagful of medicines sat as Steven Murray carefully parked himself next to Drew. The officer still had another surprise gift to offer up.

"Try this on for size," he encouraged.

He handed Drew a small elasticated blindfold. The kind that keeps out any excess light. That people use regularly to help get them a better night's sleep.

"There's a further surprise," the inspector told him. As his patient went to remonstrate...

"Put it on," was the firm, clear instruction this time.

It was duly adjusted as Andrew Curry strapped himself in and all four passengers went on their merry way.

The journey was continually interrupted by stop/start motions and twists and turns. A brief acceleration, followed by no movement at all for a while. Traffic lights, road works and a busy by-pass played their part.

How much longer? Curry asked himself. Another couple of left turns and one last right seemed to suffice. The vehicle shuddered to a halt. They'd arrived. Twenty minutes in total. So he was still in Edinburgh at least, Drew figured. He went to remove the blindfold...

"Not yet," Murray said. Placing his hand back over his passenger's eyes and repositioning the black material.

After a few seconds, Curry felt himself be reversed out from the cosy interior of the mini van. He was wheeled along a pavement with the occasional uneven bump. This would be the path to his new abode, Drew guessed. Next, he experienced gliding smoothly up a metal ramp - one that had no doubt been specially installed. His head was filled and due to burst with overwhelming thoughts of uncertainty and anxiety. It sounded like they were inside. He heard doors close and felt the breeze of the warm outside air disappear in an instant. What a difference. Now he was being pushed, almost effortlessly, along a plush carpet and unbeknown to the man himself, he'd been carefully positioned next to an impressively large bay window.

"Can I?" He asked.

This time as he went to remove the mask, no attempt was made to stop him. Through the window frame golden fingers of sunlight shone on a picture perfect day. It took the man's vision a few seconds to adjust. Gradually as his sight eventually settled and he looked outside, a fascinating feeling of horror and familiarity took over. There was no high-rise slum in front of him. No glaring graffiti or feral youths roaming the narrow streets, and no burned out cars or broken windows to be found as far as the eye could see.

At that moment, Drew Curry instantly remembered a discussion that he'd had with Steven Murray when the man had visited him in his disgusting hovel of a flat eight months previous. His DI had just sweet-talked him into coming back to the team. Though the man had no idea in advance of the squalor that his officer resided in. Or for that matter that his parents had moved away two years earlier and he'd no immediate family to call upon for support - financial or otherwise.

That day, Murray promised him that he'd get him out of there. Sadly, he'd no idea back then that 48 hours later 'the Kid' would simply be fighting to stay alive and that when he survived, he'd be crippled for life.

It was during that heart to heart, that Inspector Murray had told him, how after years of reflection and pondering that he'd realised that Edinburgh's toughest housing schemes all had one thing in common. Something that delighted 'Bunny' Reid and his ilk.

"They were all designed to give you an addiction. Each one had an abundance of bookmakers, off-licences, takeaways and chemists," he told him. Adding, "Look carefully at them, Constable. Check out the local amenities in the various areas and you'll see I'm right. It's no coincidence, Drew. It correlates perfectly with the deprivation, crime and anti-social behaviour that's rife in all of those particular places."

Back in April the inspector finished his remarks with…

"In my humble, experienced opinion, those working-class communities have been abandoned by the people in power. They simply don't want to hear about the drug deaths and the mental health epidemics plaguing those areas, never mind working toward a solution."

Today, in the beautifully decorated bay window, it gradually dawned on Andrew Curry that he recognised both the area and its familiar view. He was in the north-west of the city, in the Barnton district of Edinburgh.

"Sir. Inspector," he began. "This is your home."

"Aye, indeed it is, son. I know that. But it's far too big for just the two of us. It has four bedrooms upstairs and we've already adapted and modified the downstairs dining room to be your bedroom, with its own en-suite. So what do you say? Will you be joining us?"

He looked over his shoulder and saw not only the luxurious en-suite toilet complete with shower room in the corner. But also the specially constructed hoist by the side of the disabled-friendly Queen sized bed, and a host of other aids that were all in place to make this young man's stay as accommodating as possible. As Curry pondered on the inspector's generous words, tears began to fill his eyes and his voice quivered.

"When you say, far too big for just the two of…"

"He means the two of US, Andrew."

It was then that DCI Barbra Furlong entered the room, leaned down and gave the man an almighty hug.

"My cottage in Dirleton is currently up for sale. But what do you think, Ironside? Could the **Three Mary Wallopers** give it a go?"

Murray realised that Drew would have no idea who Barbra was talking about, either Ironside or the Wallopers. TMW were in fact the name of a lively Irish folk band that he and Furlong had attended in concert the previous week in Glasgow.

The inspector suspected that Andrew Curry would probably have guessed that Detective Chief Inspector Furlong was just trying desperately hard not to swear. As per usual.

"Nobody told me that you guys were back together?" He said in surprise. "I'm really pleased about that." Stammering to get his words out, he added. "You make a great couple and you certainly don't need me here. I'd just be a major inconvenience. A spare wheel," he joked. Pointing at his current mode of transport.

Over lunch, the inspector, Drew and Barbra Furlong chatted non-stop. Enthusiasm and excitement soon returned to the face of Andrew Curry, as his friend informed him of further news that he had for him. Murray revealed to an elated Drew how he'd spoken at length with Simon Gore regarding the partnership vacancy at his *Blood'n Gore* detective agency, and at how the man was willing to give 'the Kid' a chance to replace his late wife in that particular business venture.

Two key elements helped facilitate the arrangement. Firstly, Steven had made a down payment several months ago that had ensured the opportunity was put on hold until Drew was out of hospital recuperating, and the idea could be presented before the young man.

More importantly and even more significant, was the fact that Lizzie had agreed to help Simon Gore during that period of time with accounts, paperwork and I.T. The woman had worked tirelessly and admirably to do this in between her shifts at Queen Charlotte Street.

Murray, Furlong and the others squad members were blown away and inspired by her overall level of commitment toward helping her old colleague. Though Lizzie would possibly now admit to ulterior motives.

That July day, on and off, Andrew Curry just wept with raw emotion. In his mind he continually asked how he could repay these fine people for their kindness? On the other hand, he was once again thrilled to still have a future and a purpose in life. From that day on he was determined to make those upcoming chapters of his life story extra special. To make every 24 hours count.

As December rolled into town, Gore's new partnership with Curry had gone well. Importantly to Drew, he'd managed to pay Steven Murray back the full deposit that he'd initially put down to buy into the business.

The man's healthy compensation and his substantial Police Scotland payout package had also come through, so 'the Kid' felt that he could once again stand on his own two feet - though not literally!

As a detective agency, work had blossomed in their first few weeks together. Police contacts had tried their best to get their name back out onto the streets and Lizzie had inevitably helped increase business by creating a new modern looking website for them.

The Blood'n Gore trading name had given her creative juices plenty to work with. She was more than delighted with the artistic logo that she'd created out of a smoking revolver, two pints of blood and an extra sharp hunting knife. Blue Peter eat your heart out. Some of her popular narrative included:

"Not every case has a simple solution, but our team of agents are here to help."

That was an iconic line that she'd stolen straight from one of the Marvel Comic movies. But don't ask her which one.

The home page continued with:

"Our team of investigators have years of experience between them. We represent lawyers, executives, concerned citizens and family members."

In the final paragraph highlighting their talents it showcased: *Matrimonial relationships; Surveillance skills, plus employee fraud and theft.*

During the first 10 weeks they'd done them all - Legal work, spouses cheating on their partners, embezzlement cases and specialised surveillance operations.

'Kid' Curry was loving it. He'd been involved in stakeouts, learned most of the admin procedures and even more importantly had gotten to hang out with the sexy Lizzie on numerous occasions.

Simon Gore on the other hand, had been more than happy to see his business once again flourish and grow.

Together they'd also been delighted over the past four months to assist Steven Murray 'unofficially,' from time to time. Mainly because both felt that they were indebted to the man and also because some 'requests' were just not worth getting Lizzie the sack over. Although as she wasn't officially a Police Scotland employee, she'd simply have her contract terminated.

One thing that the 'Radical' non-member of staff missed about no longer living with the detective inspector was... No, not the raunchy sex or the hedonistic partying. Nor for that matter, the camaraderie, fun and playfulness. No, although they were all high-spirited and super enjoyable, what she missed and longed for most - was his study!

The sheer satisfaction, solitude and sanctuary, Lizzie gleaned from sneaking into that gloriously snug little room and reading a paragraph or two from one of his collection of poems was overwhelming. For the briefest of moments, she'd be transported instantly to heaven.

There was absolutely no doubting that was what she missed first and foremost from their relationship.

However, before she left back in April, she had cleverly and astutely photographed all of his currently stored hand-written verses. This ensured the female poetry addict could still enjoy short bursts of his prose over these past few months, and with discipline, it would also allow her to look forward to special literary treats throughout the dark winter nights.

At present, the intelligent and courageous woman still helped out at the agency two evenings per week. What was that all about? She knew, but Andrew Curry remained too scared to ask. That evening before bed, the I.T expert chose to open her phone, pour herself a refreshing glass of wine and read an enchanting lyric. Tonight's choice was over thirty years old. In fact, it was dated August 22nd, 1983.

By Myself:

I was a loner, I lived alone.
I liked to keep myself to myself. No fancy parties, no flash cars.
No romantic evenings by the fire.
I stared out briefly into that fearsome world.
I watched the people slowly drift away.
I let emotion take control of me. I never tried to be too brave.
I can't help retracting. I'm just so unsure.
This world is all wrong for a loner like me.
A crazy world just for lonely me.

The page was signed by a 19 year-old, Steven Murray.

Two

"I can tell the difference between margarine and butter. I can say 'Saskatchewan' without starting to stutter. But I can't understand why we let someone else rule our land... cap in hand."

- The Proclaimers

"That makes FOUR altogether, Steven." Barbra informed Inspector Murray over lunch. A snack that consisted of two expensive à la carte Tesco meal deals, and one that was currently playing havoc with her throbbing toothache.

"Whilst you and 'Babbling' Brooks were hiding off Lothian Road. Your buddy 'Sherlock' and Allan Boyd were in attendance half way down Leith Walk."

"Yes, so I heard on the radio. Another naked body?"

"Well, no actually. This one was fully clothed."

Furlong read him what Joe had sent to her phone...

"*He had his wallet on him.* That's all he said. Though I suppose it's a bit more substantial and helpful than your naked bin man offered up."

"You do know, he wasn't actually a..."

"I know, I know," the DCI laughed.

It wasn't normally in her nature, but occasionally, she loved to unexpectedly wind the man up.

"The victim was called, Mark Ziola."

On hearing the name, Steven Murray nearly choked on his 'succulent' guacamole chicken wrap.

"Ziola? Mark 'friggin' Ziola?" He spluttered out through a mouthful of food. "Fully dressed you say?"

"Indeed he was, Inspector." She looked across the desk and waited patiently for a further response.

Her DI didn't disappoint. He seldom did on so many levels. Though even she was extra impressed at his next statement...

"He'd have been wearing an over-the-top, nauseatingly bright Hawaiian shirt. Was of Polish descent and had been working in security for a firm stationed along the road in nearby Portobello. How did I do, Ma'am?"

Barbra scrolled back her phone and replied...

"Worked for DG Security, Portobello. Tick. Palm trees galore on yellow shirt. Tick. No mention of his family tree. However I'd guess with a name like Ziola, you may well be right there also. So who was this quirky sounding individual, Inspector Murray?"

"I'm surprised you've not come across him, Ma'am. He was one of Kenny Dixon's old lieutenants. I say 'old' but he could only be in his mid-twenties. He used to look after Dixon's working girls here in Leith. He'd run security for them. Keep unruly clients in line. It's not the first time that a finger, complete with a cherished wedding band attached was delivered to a client's wife. If the said client had become too physical or abusive."

"And now?"

"I believe he was still working as part of 'Bunny' Reid's crew in the exact same role, Ma'am. At least he was when our paths last crossed a couple of months ago."

Furlong pursed her lips. "Sergeant Hanlon would like you to go take a look, Steven."

Murray nodded. "I can do that."

"You do know these will be linked?" Furlong frowned.

"It's certainly looking that way," the inspector agreed. Before throwing his empty container toward Chief Inspector Furlong's waste paper basket. He missed.

"It would appear that our assailant at Bilton Lane was far more accurate than me at getting stuff inside a bin," Barbra grinned childishly.

This time it was Steven Murray that shook his head.

"Two jokes in a minute. What's got into you, Ma'am?"

"Well, it seems that I'm not the only joker here today."

"No idea what you're talking about chief inspector."

"I didn't think you would have. However, a little bird tells me that when you popped into Tesco for our lunchtime feast, you tried to help out a poor lady in distress. Would I be right? Because that surprised me."

"Ah, it was a bit more complicated than that, Ma'am."

"You were behind a woman in the queue, correct?"

"Well you see…"

"Just yes or no, Inspector. Was that correct?"

"Yes." Steven Murray sheepishly replied.

"And she was nearly ten pounds short. Correct?"

Murray went to dispute matters, but saw Furlong's hostile gaze and wisely decided against it…

"Correct," he once again replied.

"So DC Brooks told me that was when you decided to do your good deed for the day and be a kind-hearted Samaritan. Would that be correct also?"

"It would," the inspector confidently assured his DCI.

"And what did you do, Steven?"

"Oh, you don't know? Didn't Janice tell you, Ma'am?"

"She thought it best not to spoil the surprise."

"Yes, well, like you say the distressed woman was way short in terms of being able to pay for her groceries…"

"And you paid for them! Well done, very noble, Steven. I admire and applaud your generosity, Inspector."

"No, no Barbra, you misunderstand." Murray blushed. "I'd best go and get DC Brooks now and we'll head straight over and meet with Hanlon and Boyd at Leith."

"Inspector. Steven, wait. What did I misunderstand?"

"Well you see," he spoke apologetically. "My good deed for the day wasn't paying for her soapy detergents, toffee pops and raspberry ruffles. No, in making that assumption, that's where you went wrong."

Furlong rolled her eyes in preparation for an update…

"I simply helped her put it all back onto the shelves!"

The man held his stomach and let out a joyous, rollicking laugh. It was hearty, loud and victorious. Outside, Brooks shook her head. The deed was done. His laughter was infectious and she grinned merrily. As the door closed over, Barbra soon realised that the comedy duo had stitched her up good and proper.

Ten minutes later…

"Leith Walk as we know it, Janice, owes its very existence to a defensive rampart which was constructed between Calton Hill and Leith in 1650."

'Babbling' Brooks eyed her partner with scepticism. Though Steven Murray went on to tell her…

"Seemingly the attack on Edinburgh by Cromwell's army in that year was halted at that line by the Scots, under Sir David Leslie. The man whose army was subsequently defeated at the Battle of Dunbar."

Brooks still appeared far from convinced. That was until her historical narrator, Steven Murray, added…

"At least that's what DCI Furlong told me over lunch."

A relieved Janice Brooks seemed so much happier knowing that their resident walking encyclopaedia had provided the information. So much so, her features began to nod in understanding and amazement at that last particularly mundane fact.

Heading northward from the city centre, the officers parked up fifty yards short of Manderston Street. It was there in a four storey tenement building that the lifeless body of Mark Ziola was to be found.

Once again the standard scenario included vehicles with flashing lights, cordoned off streets, uniformed and forensic personnel. It also included several serious looking individuals in white SOCO suits. Murray pointed at the said items and told Brooks…

"You know these days that they come with additional self-adhesive pockets, chinstrap and a two-piece hood?"

"Did DCI Furlong tell you that also, sir?"

"Ah touché, young lady. Touché." Murray surrendered with a warm, rueful smile.

Two flights up and after donning said SOCO suits, the pair were met by Detective Sergeant Hanlon. DC Boyd also waved over to them from the adjoining kitchen. For now it was just the three of them that stood in the smaller of the flat's two bedrooms. Its red walls and bedsheets didn't quite match the rest of the decor. However, the inspector was certain that yesterday litres of blood wouldn't have been found there either.

As he'd approached the building earlier, Murray saw that a painting firm, a Turkish barbers and a launderette were all within easy walking distance. So he was certain that the owner would get all the heavy-duty stains out!

The *'focal point'* is one of the most fundamental elements in interior design. Put simply, it's the star of the show. It's the first place a viewer's eyes should land when they enter a room and it's from there that you create and build the rest of your design around.

Today's *'focal point'* was positioned directly above the bed's headboard and all eyes were instantly drawn to it. It was without doubt the most impressive and colourful feature of the tiny windowless room. Because there, attached to the normally bare, poorly decorated wall, was the normally energetic, free spirit of Mark Ziola.

The man's corpse was resplendent in one of his many celebrated and iconic Aloha shirts, just like Barbra Furlong had confirmed. This particular one however, was covered with an inordinate amount of blood and a red tartan bonnet adorned the man's shaven head.

At this point, Brooks' mouth was wide enough for trains leaving Waverley Station to exit via. Whilst Steven Murray was busy admiring the fine craftsmanship.

"What is this, Joe?" the inspector questioned. "The Leith Walk Nail Gun Massacre?" He extolled. "It's been awhile since I last saw one of those, Sergeant."

"Each one is six inches long," Hanlon advised him.

"Even the head is perfectly upright," Murray voiced.

"The nail driven in through the back of his throat, sir." Brooks nearly wretched at the overall sight and smell.

"So the front of the gun was thrust into his mouth? Interesting," Murray pondered. "Very aggressive and personal. A case of both intense rage and retribution."

"That's what we were thinking, sir," voiced the dry, brash accent of Allan Boyd, as he strode purposefully into the room. The Glaswegian, ex-military man was now the proud owner, not unlike Ziola, of a severe skinhead. But for a very different reason entirely.

A serious bottle attack two months earlier had rendered him unconscious and requiring immediate surgery. He'd only just returned to work ten days ago, but seemed to be settling back in and adjusting nicely. By comparison to his old colleague, 'Kid' Curry, Boyd considered himself extremely fortunate. Which was more than could be said for the well hung, Mister Ziola.

"It's everything that it sounds like," Hanlon informed him. "A psychopath on the rampage with a nail gun."

"That's a fine specimen of a human pin cushion, we have right there," the jovial Boyd added.

You could always rely on west coast humour to cross the line, Murray thought. And Boyd didn't disappoint.

"You do recognise him, Joe. Yes?"

"I didn't at first, sir. But sure, once I saw the 'typically tropical' short-sleeved shirt, I remembered he was one of Kenny Dixon's men. Usually a minder for groups of his working girls under 'Bunny' Reid's command if I remember correctly. Would that be accurate?"

"Fully accurate, Sergeant."

"We checked the nameplate on the door and some old bills and statements that we found in the bedside drawer, sir." Boyd told Inspector Murray.

"It would appear to be his home." Hanlon confirmed.

"And no escorts or massage therapists operated out of here," Allan Boyd stated. "And I've already checked with several neighbours, sir. It's a quiet building by all accounts. No students to be found in any of the flats."

"That's certainly unusual in itself," Joe Hanlon opined.

"DCI Furlong wondered why you mentioned to her that he had his wallet on him?" Murray lied. He simply had an itch that he wanted to scratch. Curiosity as always had gotten the better of him.

"That was wrong on my part, sir. It was a little light-hearted play on words," Joe answered awkwardly. "I had a good, but mischievous mentor remember?"

Boyd and Brooks stared immediately toward Murray, who in turn focused on a tall, cowering DS Hanlon.

"It's ON his trousers, sir. If you look carefully behind the massive red squall. It's securely nailed to what I believe was once his scrotum."

"Yes, I see it now," Murray grinned. "However, may I gently remind you that the mentor that you refer to was never mischievous, and certainly way better than good. He was thorough, meticulous and slightly warped."

"Sir," the quiet female voice offered from behind him. "Could I possibly interrupt and pass comment here?"

"Of course, DC Brooks. I'm a big fan of people speaking up and voicing their opinions. That's why you're part of our team and don't ever forget that."

With a cheeky smirk, Janice Brooks continued...

"Well that being the case, Inspector. In my humble opinion anyone who has the gall to wear ridiculous, brightly coloured hideous shirts like that out in public, fully deserves to have his palm tree chopped down and his coconuts removed by whatever means available!"

Eyes raised all around and DI Murray's bright blue ones stared in admiration at his relatively new female sidekick. He'd instantly become an even bigger fan. In fact the dazzling glint from his eyes contrasted with this woman's obvious dark sense of humour, and with her remarks not being politically correct either, that endeared her to him even more. All four officers shared grins and muted laughter before the inspector generously informed Brooks that her comment was...

"Spot on, Janice. Nailed to perfection!" He winked.

In addition to the two bodies discovered today, a further pair of reports currently sat on DCI Furlong's desk. In the past fortnight another couple of individuals, both males, had also been killed. Information about the cases and the gory details of their deaths were contained in the aforementioned paperwork. At the time the force had nothing to connect the first two gruesome deaths. But after today, things seemed to have changed rapidly.

Queen Charlotte Street police station was an easy fifteen minute walk from where the killer's masterpiece was to be found hanging. Mark Ziola's face had been smashed in and significantly altered. The loyal enforcer and gangster now looked more like a repulsive medieval gargoyle. The kind that you'd regularly find on ancient Gothic Cathedrals.

"What's with the cap on his head?" Brooks asked.

They all shrugged. Though Allan Boyd stated...

"Once we find out, you can guarantee it'll be relevant."

As they began to disrobe and depart the premises, Murray encouraged 'Sherlock' politely...

"Joe, could you please send me a rundown on your findings. Myself and the wise-cracking Brooks here are off to spend an hour or so reading up on the previous murder scenes. Hopefully we'll find a strong link to today's events. If you need us, we'll be at the station."

"It has to be a serial killer," Hanlon said. "Doesn't it?"

Murray was reluctant to give a straight answer.

"Until I've revisited those other cases, Joe, I really don't want to alarm DCI Furlong. Because at the moment, I actually think it's a series of murders that have been carried out with the victims chosen quite specifically. But for what reason and by the SAME person? I think that is too early to say."

'Sherlock' shrugged and acknowledged that was a fair point. Meanwhile, Allan Boyd had carefully moved out of sight to remove his SOCO outfit. He'd been desperately keen to hide his gaudy, yellow, Paisley patterned shirt from the prowling eyes and biting, acerbic tongue of their scathing colleague, 'Babbling' Brooks.

Although romantically linked, it was clearly noticeable to outsiders that DI Steven Murray and DCI Barbra Furlong were very different creatures entirely.

Barbra had the ability to tell you a fascinating story in two minutes flat. Sticking comfortably to its key points. Steven Murray on the other hand, could tell you the exact same tale. Yet his retelling took 20 minutes and included 37 insignificant details, 11 back stories, 6 off-topic side stories, 3 *'to make a long story short'* remarks and at least 1, 'Where was I going with this again?'

It's often quoted, but the world truly would be a boring place if we were all the same. Though it did make you wonder how many words the inspector would have used to describe his recent secret rendezvous with Lauren Naulls the week before. That house call was due to the promise he'd made earlier in the year of giving a regular monthly update to both Lauren and her friend, Al Lawrie. That deal would finish at the end of December. Each had one more visit still to enjoy.

Three

"And so long to devotion, you taught me everything I know. Wave goodbye, wish me well, you've gotta let me go - Are we human or are we dancer?"

- The Killers

Steven Murray had known Ashley Louise Lawrie for a number of years. On and off the award-winning journalist and the inspector would link up and become involved. Never actually as boyfriend/girlfriend. It was mainly adventurous one night stands, lengthy afternoon liaisons or the occasional ten minute, hotel quickie.

It was during the case to convict TV personality Colette Ford that Murray had first become embroiled with Lauren Naulls. The sexy female had been Ford's secretary at the time. A role that she'd gotten through her unlikely friendship with Colette's husband. The man had actually blackmailed his dear wife to get her the job.

Anyway, both Al Lawrie and Lauren had damning evidence that would help convict Ford at the time. In return for their help, Steven Murray had been easily encouraged to give both woman *'regular updates'* until the end of the year. Considering he and DCI Furlong were not an item at the time, everything felt okay with that arrangement. Now that things had changed on the home front, the inspector was keeping all parties happy until January 1st.

In the nine months since Curry's shooting, PC Harris had been poached by Murray from nearby St. Leonard's to join their team and was now… DC Lorna Harris.

The inspector had noticed her quiet confidence whilst assisting in the Colette Ford case and he felt it only fair to rescue her from a partnership that consisted of PC's Harris and Harrison. That was just plain cruel. The fact that the 31 year-old had two youngsters of her own, also helped greatly whilst serving alongside a female inspector who'd been expecting.

And so how does one describe exactly what Sandra Kerr has been through in the last year? She was left a single mother of two year-old twins when her husband was brutally blown to pieces in the garage of their family home. After which, she literally went armed with a knife to a gunfight to seek justice and revenge, and those are very different bedfellows entirely. She was one of the four individuals whose hands were on the knife when Sean Christie was killed in *'self-defence.'* And if all of that wasn't enough, 'Sandy' soon found herself pregnant with her late husband's child after his death.

But wait, there's more. With a valuable contract on her head, a would-be assassin captured her and her girls, plus DC Curry. However the twist was that her enemy had only wanted to keep her silent and in fear of future repercussions. So had ordered that the hit be on only one of her gorgeous twin daughters.

That was when Habib Abdullah went to open fire and 'Kid' Curry instantly threw his body across both Stephanie and Carly. The youngsters may have survived unscathed physically, but who knew what damage might stay with them in the upcoming years? As for Andrew Curry, he'd lived to tell the tale. But was now paralysed from the waist down.

He'd received a substantial payout from his employees and was thriving living with Murray and DCI Furlong, as well as growing and developing the Blood'n Gore Detective Agency throughout the Lothians and beyond.

The fact that a good-looking 'radical' female seemed to be playing with his emotions and was 'on call' around the clock was just frankly... the icing on the cake.

Today, that lady in question - Lizzie, was dressed in a nutty green and red voluptuous striped outfit. She was to be *'one of Santa's helpers for the next three weeks,'* she would tell everybody. Like anyone needed to be told? Her sexy stockings and slim bauble hat completed her sensual festive appearance. Her wavy red hair with sparkling emerald tints, had been like that for days.

In all seriousness, she'd been a rock whilst supporting Drew. No boyfriend/girlfriend shenanigans. More like a loving, caring big sister. So much so, 'Kid' Curry didn't really know where he stood with her. Although he did, because he couldn't stand anywhere. And there it was... he used humour much like his older mentor and friend, Steven Murray did. To constantly deflect from the serious, sad and reflective moments in life.

And DI Murray, how was he actually doing?

At QCS the wily inspector had commandeered an old box room. It had been used most recently for storage, though it was big enough for a desk and two chairs. It was also obscurely enough positioned on the second floor of the ancient premises, that it ensured they'd be left in peace for a couple of hours.

"I do love reading, sir." Janice Brooks announced excitedly, as she dragged her wobbly grey plastic chair closer to the edge of the solitary desk.

An impressively sized electronic tablet sat opposite each officer. Steven Murray was still getting used to scrolling through recent cases on - 'these damn contraptions,' as he would lovingly refer to them.

"It's a strange evolution of storytelling," was all the female detective had said. As a keen writer and reader himself, comments like that made DI Murray go weak at the knees.

'*A strange evolution of storytelling*' - what a phrase. He loved to hear people speak from the heart. More importantly, he loved to hear people speak from the heart with both a passion and a knowledge for the subject that had seemingly captured their imagination.

"It's a special art form. One which has played a pivotal role in transforming humanity into the animals that we are today. Don't you think, Inspector?" She continued. "We, each of us, all capable of being 'The Hulk' or 'Dr Banner,' depending on our perception of our reality."

Murray was impressed at how this officer's intelligent mind worked, and at her ability to hold and host thought provoking conversations, as well as her quick witted retorts and bold cheekiness.

In conclusion, the unconventional Brooks added… "These stories educate us in regards to virtue and vice. On how to become heroes and light up the night."

That was quite a dramatic picture to paint before they hunkered down to hopefully unearth some important facts and figures from pages of mundane crime reports. Her inspector smiled and added knowledgeably…

"Did you know, DC Brooks, that between the year 2000 and up to last year, roughly half a million people died each year in the United Kingdom."

His colleague wondered exactly where he was going with this. But as she pulled up the recent deaths on her screen, she willingly joined in and shook her head.

"The vast majority had lost their lives to illness or accident, but a significant number were neither ill nor unlucky," he said. "They were unlawfully killed."

Ah, she thought to herself. Eye contact sufficed.

"Whatever the exact figures," he continued. "Every day in the UK, lives are suddenly, brutally and wickedly taken away - as we've already once again witnessed today."

There was a troubled determination in Murray's voice. As he continued, you could hear the resolve he had to address the issue. The cadence of his speech increased.

"Victims are generally shot or stabbed, Janice. Less often they're strangled or suffocated or beaten to death. Rarely are they poisoned, pushed off buildings, drowned or set alight," he told her. His voice mellowed and slowed again. "Then there are many who are killed by dangerous drivers or corporate gross negligence."

By this point, Murray spoke in no more than a whisper. "And I've seen most of them up close over the years."

An understanding look was exchanged. Brooks appreciated the vast experience this man had garnered over time. She also understood how wisdom could be proffered from one generation to another. Just like she thought her DI was currently trying to do. However, so can hate and intolerance, she ably reminded herself. Her clearheaded thinking on the matter was…

If only people were clever enough to distinguish the positive from the negative and discard the latter. That way we'd multiply what is wise and let go of the dark places that evil leads us to. Which in turn led her nicely back into Steven Murray's ongoing rant…

"So it's our job, Janice, to ensure that there is a careful, clinical sifting of the evidence in each of these cases."

Both sets of eyes rolled as they stared at the hundreds of pages of electronic notes in front of them.

"Our role is to bring a dispassionate focus to the most terrible situations in which humans get entangled. To bring a considered examination of the how, the who and the why?"

"Would that be…" Janice saw her opportunity to contribute. "Because every unlawful death tells a story, sir? Every trial involves characters to be understood or possibly misunderstood? Motives to be unravelled? Plans and methodologies to be exposed?"

Detective Inspector Steven Murray simply nodded his head. She got it! He knew she would.

"Exactly, Janice. Each killing drops into our world like a stone into a deep, dark, unrelenting murky pool."

"And..." Brooks took up the baton once again. "The ripples widen and widen. Thus every day we continue to hear about horrific things that people do to each other that make us shake our heads in disbelief. That make us question whether we are truly human or not."

"Absolutely, young lady." Murray agreed. "And be in no doubt, that one way or another we'll be touched greatly by the stories that unfold in these particular cases."

At that, both heads bowed and they began to read.

Located directly below the 'broom cupboard' that Janice Brooks and Steven Murray currently occupied, was the substantially larger office of one DCI Furlong.

Sat opposite her right now was none other than the stocky, imposing figure of James Baxter Reid. From the hollowed depths of the evil gangster's voice box, the husky, precise words came out at a snail's pace. Each one filled with menace and distain. The message was playfully threatening, yet most alarmingly sincere.

"I don't think you understand the severity of the situation, Chief Inspector Furlong. They are missing, and I want you, Barbra, and your boys and girls in blue to do something about it urgently. Like... yesterday!"

After a short spell reading up on the other recent deaths, Murray felt another monologue coming on...

"We should've paid attention a long while ago to those red flags, Janice. We shouldn't have let it get to this stage," the man declared. "We should've asked with conviction - What exactly is wrong with our society?"

As much as Brooks was enjoying her education at the hands of this rugged, streetwise and sometimes unethical officer. She couldn't quite figure out, given his remarks today, if he was tired of the life and set to quit and simply walk away - or if he was even more hellbent on making a real difference. One minute he was super passionate, then sixty seconds later, indifferent to all of life. She thought that the next few days would probably provide the answer to that particular tricky conundrum.

"As well as punishing people after they killed," Murray went on. "We should demand clearer analysis of and better answers to why people kill. We should be asking not only how we can deter, but how we can deflect. We should wonder why we didn't offer help before it came to this. THIS being the cold mortuary slab! We should recognise that these killers are part of our society. We have nurtured them."

Those last thoughts were uttered with genuine sadness and Janice felt it was time once again to live up to her nickname, to contribute and ease some of the burden that she felt DI Murray was being weighed down by. Her 'babbling' began promisingly and at pace.

"The internet now allows those with perverted ideas about sexual contact with children to put those ideas into practise, sir. And as for the dark web, that is totally out of our control."

Murray said nothing. He listened. She made him think.

"Drug dealing breeds violence," she said. "In turn, greed breeds drug dealers and the constant pressure of our society to accumulate and flaunt our wealth, breeds greed. We have constructed a set of rules by which we expect the people of our country to live by. Sadly and most challengingly, a terrifying number of young people are opting out of it."

As his phone rang, Steven Murray nodded slowly.

Undeterred, Detective Constable Brooks concluded…

"They are disaffected. Instead they sign up to the gang. And in the world of the gang, they create their own language and their own rules, their own way of life. This, sir. Brings them into direct conflict with us."

As he answered his phone, Murray nodded gratefully toward Brooks to acknowledge her invaluable input. He was going to enjoy working with this woman, though it may involve him learning to speak less. But for now, he had a call to take. It was brief and to the point…

"I'll be right down."

He immediately turned toward his colleague and encouraged her to keep reading. "I shouldn't be long, Janice. See what you can find out by the time I get back. A certain Mr Reid is downstairs and would like a word."

Brooks' curious head gesture and facial expression, left Murray uncertain whether to exit or call an ambulance?

"Ah, Mr Murray. The very man required to help me."

"You do know you sound like an undesirable cross between the 'Grim Reaper' and 'Simon Cowell,'" the unimpressed inspector announced.

As he entered the room the DI walked at pace and stepped across confidently to be at Barbra Furlong's side. The DCI remained seated. Though she now looked relieved to have some extra moral support.

"I don't entirely know what the Grim Reaper looks like," the man rasped. "Plus, I think you've been closer to meeting with him recently than myself, by all accounts."

'Bunny' Reid gave him a mischievous, knowing wink.

"Would that not be right, Steven?"

Murray said nothing.

"And Simon Cowell, well he's a wealthy man I believe. So, sure, I can relate to that one at least."

The man paused for breath before continuing.

"And therein lies the problem. I'm being robbed of way over a million pounds and I'd like you to help get it back for me, Mr Murray."

Furlong and the inspector looked cagily at each other.

"Oh, aye, I heard you two were shacked up again," he proffered. His words were cold and delivered with no emotion. "And I'm told that you're even taking in waifs, strays and cripples these days."

As always, the Reidmeister was up to speed with everyone else's personal business. Whereas his own business had nearly doubled in size in recent times. That was due in part to when several months ago, Andrew Scott had been gunned down and killed in a cowardly attack on Benarty Hill in Perthshire.

Kerr and Steven Murray had watched the assassination footage. It had been sent directly to DI Murray's phone. They knew that Reid had ordered the hit on his long term rival. Though at that point, they were supposedly equal partners in crime. Neither detective had the proof to corroborate their claim and Habib Abdullah, Andrew Scott's actual killer, was now dead. That man would also take to his death the fact that it was Reid who had manipulated him into attempting to kill one of Sandra Kerr's children. It had been James Baxter Reid that had taken out the contract. But as usual, they had no proof.

Al Lawrie had even managed to get an article published in The Gazette about 'The Life and Times' of the dead gangster. It focused on Scott's early life growing up in the posh Glasgow suburbs. The violent killings of his mother and brother from gangland retribution and on his ultimate death and the disturbing disappearance of his body from the sweeping, misty shadow of Benarty.

Up on the plateau of the hillside they had located what remained of his two poor bodyguards. After each had been repeatedly shot with bullets fired from a high-quality, fully armed assault drone.

Andrew Scott's body was discovered one week later. It had been buried in a plot of land directly at the back of his legally run haulage yard in Dunfermline. That was the only slice of his business pie that 'Bunny' didn't take over. As for the gambling, drugs, prostitution and protection rackets, they all instantly came under James Reid's impressively burgeoning umbrella.

Up until the last few weeks things had been running smoothly and efficiently. Now however, some major challenges had come to the fore and 'Bunny' Reid found himself once again back inside a police station. This time - as a public minded citizen. Ye, right, Steven Murray thought. Pull the other one…

"What exactly is the problem, Mr Reid? Hypothetically talk us through your concerns. I'm guessing you'd like them to remain hypothetical at this point?"

"Ah, you catch on quick, Mr Murray. It's only taken you a decade or two."

The man's laugh was like an extended fire from hell. Furlong and Murray shook their heads, but edged their respective seats in closer. This would be interesting.

Steven Murray's voice had been calm, but patronising. Whilst his troubled turbulent maze of a mind, conjured up - This man was a killer, a drug dealer, a sex trafficker. A degenerate individual. One at the very root of the problem he and Brooks had just been discussing.

Watching him preening himself across the desk and listening to him continually talk down to his DCI was eating him up, and Barbra Furlong would definitely have known as such.

Having to put up with the man's arrogant, smug, self-righteous attitude and all his other unbearable character traits, led the bold Steven Murray to only one inevitable conclusion. And it was that…

Society needs to act fast and eradicate scum like this once and for all.

He breathed an unexpected, although much needed sigh of relief. His hoped for vigilante-style justice was most likely a very different scenario from the intellectual methods that 'Babbling' Brooks would no doubt support and bring to the table in the future.

Murray meanwhile shook his head and got himself focused and back in the game...

"Please enlighten us, 'Bunny.' Ya mad friggin' bampot that you are!"

At that remark, Barbra Furlong's mouth was instantly agog. Though her eyes just shone with sparkling delight.

Undeterred - James Baxter Reid smiled and went on to roll out his interesting and fully rational hypothesis. Especially now that he'd sufficiently riled the man that he often simply referred to as... Mister Murray.

Four

Upstairs as Brooks considered her surroundings in the poky, cramped windowless office. She quickly imagined for a second or two what life must be like for those incarcerated. What exactly must go through an inmate's mind in such a tight and intimate setting.

Welcome to your prison cell, she thought. *This is where you'll remain meek. You were asked to love and be respectful. You were asked to protect the weak and be chivalrous. But you chose to hunt with the glee of a demon pack. So take time to look around you. If you can't see the walls closing in...... you soon will.*

At that, Janice gave herself a shake. Her spine cracked like splintered wood and she jolted upright. Instantly returning to the reality of her situation. Had her late night the previous evening taken its toll? She rubbed at her eyes, before circling her arms high into the air and taking long elaborate stretches. All of which were accompanied by a solitary noisy yawn.

Minutes earlier the officer had been intrigued reading over the reports of the first fatal attack. Perpetrators plural, they believe, had broken into the lavish home of a Dr Ian Lennon on the outskirts of Dalkeith nine days ago. It appears they may have had a key. Because there had been no sign of an attempted break-in. No forced locks, broken windows or doors damaged, Janice read.

All of this was before DI Murray had received the call that led him to shoot off and disappear downstairs.

Brooks read that the man's family had been visiting friends. Had that been chance? Or someone with an accurate knowledge of the doctor and his movements?

There appeared to have been at least two assailants. Maybe more, based on the bruising on the man's upper torso. He'd been held down firmly whilst fully awake. There was then a drill involved and lots of screaming.

Why had the cordless drill been left at the scene? Was it a teasing clue? An arrogant statement saying… 'Catch me if you can?' Whatever it was, no attempt had been made to clean it up or remove it from the home. No prints were found on the tool. Though the killer obviously had money, because this type of high-end power equipment wasn't cheap.

By all accounts the holes in Lennon's body had begun with the agonising burrowing directly through his kneecaps. Bone and cartilage spraying like machine gun fire throughout the room. The assailants would have been drenched in bloodied splintered remnants. Brooks realised that the GP wouldn't have survived long, because the following line spoke of his forehead being the next target. It was as if they'd wanted him to wake and be fearful, for him to have no idea what was actually happening. Yet have just enough time to see his whole life flash before him - Wham! A power drill put an instant end to his forty-five years here on earth.

Janice shuddered at the very thought of seeing that rotating metal blade firing around and heading directly toward her forehead. She immediately made for the waste paper bin and threw up.

"Well, like you said, Mr Murray." Reid stated, in his familiar tone of a mythical Gruffalo, eating spinach!

He deliberately called the inspector, mister. Because he knew how much it irked him and got under his skin.

"If we're talking hypothetically, then let me take a trip back to when *'my good friend,'* Andrew Scott disappeared.

"Disappeared?" Furlong interjected. "Can I just add a little something to that, Mr Reid?"

Before 'Bunny' could even respond, the DCI had spurted out a low level rant all of her very own…

"**Sausage melting wallabies!** You piece of…"

Murray nodded and tried to restrain a magical grin as Reid's eyes darted from one officer to the other. What had he just experienced?

"Is she okay, Mr Murray? Mentally, I mean? Because I don't like being present when someone's having a stroke. It's an awful thing to witness that's for sure."

"Oh, MY Detective Chief Inspector is absolutely fine, 'Bunny.' It's just that she gets her words mixed up from time to time. What she really meant to say was that we both believe that you somehow encouraged, blackmailed or offered false promises to Habib Abdullah to firstly gun down *'your good friend'* Andrew Scott, and then to later murder one of DI Kerr's innocent children. It's just that we can't prove any of it at the moment. That's why it all remains hypothetical."

"Ye, ye, ye, I've heard it all before my good man."

And there you have it, yet another gentle dig. Reid had felt inspired to use Andrew Scott's familiar 'good man' expression. This ageing gangster had no scruples at all.

"So can I get on with enlisting your help now?"

Both officers sat back and said nothing. The arrogant Reidmeister took that as an encouraging YES!

"So it's agreed, it's all hypothetical," 'Bunny' reiterated. "Many of my fully insured dancing girls and my tax paying escorts have left in droves in recent weeks. They fear for their safety, I'm guessing. Although I suspect that they may have been given no option and have possibly been taken to perform elsewhere."

"How so?" Steven Murray asked innocently.

The ruthless gangland boss pulled out his phone and played the officers various voice messages that had been sent to him over the past week or two. Each one from a 'hypothetical,' high earning employee. He then informed Furlong and Murray, that neither of the girls recorded had been seen in recent weeks. Which wasn't surprising, listening to those upsetting clips.

Hysterical screams and desperate pleas for their lives seemed to be the gist of the audio footage. Exactly like Murray, Hanlon and Brooks had already heard. Though this time, different individuals were involved. Someone was definitely out to damage the Reidmeister's reputation and it seemed to be working a treat.

"And your thinking, 'Bunny,' would be?"

"Well, Mr Murray, I think that some of my colleagues in the East are looking for a share of Andrew Scott's spoils. Unfortunately that ship has already sailed."

"And we all know that it headed toward the *Sunshine on Leith* rather than *Bonnie Dundee,*" Murray quipped.

"Correct." Reid replied arrogantly. "And I see you still like all your musical references. So the less we have those amateur numbskulls from Dundee and Angus involved, the better." The man's voice suddenly lost its lightheartedness and its harsh criminal undercurrent resurfaced. "Otherwise, sadly… I'll show you, as well as them, *the road and the miles tae Dundee.*"

Steven and Barry Fitzsimmon are the seemingly handsome, though not identical, twin brothers that oversee the majority of illegal activities in and around Dundee. They're the 'Gruesome Twosome' that 'Bunny' Reid is certain are responsible for his escorts going missing. The 'handsome' part is obviously a popular myth that the brothers themselves like to perpetuate, because they're far from it.

Steven looks to have come from German livestock with his square face and angular jawline. His natural blonde hair is combed forward into a peaked point and trendily shaved up both sides. His strong cheekbones emphasis the brightness of his cunning blue eyes, and a spider tattoo crawls menacingly beneath his left earlobe.

Barry on the other hand, walks with a heavy limp and would appear on first impression to be at least twenty years older than his twin. The man sports a demonic skinhead and his belly-button has been oblivious to him for several years, as his finely tuned stomach muscles remain cleverly hidden behind a five stone mound of grotesque lard. The whale of a man regularly has two fish suppers for his breakfast. He'll call upon one of his favourite chip shop owners in town and kindly invite them to open up early, turn on the fryers and get busy preparing his 'most important meal of the day.'

So far, only one proprietor has ever refused the man. He too, now walks with an unsightly, painful limp.

Recent headlines from the local Dundee Courier had the name Fitzsimmon plastered all across its front page:

'Officer stabbed in neck, millimetres from death.'
'Man left with serious injuries after blade attack.'

Current police data shows that the city has the most crimes per 10,000 people. Whilst Glasgow, Scotland's largest city and described as one of Europe's most cosmopolitan and vibrant, was ranked only second.

As well as the most crimes per 10,000 people, the city that had once been famous for its jute, jam and journalism and whose stunning location places it at the mouth of the River Tay on the east-coast, now had the highest proportion of offences such as sexual assault, robbery, drug crime, housebreaking, vandalism and shoplifting. Everyone should get their *'lucky white heather'* there before it gets nicked!

In less than two decades the nasty, notorious brothers had risen through the ranks to come out on top seven years ago. That was when crime lord extraordinaire, Tam Fincher, had been stabbed to death in the street by two hooded assailants. It was just after midday and in broad daylight. No one was ever arrested or imprisoned for the vicious, fatal attack. Yet one week later, Steven and Barry took over the man's thriving business concerns. Their trademark weapon of choice was always a blade of some sort or other.

Was it sheer coincidence that on the day Fincher died, the two Fitzsimmon brothers were scheduled to host a joint 40th birthday celebration that evening? The two siblings bragged all through their festivities that they had already received their 'hoped for' gift, earlier in the day.

"Those 'amateur numbskulls' as you casually refer to them. Seem to be doing a good job at capturing, intimidating and scaring off your established working girls by all accounts, Mr Reid." The DCI interjected to remind him. "And it sounds like a bit of a 'turf war' has already broken out. So why didn't you bring this to our attention sooner? Barbra asked. "You do know that they're all most likely dead."

Her last remark was made more as a statement, rather than a traditional question.

Steven Murray sat, stared blankly and said nothing.

"Aye, I probably should have, but…"

"But, now that it substantially impacts your bottom line, you're happy to have us involved," the DI leapt in.

"Would I be right in thinking that yearly, every female employee of yours is reputedly worth around thirty to forty thousand pounds in commission, Mr Reid?" Furlong cheekily asked him directly.

"Hypothetically, Chief Inspector Furlong," the man growled. "On a good year, it can be closer to fifty. Why? Do you fancy a wee side hustle, Barbra? I've lots of willing clients that like the more mature woman."

Instantly his sunken lecherous eyes scanned the good looking female's curves. Taking his time, he slowly scanned up and down her whole body.

"However, I'm not sure that your man, Murray here, would be too happy about that prospect though. Eh!"

Actually 'her' man, now simply wanted confirmation.

"Are you telling us, 'Bunny,' that between half a dozen and a dozen of your girls have been posted missing from their established locations in the last week or so?"

He shrugged and nodded reluctantly. Whilst Barbra Furlong did the maths and blurted out…

"Seriously, 'Bunny.' You're losing about ten grand a week. No wonder you've eventually turned to us."

"And to be clear," Murray told him. "We're going to investigate this fully to ensure the safety of all those women, not to help assist in your cash flow problems."

"Aye, Mr Murray. Much appreciated. It's all about the girls and their safety. First and foremost that's why I've reported the matter. Hypothetically of course, that is."

James Reid offered up a disingenuous smile, followed by a knowing wink and an arrogant shrug.

"I've one more small favour to ask," the man rasped.

"Do you need a sub?" Murray smiled. Pulling a tenner from his wallet and placing it firmly on the DCI's desk.

'Bunny' offered him a sullen, unappreciative glance.

"Funny that, because we've never actually did you any previous favours," Barbra Furlong assured him.

"Aye, you two keep telling yourselves that. Anyhow, is the trusty, reliable and exceptionally capable, DI Nielsen in the building at the moment? I need a quick word or two with the bold, enigmatic 'Robert' also."

Furlong pointed to her door. "Goodbye, Mr Reid."

Five

"I need a photo-opportunity. I want a shot at redemption. Don't want to end up a cartoon in a cartoon graveyard."

- Paul Simon

Janice Brooks' stomach had settled somewhat as she now read the report on the second body. The one that had been dragged out of the canal a week earlier.

The deceased, in his early forties, was a Kieran Flood. His body discovered by a local dog-walker at 5.30am at nearby Fountainbridge Green.

Fully clothed, the man had received several blows to the head, yet no weapon was ever found at the scene. Investigations were ongoing, as the indents to the skull had been quite distinctive in both their shape and depth. Based on blood samples found at the scene, SOCO had concluded that he'd been struck at that spot and collapsed immediately, finding himself thrust into a small area of weeds. Half in and half out of the actual canal itself.

Those very same SOCO's had been unable to get any usable footprints from the grassy area. Which was a pity as they'd guessed that Flood's assailant had slipped into the water at that point also. Partial findings indicated one foot on land and the other in the shallow edge of the undergrowth. Though no conclusive evidence could be found to help substantiate that particular theory or assist them further with the case.

The man had been a delivery driver for a Chinese restaurant. His last known delivery was confirmed as 11.45pm and the pathologist put his time of death at between midnight and two. He had no criminal record.

Based on the circumstances, Brooks began to wonder exactly what this man had done to peeve someone off so much that they felt the need to cave his head in. She smiled - had the man delivered fried rice instead of boiled? Or possibly forgotten the prawn crackers?

Back in the 'large' office downstairs, Barbra Furlong had been left pale faced by 'Bunny' Reid's visit to the station. His naturally threatening manner would often leave people with that empty, gut-wrenching feeling. At least she recognised that they were both still alive. Because that wasn't always the outcome when James Reid left a room filled with police officers. Just ask poor Tasmin Taylor. Oh wait, you can't. She was yet another one of his innocent victims over the years that they couldn't put him away for. No proof. No evidence. No witnesses and he'd alibis a plenty. Each one claiming he was elsewhere at the time her throat was viciously cut.

Suddenly a knock at the door interrupted Furlong's angry thoughts. Murray had called Sergeant Hanlon to pop in and join them. Joe had already updated his inspector earlier that morning about some digging he had done into the memory stick. The very one that had been sent to the station for the attention of Steven Murray. In turn, the DI had filled in DCI Furlong.

"Ma'am, I played you the audible that Sergeant Hanlon, DC Brooks and I heard recently, right?"

Barbra Furlong gave Murray, a slow, knowing nod.

"Well, Joe has an update for us. Though I didn't think Mr Reid need be made aware that we'd also been sent files or that we'd carried out investigations already."

Both Hanlon and Furlong smiled and nodded at that.

"Go on, 'Sherlock,' enlighten us. What did you uncover?" His DCI asked curiously.

At that, Joseph Hanlon began…

"The motorcycle courier was given an address in Leith to pick up the stick from, Ma'am."

Before Chief Inspector Furlong could even ask...

"It's called the Big H. They do lots of mailbox pick-ups and drop-offs. They have Amazon lockers outside next to a 24 hour cash-line, as well as several other assorted vending machines."

Barbra listened with intrigue. Every day a school day.

"I suppose," Hanlon continued. "In that area those things are helpful for early-morning/late-night workers, busy students and revellers leaving the theatre and clubs. Every little helps," he said, with a wry smile to himself.

"So you're a part-time Tesco worker now?" Furlong joked with him. "What are your thoughts? What did you conclude, Sergeant?"

'Sherlock' pursed his lips. She's not going to like it.

"Unfortunately anyone could have handed it into the store to get delivered, Ma'am. Like I told Inspector Murray, the shop is literally a giant postbox. Unless you pay extra to have it sent recorded or registered, then there's no way of knowing who sent that package to ourselves at Police Scotland."

The chief inspector mulled over Joe Hanlon's words for a few brief seconds before resigning herself to a short impatient sigh.

"Thanks, Joe. I suppose it was at least worth a shot."

'Sherlock' then left the room just as the fun began. Because the station's resident origin master - DCI Furlong, began to educate DI Murray once again...

"Scotland's capital has no lack of ghost and mystery tours, Steven. Each one encouragingly offers to whisk you away on a journey into the various nooks and crannies of one of the most haunted places in the world. The city's past is often stranger and more twisted than its fiction," she calmly informed her inspector.

On cue, he waited for the next riveting instalment…

"In The Writer's Museum in the Lawnmarket, a unique cabinet was in situ. It was once owned by Robert Louis Stevenson and handmade by Mr William Brodie, a cabinet maker and city councillor. You'll have heard of the infamous Deacon Brodie, Steven. Haven't you?"

Again Murray remained mute, but offered a gentle nod.

"In 1788, Inspector, it was discovered that Brodie had been living a double life. A gentleman by day and a devious burglar by night. Copying the keys of the grand houses his job allowed him access to, he and his gang made off with money and goods to fund his gambling debts, two mistresses and five illegitimate children."

Murray's raised brow wondered where this was leading.

"After his capture and the scandalous revelations of his private life came to light, Stevenson was subsequently inspired to write one of the most famous books of all time: The Strange Case of Dr Jekyll and Mr Hyde."

Now Murray shook his head and questioned…

"And this is relevant to what exactly, Barbra?"

Furlong gave him a mighty long and puzzled look.

Murray sought clarification, "Reid's missing-in-action girls? The dead terrorised men? What? Help me."

"It's relevant to YOU," his DCI stated loudly. "You're the one with the Dr Jekyll and Mr Hyde persona, Steven. Get into character. Whichever one will help us best safeguard the lives of these men and women."

Murray said nothing, but gave an approving smile. In a strange, warped and twisted way, he felt rather proud.

DI Robert Nielsen was forty-three years old. Only a decade younger than Steven Murray, but light years apart in terms of trust and integrity. He'd joined up as an ambitious nineteen-year-old. A teenager who would have done anything to succeed.

To the outside world he'd had a very successful career. Plenty of high profile cases and lots of convictions. Yet when you scrutinised his record more closely, you would find a very disproportionate share of those were failed prosecutions. There had been rumours, plenty of rumours. Often witnesses failed to appear or testify in court. Then there were occasions where evidence had mysteriously gone walkabout, and that's not to mention the numerous trials that he was involved in where jury tampering had clearly taken place. Though as always, nothing had ever been proven.

However with the amount of unanswered questions, allegations and suspensions labelled against him, Steven Murray had no idea how 'Rab' Nielsen had escaped jail, never mind risen to the rank of detective inspector.

These days the man had the build and physique of an ageing prop-forward who'd lost his way. Extra inches sagged from a belly that hung over an imaginary belt. Even his once made-to-measure designer jackets failed to close properly and his extra-large bespoke shirts were all left unbuttoned around his burgeoning neckline.

Murray knew that Reid had only mentioned the man's name to play mind games with him. It worked. The inspector went down to the vault to set Lizzie on him.

"Discreetly mind," he'd asked.

Then as a further back-up, he made a quick phone call to Al Lawrie regarding his fellow DI.

Furlong, Lizzie and Lawrie. Steven Murray appeared to be surrounded by ex-partners wherever he turned. It made him smile and kept him on his toes at all times.

"Surely over the years, PC, DC, DS or eventually DI Robert Nielsen had popped up on your radar, Al?"

"I've no recollection of him," she said hesitantly.

"He's bound to have been involved in some of your investigations and undercover ops over the years. It's just that you haven't been looking out for his name."

"Nielsen genuinely doesn't ring a bell, Steven."

But she did also admit that maybe DI Murray was right. If he hadn't been the main man at the heartbeat of her breaking story, she could easily have missed him.

"Please check him out for me, Al. I'll do some extra digging at this end also. Ideally anything that connects him and 'Bunny' Reid. But right now I'll take anything that shows him as being corrupt. It's about time this guy was nailed and held accountable for his deeds, both past and present."

Al Lawrie listened intently…

"Everybody loves to hate a dirty cop," she said. Before adding, "Even Arthur Conan Doyle's, Sherlock Holmes wasn't always impressed by the dedication of the Metropolitan Police."

Murray held the phone closer and smiled…

"You are actually aware that a certain Mr Holmes was a fictional character and that he's not real, right?"

Al Lawrie laughed knowingly, before responding…

"Oh, I do, Inspector. Indeed I do. And any more of your sarcastic remarks and you'll soon discover that the real woman you're currently speaking with, will no longer require any future updates whatsoever."

It was Murray's turn to laugh and also to turn red.

"I'm guessing you're thinking more Yorkshire Ripper, West Yorkshire Police and a cesspit of corruption, bigotry, racism and sheer bloody incompetence?"

"Absolutely, Al. When it comes to the bold DI Robert Nielsen, that's exactly what I'm thinking. I'll guarantee not if, but when you find stuff, your exposé will not make for light-hearted Sunday reading and you'll strike gold. Even more journalistic awards, guaranteed!"

Some reassuring song lyrics made their way down the phone, as the desperate inspector burst into life with…

"If you'll be my bodyguard, I can be your long lost pal. I can call you, Betty."

Her response was immediate…

"And Betty, when you call me, you can caa-lll me-eee, Al."

Both lines went dead. Was that their hang-up code?

In recent months, Lawrie's newspaper, as well as covering the disappearance of Andrew Scott, had ran a substantial article on the attack on Sandra Kerr's family and a piece on DC Curry's heroism and subsequent disability. Seemingly unconnected, they then did a gritty commentary on youngsters being used as drug mules and couriers throughout the whole of the UK.

Several invitations to be interviewed had been turned down by Police Scotland's top brass and also high profile politicians. However, several were glad to comment on the other well researched personal supplements. The weekly stories ran under the banner heading of: **Law and Order in the 21st Century.**

The second of Lawrie's in-depth articles was all to do with tougher sentencing being required for those who harm police personnel. In days gone by, even the hardened criminals wouldn't think to endanger the life of a serving officer, never mind his family. These days no rules seemed to exist. It appeared that there was no longer honour among thieves.

Nowadays that was because they mainly consisted of greedy, arrogant, egotistical thugs. No mutual respect. No admiration for the job that they each do, and certainly no respecter of loved ones and extended families. If anything, that's a bonus - It's called leverage. Another opportunity to threaten, blackmail and kill. As was the case with Sandra Kerr's twin girls.

In recent years, Murray's team has been targeted more than most it seemed. Then again, they did regularly go up against the big guns. They often took on the might and resources of 'Bunny' Reid, Andrew Scott and even include in that Southern Ireland's finest in Sean Christie and his mother (although they're now both deceased).

So really who in their right mind would want to join Murray's elite team at this point in their career?

In fairness, Janice Brooks was about eight months in and was loving it. Plus, for Lorna Harris it was less than six months since her transfer from St. Leonard's and she seemed to be delighted at how her partnership with Inspector Sandra Kerr was working out. So it would appear that there was always fine individuals willing to step up and make a difference, and that was what DI Murray and his team were all about.

Throughout the next twelve months he wanted to ensure that Al Lawrie would have no further police obituaries to be writing home about. After their telephone conversation, Al felt compelled to email him. Her personal words included excerpts from her latest article. It was part of a transcript with an aid worker regarding using these kids as UK drug mules. It began:

Steven, these were the first words uttered by my anonymous social worker friend:

"Every young person that goes into it, is going to be a victim of violence somewhere along the line."

Murray was already welling up. Before he resumed reading it, he questioned to himself - what kind of a world do we truly live in?

"Beaten or stabbed. It's absolutely awful to think about to be honest. My organisation works with young people who are at the highest risk of going missing, being groomed and coerced into travelling across the country to deliver drugs. Years ago, you just wouldn't think about using a kid to run drugs. But now they just couldn't give a crap, as long as they can line their own pockets with money they don't care who they use. It's heartbreaking."

In fear for his life, the frightened man went on to tell me…

"Too often, too many people negatively label the behaviour of the youngsters that I work with, without looking at the reasons for their actions. I wish some people would open their eyes and look at them as vulnerable children and things may be very different."

Murray paused and pondered on the next paragraph…

"These are lost childhoods. There's always something in this person's life that led them to do what they are doing. That's what people need to look at and wonder what exactly they've each been through. The glamorisation of gang culture on social media sends the wrong message, but the connections we are making with young people is beginning to make a real difference. No kid is ever a write-off."

The inspector bit his lip and nodded positively. This worker gave him optimism for the future, no matter how briefly. The incredibly brave man left Ash Lawrie with some encouraging words…

"Lives are being changed for the better."

Six

"There's power in a factory, power in the land. Power in the hand of the worker. But it all amounts to nothing if together we don't stand - There is power in the union."

- Billy Bragg

Having survived care or more accurately - having escaped from her local authority's *'loving clutches'* after six years of hell at the tender age of sixteen. The vulnerable youngster made her way into the deeply deprived centre of Edinburgh. It was there that she first became involved in teenage prostitution.

Initially it was on dingy street corners. Then with unpredictable strangers in bars, before graduating to loitering outside seedy nightclubs and music venues. The latter she found the most lucrative earner of them all, because half the time she was able to make off with her drunken client's wallet. It was during one of those less than honest fumbles in the back alley of a famous theatre at the top of Leith Walk, that she met a fellow 'lady of the night' for the first time. They started to chat about life and the sad, sorry circumstances that had taken them to where they were at currently.

Kindred spirits, the two females had once aspired to do so much more than just exist. They were keen to turn things around and they both knew that in life, situations and circumstances could change in a heartbeat.

Relationship disputes and child abuse are still a sad, upsetting and yet far too familiar tale within family homes these days. That was a long number of years ago when those two females first confided in one another. A mutual trust that had survived to this very day.

Back then the older of the two woman, at twenty-five, extended to her new sixteen year-old friend an invitation. She'd told her that she stayed in a small council flat. It was nothing fancy. It had two tiny bedrooms. Her last flat-mate had recently moved out and it could be hers for a very reasonable rent.

It would be an expense that the teenager could pay back by lying back more often in the comfort and warmth of her own place. The naive women had no idea at that point that more than one girl in the house selling sex, immediately constituted the location as an up and running brothel. However, none the wiser, the females agreed a deal and both parties were satisfied.

Sixteen year old, Lola's first client in her new intimate abode turned out to be both a blessing and a curse. She was excited. Based on first impressions he seemed to be a very decent individual - well spoken, courteous and polite. He wore a fine suit and she reckoned that he was a professional. Maybe an accountant, a lawyer or even a school teacher. She certainly wouldn't have minded being taught in English or personally tutored in Biology by this handsome looking chap, she'd thought. The small mole under his right eye gave him a rather distinguished look.

Unfortunately first impressions aren't always accurate. It turned out that he wasn't employed in any of those professions or for that matter a very nice individual. He was something else entirely. He was a housing officer, a violent devious bully and an all-round sleaze.

In their very first meet he knocked out one of her teeth and left her badly bruised. She'd thought it had been accidental at first. That he'd just gotten too boisterous by mistake. But no, it turned out to be quite deliberate. Afterward, he wanted to role play and that would involve her speaking like a child and putting the blood covered tooth under her pillow.

She would then wait patiently and nervously as his acting skills stretched to being the generous, kind-hearted lothario. He'd be her very own 'Prince Charming.' Riding in to give her 'compensation' for her loss and to help 'soothe' the pain. His slimy, seductive attention left her feeling nauseous, numb and very sore.

Whereas her actual loss of innocence had been taken violently and unlawfully many years previously when she'd been raped by a predatory nearby neighbour. The young man had only just celebrated his 21st birthday a fortnight beforehand. He'd been asked to watch her for thirty minutes whilst her troubled mum claimed to go out and get some late night essentials.

The girl was ten years of age!

The tiny cramped, one bedroomed flat that the mother and daughter survived in, could never be described as a home. What chance did any child have under those circumstances?

The building itself was nearly fifty years old. It had been erected in the early seventies and was several storeys high. The unreliable, grubby and often vandalised lifts enhanced the blended stench of sickness, alcohol and urine wonderfully well. Whilst the concrete jungle walkway around the flats hosted and housed numerous drug dealers, thieves and an assortment of addicted hookers of all ages. On the aged dirty stairwells used condoms and needles were to be found frequently amongst the litter and junk strewn across the steep, wide and often uneven steps.

The regular postman even bribed a local teenage thug to escort him around the tower block most days. It was a gloomy bleak environment - and it easily claimed the life of one poverty-stricken individual every month.

Four hours later, the girl's mother still hadn't returned. It was at this point that the low-life adolescent decided that he was entitled to some form of recompense.

It was midnight when he began helping himself to the young primary school child. He'd stripped her naked and was halfway through claiming payment when the front door slammed and her mother finally returned.

Cigarettes and alcohol seemed to be the only essentials she'd been out to get, and lots of alcohol at that. The woman could hardly stand as she spluttered out an apology for her lateness, immediately undressed and offered herself up as payment instead. No police were ever involved and only four months later her daughter was eventually taken away and placed into care.

Six years on from that traumatic event and her first ever caller continued to visit. She would plead and beg with him not to be aggressive, but he had a major hold over the two females. He was actually a senior housing officer. One that knew that their property was owned by the local authority and that illegal activities were being run from it. Reporting them and having them evicted would be relatively easy. However, after their last couple of meetings he had offered to get them better and more spacious living accommodation. Obviously it would come at a cost. The price would be every fortnight, one or other of the girls would re-enact his tooth fairy fantasy with him.

Back then whatever he wrote and told his bosses would have been taken as Gospel. Especially over the word of a super aggressive, teenage female. One high on drugs every time he met her. At least that's what he'd say.

These days putting people out onto the street and making them completely homeless would be frowned upon, and if they'd had a young family in tow, that would be a definite no, no. At least a refuge or something temporary would be found. Six weeks later, and after several teeth had been knocked from their respective mouths. Both females fled undercover of darkness and hoped never to see the man ever again.

Over the previous months the two friends had worked and saved hard. Soon they managed to put down a deposit on a top quality loft apartment and through an 'extra special client,' who was in the banking sector, they got approved for a mortgage on very favourable terms. It seemed like things were eventually looking up.

Alongside the upmarket premises came the potential to increase their rates, get a better standard of client and a host of other positive ripple effects. After a few busy years, the older of the two finally completed her studies and entered into another career entirely. One that she would eventually become very successful in. Though it was never as financially lucrative as 'being on the game.'

Her younger friend continued to flourish in the sex industry and bought her old colleague out of their shared property. After a further few years of selling her ample wares, she also decided on a change of scenery. Settling for a mundane nine-to-five office job that would give her a taste of normality. However in recent years a major tipping point had been reached once again, and decisions had been made that saw her return to her old profession. Throughout this period she had kept her luxury pad. Thus allowing her to still meet with the more discerning, high-end clientele.

Also, she'd become far more familiar with the current laws of the 'escorting' jungle and felt it was time to give something back to society, other than standard STD's.

After her cleansing sabbatical away from the game, she had made this fully conscious decision to return. Though this time it was not only to give pleasure to a select element, but also to seek revenge and bestow pain on the extremists. Those persecutors, oppressors, tyrants and tormentors. The bully-boys who regularly preyed on and took advantage of genuinely helpless and probably desperately disadvantaged individuals.

She was determined to become the unelected Union leader and Patron Saint of Edinburgh's illicit ladies of the night. Though these days that covered early mornings, late afternoons and mid-evenings also. It was a twenty-four hour job in the new world of computers.

Her working name throughout the years had always been Lola. It had never changed. This time though, she recognised the need to upgrade to something more in keeping with her current experience and profile. So she had reinvented herself and her new slogan was to be - *'Delivering justice and wrath upon all who were deserving!'*

She was keen to create a tribe for all those desperate girls who never had a voice or a choice. For those who died too young, either neglected, abused or forgotten. She wanted to redress the balance. Surely someone had to be held to account? There was to be no more hanging about. No more talking. No more procrastinating and putting things off. No more waiting around for change. No more listening to Government rhetoric and spin. It was time for action. Time to come together. Time to unite. Time to nip things in the bud.

Like the old proverb said… **'A stitch in time, saves nine!'** Meaning: Act now and you'll save a whole lot of trouble, grief and upset later on down the road.

It had amazed the two women just how their lives had turned out. The older had now been in her chosen career for over a decade, and as one of its top performers was respected by all. With her 41st birthday fast approaching, she was loving life. Which all seemed an eternity away from when she and her mother continually traded insults at one another. Bitter disagreements and constant arguments between them, led to her leaving home for good at the tender age of nineteen. She had successfully completed her first year of college. However, things had gotten so bad at home that she'd decided that final term would be her last.

Over two decades had passed by and she'd experienced many heartbreaking and extremely satisfying moments in her life since then. Eleven years ago she'd learned that her mother had died in a fatal road accident, though she chose not to attend the funeral. She didn't see the point. They'd never spoken since she'd walked out of the family home all those years previous.

Her dad had died when she was only six. Yet over the years she had never lost her late father's ability to dream and imagine a better life for herself. Throughout the past twenty plus challenging years, she feels that she has finally, eventually managed to create just that.

Neither of the friends had ever worked for James Baxter Reid. Though they'd both heard of him and of his equally deranged predecessor, Kenneth Dixon. The Reidmeister was an importer. He would prey upon and fast-track vulnerable eastern europeans. He would acquire the majority of his working girls, his so-called executive escorts through ruthless third-party gangs operating out of Romania. 'Bunny' had always been happy with that arrangement, and until recently, so too had his Bucharest counterparts. However the continued disappearance of females in recent weeks had put both factions on edge. The way Reid told it, the women were being deliberately targeted and removed swiftly from their various locations. They would literally go out for cigarettes or groceries and never make it back. Their personal goods, lingerie and clothing remained untouched at their designated apartments.

The Romanian Mafia is made up of several groups with a network throughout Europe. They're one of the hardest enterprises to crack and are renowned for being extremely violent when they need to be, *and they certainly changed lives.*

'Bunny' Reid and Police Scotland were well aware of those facts, especially as the Edinburgh crime lord's employees were being strategically targeted and disappearing at the rate of one girl every three days.

The other side of that deadly coin was that male corpses were turning up left, right and centre in time for Christmas. Ho! Ho! Ho!

Was Mark Ziola's death a coincidence? He did work for Reid after all. But then again, none of the others were connected directly to the man himself. Like Hanlon suspected earlier, could the murders ultimately turn out to be the work of one individual or dedicated group? If that was the case, then where to begin and what was the motive? Was it part of the gang culture that Janice Brooks had mentioned during her discussion with Steven Murray? And if so, what gang? And crucially, what linked each of the dead men?

Since 'Bunny' Reid had taken over Andrew Scott's territory, business had continued to grow steadily. His dodgy dealings and his property empire were ticking along nicely and the flow of drugs and profit margins were better than ever. The efficiency with distribution since he took over the English importation side of things from the deceased Baddour brothers had helped steadily fuel profitability. The Reidmeister had reliable and trusted lieutenants in Manchester running that side of things for him. All was good. At least it was up until recent weeks.

At the moment his major challenge was much closer to home and involved livestock. With many of his female escorts disappearing - and not willingly, because that wouldn't be allowed for starters. You can't just walk away from the investment that 'Bunny' Reid made in you. Well certainly not without repercussions.

And those repercussions and consequences would most likely involve a broken nose, arm, leg or eye socket. Something along those lines. A definite injury that would disfigure you and keep you out of the business for a prolonged period of time.

Currently it appeared that someone was threatening the girls, capturing them, holding them hostage, potentially torturing and then killing them. Though strangely, as had already been mentioned between 'Bunny' and Police Scotland - no bodies had turned up so far.

What did that say, signal or indicate?

When would the first female be found or delivered?

Something was amiss. Things didn't seem to add up.

DI Steven Murray had his own doubts and hypothesis. Though a few more enquiries and answers were needed before he revealed it fully. As he and Janice Brooks left the station to seek those answers and investigate matters further, the often unconventional inspector began to sing merrily out into the ether...

"Last Christmas, I gave you my heart."

It was one of Janice's favourite festive tunes. Though that was before she heard her detective inspector follow up those words with...

"But the very next day you stuffed it under the floorboards with the rest of my corpse, until the sound of my heartbeat intensified your rapid descent into full blown madness."

Their gaze met. Murray winked and Brooks rolled her eyes and shook her head in total despair. Despite the sacrilege of ruining such beautiful lyrics, loud laughter immediately filled the air as both officers guffawed their way back toward the inspector's car.

At the opposite side of the car park there he was...

Seven

"My son turned ten just the other day. He said, thanks for the ball, dad, come on let's play. Can you teach me to throw, I said, not today - I got a lot to do. He said, that's okay."

- Harry Chapin

Sonia Nielsen was never paraded on her husband's arm these days. Yet when they had married two decades ago she was the ideal trophy wife to help enhance his career and take it up a level. Though even back then at the start of their marriage there were rumours that he had pimped her out on occasion to help ensure a speedy promotion or two.

She had been a curvy, dark haired beauty with a vibrant radiant complexion. There was a softness to her appearance, a kind of warmth interwoven with a natural shyness. Oh, how opposites attract - because in reality, she got in tow with a cold, calculating and devious thug.

In recent times she had the look of an exceptionally vulnerable soul, an individual that was hiding. The way a scared child might do from monsters, either imagined or real. Ultimately DI 'Rab' Nielsen loved nobody but himself and that became apparent to Sonia immediately after their honeymoon. The beast had turned and she quickly found herself being isolated. For he began to further his career by fully immersing himself deeper into corrupt deals with hardened criminals, did lucrative favours for the bad guys and eventually started to indulge in a selection of their products himself. By way of confirmation - that produce would include stolen goods, illegal substances and a multitude of women.

By some stroke of good fortune or bad luck, Sonia fell pregnant eight years ago and their only child, Robbie Jnr, was born. For a brief period of time his father tried to get his life back on track, but the allure of the cash and drugs was too great. By then he had set up and become a leading player in several unauthorised, highly addictive children's websites. By this point, Sonia on numerous occasions had tried to take young Robbie and leave the dangerously delusional individual. For her efforts each time, she was rewarded with a vicious, severe beating. Often to within inches of her life.

At the end of every prize bout, his broken wife would yet again be left to deal with the aftermath. She'd be expected through her severe pain and bruising to mop up the bloodied mess. To pick up the fragments of shattered glass and slowly rearrange the solid wooden furniture that had been her adversary minutes earlier.

She was grotesque. Her eyes were swollen over and spit drooled from her slackened jaw. As far as her bully of a husband was concerned, she was now as revolting as she should be, and her outside reflected the damage done within. This cockroach of a man who seemingly upheld the law on a daily basis, had once again left this poor woman to lie distraught in her own fluids. When she eventually recovered the fresh scars would once again remain, though not only on the outside.

On each occasion the destructive, heinous man would take a step back and survey the collateral damage. Then with a wrinkled nose he'd step forward and always whisper something demeaning, nasty and negative in her ear. Something that clearly highlighted the fact that she was well and truly crushed and that he'd won.

During every one of his dad's violent episodes, Robbie Jnr was thrust into his room and encouraged to keep busy by playing a host of computer games. Best sellers given to him by his 'gracious, kind-hearted' father.

Throughout the years, Daddy bear had been extremely loving and protective toward his young son, though only in monetary terms. He'd buy him gifts and lavish cash on the boy. But as for giving him quality time and playing with him like a real father - eh, no, that didn't happen. Plus he was busy physically and mentally torturing and abusing the boy's mother by this point. So much so, that even Sonia was amazed that the man was still able to function in life or in his workplace.

He'd become overweight and his once finely chiselled good looks had disappeared rapidly. His wife no longer knew the number one cause for his spiralling appearance, but she was confident that if you chose any combination of the following you'd not be far off the mark… Popping pills? Alcohol? Gambling? Women? And either injecting, smoking or snorting an illegal high? Each of those addictions had impacted Nielsen in recent times. The guy's dress sense and hygiene. His cognitive thinking and overall behaviour, including his body language and involuntary movements. It was all there for everyone to witness, and this time, finally, Steven Murray had decided to run with the ball and get Al Lawrie and Lizzie to dig down much, much deeper.

The thing is his son was getting older. He was no longer a naive toddler with no awareness of what was really going on. Nowadays after every episode, it would be the heartbroken youngster that would comfort and encourage his aching female parent to get up and keep going. As a mother and child they were now becoming desperate. There were severe lacerations to her skin each time, yet the impact to her mind would take far longer to heal. The rewiring back to empathy, to happy memories and a positive sense of self, requires the patient layering of neurones daily. The damage done in seconds can often require years of healing. Being continually beaten up, is in reality, being beaten down.

It was surely time for new measures to be put in place. She'd convinced herself of this as she sat at home and listened to a message that had been left on her mobile phone. It was a calm, reassuring and respectable female voice that spoke up…

"Mrs Nielsen if you'd like out of your marriage, may I encourage you to seek wisdom from a certain newsagent on Leith Walk. So to re-cap…"

The woman then repeated her cryptic message once again. How had they gotten her number? No matter, Sonia Nielsen would try anything at this stage in her life. It was called desperation. Within thirty minutes, Robbie Jnr had been picked up at his school gates as the bell sounded for close of day. Ten minutes later his education would continue as the couple began trailing up and down the one mile stretch of Leith Walk. Given its length, it actually only contained three newsagents.

'Bunny' had described him as enigmatic, and he most certainly was a very perplexing, puzzling and mysterious individual, much like James Baxter Reid. But be under no illusions, according to Steven Murray, DI Robert 'Rab' Nielsen was also fly, sly, sleekit and sinister. But it didn't stop there - nasty, noxious and murderous were also included in the inspector's descriptive list.

Out having a desperately needed cigarette, the man waved over at the two officers as they entered Murray's vehicle. The courteous gesture was returned in kind. Though Steven Murray grinned somewhat as he noticed that Brooks' wave seemed to resemble giving the man the middle finger.

"Did you just do what I…"

"You said he was a wrong un," Janice interrupted. "So I shan't be wasting time on him. Plus we've got plenty to be going on with and I've got plants to tend to."

Busily belting up and unable to see her inspector's grin, this independent free thinking constable continued to inspire and uplift her grumpy DI at every turn. First Joseph Hanlon, now Janice Brooks. At this rate he'd have to exchange his partners every couple of years to keep himself feeling enthused, refreshed and motivated. He'd certainly been fortunate with his last two choices.

Brooks giving Nielsen the finger had made his day. So he thought in turn, he'd return the compliment.

"I now know how much this is costing our, Mr Reid."

"Is it worth him getting upset over? Worthy of all this commotion? Does he really need DI Nielsen's help?"

That last remark didn't bear thinking about.

"Do you know how much each girl is worth to him?"

The female bit warily on her lips and shook her head.

"Vice tell us they reckon the Reidmeister rakes in between three and five million pounds per year, based on approximately one hundred girls. He himself just confessed 'hypothetically,' that they earn him over fifty thousand pounds per year - Each!"

"That's more than WE earn," she said, sarcastically.

"Aye, and it's a heck of a lot more than the girls earn," Steven Murray stated. "Try thirty quid for the day. Sure, they get bed and board. But what life are they going to make for themselves? They'll be lucky to get five years before 'Bunny' kicks each of them back into touch."

"And no severance pay, no loyalty bonus," Janice added. "Just a great big zero. They'll have paid no tax or National Insurance. They'll be due nothing from the state and in a few years they'll end up in even poorer circumstances than they find themselves currently."

"You're right. An extremely vicious circle altogether."

"So how do they escape it, sir?"

"They don't." The inspector went silent for a second or two. "Or do they, Janice? Is that what we've overlooked? Is that why we can't find any bodies?"

"You mean, they're not dead? That they've found a way out and played us all?" She offered excitedly.

"Could it be that simple?" Murray asked. "Because with his contacts, the brazen 'Bunny' will hunt them all down individually and make each one pay."

Sandra Kerr was animated and agitated. Eager to get on with things and full of untapped nervous energy. She simply couldn't contain herself and had spoken with nurses, doctors and visitors all day long. Even auxiliary staff hadn't been safe from her constant chatter.

A tiny addition for Stephanie and Carly would be making its way into the world very soon. Though given her slow, heavy waddle these past few weeks, Sandy suspected the child would be anything but small.

The baby's name had been told to Kerr's parents and parents-in-law, but currently she was once again sharing those precious details with a young student nurse called Isla. Isla had just taken her blood pressure.

"If it's a girl," Sandy told her. "It's to be called Annabelle."

"And if it's a boy?" Isla asked.

But no reply was forthcoming. The worn-out, Sandra Kerr had suddenly, yet unsurprisingly, dozed off.

How a newsroom functions, depends in part on the size of the publication and when it's due to be published. The Gazette still had a weekly print run of over 22,000. Its offices were literally a hop, skip and a jump away from The Dynamic Earth Science Museum. A whole two minute walk from the Scottish Parliament and in the ever-present shadow of Arthur's Seat. The extinct volcano which is the main peak of the group of hills which form most of Holyrood Park in Edinburgh.

Gazing out from a nearby window and supping a cool refreshing water, Ash Lawrie was taking some much needed respite from her keyboard. Her latest article had left her feeling emotionally drained. As she returned to her busy, untidy desk, she scanned her first draft with a mindful, reflective tear in her eye. It read…

Every week, children criss-cross the UK on buses and trains, ferrying drugs as part of the county lines operations.

"No-one asked why I wasn't at school," one girl told me. "I have seen a lot of things. I've seen people get kettled with boiling water."

She had been initially recruited to drug-running at the age of 11.

"I've seen people get stabbed because of the tiniest disagreement. Over things like a tenner," she added.

Before she joined the gang, she was sleeping on a filthy mattress and showering at school when she got the chance. She's now 18.

"It finds you," she said about county lines. "You don't find it."

Ash was hurting with this story. Sentiment getting the better of her, which was unusual. She was normally able to switch off and detach herself, but this one had gotten under her skin. She'd allowed it to become personal. In fairness, she'd just spent two hours earlier in the day with this young woman. That couldn't and wouldn't have helped matters. She continued to read…

The gang promised her a new bed, new clothes and help for her mother to pay the bills. She told me how she regularly saw her new friends with nice trainers, nice clothes and fancy make-up.

"I was just so jealous that I didn't have any of that. And I was at the point where I'd do anything to be able to get it," she'd said.

But the gang's promises never came true.

"We never got to the stage of a bed or new clothes," she told me.

Instead, she was initiated into a world of violence and abuse. On one devastating trip travelling north from England toward Glasgow city centre, she told me how she cried in the toilets at every station that they had stopped at.

"When I got to the location, what was planned, didn't happen," she said. *"I had to do a lot of things that I didn't want to do to get out of that situation alive. If I hadn't have done what I was asked to do - which was sexual, physical and mental - then I don't think I'd be here today."*

The violence she'd witnessed kept her working for the gang. She was told what to do and warned that if she didn't do it, she'd pay. To this day, she simply can't understand why no adult intervened as she travelled the length of the country on trains and buses alone, aged 11 and missing education.

"Not seen, not found, not asked why I wasn't at school. Not even asked why I wasn't with a mum or a dad. That is now what mostly affects me to this day," she told this reporter. *"Why didn't someone step in any sooner?"*

As Ash made a few adjustments, she continued to pour over the remaining few paragraphs…

After three years of relentless violence, abuse, fear and broken promises, just as she reached her lowest point, she was able to grab a chance to escape. One day, aged 14, she turned up at school having suffered a miscarriage. A female teacher that had been offering her showers at school and paying for her meals outside of school became aware of her pain.

"The teacher noticed straight away what had happened and she took me to the hospital. I had just had enough. I'd reached breaking point," the girl said. *"I thought to myself, I need to trust this person. She needs to know that I am NOT okay."*

Now, several years on from her escape, She is studying at college to make a better life for herself. She hopes to have a house and a family, and she says she wants to be the kind of person who doesn't look away when someone else needs help. She wants to give hope to others who may still be trapped, frightened and exploited.

"I can't stress to people enough that it doesn't matter how scared you are. You are valid. Your feelings are valid. You are never that stuck," she told me. *"If you are still living and breathing, you are never stuck past the point of no return. You can always end up at the better end of it. And I stand by that."*

Lawrie suddenly stopped typing. A satisfactory nod was offered and her head gently bowed forward. She took one last gulp of the cold water and decided enough was enough. Her jacket was removed from the rickety old-fashioned coat-stand in the corner and she headed home. There an equally cool but much more lethal alcoholic beverage awaited her. She sighed, caught the elevator down to the ground floor and departed the building. Soon back at home, she immediately tried to reach her friend Lauren Naulls. Once again, her call was unsuccessful.

Eight

"Mrs Lennon. Good evening. Sorry to disturb you. I'm Detective Inspector Steven Murray and this is my colleague…"

"DC Brooks," Janice announced politely.

The woman appeared quite startled. She'd obviously thought that she had seen the last of the police.

"We're going to being taking over your husband's case, Mrs Lennon," Murray informed her. "It's just that we need a couple of things clarified and confirmed for us, Ma'am. Then we'll gladly leave you in peace."

As both officers entered the home their warrant cards were barely even looked at. Steven Murray often wondered why they still bothered with them these days. Because any two semi-competent, articulate individuals with Mickey Mouse and Daffy Duck credentials could make it across the threshold of most people's homes. Then they'd be able to lovingly and respectfully slice you into tiny pieces in a warm cordial environment. Rather than on a cold, breezy, damp doorstep where all and sundry could witness your execution. That was the slightly warped opinion of DI Murray. One which he wisely and humbly kept to himself on this occasion.

The Belmont Oaks residential site on the outskirts of Dalkeith was a relatively new development. Two years old at most. It was built with wealthy professionals in mind and Doctor Ian Lennon fitted the bill perfectly.

The surrounding area had plenty of cycle paths and dog-walking space. There was sufficient playgrounds and family attractions nearby, plus convenience stores within easy walking distance. It also gave quick and reliable access to the Fort Kinnaird Retail Park, the city-bypass and the appealing attraction of Edinburgh itself.

The recently bereaved and noticeably flustered Charlene Lennon was dressed in a beige jersey and slacks as she led the pair through into her open plan lounge. When she did so, Janice couldn't help but notice that the widow walked with a slight limp. As the inspector sat on the leather corner suite, he would have noticed it also. The two females sat opposite Murray, and as the officers relaxed, it became apparent to them just how opulent this room was seeking to be.

A bespoke anthracite radiator ran smartly along the feature wall. Above it an all-smiling, award-winning family portrait hung, and on the the wall directly behind them was an impressive six foot wide diamanté mirror. If that wasn't enough, the authentic crystal chandelier perched above their heads added a glamorous finishing touch of bling or tat - depending on your taste!

Surely this was all make believe the inspector thought. The whole house was desperately searching for grandness, pretending to be something that it wasn't. It was part of someone's picture perfect fantasy. A fulfilment of a childhood dream. It was a clever illusion that masked the reality, and the reality was that Doctor and Mrs Lennon lived in a modern day, overpriced housing estate. Well, Mrs Lennon and her kids certainly did. It was a recent new build. How large and grandiose did they really think it would be inside? How much genuine quality craftsmanship would you be expecting? Next door would be the same. So would the one across the road and even your neighbours' around the corner. They'd all be like for like or in this case: tit for tat!

"You've a beautiful home, Ma'am." Brooks offered up.

Meanwhile DI Murray shrugged and looked back in the direction from which they'd came. The dining room was positioned off to the right as they walked by. Its frosted glass doors had been shut, though he'd witnessed two teenagers emerge from the area and head immediately upstairs. Both were High School pupils according to the information that they'd been given. The taller of the two would be Eric, aged seventeen. Whilst the shorter, his sister Emily, was only thirteen. On gut instinct, Murray found himself blurting out…

"This didn't happen to be the show-house for the development by any chance, did it?"

Charlene's head jerked in a shocked manner, though her hands remained gripped, one on top of the other.

"Wow. I don't know where that came from, Inspector. Or why you would actually have need to know? But yes, it was the first home built on the site and used as the company's showhouse. So what made you…"

"The interior design," Murray interrupted and lied. "Was it your husband that suggested this home? Did he also have an eye for detail, coordination and the planning of the inside decor and fittings? Or would you be the one with the tasteful fashion sense?"

Brooks knew Murray was up to something. Whereas Charlene Lennon was simply wary of their visit, right from opening the front door to them. She appeared to be a very quiet woman. Meek and timid. Scared even.

"It was Ian's idea to purchase the showhouse," she eventually reluctantly stated. "Though I suspect he'd an eye for more than the fabric and the interior design."

Both Murray and Brooks remained silent. But they got the gist of that rather caustic comment. The inspector rallied round and asked with a bit more brevity…

"Do you mind if I go introduce myself to Eric and Emily? I assume that was them I saw head upstairs?"

Their mother initially made to stand and remonstrate, but when Janice placed a gentle reassuring hand on her knee, Charlene Lennon exhaled and remained seated.

"Thank you, Mrs Lennon. I've only a couple of brief questions. Meanwhile, Constable Brooks here will update you with all the latest information that we have on the case. Isn't that right, officer?"

Janice offered the woman a comforting smile.

As private conversations continued at number 2 Belmont Crescent, an enterprising newsagent on Leith Walk was open late and knew that if they hadn't continually diversified in recent times they'd have most probably have closed down by now.

In recent years the local independent retailers, the family run stores and corner shops had all been decimated by the increasing growth of the 24/7, larger branded convenience outlets.

This was only the third advert added in the past fortnight. Bringing the total number of ads out in the front to an almighty - Nine! No one really used shop window advertising these days. It only worked for niche items...

The impressive header stated:
• FREE Classifieds.
• Place your advert now.
• Sell unwanted items, advertise local events, jobs, etc.

After peering at the tiny card for several minutes from outside, one of the two curious females finally produced her phone and took some snaps of the details and immediately shared them online with work colleagues. They'd already been informed by others about this particular service. Afterward, they locked arms and marched off. It was a bitterly cold night to be out walking the streets of Edinburgh.

By now Steven Murray and DC Brooks were sat back in the warmth and shelter of the inspector's vehicle when Janice's phone rang…

"Yep. Uh-huh. I see. No, we're back in the car. Sure. No, I'll tell him. Thanks, Joe. Speak soon."

Murray didn't bother trying to fill in the blanks. He tapped his fingers on the steering wheel and looked across at the woman with intrigue. He soon wondered exactly how long it would be before she decided to share anything with him?

Brooks immediately cupped her hands and breathed into them, in the hope that they'd instantly heat up.

"Janice," he said, in a sharp, clipped, raised voice. "Now I know that you're deliberately winding me up!"

"Me? Surely not, sir." Her words dripped in sarcasm.

Inspector Steven Murray licked at his lips. He liked her boldness. It always made him smile and reflect on what he himself had been like as an annoying young PC. Someone always looking to learn and develop. But not always being assigned to partners that were willing to help him achieve those admirable goals.

"It was Sgt. Hanlon," she said with the hint of a smile.

Her inspector had gathered that, though stayed quiet.

"He'd tried to reach you, but your phone was switched off, so he's left you a message."

Murray instantly removed his mobile from his pocket, made some strange noise that told you he was annoyed with himself and switched it back on again.

"He was letting us know that early preliminary results from the lab suggest that Mark Ziola was held down by several people before being drugged. That allowed them time to hold him up and pin him dramatically to the wall."

"He said, several. But did he narrow that down at all?"

"They reckon six or maybe even seven," Brooks said.

Steven Murray nodded thoughtfully, before asking…

"What do you think was going on in there, Janice?"

His colleague carefully considered the question. Her head swayed from side to side considering options.

"He would be too strong for one or two people and they had to guarantee…"

Murray quickly interrupted…

"I was actually meaning what do you think had been going on inside the Lennon family home?" He quickly offered up a mischievous grin by way of payback. "I was referring to how did you get on with his wife?"

"Well we're still waiting to confirm the identity of our naked body in the bin," Brooks smiled. "But we already know that our deceased in Leith wasn't a very nice man, sir. And from what Charlene Lennon just told me, I suspect she might order a similar themed headstone to Mark Ziola's. One which states: *Here lies a first rate sleaze ball, a second rate father and a totally abusive husband.*"

The solitary high-pitched beep, told DI Murray of his missed message. Two clicks and it was on speaker…

"Hello, sir. Sgt Hanlon here. Just to let you know that early indications on our man, Ziola, show lots of fingerprints and bruising under the skin on his arms and legs. Indicating that several people helped lift and hold him in place. This allowed our self-proclaimed 'Equaliser' time to get to work, pinning him to the wall. I'll call the DCI and update her also."

Murray looked toward Brooks. They'd all known earlier that afternoon that one man couldn't possibly have worked that magic all by himself. An accomplice of some sort was always suspected. But six or seven!

"You know, sir," Brooks chirped up. "That maybe isn't a bad comparison that Joe made earlier regarding 'The Equaliser.' Because you'll remember in that particular storyline, Denzil Washington, complete with hydraulic nail gun takes out the baddie."

"I think that was his point, Janice. The nail gun."

"Oh, I got that. But my point ISN'T the nail gun, sir. It's the fact that he always takes out the baddie."

Murray pondered on that. *'My point isn't the nail gun, but the fact that he always takes out the baddie.'* A few seconds passed before the inspector felt he could respond.

"So while we're seeing them all as victims…"

"Which each of them are of course, sir." 'Babbling' interrupted. Keen to emphasis the importance of that. "However, what if they're not quite as pure, clean and innocent as they're being made out to be?"

"Well, Mark Ziola and by all accounts Dr Ian Lennon certainly weren't," Steven Murray confirmed. "It's a valid point, Janice. Tomorrow, let's check out the others more thoroughly. A little bit more digging into the lives of our slaughtered men could hopefully bring about its own reward." He then offered up a reminder… "And what about here at number two, DC Brooks?"

They both instantly shared a look that clearly stated… *'Oh, yes, definitely much more digging required here.'*

Often in life, people do what they have to do to protect those around them that they love, and if that involves accepting the direct consequences - then so be it.

When 'Radical' Lizzie had packed her bags and departed DI Murray's beautiful home several months ago, the inspector had returned that evening to find his attractive two-storey house in complete darkness. Given their limited and extremely tepid interactions during the previous few days, that came as no real surprise or shock. He had - they had - ultimately seen it coming.

What did surprise him however, was NOT that her key to the house had been put back through the letterbox after she'd locked up. But what Lizzie had seen fit to scrawl upon the note that the key was scrunched up in.

The 'radical' six words of counsel and encouragement were hand-written in the hope that they would genuinely help Steven Murray's long term future and mental stability. They were meant to help get him back onto a steadier path than the one he was currently trying unsuccessfully to navigate. That was, should the often proud and stubborn man ever choose to act upon them. The brave words that an emotional Lizzie had felt inspired to write down back then were:

She still loves you, you know!

They were alluding clearly to… DCI Barbra Furlong.

Lizzie never felt that Steven Murray had ever gotten over the woman. In fact, she thought that the couple were still made for each other and that Furlong always ached to be back with her beloved DI. For although they hadn't always been colleagues in the same station, they had known each other for a long period of time.

Within a week of Lizzie's exit, the inspector had actually reflected on her parting words and had asked DCI Furlong out for a meal and a personal chat. The evening was cordial, extremely friendly and went well. Because the pair ended up back at Barbra's cosy, intimate cottage in Dirleton. Murray had clearly been forgiven as he ended up staying the night and was even allowed to prepare a notable and sumptuous breakfast the next morning.

One of the things discussed the evening before, was about how she felt that she now understood him better. Whereas month's ago when he wouldn't trust or share certain aspects of the Sean Christie case with her, she now got it. With hindsight she'd realised that he was doing it to protect her and the other members of his team, namely Sandra Kerr. It wasn't about fear of incriminating himself or trying to shield himself from any flack heading his way, or even shifting the blame for that matter. For he was well used to that.

Over time, Barbra had succumbed to that way of thinking. She'd finally accepted that ultimately an evil, good for nothing Irish gangster had been taken off the streets and a good number of innocent lives saved. And that no matter the suspicious circumstances surrounding his death, in many respects there couldn't have been a more fitting finish to Sean Christie's life than being knifed to death - with the hands of each of his four opponents all gripping the weapon.

Andrew Scott, James Reid, Sandra Kerr and Steven Murray never altered their stories one iota and the case was closed. Which was more than could be said for the DCI/DI romance. It had most definitely been rekindled big style and surely with some major concessions being made. Because during their meal the night before, Detective Inspector Murray nearly choked to death on his steak when Barbra Furlong boldly announced...

"I'm happy for you to still see other women, Steven."

Murray struggled to breathe after that comment.

"I realise we're not married, that there's no contract or official commitment on either part and that there's no need for us to have a special exclusive relationship."

Still trying hard to swallow his sirloin at this point, Steven Murray's eyes would have portrayed all.

"Did you really think that I didn't know about you and the others? I'm a DCI, man. Give me some credit."

Murray quickly replaced his cutlery and said nothing.

"Lizzie might not have known about your other life, your secret needs and deeds, but I was fully aware."

This time, his eyes definitely betrayed him.

"Oh, she did know," Barbra said, slightly surprised. "Or was at least privy to some of it. I suppose given her wild bohemian, hedonistic tendencies she most likely joined in. It would've been right up her street and no doubt fully embraced."

Murray blushed at those somewhat accurate remarks.

"So she did, and it was!" Barbra added with a cute knowing smile. "Well I'll be…"

How they had managed to recover from that part of the evening and return to East Lothian together later, goodness only knows. But they did, and DI Murray had gotten up early next day at dawn to fry some 'healthy' bacon, sausage and eggs. After which he took a three mile walk. Or more accurately, he would take DCI Furlong's dog, which was called '3 miles,' for a 200 yard stroll to the end of the street and back.

Whilst playing chef for the morning, Steven had been able to recall a few poignant words that Barbra had spoken to him on the run-up to Christmas the previous year. It was when they were still an item and she'd thought that whilst cuddled up to her, he was sound asleep. But he wasn't. Murray had heard her every word as she quietly whispered this sentimental toast, whilst gently stroking his forehead…

"I hope those days return when your favourite drink tastes magical. When your playlist makes you desirous to rise up and dance. For when random strangers once again make you smile and the beautiful night sky reaches down and touches your soul. I pray sincerely for those days to return, Steven. Days when you fall in love with simply being alive again."

The inspector remembered the words so vividly and well, because they were originally his words. He'd uttered them to Barbra a few days after 'Bunny' Reid had entered, uninvited, into her cottage and waited for her to return home one evening. She'd been shaken and badly affected and Steven Murray had hoped that those words of comfort and reassurance would help.

Seemingly they did exactly that.

Nine

"Sleeping sainted millions can you tell me what you know? Sing to me a song you wrote beneath your pile of stone. The writings on the granite read so trite and insincere. What do you feel you missed about the dash between the years?"

- The Rumjacks

Most evenings at the Gazette offices Al Lawrie could be found typing up copy for next day. That was her daily routine. Her schedule was filled with writing, meetings and deadlines. It was a life of countless stress that often covered graphic or horrifying events and one that constantly left her overworked, underpaid and drained.

The woman genuinely considered herself an introvert. A character trait that she also considered a major advantage as a reporter. Steven Murray had spotted it when they'd first met and she'd always remembered her initial response to him when he had asked...

"Does it impact positively or negatively on your job?"

"Well I certainly notice things that others don't. Mainly because they're far too busy being extroverts."

"Touché," the inspector had replied, before adding... "I believe introverts can excel in any career path that they choose, Al. Even those that seem to require extreme extroversion, such as journalism."

She had laughed at that. Then later that same evening they slept together for the first time.

Tonight though, a personal phone call direct to her mobile - was short, terse and anxious.

"I hear you," Ash Lawrie said. Trying to remain calm and assured. Though failing on all fronts. "But you need to find somewhere safe," she cried out.

There was a stony silence at the other end.

"Get yourself as far away from this situation as possible. Do it and do it now," Ash pleaded with her caller. "Let me know where you end up and I'll…"
The line was already dead.

Back in Dalkeith, Murray and Brooks remained in the car, talked and compared notes with regards to Mrs Lennon and her children. It became obvious that Ian Lennon was not a man to be respected nor admired.

"He constantly went with prostitutes," Brooks began.

"And he'd regularly abuse his wife, Eric told me. Both physically and verbally. The woman lived in fear of him. Constantly walking on eggshells," Steven Murray added.

"Yes, walking on eggshells with a limp." Brooks stated.

"Ah, but often we see what we want to see and get it wrong," the inspector replied. Chastening his young constable. "She had polio when she was young," he told Janice. "I asked Eric all about it. Like you, I guessed it may have been the result of more recent ill treatment. But thankfully, her son assured me otherwise."

"Well her unfaithful, philandering husband, seemingly gambled on anything that moved, his wife told me."

"Philandering. Now there's a good word for me!"

Brooks simply shook her head and pursed her lips.

"He'd scream and shout at the children every day." Inspector Murray confirmed. "They were generally delighted when he never came home for tea. Which was regularly by all accounts. No doubt, he'd be out and about - busy philandering."

Janice ignored his playful jesting and continued to add to the 'bad boy' list… "Mrs Lennon was given no access to any credit cards and literally had to beg him for money each week to feed herself and the children."

Murray seemed confused by this.

"Oh no, he ate out most nights like you said, sir. Happy to wine and dine some extra piece of skirt," Brooks confirmed.

"Well that certainly tied in with what Eric stated about him missing dinner most nights."

The inspector was slightly taken aback by the expression Brooks had just used. It would definitely be deemed wholly unacceptable had a MAN offered it up these days. But again he loved the fact that Janice was always happy to speak her mind, and that she felt comfortable enough to do so in his company. He then added slowly and solemnly…

"Eric told me to speak privately to Emily, if I could."

"You don't think that he…"

"Based on what we've discovered so far, sadly I do."

Janice nodded in agreement. It was as if DC Brooks desperately wanted this man hunted down and brought to justice. The irony being that he was already dead and what a brutal, callous death it had been.

Over twenty substantial holes had viciously penetrated Ian Lennon's naked body whilst he was still alive and screaming. After which he'd been left to bleed out in agony for a while. Then eventually, both his eye sockets and skull welcomed the four-inch, case-hardened, rotating drill-bit. Blood, skin and bone would have spewed out relentlessly. Later, the puncture wounds were sparingly filled with cavity wall insulation and smoothed over expertly, like icing a large sponge cake.

Janice Brooks instantly got a strange surreal sense of satisfaction and justice in the manner in which the devoutly unscrupulous man had eventually been killed.

Before they went to drive off, DI Murray's mobile sounded. It was Lothian's head pathologist calling. It had seemed like an eternity since Doctor Danielle Poll and Inspector Steven Murray had been in regular contact.

Possibly the last actual interaction between the couple had been at the funeral of Thomas Patterson and that had been several months previous. Reports and secondhand conversations had taken place in between, but it hadn't been anywhere near as often as before.

She'd never actually said it to the inspector's face, but he had heard through the Police Scotland grapevine that she was seemingly less than enamoured by the way that he'd treated Barbra Furlong first time around, and for his infatuation later with 'Radical' Lizzie.

All of which greatly disappointed Murray, as he'd never been anything but fully supportive of Danni Poll ever since she took up her role in recent years as Tom Patterson's second in command. Ah well, he gently reminded himself... we're all different.

"Doctor Poll,' he answered politely. "It's good to hear from you." He then offered up in a rather warmer and generally more upbeat tone. "How can I help you? And Danni, be mindful, because you're on speakerphone. Do you know DC Brooks by the way?"

Janice smiled warily as she heard Danielle Poll let out a good-natured, though rather boisterous laugh in response.

"Yes, Inspector. The ever chatty, 'Babbling' Brooks and I have crossed paths previously. She was in uniform last time we met. Good-day to you, Constable. I hope DI Murray is treating you well?"

Brooks nodded without thinking, before realising her mistake and adding... "He is Doc. Thanks for asking."

Murray wasn't overly impressed with that interaction. Was she genuinely checking up on him? Or was he being paranoid? He suspected a bit of both.

"So is it good news you bring us today, Danni?"

"Well I hope so. It's about your body in the blue bin."

"Great," Murray said. Sitting up to listen more intently.

Poll paused slightly before stating emphatically...

"Firstly, did you know DI Murray that was the wrong colour of bin for that man to have been placed in?"

She followed that up with raucous laughter. It took her fully thirty seconds to regain her composure.

"Someone, a little bird, obviously made you fully aware of my concerns in relation to that particular set-up."

"Oh you do crack me up from time to time, Inspector."

Janice Brooks patted his shoulder. Steven Murray was taking it in good spirit, but was doubtless curious at how this mild-mannered American had come to hear about his early morning rant about naked body parts.

"Anyway," Poll said. "We've identified your *bleach boy,* and *God only knows* he doesn't give off *good vibrations*."

Murray smiled at her witty, musical surfing knowledge.

"His name was George Matthew. It didn't ring any bells for me," she added. "Then again, I'm relatively new to these shores. Though to an old hand like yourself, probably pounding the beat at the time, any guesses?"

It was kind of familiar. The name lurked menacingly in the back of Murray's mind. It was crying out to him. But no, no instant recollection could be offered up.

"Sorry, Doc. You'll have to put us out of our misery."

"Well to be fair, I've already spoken with DCI Furlong and it was her that told me all about our mutual friend."

Murray bit on his tongue. She'd already spoken to Barbra. What was this? Disrespect Steven Murray Day? Now he was far from amused, but once again refused to show it in front of Detective Constable Brooks.

"And you intend to keep us in suspense for how much longer?" He curtly, yet playfully asked. "Matthew was?"

"Not a nice person, Inspector," Poll replied quickly.

Both Steven Murray and Janice Brooks had figured that part out. If DCI Furlong had been able to fill in Danni Poll, then it was because the man's DNA must have been on file. So he'd a record and it wouldn't have been for anything good... *so help me Rhonda!*

"How not nice?" A female voice piped up.

"Ah, Janice, you're still there?"

DC Brooks grinned and her cheeks glistened red.

"Indeed I am, Danni. But don't let me interrupt you."

"Well, Mr Matthew was given time for sexually abusing boys and girls that attended a residential school run by the council in East Lothian about fifteen years ago."

Murray offered up a nod. It was coming back to him.

"He only served six years, and had been out and about keeping a low profile by all accounts for the last eight."

It went quiet for a few seconds before Murray's dulcet tones resurfaced to break the silence once again with...

"Sergeant!"

Brooks looked quizzically at him. Whilst Poll said...

"Sorry?"

"I was no longer pounding the beat, Doctor. I was a fully fledged, Sergeant. One that was busy building a name for myself and steadily gaining a reputation."

"Oh, in recent times I believe you've most certainly done that, Inspector."

Murray heard yet another personal dig aimed directly at him. This time even Janice Brooks seemed to flinch uncomfortably at the pithy, personal remark. To his credit, DI Murray seemed to rise above it and continued to share some follow-up...

"Let me think. It was Polish sounding," he said. "It was in Tranent to be specific. It was something like the Walsha or the Walery. No, no, I remember it clearly now. The Walerek Residential School for Children," he recalled. Giving serious weight to those last two words: **For Children.** Whilst shaking his head in dismay.

"I'm going to get Lizzie to work her magic on this."

Brooks raised her eyes and added. "He's not so nice either, sir. That makes Ziola, Lennon and Mr Matthew."

"I hear you, Janice," Murray said, before confirming...

"There had been several abused. Isn't that right, Doc?"

"Well, officially it says only seven." Poll's voice sounded more genial and apologetic. "But DCI Furlong told me that the case notes reckoned he had abused dozens. But they just didn't have the evidence to back them all up. Lots of the children were simply too afraid to speak up or say anything untoward about a man who was supposed to be their trusted teacher at the time."

"Well I guess I'll not be losing any sleep over him," Janice Brooks interjected. "Though it certainly gives credence to a theory that we've got, that's for sure." She ended with a courteous, "Thanks for that, Doc."

"Before you go, Danni." Murray burst in. "What age would that put our ex-teacher at now?"

"He was 55 years of age, Inspector. I hope that helps?"

"Every little helps. You know that."

"You're welcome. Speak soon."

Murray looked toward DC Brooks. Who as predicted, failed to meet his eye. I thought so, he said to himself, biding his time.

Finally the two exhausted detectives drove back to the station and headed home to the land of nod. Before sleep, deliberations would be churning in the busy minds of both Brooks and Murray. It wasn't long before the DI had the images of George Matthew, Mark Ziola and Ian Lennon all fighting for headroom and questioning whether Flood was possibly also a baddie of sorts? Or was he the exception to the rule?

What actually linked these individuals was paramount to inquiries. How had they been selected and who'd chosen them as candidates? Was the fact that it's an all male line-up so far, a clue in itself? Because not one of Reid's missing females had turned up anywhere. Numerous girls had seemingly been tortured and kidnapped. Yet each of them remained well and truly off the radar, with no further audio clips of abuse being received on Murray's desk. Strange that.

It was close to midnight when the stolen, silver BMW hugged the slick, wet, black tarmac. The vehicle's brakes squeezed as it approached a speed bump the the size of an alien spaceship. Afterwards its main beam again illuminated the road ahead like an experienced lighthouse keeper. Foot to the floor it immediately gained traction and ended up taking the corner of Bridge Street, Portobello on only two wheels.

Inside the high-spec vehicle were at least four adults. The Bayerische Motoren Werke, as always had a personality all of its very own. It appeared to be genuinely sexy and feminine with its designer curves, prominent chassis and sleekly raised headlights. Its quality had already inspired some exceptionally impressive driving skills.

Unexpectedly a rear door flew open and a lifeless male body crunched and thumped down hard onto the quiet residential roadside. Its prevailing momentum sent it rolling at pace across a well maintained, yet rain-soaked gravel walkway. It was there that a gathered picket-line of green and blue wheelie bins had brought it to an abrupt halt. The man's back was thrust upside-down against them. One leg angled in salute, whilst his slender, scrawny neck had been broken well before his disheveled body had even exited the speeding vehicle.

Twenty minutes earlier this individual had been going about his business not bothering anyone. Twenty minutes later and numerous men and women, many in traditional white SOCO suits, would be happy to bother everyone in sight, as they tried to piece together the dead man's final movements.

It had been a while since DI Murray had experienced one of his hallucinatory, highly visual and extremely exhausting dream sessions.

Tonight as the concerned inspector turned out his light, little did he know that a full-blown episode lay ahead of him. It would be painful, sordid and extremely worrying all rolled into one. Ten minutes later…

He envisaged scantily clad x-ray images of Lauren Naulls, Al, Lizzie and Furlong all nibbling and biting one another at different crime scenes. Murray wondered if celibacy was an option at this point? - **What was all that about?**

Ex-secretary and office manager, Lauren was first to appear. Dressed only in black briefs and stockings, she sat astride a blue bin screaming, 'Wrong one! Wrong one! Wrong one!' She jumped off and theatrically threw back the lid, revealing a chopped up male cadaver. The head instantly began singing, 'I'm in pieces, bits and pieces.' The naked, dismembered body had been soaked in bleach and then rinsed off - **What was all that about?**

Next up, it was the turn of newshound, Al Lawrie to invade his normal sleep pattern. The journalist sat topless and tanned, typing up an article on her iPad at the home of Dr Ian Lennon. Did that mean that there was a further story there? Family and friends had gathered around the body. Then the inspector realised that none of them were friends, including the family members. Because each one of them proceeded to take turns of the cordless drill that had been left behind. They then applied the quick-setting cavity wall foam. It oozed out of the medic's every pore - **What was all that about?**

As Murray turned and tossed restlessly, he questioned his very relationship with DCI Furlong and the fact that he still continued to update Naulls and Lawrie. No wonder his mind was aching. That was when 'Radical' Lizzie popped up. She had invaded a Leith home and was kitted out in an all-in-one bodysuit under a white tunic. She held a nail gun in her hand and was shooting specifically at the tartan bonnet on the man's head. Her aim faltered slightly on the fifth nail and it exploded straight through Ziola's left eye socket. Shattering one side of his head completely. The fallout and debris landed on Mr Sheen, a nearby can of furniture polish - **What was all that about?**

Without further ado, it was the turn of a soaking wet Barbra Furlong to emerge smiling from the deep roots and murky weeded area of a local canal. She may have looked glamorous in her slinky bikini, which was cut very generously for women of a certain age, but the decaying body to be found at her feet did her no favours whatsoever - **What was all that about?**

Interspersed between all of the murder scene segments were clips of stampeding women fleeing from 'Bunny' Reid establishments. Effectively costing him hundreds of thousands of pounds per annum. Beatings, rapes and strangulations weren't forgotten. They too popped in to give fleeting Oscar nominated performances.

And who exactly were the flaky Fitzsimmon brothers? One of them was a psychotic murdering lowlife. Whilst the other one, who'd step on scales daily - had the unique ability to eat as much chocolate as he liked. Safe in the knowledge that next day his silver studded earrings would still fit perfectly! Even in his sleep that thought made Steven smirk - **What was all that about?**

'Kid' Curry appeared intermittently and like a personal host or ghost, he'd drive King Murray, complete with crown, from scene to scene. Zooming around high on speed at 110 miles per hour on his supercharged, eco-friendly, enamel coated wheelchair.

So a foam filled doctor. A decaying delivery driver. A blood soaked enforcer and a singing corpse in a blue bin - all dead. Throw in numerous extracted escorts who've had a brush with death, plus a fully masked corrupt officer and we're all sorted.

Drenched in a pool of sweat, two hours later he woke. Immediately he put notes of his mad exploits onto his phone for posterity. It was barely 1am and Barbra was still up busily preparing her remarks for the media in a few hours time. Was there meaning to be had from his almighty surreal adventure or had it all been complete madness? Unsurprisingly his first words to Furlong when he sat up were… **"What was all that about?"**

Later that day he would schedule an appointment to go visit with someone at HMP Edinburgh. Better known as Saughton jail.

Ten

"I've been all around the world. But, there's nowhere compares to my hometown. The mayhem of Glasgow is buried deep in my blood."

- Gerry Cinnamon

Next day was a busy media day. On these occasions it took much longer to get out the door in the morning. Murray always remembered that from his previous long term residency at Furlong's cute home in East Lothian.

Last night they'd stayed there and Barbra always wanted to look her best on these days where they were in front of the press. Indeed, today was a double whammy. Ash had arranged a press conference at The Gazette offices in Edinburgh mid-morning. Then the BBC in Glasgow beckoned at three o'clock to record a reconstruction of the death of Doctor Ian Lennon. Furlong was still applying her makeup when Steven Murray drove them off at high speed.

The latest body discovered dumped last night on Bridge Street, would not feature today on the live media session. *'It was far too soon to say if it was connected in any way to the other deaths,'* was presently the official line. Unofficially, all the officers knew that it was. But that they'd have to wait for forensics or themselves to discover a definitive link to all of the others.

Less than ten miles from the busy media circus, the wholly irrational and often psychopathic, James Baxter Reid was having breakfast discussions of his own. He was holding court with a rather nervous individual.

Their location was a ten minute drive from the home of Charlene Lennon and her two children. Could that be a simple coincidence? Or was there something much more sinister altogether at work?

Newbattle Abbey had remained the home of the Marquesses of Lothian until being given to the nation in 1937, and for the past 80 years it has been effectively used as a College of Education.

Currently 'Rab' Nielsen was being held by the scruff of the neck as the Reidmeister made his point in his usual no-nonsense manner.

"I'm working on it, 'Bunny.' Honest," the inspector spluttered. Trying to free himself from the man's grip.

"Well you'd better work harder." Reid told him.

As always the man's raspy, hoarse voice had a deep resonant timbre. The kind that anchored your soul to a single moment in time.

The oak-lined library that played host to the men featured a 17th-century moulded ceiling, and the young lady presently pouring them tea was anxious to make a hasty retreat. Strangling someone by the throat wasn't something that she normally experienced on a daily basis during her catering responsibilities. It was after all, supposedly an up-market educational establishment.

"Thank you, my dear," 'Bunny' offered up like a harsh sounding grandparent. Before eventually dismissing the nervous teenager with a disparaging wave of his hand.

At 11am, Furlong and DI Murray walked out to begin their grilling from the gathered crowd. News reporters and journalists jam-packed into the media suite with microphones, mobiles and big-screen cameras flashing furiously and clicking non-stop. Monitors and heavy-duty lighting set the scene for Batman and Robin's latest appearance in front of the spotlight.

The public wanted answers. The detectives wanted the public to help provide those answers, and A.L. Lawrie had been allowed to start off the proceedings...

"DCI Furlong are we saying that we have a serial killer on the loose in and around the streets of Edinburgh? Are people safe to venture out?"

As Lawrie asked those questions. Every cameraman, reporter and sound engineer edged closer. Each one shuffling for a better view. Both were fairly standard beginner questions, though a little sensationalised and dramatic. Barbra Furlong was well used to the occasional media circus and, as was often the way, she would embrace the role of juggler.

"It is most definitely safe for people to go about their daily business," she said calmly. "We're following a specific line of inquiry which would lead us to think that these current deaths are not random, but possibly all related. Though not necessarily carried out by the same person. Hence, not a serial killer. Not someone who strikes on a whim or at a minute's notice. These attacks have been carefully planned and don't look to have been carried out by one single person."

"So are you saying Chief Inspector Furlong that they are gang related? Can we expect retaliatory action?"

The officer gave the questioner a derisory scowl.

Bobby Bryant, an experienced Mirror Group journalist had been the one probing. This man confidently portrayed what most people imagined an old-school, stereotypical, newspaper reporter to look like. He was of medium build and had a slovenly, disheveled, scruffy appearance. Plus he had numerous miniature note pads hanging from every pocket. He'd deliberately thrown a hint of alarm and concern into the question, and although delivered toward the detective chief inspector, she never actually got the chance to answer it. Because the audacious Steven Murray was bored...

"The DCI never mentioned that the murders were gang related, Mr Bryant. Are you going deaf in your old age? You've been doing this as long as me, Bobby. You even wore that same suit back in the day! So let's get serious here and stick with the facts and stop with all your rumour fuelled questions and endless speculation."

Many smiled at Murray's frank exchange. They'd known the man for years and loved his plain speaking. The newer element though didn't always take to being told what to do or being put in their place. They were still young and fresh and keen to change the world. They all had aspirations of moving mountains and breaking down boundaries. Give it a year or two, Murray thought. For both he and Barbra Furlong had seen restless, unprofessional individuals with inflated egos come and go regularly over the years.

"Here's the deal," Murray told them. "We need help."

The reporters waited patiently on the follow-up.

"It's as simple as that," the inspector informed them. "Currently we have FOUR male individuals. Each one brutally murdered to death. Ma'am," was then proffered up in a rehearsed manner. Handing over an imaginary baton to an already warmed-up DCI. Barbra was all set and ready, and she continued to run at pace…

"In Bilton Lane we discovered the remains of a man that we believe to be in his 50's," she said.

"A killing carried out by one person." Murray added.

Some eyes in the media lit up at getting that little tidbit. Mainly the younger element who didn't know better.

Deliberately they'd withheld George Matthew's name.

"That same day, another body was found in a building just off Leith Walk," Furlong continued. "The deceased was a local man named Mark Ziola. Mr Ziola was a well known security worker in that part of town. His flat is in a busy area of the city, so we're hopeful that someone saw or heard something that could help us."

"There was no way that specific killing was carried out by one person," Inspector Murray informed them this time. "So a group of two or more would have been in the vicinity at the time. Granted they may have entered the apartment at different times, making it more difficult to pinpoint exactly who they were. But like we said earlier, we genuinely need all the help we can get."

Murray never failed to shake his head at how most of the public and journalists almost routinely expected the police to solve all crimes. But generally speaking, they were never willing to put their own heads above the parapet. They were happy to shirk any responsibility that they had to step up to the mark, to provide reliable evidence, to offer witness statements and actually to be involved in any way shape or form whatsoever. That's a soapbox that DI Murray could be found on regularly.

Meantime, whilst Furlong spoke to the multitude, her inspector felt the urgent need to send an important text.

"A murder occurred ten days ago on the outskirts of Dalkeith. That death we now believe to be the first killing. So it would appear that it all actually began in a rural setting," Barbra told them. "These individuals have definitely been specifically targeted. We haven't yet found the common link, but our investigations are ongoing. So you can all understand that with this particular pattern we feel confident it's not a serial killer and certainly not someone randomly killing strangers. On this occasion, Dr Ian Lennon was a pillar of the community. A trusted and valued General Practitioner. A man who was in fact dedicated to saving lives, rather than taking them. We're still appealing for anyone who may have saw or heard something untoward to please come forward."

Murray genuinely struggled to lift his head during Furlong's kind generic words. His thoughts had turned back toward Lennon's battered, abused wife and family.

He couldn't help it, but the man deserved all that he got. He was a thug and a bully. Maybe death was a bit harsh, though Steven Murray remained on the fence over that. It was an interesting double act that the pair had chosen to operate today. At the very least it kept the reporters on their toes.

"With regards to Ian Lennon." The inspector added some pertinent words, but still wasn't able to call him by his professional title. "That's yet another killing that couldn't have been carried out by a single person. So it is absolutely right and correct that you highlight the fact that others are definitely involved. There is without doubt people out there who will know some of these individuals. They'll have noticed them on edge. Possibly even posted missing on the days or nights of these brutal, cold-blooded attacks. Be in no doubt, we currently have people protecting these murderers."

The inspector went on to speak briefly about the death of Kieran Flood, the second killing. Both he and Brooks had eventually read up on the details and sure enough there were similarities, but they were slim.

Again though, based on current evidence there was a strong indication that someone was definitely meting out their own form of justice. None of these were assorted random killings, that had become clear.

Murray was getting overly emotional and passionate. The press loved that about him. What you saw, was what you got. Perhaps his team and especially Lizzie and Barbra Furlong in recent months would all tell you that was not actually the case. That if you took the time to gradually scratch away the surface of that public persona and kicked his 'black dog' into touch, you would soon discover and witness a very different side to Detective Inspector Steven Murray, altogether.

He was currently in the midst of clarifying specifics with those present, before inviting further scrutiny…

'How many officers were on the task force?'

'Did they have any further clues that they could share presently?'

'Wasn't Mr Ziola gang related?'

'Moving forward - did they expect further killings?'

The senior detectives were bombarded with another twenty minutes of questions. Many of which went unanswered. Then as their time drew to a close, the group were collectively informed that they'd only availability for one last remaining inquiry. That's when Ashley Louise Lawrie stood up, just as she'd done thirty minutes previously. Barbra was delighted that is was Al. The thought of a curve ball being thrown at this stage was not at all appealing. That's when her DI spoke…

"Miss Lawrie you got the ball rolling, so it's fitting that you round things off. What would you like to ask?"

"Thank you, Inspector Murray. This final question is probably best put to your chief inspector though, as I'm not really sure of its accuracy. It's a piece of news that has just reached me in the last few minutes."

Both officers braced themselves, exactly as planned.

"Well let me see if I can confirm or deny it for you," Barbra Furlong stated in her normal assured and professional manner.

Ash Lawrie held up a torn piece of paper and read…

"Given that you think the four heinous murders already committed may all be linked, DCI Furlong…"

The others could tell by her tone that this was the very 'curve ball' that they all wished they'd possessed.

"Could it be," Ash asked. "That the dead body tossed out of a moving vehicle and abandoned in Bridge Street last night, was in fact the fifth murder in the series?"

Loud audible gasps were prominent amongst the gathered journalists, as the two officers made their excuses and promptly exited not only the room but the building.

The Gazette Newspaper Group would be more than delighted with that finale. The crowd of tried and tested journalists would all be kept occupied on the newly discovered fifth body. No doubt busy creating links and airy fairy stories of their own speculative theories to splash up as headlines and false facts.

The two officers were also happy to now be heading across to the west with news of another body fresh in everyone's mind. Hopefully some witnesses may now feel galvanised into doing their duty and coming forward with some helpful information. At least that was what DI Murray was hoping for when he sent word via text to Ash Lawrie minutes earlier, and she in turn asked the question of Barbra Furlong.

He did find it a nice touch that she'd written it out on a ripped-off piece of scrap paper. Touché, Al. Well done.

As the number of elite officers grew on the team carrying out the investigations into the spate of unexplained murders, Barbra Furlong and Steven Murray headed over to the quayside in Glasgow to assist BBC Scotland with the reconstruction of Ian Lennon's tragic death. During their travels they were being kept in the loop regarding the body that wasn't wearing a seatbelt. A body and an area that they also knew SOCO would be busy examining throughout the day.

For themselves by the side of the Clyde, voice-overs, sound bites and appeals on camera were all part of the process. The two detectives did their recording stint and eventually returned to DI Murray's Barnton home at ten minutes to eight. Once there, they were greeted by an enthusiastic couple in the shape of 'Kid' Curry and 'Radical' Lizzie. That pairing had some very interesting and important news of their very own to share.

Eleven

"Gie fools their silks and knaves their wine; A Man's a Man for a' that. For a' that, and a' that, Their tinsel show an' a' that; The honest man, tho' e'er sae poor, Is king o' men for a' that."

- Robert Burns

Maggie Morrison stood shivering outside the popular launderette. She had managed the outlet near the Leith docks for the best part of a quarter of a century. Overhead a broken street light flickered at regular intervals onto the original thirty year-old signage. New residents to the area always got a kick out of seeing the name of the premises for the first time. Maggie was a local and had witnessed plenty of comings and goings during her tenure and not always for the better.

In the last ten years, Leith had undergone some incredible changes. Today, after decades of decline, the area is often described as being 'Edinburgh's coolest neighbourhood.' Known for its impressive dining and trendy art scene. That alone is a huge transformation from the rough part of town that it used to be. A place where Mike Tyson would once shake in fear of his life.

A little known fact that the widowed Mrs Morrison liked to impress her clients with, was that the harbour area today has the highest concentration of Michelin star restaurants in Scotland (4 to be precise).

As it fast approached eight o'clock in the evening, the grey-haired woman had one hour left of her laborious, twelve hour shift. Tired and exhausted, she'd been enjoying what was meant to have been a brief break for a cigarette. Though that was nearly twenty minutes ago.

Most of that valuable time had been taken up by a customer joining her outside with a vape, striking up a conversation and engaging her in a whole host of random subjects. At least at the time, Maggie thought she'd been a customer. In hindsight, she couldn't have been more wrong and the police arrived within minutes of her distressed and anxious phone call.

Back in the comfort of his home, Murray questioned…
"What's with you two? Have you gotten engaged?"

At that, Barbra Furlong nearly choked on the paracetamol that she'd taken for her toothache, whilst 'Drew Curry turned scarlet. Lizzie however, dressed in an all khaki combat outfit and with her blackened hair put up into a bun for the day, mulled over that particular idea and smiled wistfully.

One second before 'Ironside,' in his wheelchair could share the big reveal, two mobile phones began to ring simultaneously. That was never an encouraging sign. Murray and Furlong shared a look. This wasn't good.

"Hello, DCI Furlong speaking." Was one response.

"Hi, Joe. What do you have for me?" Was the other.

"I hear you. Thanks. Both DI Murray and I will be with you shortly."

Furlong hung up and immediately grabbed her coat.

"Cheers, Sarge. Call Janice. Tell her I'll meet her there."

"She's already here, sir. Her and DC Harris."

"Okay. The DCI and I will be there in ten minutes."

"Sorry, but your news will have to wait," Furlong told 'Drew and Lizzie. "It looks like our man is speeding things up. There's been another murder in Leith."

"We don't know it's definitely connected," Murray said.

"Well it had better be, Steven. Because the thought of another murderer on the loose would be alarming."

Murray conceded that point at least.

"We'll still be here when you get back," Lizzie said in a supportive and understanding manner. "Let us know if we can help," she added positively.

Curry, although disappointed, threw in - "Go get him."

Within seconds, Furlong's vehicle was out the driveway and careering along the surrounding streets with blue lights flashing. At that speed, DI Murray had badly miscalculated their estimated time of arrival. His recalculated ETA would be… 3 minutes!

That night a lone figure was to be found in a five star B&B in the east. He'd had a lovely meal and was now enjoying the most beautiful view from his bay window.

Broughty Castle was built at the end of the 1400's. This evening the sun cast long shadows on the ground and its slanting rays gave a warm orange tinge to the sky. This idyllic scene filled the man with excitement and enthusiasm. He'd been motivated into action, for there was work to be done. It was abundantly clear having watched DCI Furlong and her lapdog, Mr Murray at their press briefing that morning, that neither were interested in helping secure the safety of HIS girls and in protecting HIS interests. So 'Bunny' Reid had to deal with matters in his usual delicate, ultra-sensitive manner.

"And when you came back inside, the machine was still spinning, Mrs Morrison?"

"Yes. Exactly, Sergeant. Like I said, it was set on a high-rinse cycle and that would have gone on for another ten minutes easily." As she spoke, she held on nervously to her well-worn, grubby apron.

"But you chose to stop it?" The curious voice asked. It belonged to Steven Murray. The man had silently entered the cordoned off launderette. "Can I ask why?"

Taken aback, the female looked warily at DS Hanlon.

"It's okay, Maggie. This is Detective Inspector Murray."

Having given the woman the man's full title, Maggie Morrison seemed to instantly grow taller by a few inches. As if she were meeting Mandela, Churchill or Barack Obama. She even cleared her throat and began to pronounce her words more eloquently as she proceeded to respond to the inspector's question.

Behind his hand, 'Sherlock' grinned in bewilderment.

"I turned it off, Inspector, because I didn't expect to see a head and other shiny body parts being rinsed, buffeted and cleansed so thoroughly."

"Oh, I see."

Murray hadn't realised that the dead body was inside.

"I didn't get a chance to tell you, sir."

"My apologies. I just jumped in without thinking, Joe."

DCI Furlong and DC Brooks were only a couple of feet behind Murray. So the whole comedy sketch being played out in front of them had been pretty humorous.

"In the washing machine?" Barbra Furlong questioned.

"And at a high-rinse," Maggie Morrison chirped in. "When a low level, delicate wash would have sufficed."

The three others looked at her in astonishment, as Hanlon continued to grin. He then gently escorted and encouraged the woman off the premises. Maggie, having spotted all the stars and stripes on the chief inspector's outfit was very near curtsying, bowing and blowing kisses out her backside as she was led away. Though her hands still never left her apron pockets.

"CCTV footage?" Was Murray's next question.

"Nope, nothing. The first cameras are three streets away. There is nothing on this stretch at all, sir. Boyd and a few other uniforms have already checked and DOUBLE CHECKED. Before you insist upon it."

Murray shrugged and smiled. Both men knew each other well. The DI always liked to double check things.

"Where are the SOCO's?" Furlong enquired.

"I believe that they're en-route, Ma'am. Less than five minutes away."

Barbra scanned around the deserted and apparently poorly maintained premises. Surprised that the place was still even in existence.

"If this is the work of the same man then he's becoming quite brazen," she stated. "Mid-evening on commercial premises? It's cocky, arrogant or downright stupid. Steven, what do you think? Surely signs of someone that's had enough and looking to get caught?"

Brooks and Joseph Hanlon were now genuinely intrigued to hear their inspector's thoughts. Seeing as their DCI had happily aired her *'dirty linen'* in public. Murray's reply though, took them all by surprise.

"Before we speculate further, I think we should…"

By pausing, he was teasing them and they all knew it.

Furlong immediately pulled rank…

"Inspector. You think we should what?" She urged.

"I think we should get the great Afro MacDonald down here straight away, Ma'am, and seek her valuable assistance. That's what I think. And no matter what wisdom she can impart, one thing is certain…"

Furlong, Hanlon and Brooks knew what was coming…

"This is not the work of one person!"

They all unanimously nodded in agreement.

"How did THEY get HIM in here?" Murray added. "I'm guessing that it's another he?"

Brooks answered… "Yes, I can confirm it's a he, sir. Mrs Morrison in a roundabout way confirmed that it's definitely a man."

"When she arrived," 'Sherlock' told them, "DC Brooks here had a chat with Maggie, Inspector. The woman was still in shock and Janice did a great job reassuring her and calming her down."

"So what exactly did she say in her - round about way, Constable Brooks?"

"Well would you like it verbatim, sir?"

"That's preferred. Do you need to check your notes?"

"On this occasion, I don't. It's now vividly ingrained in my memory for time and all eternity," she grinned.

'Sherlock' smiled cheekily at both his DCI and his DI.

"We don't have all night." Steven encouraged her.

"Her actual precise words, sir, were - Who's gettin' that humongous, giant, hairy penis oot o' ma machine? Coz am no touchin' those soapy testicles wae a barge pole!"

'Sherlock' stifled a laugh. "I suspect if she'd spoken to yourself, Ma'am, or Inspector Murray, her choice of words may have been oh so different," he grinned. "But a man for definite, of that we're sure."

Now Barbra Furlong's question to her DI was simple.

"How did you know about, Afro MacDonald?"

Neither Hanlon nor Brooks had heard of her. But this would make for a great docu-series: Furlong & Murray (Raw and Unedited). A bit of tension was in the air.

"I still have my sources," the man said moodily. "Were you ever going to tell me and the others about her?"

"It was only confirmed yesterday, Steven. So you do have very good sources still it would appear. And we've been rather busy today or did you fail to notice that?"

Murray shrugged and said nothing.

"I was going to tell everyone in the morning. She'll be a great addition to the team and surely your ego's not that fragile DI Murray? Or is it?" She mocked.

Two other souls stood like scavengers waiting for any scraps that might be tossed their way to enlighten them.

"Aphrodite MacDonald is a criminal psychologist," Furlong threw out for them. "She is known as Afro and will be joining the team in the next few days."

Both Hanlon and DC Brooks seemed impressed by that news, much to Steven Murray's chagrin.

"In the meantime, we'll all just have to put up with our grumpy DI's improbable theories, synopsis and educated guesswork regarding this particular case."

"Yes, yes, very funny," Steven Murray sulked. "You're absolutely hilarious, Chief Inspector."

At that moment a text beeped on Hanlon's mobile.

"That's forensics arrived, Ma'am."

"Go greet them, Joe. Ensure that they're brought up to speed with everything."

After which, Barbra Furlong moved slowly forward to gaze curiously inside the drum of the large industrial machine. Through the damp moisture and steamed up window she could just about make out various body parts that had all been cut, chopped, sliced and diced.

"Much like your man in the bin, I presume, Steven?"

Murray nodded and what resembled the faintest of smiles began to gradually resurface upon his face.

"To be fair, Ma'am," Janice Brooks spoke up. "He should never have been put in the blue bin. That was just out of order. Unforgivable."

After a momentary pause, a ripple of soft laughter escaped from Furlong's mouth. Whilst infectious tears began to stream down the cheeks of Murray and the young female constable. Highly inappropriate? Absolutely. But each of these individuals had seen enough death and heartache over the past few days, and from time to time a little bit of brevity goes a long way to maintaining one's own personal sanity.

At that precise moment three scenes of crime officers arrived through the narrow doorway. Complete with their paper Ghostbuster suits on, they ambled slowly along the tiled floor. Though their look of confusion stated - Into what madness have we just stumbled?

The shamed trio of Police Scotland employees tried to compose themselves as best they could and went to exit with what little dignity they still had left in tact.

DCI Furlong headed off to speak with the two or three reporters that had gathered. One of which was the busy and extremely versatile A.L Lawrie. How had she gotten wind of the story so fast? Had Steven? No, he was with her all the way from Barnton. So how? Later, that would be revisited for definite, she thought.

Meanwhile Detective Inspector Murray had something on his mind that needed cleared up also…

"Janice, I need to ask you a personal question."

Brooks enjoyed their chats, so nodded happily.

"Is it about my 'body in the bin' remark?" She asked.

"In a purely coincidental way it actually is," he smiled.

Though Murray then caught her out with…

"Why did you feel the need to tell Doctor Poll about my animated bluster over the dead body in the blue bin? Didn't you know that I was joking about the whole wrong colour thing? I like to rant and rave and get on the occasional soapbox. To embellish, exaggerate and laugh about things. Hadn't you noticed?"

"What!" Janice Brooks exclaimed, about to deny all…

"Please don't say it wasn't you…"

"I'm sorry, sir," she immediately interrupted. "I just hadn't gotten to know you well enough at that point. It went way over my head. I was nervous and needed clarification. I had to know that I was still sane and was desperate to check up and see if you were also?"

She swallowed hard. Her face desired forgiveness.

Murray pursed his lips, nodded, considered her words and finally shook his head - all at the same time.

"I love working with you, sir, and I sincerely apologise. We have had a blast since then have we not? I get you now - I think," she added with a cheeky grin to cover herself. "Otherwise I wouldn't have referred to it as a joke two minutes ago."

She definitely had a point the DI conceded once again.

"I think we get on great also, Janice. I love your intellectual mind, your ability to mix on many levels and I'm especially a fan of your dry wit - I think. *'Anyone who has the gall to wear ridiculous, hideous shirts like that out in public, fully deserves to have his palm tree chopped down and his coconuts removed by whatever means available,'* may well go down as my favourite quote of the whole year."

The easygoing female blushed with unashamed pride.

"But the fact that I never recognised that you were gay, still rankles me. It was when you called her Danni."

Brooks instantly turned Cluedo red. Bright shades of Miss Scarlet - in the library - with the candlestick!

"I must be getting really unobservant in my old age," Murray continued. "The *'You're welcome'* from Dr Poll was directed at me, I got that. But it took a few seconds to twig that the *'Speak soon'* was proffered toward yourself. And the fact that you couldn't look me in the eye afterward, only confirmed it. So you and Poll are an item. That'll be the kept secret in town, I suspect."

Janice remained cautious. Uncertain how to play this. She certainly didn't want to let him know that he may well be the last officer in the station to know about her personal circumstances. Most of the others were all fully aware of her sexuality and of her current girlfriend. Eventually she opted for...

"You're not old, sir. It's not like we go about holding hands, raising placards or wearing badges these days."

She'd gone for humour and his vulnerable ego. She felt that those were definitely the safer options, but only time would tell. She stood patiently and waited, and waited and......

"What are you waiting for, Constable? The matter is closed. Let's move on. We've got work to be done."

His wide infectious smile said it all, and Brooks happily followed behind him as they walked over purposefully to take Maggie Morrison's formal statement.

Twelve

On the speed of light journey over to Leith, Steven Murray and Barbra Furlong had agreed that they would partner up with Brooks and Hanlon, respectively. Thus allowing Lorna Harris to finish her shift and travel over to visit with DI Kerr in the hospital. She could easily sweet talk her way in, even at such a late hour.

"Just flash your police I.D," Furlong had told her. "No matter the time, they'll always let you in."

Lorna had also been instructed to pass on the love and best wishes of all the team and let 'Sandy' know that they were looking forward to the baby's impending arrival. Steven Murray had hoped to have returned from Glasgow, quickly changed his clothes and nipped across the water to see her himself. But that phone call at eight o'clock had put an end to those particular plans. Instead, Constable Harris was more than delighted to fill in and accept the assignment in his place.

"Mrs Morrison. How are you feeling?" Brooks began.

"Aye, aye. A lot better, love. Thanks for asking." With her hands still firmly in the pockets of her works apron, she added... "It was a bit o' a shock, ken?"

"Absolutely, Maggie. It's not every day you get to find a dead body at your workplace."

"Well, sure, that's true enough," the feisty woman admitted. "Unless ye just happen to work at the local morgue," she replied with a cheeky smile and a friendly, playful wink.

She's all there and round the corner, Murray thought. Sharp as a tack, he reckoned. Then again, you would have to be to work in that environment. As he continued to listen to her responses to the questioning, he soon realised that she was also a more than capable individual. So he was very hopeful that she would surprise them and gift them something unexpected.

"You said several women had all come in right before you went out for your break. Is that right, Maggie?"

"Correct. That's spot on," she said, "But…"

"There's a but?" Brooks enquired.

Murray stood tall. He was extra keen to hear 'the but.'

"But I would swear that they all appeared to use the same machine." Morrison pointed up to the back.

"The one that the body was found in?" Janice guessed.

"That would be the one. How did you figure that?"

Brooks and Murray both withheld a potential laugh.

"So they brought in dirty washing?" Brooks continued.

"Well they certainly brought in plenty of bags, love." Maggie stated. "Which begs the question - What did they do with all their dirty laundry? Because they weren't in there long enough for it all to have been cleaned and dried."

Murray gave her a questioning look, whilst Brooks closed her eyes and screwed up her face slightly.

"Ah, geez," Maggie Morrison yelped. "You mean the lot o' them walked right past me at the door wae nae clothes? It wiz him, all neatly chopped up in assorted Asda bags. Then they randomly threw him into the machine for a final lap o' the pool. A very one-sided - Sink or swim!"

Again the officers tried hard to refrain from laughter. This woman had obviously missed her vocation in life. She would've and should've been the star turn every year at the local Christmas pantomime.

"So while that 'greasy midden' was keeping me busy talkin' at the door all that time…"

"Greasy midden?" Murray gestured. Seeking more info.

"Did ye like that wan, Inspector? Ah just made it up right there," Maggie smiled. "Aye, the skanky, skinny wan wae the dark greasy hair. She kept rabbiting oan at me. Talking pure mince, she was. But ah didnae want tae be rude, like. So ah jist listened like any auld, nut job would. They stitched me up good and proper, didn't they?"

"You're definitely not old," Brooks reassured her with a smile. Careful not to comment on the 'nut job' part.

"One final question, Maggie." DI Murray said. "The 'lot o' them.' Would be how many exactly?"

With her brightly rouged cheeks and her over-the-top strawberry lipstick, Morrison would have passed the auditions for 'Widow Twankey' with flying colours.

"How many? Aye, good question, Inspector. I usually concentrate on how many bags. So I reckon…" The woman paused for a mental recount. "There would have been five of them. Six if you include the 'chip fryer' that distracted me."

"Do you mind me asking how you got to that number?" Janice Brooks hesitatingly asked. Scared to hear the reply.

"Sure, hen. Well ah saw at least four folk wae two bags and then there must have been wan mair at least."

Steven Murray took the bait… "Because?"

"Because that huge 'Tadger Badger,' the 'Rock of Ages' that a' saw circulating in that machine would have needed an enormous Tesco 'Every Little Helps' bag all to itself!"

This time at the conclusion of their interview, there was no holding back and both detectives burst into fits of laughter. Only when they spotted the... 'We are not amused' looks from Furlong, Hanlon and the others nearby, did they even try to regain their composure.

"A Tadger Badger! Now that's classic," Murray smiled.

"That I wouldn't know," Brooks grinned with a cheeky wink of gay pride.

In Dundee the man's ten thousand pound Rolex watch glistened as its owner listened appreciatively to the 'Classics At Christmas' concert. The annual gala was presently in full swing at the city's historic Caird Hall.

As the extravaganza's stage lights caught his wrist the second hand of his expensive timepiece glided effortlessly around its circumference and showed 9pm. That was when his trouser pocket vibrated and he quietly looked at the brief message on his phone...

NEED YOU HOME - NOW! - was all it said. But that was enough for Steven Fitzsimmon to make a rushed exit and a few enemies, as he rose from the middle of the fourth row to disrupt the show and inconvenience a few up-tight music aficionados.

They should think themselves lucky. Because had it been his brother, Bazza, sat in front of them and they'd given him any grief in the slightest - he would've most likely shot them were they sat.

In the impressive eight bedroomed Broughty Ferry mansion that the brothers shared, two of their henchmen had been bound, gagged and deposited in the home's large walk-in freezer. For many years the premises operated successfully as an exclusive, high-end bespoke hotel. This evening whilst security chilled out, their overweight boss, Barry, lay slumped at the head of his extra-long mahogany dining room table.

The brief pain the man felt at his temple earlier, hadn't in fact been caused by tension or an almighty migraine, as was often the case. No, the real culprit on this occasion had been a small calibre revolver.

'When the bullet hole causes no alarm in the storyteller's art, we are the artists of hell.'

That had been the famous quote in 'Bunny' Reid's mind when he'd pulled the trigger a minute earlier. It was so famous in fact that he'd no recollection of who'd actually spoken the poetic words. But when the sibling with the spider tattoo returns, he'll have gotten the message loud and clear.

There are some people in life you simply don't mess with. If only others in and around Edinburgh would take more heed of that particular counsel.

"I've got my kids names tattooed on my right arm," Lorna informed a rather shocked looking Sandra Kerr.

"Aidan and Leah," she said.

"Wow," 'Sandy' offered. Taken aback by that revelation.

"My husband asked me why I didn't get his as well?"

Kerr remained silent. But her eyes did the asking.

"Well, I said. They'll ALWAYS be my kids, but you won't necessarily always be my... I didn't get to finish the sentence before he upped and shot out the door. If only he'd done that years ago, then our first child wouldn't even have been conceived!"

They both blushed and chuckled at that risqué remark.

Kerr's new found friend had driven over to Fife hoping that 'Sandy' was still available for a quick catch-up - and by good fortune she was.

Lorna had passed on the best wishes from everyone and sincere apologies from Steven Murray. Which then led her to update DI Kerr further about the recent developments at Leith and the 'body in the dryer.'

"There are definitely some things in life we just can't explain," Sandy smiled.

"Like someone disappearing and finding them turn up next in a tumble dryer?" Lorna responded with a giggle.

"Well, I was thinking more like sitting in a chair then attempting to lift your right foot off the floor and making clockwise circles with it."

"What! Like this?" Harris demonstrated admirably.

"Yes." Kerr grinned. "But while you're doing that, now try drawing the number six in the air with your right hand and you'll witness your foot change direction."

Straightaway her willing colleague tried it out and sure enough her foot went anti-clockwise. Three times she attempted it. Each time, she got the exact same result.

"Like I said. Some things in life we just can't explain."

After a few more minutes of family talk, work gossip and chit-chat, Harris noticed her friend's body begin to shut down with exhaustion. Lorna instructed 'Sandy' to make the most of her time before she was called upon. She reached out for an extra big hug before she left and was super excited to pop back in the next twenty-four hours to see how both baby and mother were doing.

It would be a poignant time for the inspector as she prepared to give birth, whilst pondering on her murdered husband and her remaining twin girls.

Only two weeks ago, Sandra Kerr and Lorna Harris had spoken at length about their previous experiences of child birth. Eventually both had doubled over in laughter as they dared one another to come up with only three words to best describe their 'joyful' trauma.

Constable Harris had begun. Cheerfully announcing…

"Thrilling, Empowering and Exciting."

Yep, first time around she was happy with those words. Now DI Kerr, 'Sandy,' wasn't sure that she could match that killer trio of adjectives. Eventually, she opted for…

"Painful, Terrifying and Confusing."

She did have twins after all. So they'd found that set of words highly amusing. By this point however, Lorna was inspired and she recalled the ten hour birth of her second child. This enabled her to go out with a simply triumphant double flourish… *"Sex. Never. Again."* Plus

"LONG: EXHAUSTING AND FRIGGIN' MESSY!"

That was it. They were gone. Both were in stitches. Only without the pain that accompanied hospital ones. Pairing the two woman together had been a Godsend for Sandra Kerr. She'd been through so much in recent times that it was a delightful relief for those in the station to see her smile again. To watch her embark on a completely new phase of her *'never a dull moment'* life.

Meanwhile back in the maternity unit, Harris was only gone minutes when 'Sandy' had been called into action. It was close to eleven o'clock and her new baby boy's toes were wiggling brightly as his long legs kicked out. This precious, tiny bundle of innocent joy had made a speedy appearance and would soon be held tightly and squeezed lovingly in between his two-year old twin sisters, Carly and Stephanie. He had beautiful, rosy red cheeks and the cutest dimple in the centre of his chin. A small cherubic birthmark at the base of his left ear completed his introductory CV. One that was required for when all family and friends ask… 'What's he like?'

The infant's mother had managed to keep his name a well hidden secret and currently her son was being wrapped tightly in a crisp, white linen shawl by a traumatised midwife. The newborn smiled vibrantly, rocked his tiny head back and forth and seemed in high spirits, healthy and full of life. Whilst at the same time, the baby's mother, 31-year-old Detective Inspector Sandra Kerr, lay still, lifeless and dead.

Every other minute a woman or girl somewhere in the world dies as a result of pregnancy complications or childbirth.

Thirteen

"Long hellos and short goodbyes and in between the time just flies.
It gets lonely, heaven knows - waiting for those long hellos."

- Davy Steele

The poor weather-beaten and aged street light continued to flicker rapidly on the plastic signage at the murder scene. Though the launderette's business name certainly hadn't been lost on DI Murray when he'd first arrived. *'Pound of Fresh'* - Very clever, he'd thought. But even in his book it felt an inappropriate time to comment upon it, so he omitted to take it any further.

Death was a constant we could all rely upon and Maggie Morrison had gone home to endure a troubled and no doubt restless night's sleep. That's if she managed to get any at all. How do you casually undo seeing a butchered dead body rotating at seventy miles per hour in a high-speed, high temperature, spin cycle?

It appeared that Police Scotland employee, Constable Stuart Montgomery had drawn the short straw and would be positioned outside the premises for the remainder of his shift. Inside, individuals in their spaceman outfits would be working diligently throughout the night examining the scene meticulously for helpful evidence and fresh clues.

Meanwhile, normally dressed dossers like Furlong, Murray, Hanlon and Brooks had gone home for rest and relaxation. In a perfect world they'd get some sleep and come back out to play again tomorrow. Each one feeling fully revitalised and fighting fit. Unfortunately - this world was far from perfect.

Less than a quarter of an hour after Kerr's untimely and unexpected death, Steven Murray had received notification at his home. The news had been broken to him by Sandy's heartbroken mother. The sheer anguish, hurt and distress in the woman's voice had made the inspector immediately hand the phone to the much more emotionally stable, Barbra Furlong.

The DCI had seen on Steven's face the severity of the call. She'd witnessed up close and personal the immediate impact that it had made on the man. In complete shock, the devastated officer fled in haste to his ground floor bathroom, knelt down and threw up.

"Sir?" Came the low concerned voice of Drew Curry. "What's up? What's happened? Who's on the phone?"

Steven Murray wasn't silenced too often and he knew that the man in the wheelchair, the man that had saved the life of this woman's child in recent months deserved to know at least the bare minimum. As he went to rise from his knees, he simply stated…

"Sandy's gone, Drew. She died during labour," he cried.

No more words or explanations were forthcoming as Murray walked past his friend and sought solitude and privacy. A cloud of intense darkness descended upon him as his 'black dog' gleefully appeared by his side.

He immediately made his way upstairs and didn't even acknowledge Lizzie. Who at that brief moment had resurfaced from the kitchen with a late night drink and snack, and had no idea what was going on.

Both she and Drew had been waiting patiently for Barbra and Steven to settle back in, before eventually sharing the news that they'd been sitting on all evening. Yet once again it would have to wait. It would definitely be put on the back burner for now. Though they both knew that what they'd uncovered was serious and that it had to be reported sooner rather than later. It couldn't possibly keep until the morning or could it?

Upstairs thinking about death and loss, Steven Murray couldn't believe that his close friend and ally was gone. That those children were now without any parents at all. He also found it bizarre and totally surreal that during this moment of shock and grief, he could clearly recall many of the various quotes and remarks that he'd shared with people at times like this previously.

During his time as an LDS bishop, he'd spoken often at funerals and he'd dedicated numerous graves and offered up words of condolence or paid tribute through an emotional eulogy at a service. Exactly like he'd done at the recent memorial for Thomas Patterson. Suddenly many of those words came flooding back to him, as did a reservoir of tears to accompany them...

"The pain of loss comes as a witness, to bare testimony to the reality of the love."

"In loss, the seven stages of grief come as a road of shards that can only be travelled upon with bare soles."

"We are born to love and to suffer upon loss and this comes of having a healthy soul."

"In loss, we travel the waves of grief in that most unpredictable of emotional storms. If we are blessed there is a lighthouse to navigate toward, a place to go for shelter and for warmth."

Each line had been part of an oral presentation he'd given at various funerals or memorials over the years. Tonight the emotional words conjured up fond recollections, and those clear abiding memories brought the cherished individuals momentarily back to life.

Though it seemed like an eternity, only thirty minutes had passed before DCI Barbra Furlong rose to answer the front doorbell. However she was beaten to it by the sheer acceleration of Drew Curry in the very latest Optimus off-road chair. An electric-powered wheelchair that cost more than an average secondhand car.

When the door was unlocked and opened, it revealed a familiar figure. Their umbrella had been pulled down and briefly shaken. The playful sound of its dancing droplets scattered across the front doorstep. It was as if a raindrop's sole purpose was to bring a sense of ease and calm to the day. Which was exactly what this rain soaked individual was hoping to bring into the life of her respected colleague.

The heavy downpour had run off her 'Royal Bank of Scotland' sponsored brolly and soaked the bottom of each pale blue jean leg from the thigh down. Deepening the denim to a stronger hue and giving her favourite brown boots a glossy, transcendental water-sheen.

"Can I speak with him?" The voice asked politely.

She knew it was late to call by. But needs must.

'Kid' Curry smiled, but said nothing. He could feel a strong presence by his shoulder. Gracefully he turned his wheelchair around and deferred comment to Barbra Furlong. Both woman appeared to have tears in their eyes. However, given the weather, it was much harder to ascertain the true culprit behind Janice Brooks' facial make-up.

She was instantly waved inside and it was there that they first hugged. Furlong proceeded to help her guest out of her drenched raincoat and both females embraced for a further thirty seconds. Drew Curry made himself scarce at that point, offering to happily help Lizzie brew a cuppa for everyone in the kitchen.

"I doubt he'll see you, Janice. He's shut himself away and told us in no uncertain terms to leave him alone and that he didn't want to see anybody. He's filled the last half hour with music tracks, talking to himself and the occasional crazy howl or two."

Brooks was a bit taken aback by that news, but simply listened and nodded.

"I don't have to SEE him, Ma'am. But hopefully I can share a few words with him. What's the worst that can happen? He'll blank them and take no notice? I think we can all live with that if that's the worst case scenario, yes?"

"The challenge is DC Brooks, and I know you've worked closely with him lately. But you never actually know what is going on in the mind of Steven Murray. So although we might think that may be the worst case scenario, I very much doubt that it is. But I'm with you on this one and I'm more than happy for you to at least give it a try. It's worth a shot, I agree."

Upstairs the deeply agitated man wept openly and his bloodshot eyes were closed tight. The frantic flickering underneath his eyelids gave a clue to the fact that he continued to witness a crazy black kaleidoscopic mix of fragmented shapes. He lay on the bare mattress fully clothed. Sweat oozed from every pore and his hair stood to attention like a cross between a 'teddy boy' and the Eiffel Tower.

In this depressed, confused state, he'd sought refuge from the world in one of his spare rooms. He'd grabbed a fresh quilt set, two sheets and pillowcases from the bathroom cupboard to make up the bed, but he'd never even managed to get that far. He'd simply collapsed in a heap as soon as he walked inside and closed the door. These days who still has a lock on their bedroom door? Well, Detective Inspector Steven Murray certainly does.

Nearby a circular extension gathered dust as it jutted out from beneath a bedside cabinet. Three of the four sockets were occupied. A weirdly shaped black plug with a high-backed ridge was the first to escape. It ran along the floor leaping up onto the aforementioned cabinet and finding itself attached to a rather dated, yet still fully effective bedside lamp.

Keeping it company on the unit, sat a paracetamol packet. Four tablets taken in the last half hour. A pile of crime novels, a green spectacle case, ticket stubs and an old leather wallet also surrounded the appliance. The untidy look was completed with crumbs from two packets of crisps that he'd found in a bedside cabinet.

Comfort eating would always be a default setting for the DI. He'd done enough binge eating over the years to ensure food and drink was always available in each of his bedrooms. It had always been an ongoing temptation to Lizzie when she'd stayed with him.

On top of the empty crisp packets which his OCD had made him fold into neat little packages, sat his well used mobile phone. He'd at least seen sense to have it get charged up. The dainty white plug that took up the second space was taking care of that business.

The remaining socket being used in this hoarder's paradise was occupied by a familiar shaped black plug. The two foot long wire that protruded from it was definitely for connecting to an electronic device in some form or other, but the inspector had no idea which one. In fairness the wire had sat there, plugged in and untouched for about four years.

If Murray had lived in America he knew he'd no longer be alive. The perception is that every adult in the States seems to sleep with a gun in their top drawer and given this man's ongoing mental health issues, he was certain that he'd have removed the loaded gun from its nearby location and blown his brains out twenty minutes ago. At the very least, he'd have destroyed his house with a host of 'Elmer Fudd' gun shots. Each one aimed at taking out his highly frustrating 'black dog!'

For support, comfort, reassurance and guidance the inspector had Barbra Furlong, and he was always very considerate around her. Knowing that her own brother had committed suicide a few years back.

In financial terms, Steven Murray was not poor. Plus physically he was still in good shape, fit and mobile. Certainly compared to the likes of Andrew Curry.

But the problem was - he had no feelings, no emotions. His heart and soul were gone completely. He was always drained of energy. These days he felt completely empty inside. He would continually ask himself…

"Why am I here? What's the point?" And this was usually followed up by some desperate pleading…"Lord, please take me. I'm ready for the departure lounge. Just let me say my short goodbyes and thereafter give your right-hand man the nod. Beam me up, Scotty."

"Barbra. Me and Lizzie had something important to tell you and Steven earlier when you got called away…"

"Drew, DI Kerr has just died. I don't think…"

"Oh, I think this is exactly the time. This is most definitely what 'Sandy' would've wanted me to do right now. I don't always wear my cape, but she always reminded me that I could always make a difference."

"Go on up, Janice," Furlong instructed DC Brooks.

That was the moment that Barbra realised Andrew Curry was grieving also. Like Inspector Kerr, he also had been through much in recent months. Sandy and her twin girls had been a massive part of 'Kid' Curry's recent life. His mentoring, his well-being and his recuperation schedule had all been high up on Sandy's list of priorities. Only outdone for some strange reason, one that she's still never figured, by a certain 'Radical' individual's personal assistance.

"Lizzie said we should leave it until the morning. Until the dust has settled and everyone is aware of Sandy's tragic death. However, I think that every minute we don't act on this might impact on a young child's life.

You, Sandy and DI Murray have set the example to me over the years, Barbra. So I know that leaving something unsaid overnight could be the difference between someone's safety and survival, and someone's death and ultimate demise."

Barbra heard him. Yet couldn't grasp the severity of what he was saying. She knew that they had all these recent deaths covered and that they were all connected. So was that it? Had Blood'n Gore discovered the link?

Investigations were ongoing. Even tonight, everything was in hand. Detectives, forensics and those officers on the beat were all fully aware of their roles and to the best of DCI Furlong's knowledge they were currently carrying out those instructions. So what was so important that couldn't wait until the morning?

Regarding DI Kerr, it didn't take the media, gangster and police hotlines long to go into overdrive. Al Lawrie was brought up to speed at the sudden death of the woman that she'd recently written an article on. Whilst in Dundee the news was even deemed worthy of interrupting the Reidmeister's sleep for. After hearing it, the man immediately hung up and allowed a satisfying smile of contentment to reign across his smug mug for the remainder of the evening. Because from the quartet that had gripped the knife that killed Sean Christie in 'self-defence' several months ago, only he and one other remained alive - DI Murray. Speaking of which...

Combining natural oak posts and handrails with panels of glass, the modern balustrade of the staircase lifted its whole surroundings. It gave it a bright, breezy and trendy feel. Barbra Furlong had overseen the hard work and professional craftsmanship that had gone into the project. It had been completed two months earlier and had transformed the heart of their stunning home.

Tonight Janice Brooks walked slowly up the impressive steps and down the newly decorated hallway. She deposited herself outside the one bedroom where she'd guessed that her troubled mentor was holed up. Each of the other room doors were slightly ajar, so no real detective work had been required.

Furlong was busy listening to Andrew Curry's concerns, but was still curious as to what magic this woman could work? On the other hand, Joe Hanlon had been banned completely. The grieving detective had made it clear to both Drew and Barbra that under no circumstances was the man to be allowed into his home. He hadn't given it a thought that Brooks would turn up.

The man was hurting. His eyes remained firmly closed due to the pain and overwhelming tears. His heart was broken and his thoughts kept returning instinctively to his Godchildren, Carly and Stephanie, and to their new born baby brother. In an instant they had become orphaned on her death. That was harsh. The inspector had experienced lots of 'harsh' in recent years.

His 'black dog' was back with a vengeance and had invited a stream of negative vibes and emotions to visit, congregate and wallow. The man's head pounded and every nerve-end burned with anger as an aura of emptiness permeated the room's dense, stuffy atmosphere. Life was dark and his intrusive thoughts continuous, uncontrollable and distressing. The grieving individual soon began to recognise again that heartbreak was without doubt, one of the hidden landmines of human existence. It was carefully concealed in the vast undergrowth of relationships and could readily explode at the most unexpected moment. It may be over dinner, at a wedding or even in bed whilst preparing to make love. In its wake it left a devastating trail of increased anxiety, poor impulse control and potential early death.

Murray knew from many previous experiences that when this peculiar pain is studied the findings are often as shocking and poetic as the art they inspire. For example, scan the brain of a heartbroken, grieving person and the same parts light up as somebody who has suffered a burn. Like the pain of returning to a fire, of reaching across a double bed and smelling smoke.

At that moment the deliberate tap on his bedroom door increased in volume with each steady motion. Had the inspector simply imagined the sharp, intrusive sound? He allowed a second or two to pass, but no, there it was again. This time more determined and most definitely not imagined.

"I thought I said no contact. Leave me to get my head around things and work my way through this, Barbra."

"Inspector." The quiet voice was tinged with emotion.

He recognised it, but chose to remain silent.

"Sir. Did you know that the idea behind a kaleidoscope was to offer up hope? That even although its central structure may appear to be filled with unwanted, broken and fragmented bits and pieces. That when someone looked through it they were still able to witness and view something truly spectacular and beautiful?"

Unsurprisingly, Murray still said nothing.

"Well that's exactly what I have witnessed working alongside you, sir. That no matter how low, irritated or besieged by other issues and problems. No matter what you're personally going through or experiencing, you brighten up my day. You give me hope, you continue to teach and inspire me to do better and to become better. You consistently allow me to develop. To keep asking questions, not only of others, but also of myself."

On the other side of the door, tiny delicate pools of emotional tears swelled in the aquatic blue eyes of DI Murray. He'd become deeply touched and emotional. Sandy had been his go-to default setting in recent years.

"Even now, you work tirelessly on behalf of all those dead men. Even although it would appear from our findings that they aren't necessarily deserving of your help. And before you say it - I know you do it first and foremost to give closure to each of their families and that is because, like I said - You want to offer them hope and ultimately, because you're a good man. We're often told in life, that the only thing necessary for the triumph of evil, is for good men to do nothing!"

Both Furlong and Curry had heard all of this. In fact the DCI had made her way half way up the stairs to get a closer listen. They'd both been drawn in and 'the Kid' could make out about every second word. They'd decided that his news could wait for another few minutes and that Steven Murray's welfare came first.

The chief inspector couldn't help but be impressed by this woman's handling of the situation. By her maturity and wisdom. Her ability to be upfront, kind and honest. There had been a momentary pause before the natural sound of the 'babbling brook' continued to flow gently downstream and impact profoundly on the DI's life…

"I'm heading home now, sir. But I just wanted you to know how I felt," Janice shared. "And to let you know that we all, every member of the team, share in your grief and pain. Maybe each to a greater or lesser degree, but we feel it. Be under no illusion about that."

Her inspector remained quiet, but had listened intently.

"And before I go," she reflected softly. "I need you to be mindful that the reason why some people are so kind, is because the world has been so unkind to them. So in turn, they don't want others to experience that same cruel, excruciating pain."

Two, five, ten seconds possibly elapsed in silence, before Janice saw the door handle gently turn. An audible creak echoed down the hallway, accompanied by a splintered streak of yellow light.

Suddenly, Furlong's eyes and ears were alerted by the sound and vision of both. She moved instantly to carefully peer down the corridor, whilst Drew made his rapid escape via his wheelchair back through to the spacious lounge. A tall, emotional figure now stood in the upstairs doorway and listened as his friend continued to share her feelings…

"Sir. 'Sandy' worshipped you. She admired you and had enormous respect and love for not only Steven Murray the dysfunctional, perplexing police officer, but equally for Steven Murray the man. The loving father, the experienced professional. That gregarious, comedic individual filled with tenacity, integrity and determination. The man with a wanton desire to do the right thing. The principled man of faith and good judgement."

The inspector's shoulders could take no more and they began to shake and tremble uncontrollably. Sentiment and remorse had once again gotten the better of him.

"There's no greater time than the present to rise up and make her proud of you, sir." Brooks went on. "To show her children how much you valued their mother's loyal friendship, than by tracking down the killers of these men and bringing Robert Nielsen to justice also."

Interestingly the piece of news that Blood'n Gore's intrepid investigator, Andrew Curry, and a certain 'Radical' Lizzie had been desperate to share all night, revolved around a fascinating discovery about that particular excuse for a human being. One that was now worth Drew, Lizzie, Barbra, Janice Brooks and Steven Murray all sitting around the kitchen worktop until after midnight to hear about. If it helped to divert their minds away from other current affairs, then surely that was a much needed added bonus.

Fourteen

"When you pass by, then you'll know that this is gonna take a bit of getting used to. But I know what's right for you. Please let me go......"

- Gary Barlow

"Detective Inspector Robert Forrest Nielsen. Born in 1974 in Stockholm," Lizzie announced.

"Wow." DI Murray replied. "That's something I never knew. The corrupt lunatic was actually Swedish."

When you think of Swedes, often the first things that comes to mind are that they are blonde, tall and blue eyed. Rab Nielsen currently possessed none of those noble character traits. He had noticeably dyed black hair, was overweight and had a pair of the meanest, piercing green eyes you could wish for.

Inspector Murray's adrenalin was still pumping from all his earlier exertions of the evening. His brain needed to rest and relax, but currently it was going into overdrive.

"The man's parents, Stella and Lars Nielsen moved to Scotland when their child was only two years of age. They were both science professors in totally separate fields of study and came over to take up jobs at St. Andrew's University in early January 1977."

This time it had been Andrew Curry's turn to impart the information.

"Guys, why are we talking about Robert Nielsen," Barbra said. "Who asked you to investi…"

Janice watched her stop mid-sentence and slowly turn her gaze upon Steven Murray. The inspector shrugged his shoulders.

"Trust us, Ma'am. You'll not want to miss out on this."

Her reddened face and angry demeanour seemed to imply otherwise. But from 'Kid' Curry's tone, she knew it must be important. It wasn't going to be a minor road traffic offence or a social media fall out with a member of the public. She was convinced that it was going to be serious and a reassuring, simmering smile from Drew perked her up nicely to receive further details.

"Let's cut a long story short," Lizzie began. Jumping awkwardly from her high stool at the breakfast bar to parade around the expansive kitchen doing what seemed like a fully animated hip-hop dance and then some. She had watched Steven Murray take centre stage often enough to know the score. With her hair still tied up in a bun and dressed in her designer, khaki, all-in-one combat suit that would have cost the earth, she looked stunning. A bit like throwing Britney Spears, Sporty Spice and Siouxsie Sioux into a melting pot, adding a bit of moody Goth and raucous Punk, and bringing it all simmering nicely to the boil. *'If you could turn back time,'* she gave the impression of a very young looking Cher. But then again that particular megastar wouldn't have lasted two seconds in a melting pot!

"Simon helped us as well," she began. "It was a team effort." Her hands were still tapping furiously on the worktop and going full pelt between her head and her chest. Now she was in full aerobic teacher mode.

Steven Murray felt the urgent need to step in.

"Lizzie, slow down. Take a deep breath and speak to us calmly and in measured tones," he said. "Just imagine that we're all sitting down in 'The Vault,' in your happy place at Queen Charlotte Street. Remember this is your domain and you're in total command."

He took hold of her hands and placed them flat on the granite work surface, allowing his own palms to remain firmly on top. She desperately needed that reassurance and physical contact. It seemed to work instantly.

Within seconds her shoulders dropped as she relaxed her breathing. In turn her legs had stopped disco dancing on the highly polished tile flooring and she soon looked more like her old self again.

Curry nodded in a gesture of grateful appreciation.

"I'm okay," she said, with a heavy sigh. "But Drew, why don't you continue for now."

Andrew Curry gently backed his wheelchair away from the worktop. He too needed space to talk with his hands. Steven Murray had obviously been a big influence on both their lives when it came to public speaking and sharing remarks.

Drew took over and immediately spoke with passion…

"We began reviewing a number of the old cases that DI Nielsen was involved in. Many of the ones that you had told us about, sir."

Murray pursed his lips and grimaced, as his friend had now made it impossible to deny any involvement in their investigations. Barbra instantly shook her head, but appeared keen to hear what they had discovered. The illicit twinkle in her eye however, seemed to all but confirm the inspector was in for a hard time later.

"We looked at the witness tampering," Drew continued. "And found a barrow load of discrepancies there alone. Then with regards to key evidence going missing, it would appear many of the officers involved in those cases have also gone missing in recent years. We tracked a few down to sunnier climes initially, then in the past couple of years they'd vanished altogether. Someone has definitely been cleaning house."

"I'm guessing these are all the niceties, Drew," Barbra Furlong interjected. "But I really need you to share the big reveal, because we all have a very busy time ahead of us tomorrow. Remember, Sandra Kerr's death, a host of missing females and an assortment of murdered men are all vying for my attention for the top spot!"

"Let me," said Lizzie. Her voice excited, but her emotions much more in check. "Well Ma'am, while we were investigating a Sergeant Craig Dunlop, who had disappeared to Cancun…"

"In Mexico?" Janice blurted out. Taken by surprise.

"The very same," Drew confirmed. "And here's the BIG reveal coming now," he informed everyone, as Lizzie continued…

"This man, Dunlop, either wasn't security conscious, or I suspect more likely, it was in case anything ever happened to him and people like ourselves could find it all easily and bring down others in the group. He definitely wasn't going quietly and in a very simple but covert way he was taking lots of others with him. The network ran throughout the whole of Scotland."

"And by lots of others, you're including the Swedish born reprobate in that I hope?" Steven Murray questioned.

"Oh absolutely, sir." Curry confirmed. With a smile the size of an Oscar winner.

"And for what?" Janice Brooks felt emboldened to ask.

Furlong and Murray both raised their eyebrows and paused their breathing for the second that it took the 'Radical' genius in their midst to answer.

"I uncovered substantial evidence that indicates Nielsen was a mover and shaker, if not the head honcho in an illegal group that involved underage teenage girls," Lizzie told the small gathering of Murray, Furlong and Janice Brooks.

To the experienced old hands in the group, the DCI and the inspector, this was nothing new.

To Janice Brooks it felt like she had arrived. That she was now part of the in-crowd. That she'd been invited to a seat at the top table. This evening that 'top table' may manifest itself as a kitchen worktop, but you got the gist of her emotions. She was in her element.

"In a nutshell, sir." Drew Curry continued. "We believe we have enough hard evidence on him to have him charged with rape, aiding and abetting a rape, sexual assault, trafficking for sexual exploitation and conspiracy to engage in sexual activity with children."

"We've got him," Murray declared. Pumping both fists high into the air. Lizzie then took back the baton and swiftly continued…

"The victims were vulnerable teenagers. Usually from deprived and dysfunctional backgrounds. They'd be specifically targeted in 'honeypot locations' where youngsters congregated. Local convenience stores, takeaways and off-licenses were always popular haunts."

The impressive IT specialist stopped briefly to come up for air and see if any of the invincible trio had any relevant questions that required an answer. Instead she was met with a more than capable group of minds that had been temporarily suspended. Their collective brains had seemingly stuttered at the same time. Every part of them paused to allow their thoughts time to catch up. 'Kid' Curry was smiling with satisfaction as his role in this midnight presentation continued…

"He, Nielsen, helped procure girls as young as 13 for the gang. Victims were coerced and bribed into keeping quiet about the abuse by a combination of alcohol, drugs, food and small sums of money, plus other gifts. It's all there. We have social media documentation, emails and texts. Lizzie is pretty good at her job, folks."

Furlong and Brooks smiled in agreement. Whereas a certain, Steven Murray, fixed the woman herself with a large knowing grin and offered up a wink that said, *Just between us, line crossing and thank you!'*

"We have video evidence,' Curry continued. "One occasion was where Nielsen ordered a 15 year-old girl to have sex with an as yet unidentified friend. It was a 'treat' for his birthday – The man then raped her."

Before another gasp could be expressed. Lizzie was back in commentary mode…

"Victims were physically assaulted and raped by as many as five men at a time, or obliged to have sex with numerous men in a day, several times a week. The victims, plied with drugs and alcohol were passed systematically around friends and family, and then taken to various locations throughout the country. It's a small enough nation to do exactly that. The abusers paid small sums of money for the encounters. One 13-year-old victim recounted on a text message that after being forced to have sex in exchange for vodka, her abuser immediately raped her again and gave her £40 not to say anything about the incident. Among the other horrific assaults recorded there is one that stands out. It's where a 15-year-old victim was too drunk to recall being gang raped by about twenty men, one after the other!"

"There's footage," Curry added. "Of another victim so wasted that she's vomiting over the side of the bed whilst being violated by two men. And in a different clip," he added. "We see a desperate 13-year-old victim tell how she was forced to terminate her pregnancy. The rapist had threatened to kill her parents otherwise."

Hearing that, Steven Murray had his suspicions…

"I know you well enough Drew," the man spoke in hushed deliberate tones. "Well enough to know that you didn't just leave that final piece of information until the last, without there being good cause for you to do so."

"No!" Janice Brooks exclaimed.

Furlong complemented that with a… "Surely not?"

Drew looked at Steven Murray, his eyes angry and upset. He nodded vehemently before speaking…

"Chances are it's certainly not the first child that Robert Nielsen has fathered with one of those girls."

Fifteen

Next morning at Queen Charlotte Street Station, news of Sandra Kerr's death had spread rapidly. A solemn air of sadness permeated the corridors. Grief after all created an intense sorrow. People were hurting. There was obvious, poignant distress. The doleful, unsmiling faces of Joe Hanlon and Allan Boyd had found themselves in the company of Lizzie and the others, in a larger room designated mainly for news conferences.

'Sherlock' wiped away a tear as he recalled his first interaction with 'Sandy.' It had came about during the investigation into the death of a student named Penelope Cooke in Inverleith a few years back.

"I only found out by default, some six months later," he said. "But it had been Sergeant Kerr as she was at the time, that had quietly and privately told DI Murray about my wife Lauren's cancer diagnosis. He in turn, reached out to me, befriended me and ultimately created an opportunity for me to serve here in the team. That had all been done in consultation with 'Sandy.' Because up until that point, she'd been the inspector's unofficial wing man."

Both Lizzie and Allan Boyd had heard those tales related to them before from other sources. But the one common denominator that held firm in the various revised editions was the testament to Sandra Kerr's good heart, to her natural kindness and fierce loyalty to the members of her family and to her work colleagues.

When the door to the busy room opened, Detective Inspector Steven Murray walked in. His head was held high and he wasted no time on formalities. He immediately began to address his team, plus a few others officers that had joined them to get an update.

"Late last night, DI Sandra Kerr died due to serious complications whilst giving birth to a healthy 6lb 3oz baby boy named, Andrew Steven Kerr."

A muted response was offered. When in actual fact people genuinely wanted to clap and celebrate. Maybe by way of a respectful acknowledgement to Sandy's life, but also as a greeting to young 'Andy.' To welcome him into this beautiful, yet often cruel world. It was without doubt an awkward, yet emotional moment.

Neither DI Murray nor Drew Curry were aware they'd be honoured in such a way. She had proudly named the infant after her two most influential colleagues and it had been a complete surprise when her late husband's mother had called them separately to inform them.

It was at that point Murray shared some other news with the team that he'd also been notified of…

"In the last two weeks, Sandy, had seemingly been made aware of some crucial challenges ahead by the doctors. One of which was that they'd discovered she had a very irregular heartbeat. But not wishing to make a fuss, our DI chose not to involve anyone else and decided to keep it private and under wraps."

The majority of those gathered realised that there were now three orphaned children for their police family to look after. In the interim, they'd try their best to continually support and assist them on an ongoing basis. Though it transpired that her in-laws would be temporarily caring for them. However, as they're both in their mid-sixties that would be no long-term solution. This had been a heartbreaking turn of events that no one could have predicted twenty-four hours earlier.

Murray carefully steepled his hands under his chin...

"I was persuasively reminded yesterday by a friend about the opportunity that we each have to make Sandra proud of us. About the enchanting legacy that we could leave behind for her, by catching the deranged killer or killers of these men. Sandra was a great human being, though she had suffered greatly this last year." The inspector paused. "I regularly ask too much of people. I know that. I too often forget that you all have personal lives and I sincerely apologise for my selfish expectations." The room was stilled.

No one was willing to agree with him on that score today, even if they had wanted to. Because there were far too many sentiments and feelings already on display.

"The silence says it all," the DI concluded, angry at himself. "The thing is - Sandy always fully supported me and although each of us here may be hurting at this particular moment in time, I know that we can collectively come together and do her proud."

Tears began to appear. Not only in the eyes of Steven Murray who was struggling to keep his emotions in check, but in the eyes of those gathered as they bowed their heads and wiped away at their respective faces.

"Let us strive to double our efforts and bring the individual or individuals to justice that we are presently hunting down."

On that note, the man possibly once again expected too much. He turned on his heels and exited the room.

It might not have been the best time for introductions, but at the start of the lengthy corridor and just ten feet away from all those who had gathered, Murray made his way across to yet another little exclusive 'broom cupboard.' It was no more than six feet square and lacked windows of any description whatsoever.

The nameplate currently being clumsily screwed onto the heavy oak door by a slim built, frizzy-haired woman in a brown business suit, complete with a trendy beige polo-neck underneath, READ: 'Afro' MacDonald.

So there you have it, the DI thought. Game on…

"Would you like a hand with that?" He softly enquired.

The woman had obviously seen him approaching, because she was already in mid-sentence before she'd turned around fully.

"Well if it isn't the man himself," she remarked. "No, I'm more than capable. Thank you very much."

"I didn't mean to imply that you…"

"I've heard some wonderful things about you, DI Murray and I'm looking forward to working alongside you and seeing for myself what exactly makes you tick."

She dipped her head slightly and ran her eyes up every inch of the man's healthy, six foot plus frame.

"Any thoughts on that?" She added matter-of-factly.

Murray knew it was a deliberately loaded question. But then again that's exactly why this fine looking, sallow skinned female had asked it. It was also why she'd set about pretending to attach the nameplate. Because she was curious to see if he'd offer up assistance. At this point he was still happy to play the game, so he stepped forward to politely shake her hand. However, as if lighting the blue touch paper, she shook it weakly and took a giant step back.

It was now the turn of this experienced and often playful officer to study her thoughtfully before responding. His voice got gradually faster and faster as he did so…

"To be honest I have no particular train of thought on that proposal right now, Ma'am. However what I do have racing around in my crazy mixed up mind currently creating mayhem and havoc are… trains!"

MacDonald certainly wasn't expecting what came next.

"… nine fully charged electric trains travelling at high-speed on three separate tracks. Each narrowly avoiding one another when their busy, hectic paths cross. On every engine their busy overworked and overweight conductors are screaming like mental, mad banshees. They need to blow their whistles and regain control."

The man instantly stuck an assortment of fingers into his blabbing mouth and blasted a loud shrill. Soon afterward, he sighed with relief and gradually exhaled.

Throughout all of this, MacDonald never flinched. She'd simply beamed wider than a Mississippi river bed. Ah, he was a responder, she thought… Interesting.

"No need for, Ma'am, Steven. Afro will do just fine."

"Really? Well, I'm Detective Inspector Murray to you!"

As the mischievous officer walked off. There appeared to be a definite touch of oneupmanship in his step.

"Touché, Inspector. I'll give you that," 'Afro' MacDonald whispered softly out into the ether.

Within minutes, Murray had returned to his car, though he couldn't help but remind himself that 'comparison' is not actually an emotion. It does however, drive all sorts of bigger feelings that can affect our relationships and our self-worth. More often than not, social comparison falls outside of our awareness and often we don't even know we're doing it. On this occasion, the experienced officer figured Afro MacDonald knew exactly what she'd been doing.

Once inside his vehicle, a special assignment and invitation had been hastily extended by phone to DC Lorna Harris. Both were excitedly noted and accepted.

Barbra Furlong on the other hand, didn't wish to appear callous. But knowing that Inspector Kerr would no longer be coming back to join the team, she wasted no time in drafting another officer in to replace her.

The DCI had been given a shortlist of four names that would be made available immediately. By immediately, they meant that very morning. The individual would be told to ship out from wherever he or she were based, and sent along posthaste to Queen Charlotte Street.

They were all on the TABB list. Barbra had shown it to Murray ten minutes before his remarks and they both chose the same man. So great minds and all that, or simply the best of a very special group. They didn't call it… the Troublemakers And Bad Boy list for no reason.

Sergeant John Black was top of the list and would be joining them from St. Leonard's within the hour.

Hanlon and Boyd were back at their desks reviewing the previous evening's dry cleaning business in Leith. They compared events with those on Bridge St. Where an 'escapee' had sought freedom from a silver BMW.

"Any joy?" Steven Murray asked. Having returned back indoors to tie up with 'Babbling' Brooks.

"Well the bold Mrs Morrison said that there was about half a dozen females," Allan Boyd replied. "That between them they'd distracted her and put the man's body parts into the washing machine."

"Can we believe a word she says?" Joe Hanlon asked. "I thought she was a bit strange and out of sorts."

"A bit strange? If that's your standard in judging witnesses then we'd have very few ever in any outstanding cases. Plus what chance would I personally have in life if that was to be your criteria?"

"I suppose," 'Sherlock agreed.

Boyd could only smile and nod in total agreement.

"So I ask again. Any joy?"

"We might well have something," Boyd offered up. Scratching nervously at his own ever growing hair. A style described as a buzzcut these days.

"We're waiting on Lizzie getting back to us, sir." Hanlon added. "The hand that closed the car door appears to have a small blemish near their thumb."

"And she's going to enhance it for you?" He asked. Before adding... "Where did you get that actual footage from?"

"A top of the range security camera installed by a wealthy neighbour, sir. Their home was directly in line with the vehicle as it unleashed the poor gentleman back out into the world. It turned out to be the worst guided tour the man had ever been on," 'Sherlock' grinned. "And no refunds! Plus remember, Inspector, I learned all these irreverent quips from the very best in the business. I'm only reminding you of that, sir, before you decide to make an example out of me."

Murray pursed his lips with the merest hint of a smile.

Last night's icy weather forecast had turned out to be pretty accurate. Though the roads and pavements had been gritted from early morning and all major thoroughfares and motorways appeared to be fine. But it still wasn't the ideal day to be venturing out, if not required. At that moment, DC Brooks received a text from Charlene Lennon. The recently widowed woman had simply stated... *Arrived!*

Be right down - was Janice's curt, but polite response.

The Lennon family had all travelled in from Dalkeith. By car that was a relatively short distance in normal weather. Today's conditions had possibly added a few extra minutes, but nothing of any significance. Mrs Lennon had been adamant that they would much rather come into the station this time round. Preferring no doubt to keep both sets of neighbours, those living nearby and those just fiercely nosey - well out of the loop on this particular occasion.

Speculation throughout her estate with unsubstantiated theories was rife. Unwanted attention from media and police over the past ten days had also been immense and had only added fuel to the fire and heightened the latest malicious gossip. Such as, the doctor had caught his wife in bed with another man and her lover had lashed out, killing the homeowner. That one was the current favourite in the local sweepstake.

As Janice watched the mother and her two children walk cautiously along the icy pavement. She could immediately spot the easygoing camaraderie and closeness they enjoyed as a family. The taller, older brother laughed and joked freely. He made comical facial gestures at his younger sister as she walked arm in arm with her protective mum. All three had wisely chosen to wear hat, scarf and gloves. Each pattern and design different. So not quite the perfect Stepford Family that Ian Lennon wanted on display at any given moment. Between the females, one wore trousers and the other a full-length skirt. This displayed quite clearly that they each had their own unique personality.

From an early age, Janice Brooks was taught the beauty of cold winter days. How they could show us what we'd otherwise never witness. A warm smile soon crossed her face as she watched the family rub their hands and blow out into the air. Their actions reminded her of an 'old saying' that her own mother saw cause to mention every winter… *"From the warmest lungs came the whitest of clouds, and a humble gift of myself I send heavenward."*

The officer greeted the family at the front desk and kindly ushered them upstairs into another one of Police Scotland's snug, pocket-sized cubby holes. Herself and Murray had agreed that an interview room would have been too cold and clinical for their chats. Especially for a potentially difficult discussion with Charlene's youngest child, Emily. The female wearing the skirt.

Whilst waiting on Eric Lennon returning from a toilet stop across the hallway, Steven Murray felt inspired to offer Afro MacDonald a *'no time like the present'* invitation to join them. The woman jumped at the opportunity and accepted gladly. She was still busy introducing herself to Mrs Lennon, Emily and DC Brooks when the oldest sibling ventured back through the door and the first interview was all set to begin.

The family were in the process of removing all their warm winter gear. Although Mama Bear, Charlene Lennon, chose to keep on her pretty individually fingered lemon gloves. She soon tucked hers hands into her trouser pockets and was ready.

"I have poor circulation and chilblains," she explained.

Her children sighed with embarrassment.

"No problem," Steven Murray acknowledged. "We want you all to be comfortable," he added.

"Oh, and now that you're back, Eric. Would you be so kind to sit with Emily outside for a few minutes," Janice said by way of instruction rather than a question. "We're going to chat with your mum first. Thank you so much. That'll be a big help."

Eric instantly looked worryingly across at DI Murray. In his wisdom the inspector's eyes caught the boy's and a reassuring nod of his head told the lad that everything would be fine.

Sixteen

"All aboard, stitch in time. Get yours, got mine. Tell my story and Charlie's makin' me...... and Charlie's makin' me smile."

- Red Hot Chili Peppers

"Mrs Lennon. Would you like a glass of water? A tea or coffee, perhaps?"

Janice Brooks' soft honeyed voice was both rhythmic and melodious. Singing each word as she spoke. Her detective inspector got the impression that she was trying too hard to be nice. Whereas Steven Murray on the other hand was hoping to have the doctor's wife speak to him with her eyes and through her breathing.

He was anticipating tell-tale whispers from the subtle motions of her body language. Like he had initially watched the woman eye-up the water dispenser in the corner of the room and soon afterward he'd happily brought a refreshing H2O across for both her and DC Brooks. 'Babbling' never even acknowledged the gesture and that made him smile. But he did begin to wonder why their visitor was quite so nervous?

"Thank you," Mrs Lennon politely responded, as she happily received the plastic cup in her hand.

The temperature was rising rapidly as the radiator in the room soon became burning to the touch. The low unventilated ceiling didn't help matters, yet the woman's gloves remained intact. Charlene certainly appeared much calmer and far more assertive out-with her own home. Steven Murray found that intriguing and took a mental note of it. Because with ninety percent of people, it would have been the other way around.

"Thank you so much for coming in to see us today, Ma'am. You really didn't have to do that. We would've gladly driven back out to visit with yourselves."

"It's no trouble, honestly. And please, it's Charlene."

"Well, Mrs Lennon, sorry Charlene. Let's begin…"

"Don't you have to record everything, Inspector?"

Murray and Brooks stared at each other in alarm…

"OH!" they exclaimed in unison. "This isn't a formal interview, Charlene." Janice quickly tried to reassure her.

"It's just that we have concerns regarding the health and well-being of you and your children, Mrs Lennon."

Murray's words carried weight and he'd deemed the use of her Christian name too personal, so opted for officialdom instead. He was happy with his choice.

"I see," the woman said in no more than a whisper. "Can you help me understand what you mean by that?"

"Well Charlene, do you need anything from us right now? Because we have real fears that Emily may have been the subject of abuse from her late father. Now be that physical or purely verbal we should be able to ascertain that one way or another, once we've spoken with her. Ms MacDonald here will assist us in that."

Afro was pleasantly taken by surprise at that news. But she remained unfazed and didn't bat an eyelid.

Charlene Lennon stared at him in disbelief. Though the DI was confident that he'd witnessed that look on numerous previous occasions. It was a shrewd uneasy glance. He knew that he'd quite clearly touched or possibly even severely pinched a nerve.

Janice had also seen the immediate recognition on the woman's face. It was then that she found from somewhere deep within the following words…

"No-one expects someone close to them to be raped or sexually assaulted, Charlene. Especially when that person looks totally together on the outside."

The colour immediately drained from the anxious mother's normally bright-eyed, bronzed complexion and there was uncertainty in her eyes Murray reckoned, as the articulate Brooks continued with her remarks...

"Sexual assault can often shatter a person and fill them with a shame that they may well carry with them forever. Remember, Mrs Lennon - Charlene, that it's a crime. No matter who commits it or where it has taken place. Don't be afraid to get help."

Although physically unmoved, MacDonald couldn't help but be emotionally moved and impressed by Janice Brooks in equal measure. Here was a woman capable of articulating empathy, understanding and compassion all rolled into one. She had focus and a definite understated, yet very noticeable passion for her job and in particular what her role involved. Detective Inspector Steven Murray was a very lucky man to have such a capable individual by his side, and she'd not be slow in telling him her thoughts on the matter.

Nervous, scared feelings are there to protect you; yet all they are really asking you to do is check for traffic before you cross the road. It's a protective mechanism. Traffic lights that turn green once you've done your due diligence. Yet Charlene Lennon was stuck at amber. Murray could see a desire to speak, but did the woman have fear or concern at what may ultimately come out?

"Can I ask," she eventually stuttered. Her voice low and apologetic, as if she'd missed something and sought clarification. Her words were delivered with a deliberate pause between each one. "Are - you - still - referring - to - Emily?" She questioned.

Neither police officer spoke and Afro MacDonald remained static. Her hands clasped on her lap. Each of the three could sense a breakthrough and it took all Janice's willpower to bite her tongue as it protruded with dangerous intent between her lips.

In the next twenty minutes they were confident that Charlene Lennon's true story would finally be revealed.

Meanwhile Robert Nielsen had gone to ground. Several colleagues had left furious voice messages and numerous calls from Furlong had gone unanswered.

He knew his time was up when keywords like 'Cancun,' 'Romania' and 'Mafia' were mentioned, and that's before others questioned why they'd been getting asked about their involvement in teenage trafficking, child abduction and sex rings. Suddenly he'd more than just a few unhappy officers looking for answers. Several ex-production keepers had also left him some rather choice words. 'Back-handers' and 'bribes' were the words being described in their voicemails. The man's past had caught up with him big style. He needed to help 'Bunny' Reid deal with his missing girls, and in return get rewarded for that result. After that he could take off and vanish without trace. Though, he'd be without pension and perks and that would hurt him greatly. He sought vengeance. Someone had to pay for taking him down and he'd one particular individual in mind. A man - head and shoulders above the rest.

As a young newly qualified doctor, Ian Lennon had paid for sex with her on numerous occasions. It had normally been once or twice a month. By about month five, he'd forgotten his wallet and was the worse for drink. Back then, so-called 'Ladies of the Night' didn't get to hide behind the fancy modern moniker of being an 'escort,' a 'masseuse' or an overly familiar 'friend with benefits!' She was simply a hooker. A wanton whore. A hussy. A cheap tramp. So when she refused to entertain the man. He raped her.

Of course, he never felt any guilt or remorse. He was a coward after all. Next morning, once sobered up, he realised what the consequences of his actions may include and that made him fearful for his future. He wasn't willing to take the chance that she could ruin his career before it even got underway and properly started.

Things were beginning to take off for him. So he married her. He never actually asked her at any point to become his wife. She was a young, vulnerable individual who needed love and protection. Instead her coldhearted attacker simply instructed Charlie that was what was happening. And Charlie, her actual name back in the day, that was to be consigned to history also.

Within days he was introducing the innocent, *Charlene,* to his extended friends and family. A group of individuals that she never hit it off with. Excruciating snobs as far as she was concerned - every one of them.

She was certain that Ian Lennon had no idea what her actual maiden name was. However, marriage gave her a way out of the gutter. An opportunity to improve her lot in life and hopefully to have children. That was something that she'd always dreamed of. Mainly as her own childhood years had not been the greatest.

Raised by a kind-hearted single mother named Mary, things had been tough. Their relationship was good but they had nothing. It had been Charlie's idea to go on the game. She was a good-looking girl or so she'd often been told. It had ultimately helped them both survive. Her lone parent had been allowed to attend their wedding ceremony. Yet only days later, Lennon told his new wife to cease all contact with her mother altogether or he'd ensure that family, children of her own would never enter into their relationship. That was nearly 20 years ago and she was left devastated at the time.

The three individuals listening were already heartbroken at what she had disclosed to them so far.

From that day forth the deceitful doctor was in complete control. Who would take her seriously? He was in charge of everything. She had no finances of her own. She was fully dependent on him and that never altered throughout all their years together. She'd become his wife and he was ultimately safe from the consequences of his previous drunken actions.

Nonetheless, no matter what she did over the years, it was never good enough. She was always the local slapper that he'd picked up and rescued from the gutter and then callously paid off at will. She'd been well compensated over the last two decades as far as Ian Lennon was concerned. She couldn't compete with any of his later conquests. And as his wealth accumulated, his need for new physical companions continued unabated on a regular basis over the intervening years.

Charlene had gradually accepted her role in life. She'd been blessed with two wonderful children that she adored and was a super mum to. One that supported and helped her kids in any way that she could. Be it hospital appointments, dentists or parent/teacher evenings - there she was. The ever reliable Charlene Lennon was always in attendance. Today being yet another perfect example. If only her own mother could have seen how things had turned out?

Appropriate or not, Brooks held the woman tightly in a comforting hug. An acknowledgment of how difficult her words had been to share and an encouraging gesture to feel pride in herself and her family. Though sadly, she felt confident that the poor mother would also be sharing a tight embrace with her own daughter very shortly, should things turn out like they expected.

As all four exited the room for some respite, Steven Murray immediately went to update DCI Barbra Furlong. While Afro MacDonald would return imminently to chat with Emily and her brave mother.

A mother that had one last poignant word to share with the group as they headed out from the room.

"Murphy," she said. The single word was offered up with a sense or purpose and pride. No prefix, nor nothing to follow it up or to offer further explanation.

As Brooks and MacDonald pondered on it simultaneously, their older, male colleague nodded with a sense of satisfaction and reflective understanding.

"That was your maiden name, Mrs Lennon? The one that had been discarded by Ian and never given a second thought?"

The woman nodded, and as her children came into view she quickly lifted her head higher and walked taller than two seconds previously.

"Absolutely, Inspector," she confirmed for him. Before adding… "I was Charlotte Murphy and proud of it."

That's when her thin muscular arms and glove-laden hands were flung lovingly around the necks of two teenagers. All three others smiled in an unrehearsed show of solidarity in support of the abused woman.

At the age of 27, Aphrodite Georgiou had moved to Scotland from her Cypriot home to marry the man of her dreams. After five difficult years together, she'd kicked him into touch after his continual lies, womanising and wildly temperamental mood swings.

She did keep the lovely patriotic surname, however. And now a further seven years down the line and with life just about to begin on her next birthday, the sultry, sophisticated woman found herself working in Lothian.

Criminal psychology was a field of study that focused on behaviour. It included the study of ideas, thoughts, views and the related actions of individuals who engaged in criminal acts. Though it was mainly centred around the criminals themselves.

Due to this fact, psychologists in the field commonly contribute insight and expertise to the development of criminal profiles for police and the Procurator's Fiscal officials to use in the apprehension of suspects. These talented criminal psychologists also work closely with offenders to gain a better understanding of their motivation for committing crimes and to evaluate their overall risk of re-offending. Oh, how the bold inspector was going to relish working with this woman.

This mad keen football fan's specialist field was in fact criminal profiling. Doing exactly what it says on the tin - developing psychological profiles based on personality and behavioural traits. It was a finely honed skillset. One that could be exceptionally helpful in assisting police and other legal auxiliaries in the apprehension of criminal offenders.

At this juncture in her career, it looked likely she was going to draw on her expertise in psychology and her understanding of criminal behaviour to help analyse crime scenes alongside her new Queen Charlotte Street colleagues on a more regular basis.

So would Afro MacDonald and Steven Murray be a match made in heaven or hell? The coming days and weeks should reveal a clear answer to that particular conundrum one way or another.

Today, both individuals were closely followed down the corridor by DC Brooks, Emily and 'Charlie' Lennon. This time they did head for an official interview room. One where the Cypriot born woman would duly push the appropriate button and record the date, time and all of those present. Before eventually beginning with -

"So Emily, let me start by asking…"

Seventeen

"Baggy trousers, dirty shirt. Pulling hair and eating dirt. Teacher comes to break it up. Back of the head with a plastic cup."

- Madness

After a somewhat emotional dialogue with Emily Lennon, Afro MacDonald felt it was best to officially interview Eric also. Both DI Murray and DC Brooks agreed. Meanwhile their fretting mother, Charlene, simply wanted it to be all over and to get on with raising her children unshackled and free from a man that had continually made their life a misery.

'Charlie' Lennon didn't need a highway to hell. In her vulnerable tormented mind, she'd already been condemned to existing on a secluded, miserable plot of land there for years. Alongside Ian Lennon, that reality looked like a scorching hot furnace. One that consisted of being thrust into a delicate situation and on the edge of danger every minute of every day. The man was vile. The poignant line that stood out during their chat with Emily was when her mother quietly added…

"Have you not seen the emotional purgatory that an increasing amount of humanity call home?"

All three individuals, including MacDonald, reflected on that sadly accurate, yet profoundly true statement.

"Ian had always been good to the children," she added.

Though given what Emily had told them during the interview, her father had crossed way over the line with his affection toward her.

After Eric's interview, Murray and MacDonald went to further update DCI Furlong on all three discussions.

Meanwhile Janice Brooks in her inspired wisdom and seeing the opportunity to bond closer with Charlene Lennon, chose to slide alongside the family back to their parked car on the icy street. As she began to shiver whilst chatting to them, she came to appreciate what a benefit warmer clothing made on a day such as today.

Before turning back to the station, she thanked the family once again for coming in and for giving statements and going through what must have been a difficult experience. She appreciated that it couldn't have been easy for them and expressed just that.

"It was easier and much more cathartic than you'd think." Charlene replied.

Brooks nodded and offered up a surprised smile. She'd never really thought about it like that. It was at that moment that Mrs Lennon opened the car door…

"By the way, I wasn't sure if it was important," she said. "And it never came up during our discussions, but I brought this with me today."

She stretched over to open up the glove compartment.

"I'd forgotten to bring it in earlier."

The woman handed over what looked like a small business card, and the puzzled look on the officer's face obviously did the trick.

"Oh, yes, sorry. I found it in one of Ian's shirt pockets from the night that he was killed."

Brooks stared at the simplistic paper card in front of her. It looked just like a hundred and one other bog standard business cards that you might see every day. It contained a picture of a horse rearing up on its two hind legs in one corner and the word CHESTNUT prominently printed in the centre. In matching brown font along the bottom was a mobile phone number.

"Why the long face?" Charlene asked.

Brooks looked down to meet her gaze.

"What?"

Mrs Lennon nodded toward the horse pic on the card.

It took a further two seconds to click. Brooks laughed. Wow. How was this lady able to make jokes at a time like this? I guess it must've been liberating right enough to get everything out in the open and especially to be free from such a manipulative bully. Fair play to her.

"Why the long face? Good one, Mrs Lennon," Brooks continued to smile. "So the significance of this card is?"

"Well, that's just it. I don't know if it's important or not. But what I do know is that it wasn't in that shirt's breast pocket when I ironed it earlier that day."

"Wait. What! Are you saying that someone put it into his shirt at some point later in the day."

"I suspect what I'm actually saying is that whoever murdered my husband placed that card, for whatever reason, into his shirt pocket before or after they killed him. We slept in separate rooms Constable Brooks and his newly ironed shirts were hanging outside his wardrobe INSIDE his room. So whoever delivered it must also have made their way into his room."

Janice Brooks was aghast. This was an amazing lead.

"I've tried ringing it. It just goes dead."

The officer's head sank on hearing that news.

"However," Charlene added, offering hope. "You should contact his receptionist at the surgery in Portobello. She was forever updating contact numbers for him. People lose, swop and upgrade their phones so often these days, including changing numbers. What a hassle, I couldn't be bothered with that," she concluded.

Brooks reached out and gave her and each of her wonderful children another great big, spontaneous and wholly inappropriate hug. 'Babbling' was on cloud nine with this potential breakthrough.

"You're a star. Each of you," she shouted as she skated off at speed in the direction of the police station car park. "Byeeee."

"So give me the highlights," Furlong encouraged.

"It doesn't make for pleasant listening. To a greater or lesser degree all three remaining members of the Lennon family should seek immediate counselling," MacDonald encouraged.

"Eric was by far the luckiest. If that's even the appropriate word?" Murray stated. "His father had a predilection for females, and younger females at that. The man had been using prostitutes from an early age. In reality, 'Charlie Murphy' never stood a chance."

"Charlie Murphy? I thought her…"

"Long story, Ma'am. I'll update you later."

Afro raised her eyes at that remark and wondered if it was a cheeky euphemism being thrown in there between two lovers? Whatever? She remained silent.

"Like I said, Eric never seemed to experience any untoward sexual advances whatsoever. But he's a clever lad and knew that things weren't right. I suspect Emily has probably told him far more than she's told us."

"And what did she share with us?" Barbra asked.

Afro cleared her throat and Murray happily gestured…

"Be my guest…"

"Well chief inspector, the mother and daughter have been through a lot, and each in very different ways."

Both Furlong and Murray nodded in understanding.

"For Emily it has been life altering, although the poor girl is only about to realise that as she goes through her teenage years and as maturity and hormones hit her in powerful doses. Dating, affection, cuddles, hugs and feeling safe and secure with someone other that her mum will be challenging. So many facets of her life will have been impacted that's for sure."

"She's definitely been raped by her father on numerous occasions, Ma'am. Murray wanted to confirm. "At her home, in the car and out and about in secluded, yet public areas."

Furlong rubbed her brow intensely in sheer disbelief.

"On one such public occasion, it sounds like numerous individuals may have been involved in a frenzied, brutal assault on her several years ago," MacDonald disclosed.

"I know it's the most stupid and backward hypothetical question," Barbra exclaimed. "But I don't suppose we can castrate and kill the sick father all over again?"

The vengeful remark clearly illustrated Furlong's fury at the warped, misogynistic, dead individual. A disturbed father-figure whose legacy gave good men a bad name. The chief inspector turned to inhale sharply, before exhaling at a much more calming and measured pace.

"And the mother?" She eventually managed to utter.

The other two glanced at each other. Steven Murray opened the palm of his hand and swept it smoothly out from his midriff, allowing MacDonald to carry on...

"Ma'am, bear with me, but pornography has created cultures that consume women. They treat their images as entitlements, as a form of public property. This is even worse than the concept of a woman as the *property of a man.'* This is woman as the *property of commercialism.'* Women's rights in this age of sexual imagery for sale and consumption, of pornography to control and shame women, has gone into reverse gear. It is little wonder that so many women have lost faith in men."

Both Steven Murray and Barbra Furlong knew she was on a roll and that there was no point in interrupting her.

"Thus we need a movement for chivalry led by men, because this is the antidote to patriarchy. Support and protection is the opposite of exploitation. In this environment, society can heal women and men. What other world do our children deserve to inherit? Let me quote you verbatim, exactly what Charlene Lennon said earlier... *'Have you not seen the emotional purgatory that an increasing amount of humanity call home?'* That's a mighty powerful statement to make, Ma'am."

Detective Inspector Murray was impressed by her ability to recall to memory, lengthy quotations such as that. He reminded himself that he'd need to be extra careful with his responses around her in future.

"I think she and her son will cope and will ultimately blossom at being free from her husband's overbearing influence and no doubt vocal and physical abuse. With regards to Emily on the other hand? I suspect it will take a fair while longer."

Afro tapped her head by way of an informal salute.

"Thanks to both of you," Furlong announced. "What's up next, Inspector Murray?"

"Well OUR plan of attack," Steven answered, whilst reading an incoming text. "Is to go visit the old head teacher at Walerek School and see if she can shed some light on our 'blue bin man,' George Matthew. And when I say OUR, that would be you and I, Afro. For going by this text that DC Brooks has just sent, she's whisked Black off to a doctor's surgery on the coast!"

"I hope he's okay," MacDonald said in a serious tone.

Furlong exchanged a coy wink with her DI. Both knowing that it may take Afro a while to get up to speed with her colleague's sense of humour and how it ultimately worked.

John Black, who normally went by Ian, had been having a sneaky cigarette whilst pacing briskly under cover on the frosty inside walkway of the station car park.

"No ice," he pointed out to the overly enthusiastic female heading directly toward him at speed.

"Get in your car," she instructed him. "Orders from the DI. We've to get down to the doctors surgery in Portobello as quick as we can."

"I thought you and him were heading out to see some retired ex-headmistress?"

"Oh, he'll be safe in the gentle, smooth hands of Aphrodite MacDonald. Of that I'm quite sure."

A knowing glance was exchanged between the two colleagues. Janice wondered if Black knew half of Murray's sordid personal life over the past 12 months.

"Anyway," she continued. "I have a gut feeling that we'll be in the good books after our medical check-up." Along with that remark, she offered up an impish smile.

"Yes and I have a gut feeling that we may both be in need of surgery, if we don't get the right result and Steven Murray eventually gets his hands on us."

"You're a daring troublemaker and a bad boy from what I hear, Sarge. So what say you put your foot to the floor and get us out of here, pronto?" Her voice was a little Dukes of Hazzard meets The Apprentice.

"If truth be told, Janice, I'm an ageing old copper with very little fight left in me. And as far as relationships between couples go, they are often very psychological."

"Sure, that they are," she replied. Still obviously high on adrenaline and intuition.

"And from what I've heard from you so far, Constable, it would appear that in our relationship - You're the psycho and I'm very much the logical one!"

He turned the key in the ignition and gently revved the engine over. Gradually he pulled out from the car park at a slow, steady pace. Second gear wasn't even invited to the party. Janice rolled her eyes. Oh yes, what a bad boy Black was right enough, she sarcastically thought. Though she'd immediately began to warm to the man after that frank exchange of views and dry wit.

The interview with Tabitha Thoroughgood had been pre-scheduled and the ex-headmistress was expecting the officers within the hour. It was an easy thirty minute, 15 mile drive from their Leith based offices.

These days the well-heeled town of Haddington had a population of fewer than ten thousand. Yet many years ago in the High Middle Ages, it was the fourth biggest town in Scotland. Back in the day, it trailed in behind Aberdeen, Roxburgh and the mostly rural Edinburgh.

John Knox the great reformist and founder of the Presbyterian Church of Scotland was born in the town. Knox Academy, the local high school, is named after him and it's in the shadow of that aforementioned establishment that Steven Murray and criminal psychologist, Aphrodite MacDonald find themselves.

Located in a nearby side street, from the outside, Ms Thoroughgood's run down building definitely gave the impression of being an ex-local authority property. One at which Murray instantly screwed up his face in horror.

"Were you expecting something different, Inspector?"

"Weren't you? I won't lie Afro, my expectations have certainly not been met on this occasion. Maybe I'm just too much of a snob at times. Who knows? But when I hear, ex-head teacher of a 'School for Children,' I'm thinking older established cottage with its own small grounds. At the very least, a garden with trees and possibly even a path with a front gate that works."

However, this particular home that the pair had arrived at was badly in need of some special TLC. Though it did look as if the woman was now getting around to providing it with some much needed maintenance. Because her two visitors had parked up behind a van which had a local DIY/Handyman's contact details plastered all over the outside of it. As they proceeded to walk by it, the man inside was busy scoffing snacks and reading a daily tabloid. Many similar individuals had served gruelling four years apprenticeships, only to experience that very same lunchtime ritual.

"And who said men can't multi-task?" MacDonald mumbled under her breath.

Those words were uttered whilst desperately trying to avoid breaking a heel on the growing family tree of cracks that the narrow *'crazy paving'* presented her with.

The van's radio blared out... *"It sounds like an empty house, standing still. And it's quieter than a mouse, standing still."*

Steven Murray loved The Stranglers. Though his thoughts were more about how this house was *still standing?* Never mind, *standing still.* The west coast man was also a big fan of Lee Child's 'Jack Reacher' series of books. So as he followed Afro MacDonald up through the broken gate and across mini craters, it was no surprise that he smiled gently and... 'said nothing.'

Before they rang the bell, both visitors had to squeeze under the very low scaffolding that had been carefully erected around the entrance to the woman's home.

"Dampness, dry rot or possibly just replacing parts of the old roughcasting," Murray mentioned. This time looking both seriously disappointed and mighty curious by his current surroundings.

It was a fully detached property MacDonald had noted, and *'still standing and standing still'* toward the rear of the property were a large garden shed and an empty dilapidated greenhouse. Each clearly visible from the front steps.

Suddenly movement could be heard from inside and the sturdy door which had once been painted bright red, opened with a loud huff. As it was drawn back, several more aged remnants of paint saw their chance, and made a mad, frantic, desperate dash for freedom.

"Detective Inspector Murray," the cultured, authoritative female voice exclaimed brightly. Her vocal welcome was accompanied with a gracious smile and a firm hand extended in the detective's direction. Her stern disapproving look and withdrawn hand, she kept especially for MacDonald. And the poor woman hadn't even opened her mouth yet.

"This is my colleague, Ma'am. Ms MacDonald," Murray informed her.

"Not an actual detective then?" The woman said scornfully. Offering her a brief dismissive glance before turning and marching hastily down the uncarpeted hallway. "Well come on in. Don't stand there all day. My builder will be back on shift any minute now."

The steely look exchanged between Murray and MacDonald said that this was either going to be a bundle of fun or a very exceptionally long day. Or both.

As they entered the airy, yet compact front room. Three cups of tea had been poured. Was that a lucky guess or a woman sat by her window watching out for their arrival? A female who enjoyed hosting guests or simply a retired academic who liked to be in control?

Two decades had moved on since she'd retired, but life seemed to have stood still for this particular woman. With that said, maybe Steven Murray based too many of his thoughts on first impressions. Possibly once he'd spoken with the lady of the house for a bit, his initial fears and concerns may well be allayed. As he sat down, he crossed his legs and sincerely hoped for that to be the case.

Eighteen

"Qué será, será. Whatever will be, will be. The future's not ours to see. Qué será, será."

- Doris Day

"Who knew Portobello had so many eating places?"

It was Janice Brooks that asked the question as she carefully guided Sergeant Black through its busy maze of upmarket streets, avenues and terraces. Whilst ultimately searching for the local doctor's surgery.

"The Coastal View; Milo's Bistro; The Beach House Eatery," she began to rhyme them all off.

"Next on the left you said," Black interrupted.

"What? Yeh! Sure," she replied.

Paying far more attention to the frontage of St. Andrew's Restaurant on the main drag as they slowly drove past.

As soon as they turned the corner - WHAM! - There it was on the right-hand side, and the words: Lennon; Lambert & Lawrence dominated the impressive glossy fascia of the ultra-modern medical practice.

"That's an 'L' of a sign," Brooks joked.

"Aye. Failed football managers every one of them," Ian Black moaned.

"Ah, you're obviously a Heart of Midlothian fan. Nae luck." For comedic effect, the female officer liked to throw in a little slang word every now and again.

"This is a mighty strange and unusual location for a doctor's surgery," Black announced. "It's got absolutely nowhere to park. I certainly don't fancy having a gammy leg and having to walk 200 yards up Portobello High Street to get here."

The man mounted the pavement directly outside the premises. The officers then quickly exited the vehicle and purposefully made their way inside.

From her vantage point behind a huge window, the receptionist gave them both a 'frosty' look as they walked together through the automatic doors. Though before she could comment on their parking strategy…

"Police!" Black opened with. He was in no mood for some jumped up jobsworth giving him a telling off.

"Hi. Really sorry to bother you," said the female voice.

With a different approach entirely to her colleague, Janice Brooks offered the lady behind the high counter the largest, friendliest and most welcoming grin she could muster. It was a down payment to offset Ian Black's earlier bulldozer approach. The book - *How to Win Friends and Influence People* had just been added to the cart for this man's Christmas stocking.

With her smile fixed firmly in place, Janice figured that she could endure a few more minutes being happy…

"We need to speak with Dr Lennon's secretary. It's urgent and in relation to his death." She managed that whole statement in a sobering understated tone.

"It's terrible. We're still all in shock. Murdered! What is the world coming to? What a place. What a tragedy…"

"What about pointing us in the right direction," Janice jumped in. Her smile slightly less energetic now.

The ageing employee behind the desk had no doubt been in the post forever. Her poor dress sense made her look in her eighties and the imitation pearls that hung from her neck were far less flattering than she'd surely wanted. Her hair added to the appearance of a surly Miss Marple lookalike. Also not helping was the pale pink lipstick which seemed to have been purchased directly from an ancient Woolworths store of the 1970's. The woman looked right and left, not wishing to be overheard. Then she began to voice quietly…

"Well, actually I'm the secretary, receptionist, HR, PR, cook, cleaner and general dogsbody for all three doctors," she merrily informed the officers.

It would appear from her fluid remarks that she seemed just a tad under appreciated. Both Black and Brooks knew this was the ideal time to give her their special, 'we feel your pain' nod. They both did so.

"Well we were wondering if you could give us un updated number for one of his clients?" Janice asked.

With hope, she handed over the business card that took them to the breezy coastal town in the first place. The receptionist stared at it for the briefest moment.

"Ah, you want Chestnut's new number?" She exclaimed with a rather surprised and high-pitched response. "Apologies," she said. Immediately lowering her voice.

Several patients in the waiting room had already clocked the presence of the Police Scotland duo and others were now busy checking outside, searching for the TV cameras and reporters.

"Do you know this popular, Chestnut?" Brooks asked.

The woman played nervously with her fake pearls for a second before gesturing to the officers to come closer, to avoid raising her voice. A mischievous smile arose…

"You know this filly may well be lively. But we're not actually talking about a four legged creature, right?"

The bemused, dismissive looks from both detectives told her that they had already guessed as such.

"And she is not HIS client." The woman's eyes raised.

Now that they didn't know. Miss A. Walker, at least that's what was stated on her name badge, curled her right index finger and again summoned them closer still. Janice Brooks and Ian Black duly obliged and lowered both their faces down toward the desk and the secretive medical dominatrix.

When they got within inches of touching distance the whimsical woman once again purred…

"He, Doctor Lennon - was in fact HER client," she added with a quick wink. "If you know what I mean?"

Both Police Scotland officers jolted upright. As if told to stand to attention. That had thrown them. Neither one had been expecting that. Janice Brooks immediately wondered if Mrs Lennon had been aware of that? Had she deliberately sent them down this rabbit hole to do her detective work for her? She'd have had her suspicions. After all, she knew he saw other women. She herself had been a prostitute. So what was different about this one? Someone had deliberately left her calling card in his shirt pocket on the very night he was brutally killed, at least according to Mrs Lennon.

After refocusing on what they'd just been told, Ian Black tried to make amends for his earlier brusque manner by asking pleasantly...

"And do you have a new number for her now, Ma'am?"

However, calling a forty-something year old, Ma'am, probably didn't help his cause any. The surgery's official 'Jack of all Trades' scowled at him, before eventually uttering in no more than a whisper...

"I should do. He would have me call her most weeks."

"He would have you, YOU call her?" Janice needed clarification that she had heard her correctly.

The officer's dulcet tones were nowhere near as quiet. Mothers and toddlers turned around. The man holding a makeshift bandage to his eye looked up in discomfort.

"Indeed, he would," Walker said. "Not a very nice man was our Doctor Lennon, if truth be told. His wife though, she's the salt of the earth. A kinder woman and a better mother you couldn't find anywhere."

Black simply nodded in acknowledgement. And before Janice could follow-up and question her further on that, the capable, wise and more than able Miss Walker, had handed back two surgery business cards. Each with new numbers on the back. She also felt inspired to add...

"Actually, none of the doctors here are very nice. If you're looking for a new place to register, go elsewhere. I need the job and the money, plus I only stay two streets away. I was born there and I've lived there all my life. Even when my late mother passed away, I chose to remain…"

"Thank you for your help, it was invaluable," Brooks jumped in quickly. "But we have to be going now."

Both officers bid her a hasty adieu. Janice knew that Walker's whole life story was about to be revealed, but they didn't have time to listen. Outside she added…

"That woman did genuinely help me understand one further puzzling question, Sarge."

Black's confused expression spoke up on his behalf.

"Her outdated dress sense," Janice declared. "She obviously still wore her late mother's clothing!"

"I found it quite cute actually," the elder statesman of the team replied. "Strangely seductive."

Brooks laughed. She in turn, found that charming.

"Cute you say," she giggled, opening the car door.

Inside the vehicle, a more serious and constructive tone immediately came over both individuals. Black was just about to begin driving away when Brooks went into full 'Babbling' mode…

"So 'Chestnut' was a call-girl, a hooker, an escort," she began. "And he made his receptionist book the appointments. Words actually fail me." The constable then turned her card over to check out the new number.

"What? What is it?" Black asked. Knowing full well from his partner's facial expression that something was obviously amiss.

"Miss Walker, I love you," Brooks exclaimed proudly.

She handed the card to Black and shook her head in disbelief. Could this day get any better, she thought. For not only had the middle-aged secretary, come general dogsbody, written down the lively filly's current number.

She had gone out of her way to put a little smiley face next to… an address.

"What a star!" Brooks added. "10 Quarry Close."

Both officers were familiar with that location. It was just off Nicolson Street in the centre of Edinburgh.

"That needs to be our next stop, Sarge."

"You do know that Steven Murray is going to drag us both over the coals for today, Constable Brooks, yes?"

The man turned the engine and shook his head.

"It's my first day with you guys and at this rate, I'll be lucky to manage a week."

"I think you'll be surprised at DI Murray's unique style of man-management," Janice oozed excitedly. "I believe he values giving his team full autonomy to go with their gut, to act on instinct and intuition. Or at least today, I hope that's his preferred philosophy," she grinned.

Both colleagues laughed heartily at her believed understanding of her boss's parameters.

"Que sera sera," Black expressed, as he hastily departed Portobello and headed back into the bustling streets of Scotland's capital.

Back in Haddington, Ms T's front lounge could barely cope with three adults, a chair, a tiny floral settee and a coffee table. The latter, the inspector figured, had been brought in on secondment from another room entirely. No pleasantries were to be exchanged, for as soon as sugar and milk had been added to their drinks…

"George Matthew was an evil man," Thoroughgood declared confidently with an unsurprising arrogance. "A jury of his peers agreed," she continued. "But I personally was brought up in a household that taught 'forgiveness.' That was also one of the guiding principles that we regularly tried to encourage throughout my tenure as head of the school."

"For pupils and teachers?" MacDonald asked. Though she had phrased it rhetorically and no answer was given.

Thoroughgood turned toward DI Murray. She had taken an instant disliking to the ancient Greek goddess of sexual love and beauty it would seem. When Steven had spoken to the woman on the phone, he'd told her the main reason for their visit. Though he had quietly explained that her ex-teacher's name had come up in fresh enquiries that they were conducting. So she was aware that the visit would be focused on the man himself, but nothing more than that.

"At the trial, Inspector, jurors heard how physical and sexual attacks were 'rife' with the children. The school was never going to survive long term after that."

Both visitors acknowledged the truth in that statement.

"The pupils were seemingly too scared to report their ordeals sooner to either myself or to others in charge."

"They were terrified victims," Afro jumped in. "Fearful that if they complained, there would be further immediate repercussions." She'd spoken rationally and in a quiet, understated tone. "Mean, dismissive teachers should always find a new profession," she added. "If you aren't there to love and nurture, then simply find another job. That said, many strict teachers are the most loving and stable, though there is a difference."

Murray waited to hear what that difference was. Whilst Thoroughgood was incensed that this mere slip of a woman would dare to interrupt her while she spoke.

"The key is intention," Afro said. "And if they have the capacity to care in a genuine way. Sometimes the more serious teachers are more serious about student welfare too. Heroes come in all forms you know. Yet your seriously frightened pupils couldn't find a trusted adult. That was quite alarming, Mrs Thoroughgood."

Murray held back a smile. Because she didn't know 'How to win friends and influence people,' either!

176

"It is Ms Thoroughgood," the woman snapped back. "You'd do well to remember that Miss McDonald."

Afro kept her grin hidden, before she responded…

"It's MacDonald actually, Ms Thoroughgood. M.A.C."

The bold Tabitha T sniffed at her response with an air of indifference.

Steven Murray meanwhile was beginning to think that the retired teacher was a racist. He adjusted his listening brief accordingly and set out to reel her in with…

"If memory serves me right, lots of specific incidents came out in court, Ma'am. Wasn't that correct?"

MacDonald was confident that Murray would already be fully aware of all the 'specific' incidents, but that he just wanted to test out the wily Tabitha Thoroughgood.

"I remember some of the abuse highlighted, yes."

"Go on," Murray encouraged. "It could be vital to our ongoing enquiries, Tabitha. May I call you Tabitha?" Murray asked with a radiant, yet charming smile.

"Please. Please do," she instructed him. In a very scholarly, formal manner.

She was now in her element and turned her back even further away from the other female in the room. She had to refocus to impress a detective inspector no less. She hesitated only slightly before beginning to recall numerous horrendous events, as if she were a nervous contestant participating in a live televised edition of The Generation Game.

"Golf balls were thrown at lined-up pupils/A boy had been regularly battered by a mop and forced to eat soap/A mallet attack on four other random pupils/A cigarette put out numerous times on a vulnerable female's lips and mouth/Whipping boys with towels during monitoring duties in the changing rooms."

Whilst the two visitors to her shoddy, rundown home sat and shook their heads in disbelief, she continued…

"These were certainly the more isolated cases. Things that happened over and above the sexual and physical violence that he'd continually and regularly 'doled out,' including raping two teenage girls."

Hearing this well-spoken and highly educated lady use the words 'doled out,' didn't quite fit with her upmarket, toffee-nosed demeanour. There had been a definite bitterness to her words as she'd spoken openly and freely about George Matthew's gross, appalling actions.

"You spoke earlier about forgiveness, Ma'am. Before Miss 'MAC' Donald here, so rudely interrupted your train of thought." He then gave Afro a knowing wink.

His sidekick for the day looked at him with disdain. Does he really think a little nod and a wink makes that comment okay? Against her better judgment however, she sat on that thought and gave him the benefit of the doubt.

"So had you been in contact with Mr Matthew?"

"In his early days behind bars I had, Inspector. But from when he was released - Nothing. There had been no interaction whatsoever."

Murray nodded. MacDonald frowned with suspicion.

"Who initially made contact," the inspector asked.

Thoroughgood pondered on the question briefly...

"He had sent me a short note in the post. It was filled with apologies and what seemed like genuine remorse at the time for his actions."

"And you instantly felt the need for a sadistic pen-pal after that, Ms Thoroughgood?"

MacDonald's question seemed harsh and somewhat abrupt. Had this been the desired input Murray had sought? His pursed lips and brief furtive glance in Afro's direction, seemed to indicate yes. She shook her head. He had reeled her in. He really was a sly old dog. Although he'd probably have preferred less of the 'old.'

178

"I felt the need to be polite and respectful," the woman responded. She had remained surprisingly calm and unfazed. But then added... "The least I could do was acknowledge receipt of his letter and its contents."

"I understand, Tabitha. Thank you," Murray gestured.

The door had now been fully opened to discuss staffing levels, mistakes and opportunities that had been missed to spot the pattern of abuse being systematically handed out by George Matthew. A common ground and territory of mutual respect had been established between the two passionate females. Especially when MacDonald and Steven Murray learned of the set of trying circumstances, that eventually led Tabitha Thoroughgood to take shelter in her current East Lothian abode.

Nineteen

"If I should fall from grace with God where no doctor can relieve me. If I'm buried in the sod but the angels won't receive me. Let me go, boys, let me go, boys. Let me go down in the mud, where the rivers all run dry."

- The Pogues

Sounding like an unconventional cross between an expensive power-tool company and an upmarket chain of lawyers - Black and Brooks arrived in good time at number 10 Quarry Close.

The nearby Kilimanjaro coffee shop was a favourite haunt for Brooks' colleague, Sergeant John Black. The man would visit at least twice a week, depending on his shifts. During this time the caffeine loving, coffee aficionado, could always be found in one of its quirky back corner booths. The premises had offered an ultra-relaxed hangout with comfy sofas and rustic wooden tables since it opened in 2005.

Take a brief three minute walk around the corner from the cafe and you'd arrive at the four storey high tenement building that the pair were currently parked outside.

"I've been thinking," Brooks proffered aloud. "Why did our receptionist pal feel the need to give us two dental surgery cards back? Why write out this woman's new number twice? That doesn't make sense."

"She did write the address alongside it for us, sure."

"That's as maybe. They were both on the card she returned to me. Was yours different?" She asked Black. "It's just that she seemed extremely efficient and I couldn't get it out of my head as we drove over here."

"Well let's satisfy your curiosity," the sergeant said. "Because I'm now equally intrigued. I put mine's straight into my wallet as you had all the details we needed," he said, matter-of-factly.

Wedged between his remaining two five pound notes, Ian Black removed the card, turned it over and began to gradually turn bright red.

"What's wrong? What is it?" Janice asked immediately. "Did she write a phone number and address on yours too? Come on, speak up man."

As the female constable began punching her sergeant playfully on the shoulder, Black nodded his head, began to grin and turned the card slowly over to show to Janice Brooks. She gave her colleague a puzzled look.

"I believe she has given me HER phone number and address, Detective Constable Brooks. How about that?"

"April Walker, who'd have thought it? Shooting from the hip. The sly old man-eater that she is." Brooks laughed.

"I suspect it was referring to her as, Ma'am, that won her over," Black added. They both laughed out loud and exited the vehicle.

At the main entrance to the building, eight random nameplates presented themselves to the officers like a police identity parade. Yet instantly, both Police Scotland employees stretched out to push the exact same buzzer in unison. What was that all about? The pair laughed once again at their antics. They'd both recognised that the nameplate they had chosen was the only one displaying an artistic etching instead of an actual name. The engraving was of a solitary horse leaping over a fenced hurdle. The flat number was 3/3.

"Hi. Who is it?" Came the perky, upbeat response.

"Police Scotland, Ma'am. Can we have a word please?"

Silence. Was the female considering doing a runner? But to where? And why? Had she wished she'd just ignored the doorbell altogether?

A further second or two went by before a long buzzer sounded and the two intuitive officers began to experience their very own Kilimanjaro experience for the day. One of them took the stairs two at a time. Possibly her enthusiasm getting the better of her. Black meanwhile plodded along diligently, a few paces behind.

From inside her apartment the so-called 'equestrian' escort had been watching events unfold on her doorstep through her spy hole. DC Brooks had arrived bouncing up and down on the soles of her feet. She appeared ready to go ten rounds in a boxing ring. In her mind she was lying back against the ropes, ducking and diving whilst throwing some punches. When in reality, she was leaning against 100 year-old metal railings at the top of the stairs. The very same stairs that an out of condition police sergeant was just about to summit.

"Constable Brooks," he wheezed, taking a deep ragged breath. "Do you know how they built these things?"

Taking a look down the middle parting of the three flights, Janice simply shook her head in dismay. She had no idea why the man would even think to ask such a strange question. As he responded, she realised that she was still getting to grips with his deadpan sense of humour. Because his face was impassive and expressionless, as he delivered the line…

"By using step-by-step instructions."

Brooks groaned, a door opened and Ian Black's jaw just about hit the downstairs landing!

They both immediately knew why this stunning woman went by the moniker, Chestnut. Her gorgeous shoulder length hair was a rich, dimensional shade of brown with beautiful warm red undertones.

"What's up officers? How can I help you?" The positive vibe in both her first questions was then continued with… "Would you like to come in?"

As Brooks went to step forward she literally had to push Ian Black's mouth closed. Her face was smiling, though it was actually crying out to the man to pull himself together.

In his half century plus life, he genuinely wasn't sure if he had seen a prettier girl. He was in awe… in admiration… possibly even… in love!

Shaking her head, Brooks shoved the aged, adolescent, love struck baby boomer inside. She instantly produced an imaginary handkerchief to wipe away his drool as they crossed the threshold. Now it was Black's turn to shake his head and quickly come to his senses.

"Thank you, Ma'am," he said. Still getting his breath back from the double whammy of climbing the stairs and then gazing upon this fine looking young female.

"We're looking for Chestnut." Brooks said. "However based on your terrific hair colouring I would guess…"

"Yes, you'd be correct. I'm Chestnut," she interrupted. "I always try to keep it in tip-top condition. Thanks."

Black seemed to apologetically stumble over his words as he asked… "Do you have a proper, non-business related name we could perhaps refer to you by? Chestnut is a lovely vibrant name and it no doubt matches your personality," the man quickly added.

He could feel his face turn a fiery red, as this time Brooks gave him the *'you're unbelievable'* head shake.

"It's Kirsten. Miss Kirsten Beale, Constable."

"And it's sergeant. Sergeant Ian Black," came his reply.

Both smiled knowingly at each other and Brooks felt nauseous. It was mid afternoon, yet this twenty-something female was still draped in a silky, olive green negligee. If it reached her knees you'd be lucky. Never mind luck, Black already swore that he was in heaven.

"We're led to believe that you knew Doctor Ian Lennon, Ma'am." Janice stated in a low, respectful tone.

Some of the confident wind seemed to depart swiftly from Beale's sails for a moment. Her head dropped and she expressed genuine grief as she responded...

"It was horrible. Such a shock. Murdered. Who'd have believed that actually went on in real life?"

We would! Said the puzzled expression on the officer's faces. But she was right, for the vast majority of the public they think violence and sadistic murder scenes only ever happen in books or on TV and film. So they find it difficult to relate to these events in real life.

As the woman went to speak, all three had now sat down on Beale's expensive red leather corner unit...

"I had met up with him on a regular basis over the past few years. He was a really lovely man. A very unique and special human being."

Messrs Black and Brooks, the independent tool wholesalers, glanced at each other with great intrigue at that final comment from Miss Beale.

"May I ask you two quick follow-up questions with regards to your answer there?"

"Of course, Sergeant. Fire away." Her smile had immediately returned to its familiar spot on her face.

The female officer perched beside Beale on her settee was most impressed that her sergeant had so far managed to maintain eye contact with the girl, whilst her cleavage, slim waist and shapely inner thigh all fought for his attention. Kirsten Beale was small and cute with bright blue eyes and a broad eager to please smile. In truth, even Janice Brooks was falling under her spell. She was a literal ray of sunshine.

"When you say regular and a few years. Can you be even more precise, Miss Beale? What does that look like?" Black enquired. "Because that part I believe."

Kirsten Beale was rather taken aback at his comment, but was happy to clarify and be more specific…

"Sure," she said. "It would look like twice a week and coming up close to three years. I remember it well, because our first meeting consisted of us going out for a meal on Valentine's Day. So approximately two months short of three years, Sergeant." She paused nervously before continuing. "Can I then ask you what you meant by… *that part you believed?*"

Brooks was in disbelief at the well-mannered pleasantries being exchanged between the couple. She had decided that she would give her sergeant two more minutes before she'd jump in and ask more difficult and pressing questions. She didn't care that he was the SIO on the case. Her countdown on him had begun…

"You can ask, Miss Beale. However, may I share my thoughts on what I've gleaned about you so far, firstly?"

Again with the niceties, Brooks sighed. By this point she'd internally counted down to one minute forty-five. At her side, the delicately demure and well toned figure of Kirsten Beale crossed her tanned legs, blushed and nodded excitely.

As Ian Black lifted his left hand to his chin to ponder and speak with authority, both females could clearly see the woven tapestry of darkened, historic scars that were prominently displayed upon the back of it. There was a definite story behind those horrific marks, Janice reflected. Whilst Beale had thought: Virile. Macho. Heroic. A real man.

"I believe that you live in a world full of ideas," the sergeant began. "One where you value meaningful relationships."

Is he having a laugh, Brooks surmised. Is he mindful of what she does for for a living? Several men a day being the answer. He had less than ninety seconds remaining. She was getting geared up to take over…

"People love to be around you because of your warm personality and bubbly nature," Black continued. "I believe that your alter-ego is a unique mixture of sociable introspective, always looking for deeper meanings and questioning concepts that others might not think to question."

The girl smiled appreciatively. Agreeing and buying in immediately to all that he was saying. Here was someone that got me. That was exactly what her body language was expressing. Brooks on the other hand, had only sixty seconds of patience left.

"You appear to be an expressive communicator," the Senior Investigative Officer reeled off. "Using your wit to create engaging stories. Curious and original, you definitely have an artistic side. No doubt drawn to creative pursuits because they'll allow you to express your ideas and flair."

This has to stop. Brooks looked at her watch. He was moving into the final thirty seconds and she shuffled her feet in readiness.

"I'd imagine that the beautiful Chestnut, places great importance on personal freedom and self-expression. Would I be right?"

Beale pursed her lips. The man was spot on once again.

"Plus, she obviously can't stand feeling tied down or living a life that isn't in alignment with her values."

What values? And I bet she's been tied down often, Brooks thought unkindly. The frustrated constable was beginning her final countdown as Miss Beale spoke...

"Sergeant, what was previously perceived as nerdy is now viewed as original. And what I love about nerdiness or geekiness, as some people call it. Is that it doesn't really matter what you're into – it just means you're not a follower."

"Time out," Janice said and made to stand. But Black signalled her to remain seated. His gesture decisive.

"So getting back to your question, Kirsten. Which is a lovely name by the way." His voice crisp and inviting.

The girl nodded, quite taken aback at the precise nature and accuracy of how this ageing police sergeant had described her. She was also in awe, if truth be told and so was Brooks. Who knew that Afro MacDonald would have a rival profiler in the team, she thought.

"Well that has firmed up accurately the frequency that you met with the deceased. Thank you for that, Kirsten. However it's the second part of your statement that both myself and DC Brooks have a problem with."

By this point, Janice couldn't even remember what the partially clothed, yet freshly scented woman had said.

"It's the part where you described Ian Lennon as - *'A really lovely man. A very unique and special human being,'* I believe your exact words were, Miss Beale."

"I don't understand, Sergeant, what do you…"

"Never mind all the earlier character traits that I described you as possessing, Kirsten," Black carefully interrupted. "Just focus on the latter part, the most important part of your psyche. The part where you stated clearly that your whole make-up enabled you NOT to be a follower. With that in mind, remind us again of what Doctor Ian Lennon was like."

Back in Haddington, a lunchtime bell could be heard sounding at the nearby John Knox High School. It was there, within the sound of it, that Detective Inspector Steven Murray had been digging a little further into Tabitha Thoroughgood's unscheduled retirement plan. It wasn't a good one and without doubt it had been the beginning of her sudden and almighty fall from grace. It would appear that she'd been let go several months before the school actually closed. At the time she felt she'd been used as a very convenient scapegoat.

Listening, both Murray and MacDonald thought that was a strong possibility, but who could say for certain. After all, Tabitha had been in charge throughout the previous two decades. The whole time that George Matthew had successfully carried out all his heinous, beastly assaults. So was it terribly wrong that the head teacher should also be held accountable? Hadn't she clearly been responsible for some form of gross negligence? Didn't the buck ultimately stop with her?

A disciplinary meeting had been held and she'd been found culpable on several counts and dismissed. That in itself wouldn't have been too bad. Yes, she would have been mortified, embarrassed and ashamed by the events. However, it was the fact that her pension was declared null and void that was to break her. And although later on appeal, a smaller lump sum was granted and agreed upon. She struggled financially ever since. Her upmarket home in North Berwick was first to go and in the intervening years, a further three house moves, each one downsizing, had eventually found her in her very latest dwelling.

Not the ideal scenario. Not what an influential headmistress would have wished for at the end of her up until then, unblemished career. With that said and for whatever reason, she had resolutely accepted no responsibility whatsoever for the neglect and abuse of those pupils in her care. So possibly like they say - karma can be a real ***** at times!

In Edinburgh's south side at Quarry Close, Kirsten Beale, aka Chestnut, had hesitated before responding to Black's question regarding her honest thoughts on the dead doctor...

"I'm twenty-four and I'm very good at what I do."

Neither Brooks nor Black doubted her on that score.

"I get paid to accompany people to dinner, to attend business functions, corporate gigs and concerts or simply engage in spending time with the individual chatting and listening. In essence I'm retained to socialise with the client and ensure that he, or she," she said, gazing admiringly toward Brooks, "has a great time." She paused again. "So I can truthfully say that Lennon was the worst human being I have ever met."

Ian Black smiled. Job done. Brooks was gobsmacked.

"He probably paid for most of what you see in front of you," she went on. "But he wasn't a nice individual."

As the two officers scanned the contents of the flat, they both began to fully realise just what two nights per week over three years amounted to. In Black's book it was approximately £30,000. Whereas the female of the species saw it very differently. DC Brooks noted a high-end watch and bracelet adorning the petite home-owner and the tall walls of the beautifully decorated apartment were festooned with large expensive artwork, not to mention the massive seventy-inch TV set. Plus her extensive wardrobe would be bulging at the seams with designer outfits to showcase her pleasing lithe figure.

Brooks grimaced, she tried to tell herself that she wasn't envious in the slightest. Maybe I should go on the game, she thought. Then she saw her reflection in the crystal framed, full-length mirror and thought better of it. Getting back to reality she felt compelled to ask…

"Did you ever meet his wife at all? You did know that he was married presumably?" Brooks enquired.

Beale shrugged. "I never asked." Her halo slipped for a full second or two. "I know that I present this very cheery, outgoing person, but in my line of work I also do a lot of thinking introspectively," she revealed. "I shatter a little bit when I think people don't like me. So I stay clear of any overly inquisitive or personal questions. I stick to the generic and bland."

"We quite enjoy the direct approach, Miss Beale," Black declared. "I bet Constable Brooks even has a few more uncomfortable questions for you right now."

The man smiled and swept his open palm gracefully toward Janice. She in turn nodded keenly and asked…

"Do you know a Mark Ziola, Miss Beale? And do you work for 'Jimmy' Reid? A.K.A James Baxter Reid?"

The girl's confidence and bubbly demeanour were definitely rocked by that quick one-two delivered by Brooks. 'Chestnut' was silenced for the first time as she pondered how to respond. Her sheer stupor of thought was an answer in itself.

Suddenly, scurrying through from a bedroom to her rescue came an excitable, newly awakened golden retriever. With its shining coat and outgoing easy to please personality, it wasn't hard to see how these two were paired up. The fact that the breed often maintain their fun-loving, young at heart, puppy attitudes into adulthood made this team a perfect combination.

"I adore dogs," Kirsten Beale announced. Quickly regrouping and ignoring the Ziola and Reid questions for now. "I truly believe that they are nature's antidepressants," she added. "When I'm responsible for caring for an animal, it gives me a lot of self-esteem. I gravitate towards dogs so much. I think because they're nonverbal and sometimes I feel I can't always find the words."

Sergeant Black and DC Brooks both found that last remark hard to believe. And she had did rather well up until now.

"Where were you on the night Ian Lennon was killed?"

Janice Brooks could easily have used the word died, but she wanted to remind this young girl that they were dealing with murder and that whoever was responsible, was still out and about walking the streets.

As Kirsten Beale tried to respond, her playful companion bounced vigorously all over her. Revealing to Black and Janice Brooks that she wore no underwear below her silky, skimpy nightwear. Interesting that when it came time to choose essential accessories to be worn that day, that her matching designer watch and bracelet made the cut way before a bra and briefs.

"I was with a client that evening," she said in a fairly relaxed manner. "In fact I had been with two clients that night," she went on to confirm. This time her face reddened somewhat. "And unless push comes to shove, I'll not be sharing any names or addresses."

"You have names and addresses?" Brooks asked in a surprised tone.

"Well on reflection, no. At least not for the ones who visit me here."

"And did they both visit you here that night?"

"Just the one," Beale confirmed.

"Which means you have at least one address," Janice smiled.

"I can increase it to two, if you'd like to share yours?"

Brooks blushed. Black's eyes widened and Chestnut winked teasingly. Touché, Ian Black thought. This girl knew that Brooks was trying to get information out of her, but she was having none of it.

"We need you to come with us to the station, Kirsten. There's someone we'd like you to meet."

"Someone I need to meet?"

Janice had no idea what this man was now up to. But seeing as he had supported her 'gut feeling' all day, she would now happily go along with his. What she hadn't realised was that during her conversations with Kirsten 'Chestnut' Beale, Sergeant Black had text back and forth with DI Murray and had asked him to bring someone back into the station also. The inspector had agreed and would see them in an hour.

"Can I get changed first?" The girl asked cheekily. She then added, "And no looking, Constable. I know your sort." Beale winked.

Did she genuinely know my sort? Detective Constable Janice Brooks questioned to herself.

The clever, alluring 'Chestnut' had been broken in many years ago. So she'd seen it all before and been able to read people extremely well. In fact, was she doing a number on them right now? She performed for a living. Had the last ten minutes all been an act? A charade? A special 'Police Scotland' private, behind closed doors performance? If so, she was really good - though she had already told her visitors that she was 'very good' at her job. So there's a thought or two for Black and Brooks to consider. Meanwhile who did Kirsten Beale expect to meet during her brief sojourn at Queen Charlotte Street Station in Leith?

Five minutes later, dressed in casual jeans, white trainers and an unbranded t-shirt, Kirsten Beale looked like any normal, average, twenty-four year old female. As she locked up her flat both detectives noticed that the expensive watch and bracelet had been deliberately left behind. She was 'very good,' and was now playing strongly to her girl-next-door features. With her neat, tidy hair tied into a cute innocent ponytail and little make-up on, any future mother-in-law would be absolutely delighted if this diminutive female walked through the doorway on their son's arm.

"What's your dog's name by the way?" Ian Black asked.

"It's Conker," she replied. "Though not like William the Conqueror," she joked.

The police sergeant nodded wisely. "No, like Chestnut and Conker, I get it!" A huge grin spread across his face. "That's brilliant, just brilliant," he exclaimed.

"Remember Reid and Ziola?" A mindful DC Brooks threw in… "You never answered those questions."

Twenty

"Duch of the terrace never grew up, I hope she never will. Says she's an heiress, sits in her terrace. Says she's got time to kill, time to kill."

- The Stranglers

Over the past 48 hours an experienced officer had been working hard meeting and speaking with many of Reid's escorts. He was also well aware of several of Ziola's close friends and allies. So they too had been interviewed, interrogated and threatened by the man.

He'd been directed to try a few possible locations. One in particular was only yards from the dead man's flat and it was there that he'd stumbled across a key factor in the disappearance of Reid's girls.

However, why do criminals and those up to no good still insist on meeting in the dodgiest, most questionable areas? Why not just sit and chat in a Burger King or a McDonalds? Surely that's much less conspicuous? That being the case, it was late afternoon and the two men couldn't help but cast sinister shadows as they spoke on the dimly lit street corner. Arousing no suspicions at all!

"She's called The Duchess, 'Bunny.' That's who's enticing your girls away. I have it on good authority," Rab Nielsen informed him. "It's a revenge thing."

"And you know this how?" Was rasped in return.

"I still have means you know. I'm not done, quite yet."

"My sources say that you are. So after this I'd get as far away from here as possible." The Reidmeister's voice was harsher than ever. "In fact that's a direct order by the way, not some wishy-washy encouragement. Get your family and leave Edinburgh for good."

"Don't you want to meet her? To possibly sample or destroy the goods personally?"

"You are one sick individual," Reid declared. "Just you take care of it and keep me out of it. The less I know the better. By the way, did you beat Murray and Furlong to this information?" The gangster added with a smirk.

"I did. Because my methods are a little more direct," Nielsen added with a twisted, sadistic arrogance.

The vicious, unlawful pair had arranged to meet in secret by an abandoned warehouse at the bottom of Constitution Street in Leith. A whole five minute walk away from Nielsen's previous stomping ground at Queen Charlotte Street. Reid had insisted on the location, and one couldn't help but think that he was definitely playing mind games with the corrupt cop.

Not only had Lizzie and Drew Curry uncovered this man's involvement in a child sex ring, but the now green-haired 'Radical' I.T consultant had illegally accessed his private email account, which highlighted numerous dodgy, illicit deals and rackets that Robert Nielsen had been involved in throughout the years. Although this actual evidence may not be available to use in court, it at least showed them where to look to uncover further corroborating facts to back up and confirm the truthfulness of his involvement. The man was finished regardless. He was already on the run. Now he was simply trying to avoid arrest and a lengthy prison sentence. He did however, have one piece of outstanding business that he was desperate to take care of and complete. This 'Duchess' had caused him an immense amount of grief and he was about to lose everything because of her mercenary actions. Actions that had led to his sudden fall from grace with 'Bunny' Reid. The man had some specific theories of his own regarding her and he was determined to follow up on them.

MacDonald was reflective on the journey back with DI Murray. The inspector had casually informed her they'd need to take a slight detour. Someone was to be given a special invitation to return with them to the station.

"Think of it as a surprise," he teased her.

The man was delighted that Ian Black had shown the initiative to follow up on his instincts and was happy to be both supportive and surprised by his actions.

Afro had opted for some historical informative chat with Steven Murray. She was keen to find out about the rest of the team, to get to know their backgrounds and how they'd arrived to be part of his squad. But every conversation seemed to come back to the recent members of his unit that had died, fair or foul, over the last couple of years. Names such as Tasmin Taylor, Mac Rasul, Keith Brown, 'Ally' Coulter, Doctor Thomas Patterson and Susan Hayes to name but a few.

Each individual still meant something specific to Steven Murray. That's the kind of man he was. Even those tainted colleagues that were rotten and briefly travelled the wrong path. He remembered happier times with them. The things that he'd learned from them and the lovely experiences that they had shared together.

Their taxi-run diversion would take them an extra twenty minutes. En-route MacDonald wrote down her address to her Linlithgow abode and offered it to Detective Inspector Murray.

"Just follow the postcode," she smiled. "When you arrive - turn around!" She cryptically instructed him. "I look forward to seeing you both later," she added.

Soon they reached their scheduled pick-up point. The individual concerned had no idea that they were coming. Which was exactly what the inspector and Ian Black had intended.

"Nice area," Afro commented, as they parked up in the driveway outside of the luxury home.

However just before they could exit the car, the gentle lilt of a mobile could be heard. It was in that instant that the inspector reminded himself that he urgently had to choose another ring tone. He'd most recently changed it to the hauntingly atmospheric piece of stringed music currently playing. It was Lord of the Rings meets Game of Thrones. But now every time he gets a call, Steven Murray gets a three second animated clip in his mind. The scene, resembling a dream, was a BBC black and white musical production of a very camp, perspiration laden Gollum chasing King in the North, Jon Snow, over the drama-laden cobbled walkways of Coronation Street. Whilst at the same time singing *"I'm a Yankee Doodle Dandy."*

However, thankfully on this occasion when Murray answered the call, it was Tabitha Thoroughgood.

As the inspector put her on speaker, MacDonald pulled an imaginary zipper across her closed lips and remained quiet in the background.

Steven Murray greeted the woman pleasantly enough, though he still couldn't quite believe that she wouldn't accept any responsibility or blame for not spotting what George Matthew had gotten away with under her watch for numerous years.

In fact, she was actually calling because she'd remembered an update that the now dead Matthew had given her during a phone call a while back, and she'd wondered if the DI would like to be made aware of it? Because she had omitted to mention it earlier.

"It was to do with the two Mathieson sisters," she said, in a low apologetic voice. "How their respective lives had taken vastly different paths in the intervening years after his rape and abuse of them."

Murray thought he detected a tear or two being shed at the other end of the line before he duly asked…

"And those separate paths travelled Ms Thoroughgood. What exactly did they look like in the real world?"

There was silence. Was she wavering? Had she been cut off or thought better about sharing their stories?

"Ms Thoroughgood. Hello. Are you still there?"

He eventually heard movement. A handset being adjusted, perhaps a faint coughing or clearing of the throat, he suspected. Ah, she'd been composing herself before continuing, he'd guessed.

"Yes, I'm still here," she finally replied. Her response low, but firm and clipped.

She couldn't possibly be heard displaying raw emotion now, could she? Murray smiled to himself.

"The younger of the two girls married in her late teens, but lost her life a few years later after drugs, drink and a messy divorce led her down the road to prostitution I'm afraid, Inspector. Quite a *harrowing* tale altogether.

"Quite." DI Murray replied. Though he thought *heartbreaking* a much more suitable word to describe her short, eventful life.

"Whereas her older and much brighter, more capable sister, seemed to adapt and deal with her own trauma much better," Thoroughgood enlightened him.

Steven Murray couldn't quite believe the dismissive, detached manner in which this woman spoke about the dreadful experience that both girls had been subjected too. Good grades and academia was how this ex-head teacher seemed to measure individuals, the *'much brighter, more capable sister'* remark appeared to sum the woman up perfectly. The fact that the girl's skin wasn't dark was probably also a big asset, based on how this particular female had treated Afro MacDonald earlier. When the privileged Tabitha Taylor Thoroughgood first started teaching, it was a completely different era entirely.

"She had graduated with a medical degree, George Matthew informed me."

The fact that the man had obviously kept tabs on the girls concerned the inspector somewhat. Had anyone else known this? Had one of those he abused sought retribution? It certainly wouldn't be a surprise. But then again, he was only one death in a handful that had seemingly no connection to each other.

"Was there anything else?" The DI asked politely.

Again there was a 'time out for recovery' pause.

"I remember that particular sister being in attendance at both the school inquest and at George Matthew's legal trial also. During the inquest at the school…"

"You held the inquest on the school premises?" Murray snapped. "At the scene of the alleged assaults?"

"Eh, like you've just said, Inspector - alleged assaults," the woman said sniffily. "We had no way of knowing at that point if the so-called allegations had any substance or merit. Or if they would even stand up to scrutiny?"

"And like you just said, Ms Thoroughgood - allegations plural. So no matter how many complaints, it should surely have been conducted on neutral territory."

Murray calmed down and immediately offered up an apology…

"I'm so sorry, you took me by surprise with that fact, Ma'am. I cut you off, you were saying…

"Yes, well, when she appeared she told those gathered about how she'd been a victim of abuse at the school and how her ordeal had left her 'permanently scarred and scared' for life. She and her sister had been twelve and thirteen when they'd first arrived in 1997."

"I have to say," the inspector began, "I found it absolutely amazing that having been convicted of a string of offences against all those young people back in 2003 that he only served six years. Then by 2009, he was out walking the streets again as if nothing had ever happened."

Thoroughgood said nothing.

Murray was aware that the school eventually closed within a year of Matthew being found guilty of a string of prolonged physical and sexual assaults against numerous vulnerable children over that twenty year period. But how many others had never came forward? And how did those individuals function in society today? It was interesting that the inspector should think that, because the very next thing Tabitha T said was…

"George Matthew told me that he didn't believe for one minute that his actions had damaged the girls in any way whatsoever. It was just sex he'd say over and over again."

Murray shook his head in disbelief.

"Please confirm for me, Inspector, that the man was deranged and a downright nasty piece of…"

"Absolutely, Tabitha." The officer confirmed for her before she could actually finish asking the question.

"He even had the gall to add to that comment."

"Go on," Murray replied. "What did he say?"

"I bet they've had sex with plenty of others."

That was it. Short and sweet. Murray had thought that she'd finished, but there was still one final part of his comment to be added.

"What difference did one more really make?" She paused briefly. "That did it for me, Inspector. That was to be my final conversation with him. I never heard from him again. In hindsight, he really wasn't a very nice man."

"I don't think you'll get any argument from anyone on that score," DI Murray added.

"I'm so sorry that I didn't think to mention this to you when you popped by earlier. I can only apologise. I hope it may be helpful now in someway?"

"Oh, I'm sure it will be Ms Thoroughgood, Tabitha," the inspector offered up with a smile.

The woman was gone already.

"That was unexpected," the psychologist exclaimed. Relieved at being able to breathe normally again.

"Yes," Steven agreed hesitantly. "I think our retired headmistress was feeling a bit guilty and trying in her own unique way to make some sort of amends."

"By?" MacDonald asked. Still none the wiser.

"By... my dear, Aphrodite - telling us the names of the two girls that were raped. That had all been kept under wraps at the time to protect the children involved!"

MacDonald shook her head in disbelief that she'd missed that. She was genuinely gutted that she'd been oblivious to the help Thoroughgood had just proffered.

Murray meanwhile quickly looked around outside and observed many of the other gardens in the estate. He was impressed at their immaculate condition considering it was the run up to Christmas. No leaves or branches to be seen anywhere.

"So who lives in a house like this, Inspector? Afro quizzed him. Sounding like a throwback to the old TV show, Through The Keyhole, with its ever popular catchphrase... *who lives in a house like this?*

When the door opened, Aphrodite MacDonald was amazed at who stood in front of her. The homeowner stood in fashionable corduroy trousers with a beige jersey. The sleeves of which had been rolled back to accommodate a pair of less-fashionable, elasticated marigold cleaning gloves.

"I thought we were finished?" The voice questioned.

"Inspector?" Afro quizzed.

"Yes. Sorry," Murray apologised weakly to both. "It's just that someone at the station really needs to see you, Mrs Lennon. We'll take you in and bring you back in no time at all."

It had to be said, he'd been disappointed to find her cleaning up. MacDonald had noticed his shoulders slump as soon as she answered the door. But why?

Twenty One

"He walked as if upon a breeze, a guy with a hood and a scythe. He said, won't you take a walk with me. She said, I'm sorry but I'm busy tonight."

- Jess Silk

Kirsten Beale's chauffeur driven excursion across North Bridge and down Leith Walk, consisted of her telling the officers all about the late Mark Ziola in more detail.

"He was always violent toward us. Always having to prove his masculinity," she said. "He was just muscle - and not very nice muscle. No wonder he stayed alone."

That was interesting. Both Black and Brooks glanced at one another. Kirsten knew where he lived. Surely that was unusual. A working girl knowing the private address of someone employed to look after and protect them. Neither officer remarked on it and the rest of the journey consisted of a running commentary, rant and abusive monologue on the late departed Ian Lennon.

Didn't she realise that this would put her high up the pecking order of possible suspects. By this point, 'Chestnut' really didn't care. It looked and felt as if it was such a relief to air her thoughts and true feelings about the man.

"What a despicable human being," she started with. "Who leaves their wife at home on Valentine's Day to spend time with a hooker? He was a verbal and physical abuser of the highest order."

Her terminology certainly surprised her hosts.

"He was a bully, it's as simple as that. No matter what, it had to be done his way. As a father, a husband and a lover he always dictated the rules."

She continued unabated…

"The games we'd get up to, the appointment times, the locations and all that that involved - he would be in charge. He'd tease you. He'd give you a gift and then by the end of a session he'd take it back and talk about how he'd actually bought it for his wife. He was normally always sadistic, sick and violent."

The two Police Scotland colleagues had never fully appreciated, until this point, quite how awful this man seemed to be. As Sergeant Black pulled into the station car park, Kirsten Beale summed him up rather nicely…

"Put it this way," she announced defiantly. "The world is a far better place without him. 'Bunny' Reid's a better man than him, and that's saying something. Is it not?"

Only twenty yards and sixty seconds behind them, MacDonald and Murray also drove in to park. There appeared to be four individuals in the inspector's car. One more than Ian Black had expected to find.

Janice Brooks had taken Beale inside the premises immediately. Her DS had instructed her to get 'Chestnut' settled into an interview room as quickly as possible.

As Steven Murray and Afro exited their car, a tall youthful looking male held the back door open. It was then that his mother, Charlene Lennon, proceeded to hoist herself to her feet.

"Thank you, Eric," she nodded. "Where are we going this time, Inspector?" She asked. Curious as to why she was there and who specifically had asked to see her.

Within minutes of their arrival both ladies were sat on opposite sides of a desk sharing a room. It had the standard two way mirror that you'd often see in so many police procedural programmes. Anyone watching would have spotted that 'Chestnut' grew noticeably more agitated as soon as Mrs Lennon was brought in.

After Aphrodite had escorted Charlene into the room and beckoned her to take a seat, the criminal psychologist departed the scene. Offering up…

"Detective Inspector Murray and DS Black will join you shortly ladies. Just sit back and enjoy the…"

"View!" Mrs Lennon seemed to sarcastically voice, as she stared at the four walls.

"I was actually going to say… the solitude, Ma'am. Take some time out to reflect, Charlene."

Did she just wink? Afro seemed to make a habit of that. She reckoned that it put people off their game and it almost always upset their train of thought. Take time out to reflect she had encouraged the two women. Reflect upon what? That was the thought now running through both their minds. A seed nicely planted.

"Wouldn't you normally start chatting to the other person about now?" Brooks asked MacDonald as she partnered her behind the mirror in the adjoining room.

"You certainly would if you didn't recognise them," Afro affirmed. "But your prize 'Chestnut,' she definitely recognises who's been placed alongside her. Now isn't that interesting?" Because they look like polar opposites. From their age, their colouring and even their dress sense. Kirsten Beale with her t-shirt, jeans and casual trainers - compared to Mrs Lennon's heavy duty trousers, winter jacket and leather gloves. They did, or at least had shared one thing in common - the late, lamented doctor. They then sat in silence for two minutes, as Kirsten Beale drummed her fingers nervously on the desk.

When Inspector Murray finally entered alongside DS Black. It was clear that he was in no mood for further niceties. He sat next to the younger of the two women and directly across from them - the opposing team consisted of Detective Sergeant John (Ian) Black and the newly reinstated 'Charlie' (Charlene) Murphy.

"Would you take your gloves off please, Mrs Lennon."

"It's okay, Inspector, I'd rather keep them on. Thank you. I think I told you last time about my chilblains."

"Oh yes, indeed you did," Murray stated. "But here's the thing, Mrs Lennon… I don't believe you!"

Charlene instantly jerked back at that candid comment. Beale stopped slouching and sat upright in her chair. Ian Black remained expressionless and unmoved.

"I don't believe you have chilblains and I don't believe you were cleaning up when we arrived at your home either. I think you saw us arrive and grabbed a pair of your trusted Marigolds to give us that impression. Your place was spotless only twenty-four hours ago. Plus on that visit, do you realise how long that you sat answering questions with your hands tightly clasped one over the other? In fact, not unlike, 'Chestnut' here."

Murray had deliberately used her 'stage' name by way of an introduction and Kirsten Beale's complexion swiftly changed. Not to a gentle understated blush, but to a full-on 'strawberry jam.' Her hands also parted.

"Chestnut!" Lennon exclaimed in surprise. Pushing her chair back from the butter wouldn't melt/girl next door female sat opposite her. She in turn looked across at both Black and Lennon and rose abruptly to her feet.

Charlene though confused, remained seated. She was feeling rather light-headed and at the same time terrified. Even though she knew that she was in no actual physical danger.

The auburn mane on the spectacular looking filly had come undone and was glowing. It obviously had a lot of money regularly spent on it to keep it in such good condition. Normally paid for, no doubt, by the seated woman's late husband. Kirsten's halo was slipping again.

"Well what are the chances of that?" Janice Brooks questioned aloud from behind the mirror.

"She obviously knows or at least recognises Charlene Lennon," Barbra Furlong offered up. "Surely the doctor never showed her images of his wife?"

"I wouldn't put anything past him," Brooks said.

"Though more likely she's been in her house and spotted her in one of the family photographs there."

"Are you thinking on the night of the murder, Janice?"

"Well that would certainly explain how numerous people gained entry without forcing any locks or causing any damage," Afro added.

The females watched proceedings unfold with intrigue. Janice nodded in agreement and went on to say...

"At some point in the evening during a break in riding lessons, the beautiful 'Chestnut' could easily have galloped to the front door and left it off the latch for all the others to trot inside when they arrived."

Furlong raised her eyebrows. "Now there's a thought," she whispered quietly under her breath.

Like the start of a poor joke - there was a chief inspector, a criminal psychologist and humble DC all stuck in a tiny room. It was from there that they would continue to watch as the gloves literally came off.

"So Mrs Lennon from hands clasped, winter gloves earlier, Marigolds at home and now a fine leather pair on this return visit. Please remove them."

Charlene Lennon/Charlie Murphy hadn't even heard a word the inspector had said. She was still seemingly in shock. So this was 'Chestnut!'

Had she been younger than Charlene imagined, Brooks wondered. And how had that card gotten into Lennon's shirt? Now Janice's own thoughts went into overdrive. All three on the opposite side of the glass now thought she'd been in the house the day the doctor died?

It was Ian Black that duly reached across and said...

"Excuse me, Ma'am." As he gently tugged at each of her fingertips. There was no resistance on her part.

In fairness, she was still mulling over the night of her husband's death, realising that this was the elusive 'Chestnut,' and that she had once been this very person.

Suddenly both her hands were free from leather and there it was, prominent for all to witness - the bucking bronco, the fun-loving filly or in Charlie Murphy's case, the secret stallion. Whatever she called it, she had the ink. In her case it was from back in the day when 'Bunny' Reid was only the lieutenant to Kenny Dixon. But there it was, she had been branded nonetheless.

"Mrs Lennon," Murray raised his voice sharply to bring her back to the here and now. "Why didn't you tell us? This could have made a big difference to our enquiries."

His tone was sympathetic and understanding, but definitely tinged with disappointment and frustration.

The woman could only stare blankly at the back of her bare hands and there it lay nestled between her right thumb and index finger. She had obviously tried to cover the small, tacky reminder of her past with makeup, but with little success as her tight fitting leather gloves had made short work of rubbing it mostly away.

Steven Murray remained curious as to why she still had it. Why hadn't she had laser treatment or some other form of tattoo removal? They weren't exactly short of money. Though he remembered Janice had mentioned that Ian Lennon never gave her any excess with regards to her household budget, etc. So maybe that was…

"It was his way of keeping me in my place," she said harshly. There was real venom and resentment in her voice now. "It was to remind me of where I'd came from," he would constantly tell me. "Years ago, I told the kids that I got it done on a drunken holiday."

The three others were silent. Beale shook her head and as both women carefully weighed each other up, Kirsten slowly proffered her hand across the desk. Charlene poignantly remembered her time as Charlie.

She knew what that swine of a husband had no doubt put this young girl through, both physically and mentally. They interlocked fingers and stayed quiet.

"I really do wish you had told us about this sooner."

The man then leaned over and whispered quietly into her ear. Although unheard by the others, the DI's tone was understanding and surprisingly sympathetic.

On the opposite side of the mirror, the trio all smiled at being privy to witnessing such a sight.

"We are a million miles away from linking any of this to 'Bunny' Reid, sir." Black inadvertently mentioned loudly in the presence of Beale and Lennon.

"Yes. Quite," Murray said, seemingly upset with him. "Please escort both our guests out into the waiting area at the front desk, Sergeant Black. And try to do so without offering up any more thoughts or opinions. Thank you ladies, you are free to go and discuss the doctor at your leisure now. Should you wish to do so."

Chairs scraped the floor. Shoes shuffled and jackets and gloves were put back on. Three bodies removed themselves from the room, whilst the ringmaster popped next door.

"You knew she had that specific tattoo, didn't you, sir?" Janice asked.

"I was pretty confident," he nodded. "I've seen many of them pop up in the most unexpected places over the years. You'd be amazed Constable Brooks just how many graduates and professionals have the 'bucking bronco' inked below or beside their thumbs. The most surprising one I ever saw was just last year when I interviewed Bernie. It was when that dead body was discovered outside of St. Cuthbert's church.

"Bernie who?" MacDonald innocently enquired. "And what made it unusual for her to carry the brand?"

Barbra Furlong knew the answer. She had spearheaded the team on the case. She smiled and nodded gently...

"Best to tell them her title these days, Steven."

Brooks wasn't around back then. So even she was shocked to hear the inspector reverently state…

"Ah, yes, quite. Sister Bernadette to be precise!" Murray added. Before irreverently crossing himself.

"And that's a true story," DCI Furlong confirmed.

"Anyway we digress," Steven Murray said. "Do you think that went okay?"

"You were certainly firm enough, Inspector" was Afro MacDonald's endorsement.

"And you think one of them will tip off, Reid?" Was Janice's contribution.

"Oh I do. I do indeed," said the wise old DI.

Meanwhile, Ian Black had taken both women back to the waiting area at the front desk. There Kirsten Beale perched herself down beside Eric Lennon, unwittingly separating him from his mother. The Sergeant asked them to wait patiently while he arranged transport home for each of them. They all nodded and watched as the officer immediately walked off again.

Mobiles were instantly brought out. All three had one.

However, it wasn't 'Bunny' Reid that got the tip-off.

It was Rab Nielsen's phone that rang.

Twenty Two

"Good as gold but stupid as mud, he'll carry on regardless. They'll bleed his heart 'til there's no more blood, but carry on regardless. Carry on with laugh. Carry on with cry. Carry on with brown under moonlit sky."

- The Beautiful South

Having watched from behind the mirror, DCI Furlong went straight back to her office and wasted no time in contacting Edinburgh's number one gangster. He had, after all, initially sought their assistance in finding his girls or at least who was responsible for taking them. Even although he'd already decided upon the guilty parties - hence the dead bodies in Dundee. Murders that so far, unsurprisingly, remained unsolved. However based on the information that Robert Nielsen had recently passed on to him, they were also killings that would ultimately be deemed unnecessary.

Reid's voice was its normal rough, harsh self…

"Many of my girls have remained, because they know how well I look after them detective chief inspector."

Furlong said nothing. The irony is that Andrew Scott's girls he'd taken over throughout Perthshire and Fife, genuinely did stay in top quality apartments and were treated brilliantly. Scott was a clever thinker, as well as a crook. A true businessman. He knew that it would allow them to charge a premium rate and would bring in a better class of clientele. Plus it presented the crime lord with a host of new business opportunities. Because a wealthier, more professional client base would give his organisation much better bargaining power whilst in the midst of discussions over blackmailing rates!

Unbeknown to many outsiders, Bunny's list of established direct debit payees now included married police officers, significant business leaders and highly paid celebrities. Annually his 'friendly extortion' equated to a nice little earner. The beauty for Andrew Scott and now his successor Reid, is that these individuals don't require to pay in cash. Council leaders, chairmen of committees and the like, including corporate directors and senior politicians were always handy to have on speed dial and in a position to do you a favour. Certainly better positioned than the uncompromising one that they'd obviously been caught up in initially.

"I need you to check out a couple of people for me, 'Bunny.' Firstly a Kevin Smith - is he involved in anything dodgy? Do any of your girls know his name? I'd send you a picture, but it was ruined in the wash," she said. Regretting the remark as soon as it left her lips.

Reid's response was that of a wise, old sinister sage…

"I was about to say that if he's responsible for my missing girls then I'll handle it from here, Chief Inspector. But from what you just said, it sounds more like he's the dead man in the dryer and that you want me to do your dirty laundry for you. Would I be right?"

The drug-dealing doyen was spot on. The circus act doing somersaults in the launderette had been identified as one Kevin Smith, but the police had absolutely nothing on him. By all accounts he was a model citizen.

"He's a welder to trade, 'Bunny.' He's been employed as such ever since his apprenticeship over forty years ago. He's not married and has no long term partner or children that we're aware of. So I'm intrigued to know if he raises any red flags with any of your working girls? Escorts!" She quickly corrected herself. "He appears to have had no enemies. His work colleagues and friends all speak highly of him. I think knowing more about this man is central to us finding your missing girls."

"Really? And I think you're playing me for a mug, Detective Chief Inspector Furlong. Because I now have it on good authority who is fully and foolishly responsible for my missing girls."

Barbra was flummoxed at that last comment and momentarily the line went silent. However, DCI Furlong was far from finished…

"I most certainly would never take you for a mug, Mr Reid. But I did say a couple of people. Remember?"

"Oh aye, I'm waiting," came the gravel etched chant.

"This one's easier. I was given this on good authority also. Indeed, I believe she was a star pupil and that you taught her personally."

The detective literally felt 'Bunny' Reid sit up, tense and square himself in preparation at the other end of the phone line. He'd be questioning in his mind, what exactly did the police know? And why were they asking me about a specific girl?

"Her name's Chestnut," Furlong said, "And she has…"

"A small horse tattoo on the back of her hand," Reid answered confidently in the form of a Gregorian monk. "Many of my girls have them, Barbra. Can I call you…"

"So it's like a brand?" Furlong snapped. Raising her voice disapprovingly. "It's your proof of ownership?" She suggested in a rather disgusted tone.

"It's been ongoing since Kenny Dixon's days. I like to think of it as a proud reminder of the elite group, the special select tribe that they each belong to."

Furlong made a garbled confused sound of disdain.

"But you know what? I'm feeling generous and in the spirit of better police relations, I will confirm for you that yes, 'Chestnut' is one of the best in my stable."

"Thank you, Mr Reid, but I wasn't going to ask you about her. For I already know that you broke her in," Furlong said abruptly. "I'm just surprised that she's not called you already."

"Oh, touché, Barbra. Nice going continuing the equestrian theme," 'Bunny' rasped. "But I'd figured as much. So not only have I to check out some weird welder called Smith. But you want me to confirm that my beautiful highly priced filly, 'Chestnut,' was being ridden by another jockey? One that had paid a yearly retainer for her services, and in advance may I add?"

Furlong swallowed hard. Don't let anyone ever tell you that this man was a fool. He may not be tech savvy like Andrew Scott, but he more than made up for that weakness, by being extra street smart and so often well ahead of the game.

"I wouldn't have worded it quite so crudely, but I guess you got the gist of it. And the fact that you said HAD, has already confirmed things. Thanks."

"Well I'll not be receiving anymore bonus payments from him, DCI Furlong. So sure, 'Chestnut' was one of Ian Lennon's regular mounts."

That was more than Barbra had been expecting and possibly easier than anticipated. What was he up to?

"So with that offered up and me getting the man Smith checked out for you also…"

Ah, here it was. The back scratching part that Furlong was waiting patiently for.

"In return…" the man began, before pausing.

"I'm listening, 'Bunny.' And in return…"

"And in return I need you to check out someone trading under the name of The Duchess."

"The Duchess?" Furlong repeated. "Like - of Cornwall?" She asked.

"Aye, very funny," Reid replied. "But yes. Correct. Because that is who I've been told is taking an overly keen interest in my girls and costing me a small fortune."

Barbra didn't like the sound of that at all.

"Okay, I'll see what I can turn up," she offered halfheartedly and then hung up. She was still busy mulling over and thinking about a certain Mister Smith.

With all of those particularly positive character traits under his belt the man was a definite outlier. Yet, he'd obviously been targeted for a reason. So what was the catch? In essence - He should be a baddie. Yet here he was as good as gold. The chief inspector was having none of it. Her mobile was brought out in a flash, swiftly scrolled through and a familiar number rang. After only two rings it was answered.

"Simon? It's Barbra Furlong here. I wander if you can help me with something?"

The DCI talked to Simon Gore about Police Scotland's lack of resources. She explained how Lizzie was already stretched checking the background and history of several other dead men, and that didn't include her occasional forays digging deeper into the noxious, nasty private life of the unmentionable Robert Nielsen.

Gore was well aware of the extra work that Lizzie was doing. Barbra also confirmed to him that Drew was being paid by Police Scotland as an outside consultant, double checking all that they had on DI Nielsen, and ensuring that it would stand up in court after his arrest. Again, Simon was up to speed with all of that.

"Both 'Sherlock' and Allan Boyd were also busy trying to discover who the victim from the BMW was. I could really do with your help, Simon. I'd like you to take *'the Daz challenge,'* and find out all you can about our super clean Kevin Smith. He of the **Pound of Fresh** laundromat."

Gore was more than happy to help. She'd known that he would be. Herself and Steven Murray after all, had supported the man on so many fronts in recent months. Currently he was well positioned to help repay the faith that they'd shown in him and in his business.

Blood'n Gore was once again thriving. Murray and Co. had unofficially promoted the agency to many of the legal firms in town and ensured ongoing work from Police Scotland. Minutes later, Simon was in possession of all the pictures and info he needed to get started.

With their discussion ended and Furlong taking a ten minute time-out. It only now fully sank in with her that they actually had a very strong crossover link between the 'Bunny' Reid stable of fillies and some of society's less salubrious stallions. Why and what relevance did it play? Who stood to benefit? And what about the branding? Surely that would be a major help? Or would it? And how come the Reidmeister was so keen to help out anyway? What was he really covering up?

Meanwhile down in 'The Vault,' Murray was catching up with Lizzie regarding some of the discreet work that she'd been carrying out for him. Unsurprisingly, she wasn't the only one operating covertly for DI Murray. The inspector's phone rang and it was his colleague, George Smith with some breaking news.

"Sir, I've got that footage from the waiting area that you requested," the desk sergeant told him. "It's as you suspected. Although I think you might have gotten an extra unexpected bonus into the bargain. You're some man when you follow those darn strong hunches of yours, Steven. Well done."

"Brilliant, George. And a surprise bonus, I shall look forward to spotting that. Can you please send it direct to my phone. Then call the DCI and tell her I'll be joining her shortly. Thanks. I'll get hold of Black, Brooks and MacDonald - that well known group of solicitors and notaries that we have stationed here," he laughed aloud. Both men hung up and Murray bade farewell to Lizzie, before leaping upstairs to round up 'the three musketeers.' By the time they all entered DCI Furlong's office, Barbra was already prepared for them.

"Remember it's a world premiere," Murray told them. "I've not seen any of this. It was sent direct to me by George Smith. So if you have any problem with the production quality, you know where to go and com…"

"Oh please shut up, Inspector. Just play the footage," his DCI encouraged. "Its been **a cherry-picking, barn buster of a day**," Barbra yelled in a fake Texas accent for no reason whatsoever, except that she could.

Murray placed his mobile on the desk and they all huddled tightly around it. They watched the scenes slowly unfold before them. First Ian Black turned his back on Beale and Lennon as they went to sit down. Surprisingly the auburn haired beauty sat next to Erik, separating him from his mother's side. In fairness, Charlene never rushed to be by her son's side. Which surprised all three of the females that watched the proceedings. It didn't surprise DI Murray however, and Ian Black was nonplussed. This was where a new story was about to begin and a fresh 'modern family' chapter added to the narrative. George Smith had briefly edited the clip before he'd sent it to the inspector. Or at the very least, he'd known how to work the zoom button to great effect. The hunch that Murray had was just about to play out and his colleague had captured it perfectly.

Within seconds of sitting alongside Eric Lennon, the boy's fingertips could not resist running up and down her jean covered thighs. This may have been hidden from his mother's view, but it was spotted brilliantly on the internal CCTV. Four out of the five viewers had been taken by surprise by the teenager's reaction, not Steven Murray. And just as they were expecting Kirsten Beale to react negatively and swot his lusty hand away, she made the inspector's day, because instead, her nimble fingers brushed against his and the very next second they intertwined and sat perfectly still in the secret valley between the couple's bodies.

"And you knew?" Janice Brooks pressed her inspector.

"Well I certainly had my suspicions."

Each head in the room nodded acquiescently.

"But how?" Furlong pursued. "What led you there?"

"I'll tell you in a second, Ma'am. But for now let's concentrate, because George told me that there was some unexpected bonus footage that I'd enjoy."

All eyes refocused on the mini screen and the trio sat trying to make out that they were oblivious to all around them. The next audible gasp to be heard seemed to have been synchronised to perfection. The defensive line-up of Furlong, Murray, Black, Brooks and MacDonald all cried 'Offside!' simultaneously. Because NO ONE had been expecting to witness 'Chestnut' and Charlene Lennon grip hands also. Fingers tightly embraced, thumbs rubbed passionately against one another and a knowing nod between the two females had been caught briefly on camera.

"Oh my!" Was all that Ian Black could conjure up.

"Sergeant, you and Constable Brooks get them back into separate interview rooms right away," Furlong ordered. As a soft cough spluttered up from her side...

"I would prefer to let each of them return home, Ma'am. We've nothing to lose. This evidence isn't going anywhere and they've already slipped up here. So maybe another mistake or two is just around the corner?"

"You might even be able to use the fact that Beale is known or familiar with both mother and son to your advantage, Inspector Murray," Afro piped up.

"That never even crossed my mind, Ms MacDonald."

"No, I bet it didn't," Barbra Furlong smirked. Whilst nodding in agreement to his suggestion.

Babbling Brooks thought this the ideal moment to ask Detective Inspector Steven Murray once again...

"And what gave you an inkling regarding Eric and Kirsten Beale in the first instance, sir?"

"I recalled some equestrian paintings, Janice. The ones that he'd shown me whilst we spoke together up in his bedroom when we first visited?"

"And that helped, how?"

"Well, he told me that he'd hoped to study art next year at University. However, he'd also informed me that he'd painted them earlier in the year as part of an exam."

Heads nodded. But they still heard nothing untoward.

"Exactly. That may not seem unusual in itself, but if that was the case, then it would suggest that Eric's affair with the female jockey had been going on for at least six months or so. Because it was 'Chestnut' in the saddle of every portrait that he had painted. Especially in the nude 'Lady Godiva' style caricature."

The others all remained gobsmacked.

"And your thinking currently is?" It was Barbra that spoke. She knew he'd have further thoughts.

"All conjecture and it'll need fine tuning, Ma'am. But I'd be inclined to put money on it being Eric that put Chestnut's card in his father's shirt pocket that day before heading out. An adolescent form of revenge. An - Anything you can do, I can do better scenario!"

"He's only seventeen, Inspector." MacDonald sighed.

"And your point is caller?" He smiled. Somewhat amazed at her innocent naivety.

"I was married with two kids by then," Black told her.

She could only shake her head at that personal information. She had, after all, wanted to get to know all about the rest of the team, Murray figured. Although himself, Furlong and Brooks all knew that comment to be completely false. He was winding the poor woman up. A task that was never to be underestimated in the police force. It reminded everyone to always be on their toes and keep their guard up. On this occasion unfortunately, Aphrodite MacDonald had let her guard slip all the way down to her fallen arches!

Janice however, got it… "He told us that he wasn't with his mother and Emily all night. That he'd gone out to meet some friends, sir."

"That's correct, Janice. I believe he was with 'Chestnut,' and then she had went off to be with his father."

Afro thought she'd heard everything. But even to her, that was perverse.

Black offered a shrug of indifference. He'd genuinely felt over the course of his career that nothing could surprise him anymore. Furlong rubbed at her chin. She liked where this was heading, so she simply asked…

"And?"

Everyone in the room knew who this solitary, single word was directed toward.

"And… It's hypothetical at this stage, Chief Inspector."

"Spit it out man," she promptly hastened Murray.

"At some point before or after sex with the doctor, I believe as has been suggested, that Kirsten, our pretty little 'Chestnut,' let a group of others into the Lennon family home that evening to commit murder. Plus having just witnessed that footage, Ma'am. I believe she done it with the help or certainly the knowledge of Eric, his mother Charlene, or possibly even both."

A further lengthy dialogue testing and analysing that particular theory was discussed and entered into for at least twenty minutes. After which, all the players decided that home should now be on the horizon. They had plenty to think about and ponder overnight. But they definitely felt progress was being made and that they were edging ever closer to the finishing line.

It took some doing, but Barbara Furlong eventually convinced Steven Murray to drive out to Afro MacDonald's place. The inspector had wanted to drive straight home, rest and mull over the events of the day.

Whereas Barbra on the other hand, had encouraged him to be more sociable. Convinced him that he might actually glean something from what Afro could offer to the conversation and her take on the last few hours.

When they arrived at 12a Canal Walk. Both officers gazed up at a rather tired and weary looking home. The old house appeared to rise up from the ground surrounded by a strange mixture of untended wild flowers, shrubbery and shrivelled, forgotten plants.

"It's possibly nicer inside," Furlong offered.

Murray's shrug was unconvincing. "Oh, I was to tell you that when we got outside, we were to turn around."

Furlong's face was far from impressed. When both figures turned around in the dark of night, there it was, complete with glass nameplate above the tiny doorway which had begun to open. The fresh wording boldly stated *Dite's Dingy* and the ageing barge was a confident celebration of colours. It had the kind of red that invited summer blooms and London buses to play in your imagination, and that was coupled with a splendid sash of gold wrapped around the bow. Though the most important selling point for DI Murray was the fact that it seemingly had every intention of obeying Newton's laws. Especially the one about remaining still, unless a force compelled it to move.

The dusky pink baseball boots were the first sign of life onboard. The red eyelets and extra long arctic white laces belonged to a member of the Converse family. MacDonald's casual dress was certainly a lot trendier and modern than either Furlong or the inspector had been expecting. Her fashionably long T-shirt had no sleeves. On its front it promoted a rather menacing leopard prowling intensely through a hostile jungle.

"So glad you could both make it," she enthused. "But it's freezing out here," she exclaimed. "Quick, come inside and join me for a refreshment."

Furlong's eyes lit up instantly, like a pair of rotating spotlights. Murray was uncertain if it had been the offer of a drink or the decor of the barge down below that made her eyes sparkle with delight. His canny instinct told him that the most likely cause was the latter. The DI could see that Barbra was mightily impressed.

The clever use of mirrors and cultural artefacts had made the boat look twice as big. Murray had thought on them kindly as *'nik naks.'* When in reality, if he'd known Aphrodite MacDonald longer, familiarity would have allowed him to ask her... 'Why do you have all this tat?'

However, the detective inspector played nice for once.

"It's certainly different from what I expected."

"And what were you expecting, Steve? A traditional three bedroomed semi-detached?"

No one spoke. Murray flinched. She'd called him Steve.

"My ex, Ronnie got the house." Afro informed them. "I was happy to take this. Before, we mainly used it for long weekends and short holiday breaks up north."

Barbra was busily admiring all the 'tat' on the walls and surrounding areas. The criminal psychologist certainly wasn't going for the uncluttered, minimalist look.

"What's up? Why the big cheesy grin, DI Murray?" Afro asked in a friendly affable manner.

Barbra glanced at the man as he raised his hands in an innocent enough gesture. Though the DI was most definitely in a mischievous mood. He was starving and those hunger pangs made the man extra tired and irritable. But his DCI did wonder what exactly had tickled his fancy? Gentle laughter began to filter the airwaves and it became even stronger as Murray tried to explain his dilemma...

"I'm sorry, but I can't quite get over the fact that you were actually married to Ronald MacDonald."

"Oh, that's nothing," Afro exclaimed. "Ronnie was also terrified of my snoring - especially when I drove!"

Even Barbra began to smile gently at that notion.

"But not only did you sleep with a clown," Murray let rip. "You actively encouraged the ultra innocent Ronald to get out and about in the summer nights and go CRUISING... that was very open-minded of you!"

Furlong's smile turned into laughter and even their host saw the funny side to his light-hearted remarks.

"Well you certainly hammered the head on the nail," Afro announced questionably.

Her guests howled even louder at that slip-up.

"How much have you had to drink?" Murray checked.

MacDonald put some music on. She poured out a lovely chilled wine for Furlong and handed it over.

"I've not forgotten you, Inspector," she told the man. She returned to the miniature fridge located directly under the ten foot long window sill. When she closed it and got back to Steven Murray, she was clasping tightly to an equally chilled pint... of semi skimmed milk!

This woman had obviously done her homework.

They moved on to speak about the events of the day and their various impressions and theories. But mainly they drank and turned up the music. They drank more and adjusted the volume, they drank further and the singing started. And when Afro MacDonald sang, her friends Johnny Walker and Jack Daniels ensured that she was in perfect pitch, harmonious to the last note.

They lasted two hours before heading home. Barbra Furlong was slightly merry, whilst the inspector was simply desperate to get to his own private loo and have his udder milked. The biggest reminder of the night however, was the fact that everyone has at least one vice. On her very first day it seemed that Detective Inspector Steven Murray and DCI Barbra Furlong had discovered Afro MacDonald's inherent weakness. One that involved the taste of neat single malt and plenty of it!

Twenty Three

"Daddy, is he a goodie or a baddie? Leave a light outside your door. Once upon a time there were cannibals, now there are no cannibals anymore."

- Mark Knopfler

Next morning, DI Murray was in work by 7.30. He'd travelled in long before Barbra Furlong was even awake. It had been a restless night and he was extra keen to gather his thoughts during the drive, especially as he intended to drag out the whiteboard and picture gallery. He felt it was time for some good old-fashioned visual stimulation and conjecture during the first part of the day. In doing so, he'd hoped to gee up and motivate the team for the busy twenty-four hours that lay ahead.

It was Sandy's funeral tomorrow. Only three days after her unexpected death. The crematorium had a spare slot and it was either accept that particular space or the next available time was over a week away. Her grieving family had requested that it be done as soon as possible. So the earlier time had been agreed by all parties.

The investigation had progressed nicely, but it was turning hectic. Before the others arrived the inspector had written all the runners and riders up on the board.

Where:	Person:	Job:	Rating:
1. Home:	Ian Lennon:	Doctor:	POW
2. Canal:	Kieran Flood:	Delivery Guy	?
3. Bin:	George Matthew:	Teacher:	POW
4. Flat:	Mark Ziola:	Security:	POW
5. BMW:	? ?	?	?
6. Dryer:	Kevin Smith:	Welder:	?

"Nothing is being ruled in or out. So feel free to shout away until your heart's content," DI Murray encouraged bang on 8.30am. "Be it gossip or wild hunches. Hell, even suspicions, speculation and guesswork are all invited to the party. Plus the odd conspiracy theory or gut feeling will be made most welcome too. Oh and by the way... P.O.W stands for a nasty - Piece of Work."

The gathered crowd of DCI Furlong, Murray, Black, Harris, Brooks, Lizzie and one Aphrodite MacDonald, all listened avidly as Joe Hanlon and DC Boyd got the ball rolling when 'Sherlock' happily announced...

"We've had confirmation that the man surplus to requirements in the BMW was named Charles Reid, sir. And the image on the hand seen closing the door after he was pushed out was confirmed as that of a horse."

"Yet another of Reid's runaways?" Brooks questioned.

"Well at least one of the entourage it would seem," Joe nodded in agreement.

"He was an ex-council official of some sort," Boyd added. "He'd taken an early retirement package two or three years ago."

"Which one is it?" The inspector asked sternly. "It may well be highly relevant, Allan. Remember, we're putting everything into the mix. Nothing is to be excluded, so relevancy will be important."

The ex-military man was already busy scrolling through his assorted notes on his phone...

"It was July, two and a half years ago to be fully accurate, sir."

Murray said nothing. But he immediately added the man's name to the board with the slightest of smirks.

5. BMW.   Charlie Reid.   Council Worker.   ?

"So you reckon he's a Proclaimer, sir?" Joe exclaimed.

"We can't rule anything out just yet, DS Hanlon," Murray smiled. Though the inspector had omitted to write 'pop singer' as his occupation on the whiteboard.

Boyd then stated, "We don't know if he's a goodie or a baddie yet, sir. Though we intend to find out today."

"Thank you," DC Boyd. "I appreciate the update."

"I thought it may be highly relevant," he added. Close to crossing the line with his Glaswegian '*gallusness*.'

As all eyes refocused on the board the troubled voice of their senior officer, Barbra Furlong opined...

"There would appear to be no rhyme nor reason to it all still, Inspector." Her words were accompanied with moistened pursed lips and a baffled head shake.

Amongst the others, Lorna Harris and Janice Brooks appeared to nod in agreement. Whilst Ian Black stood rooted to the spot as if on official police duties. With his feet apart and both hands firmly held behind his back, he did manage to grumpily offer up...

"In his home. Outside on a path. Outside in a bin. Inside on a wall. Inside, then outside a car, and finally inside an old industrial washer!"

With the exception of Janice, most of the others hadn't heard the man speak at length before. Even though he seemed to just state the obvious regarding the location of each of the deaths, for Steven Murray, it was actually quite reassuring. Because Sgt. Black had obviously gotten himself up to speed with the case. On the other hand, the inspector screwed up his face and wondered briefly for a second if the bold sergeant had literally just read everything that had been written up. The DI so hoped that it was the former.

Ian Black had a short military style haircut and both DCI Furlong and DI Murray had worked with the man on and off during the years in different investigations. Neither knew why he'd been shortlisted and put onto the troublemakers and bad boys list and made available for immediate recruitment. Though that may well become common knowledge in the weeks ahead. But for now, all they knew was that he was a good solid cop.

He was without doubt a surly, moaning faced man most of the time, but the team could work with that. It meant you knew what you were getting. No airs nor graces, just a plodder. A man that would try his best. One that would generally offer no more or no less. Don't expect to see him go out on a limb for you, to work on beyond what was required or to go the extra mile without seeking recompense. Though Brooks would probably already argue those particular points.

He was short in stature and exceptionally scrawny. This however gave him a great advantage during stakeouts and when trailing suspects, because he could easily don his cloak of invisibility. No one generally noticed him - he was your regular punter walking the street. An office worker, a road sweeper or a local miscreant seeking his latest fix. He was definitely a man for all seasons.

"Quite," was how Murray responded to Black's earlier observations. "But like I said, let's brainstorm and let's speculate to accumulate," the inspector added.

Silence filled the air for at least ten seconds, then…

"I'll take wild, random and silly to start us off," Murray announced. Like a poor man's auctioneer selling of the cubic zirconia before the diamonds finally appeared.

"Are they all gay conspiracy theorists? Boyd shouted.

Afro MacDonald and Furlong could only shake their heads in disbelief. Whilst Janice Brooks punched the overly cocky Glaswegian on the shoulder. Black had already personally experienced that playful revenge, so realised that was obviously her - 'go to' default setting.

"Or the exact opposite?" Lorna Harris questioned. "Were they all members of 'Gentlemen Only' clubs?"

"Or low handicappers at Bunny's Golf Club, and he'd sought revenge for the numerous 'gubbings' they'd each given him over the years?" Barbra Furlong thought it best that she should join in with the warm-up banter, before things turned serious.

A host of topical theories quickly hit the proverbial fan. They came at DI Murray with such force and frequency that he'd no idea who said what or who, who even was! He grinned and the shouts continued…

"Climate change or Brexit supporters seeking refuge?"

"Pole dancing immigrants identifying as males?" And -

"A group of rebellious freemasons, each desirous to change the colour of their aprons?"

With a slight pause in the far-fetched, preposterous proposals, a female voice looked to instantly restore sanity and bring perspective back to the table…

"I still think they're some sort of vigilante killings," DC Brooks said bluntly and in a downbeat, austere manner.

Silence - as everyone initially looked around the room.

"Yep, me too," 'Sherlock' agreed. "But why and for what purpose, I've no idea. Plus we're all agreed that it's definitely more than one person, right?"

Heads in the room all seemed to nod simultaneously.

"Well, I think that's clear," Murray confirmed. "But is it the same individuals each time? Or do they take turns? And who are THEY? What or who do they represent? And how many are involved?"

"The tattoo would indicate that at least one of Reid's working girls was in the car. Wouldn't it?" Boyd said.

"Where was 'Chestnut' that night," Black routinely addressed his remark to Constable Brooks. He knew that they had asked and noted it down.

"She was seemingly home alone," Janice answered, after a brief recap of her notes.

"Bad guys get their just deserts, good guys win, and everyone gets home in time for Christmas. Perfect!"

Murray took from that, that Afro MacDonald was obviously a movie buff. Otherwise how else could she quote such a famous line from the iconic holiday film, Home Alone?

Janice raised a hand and politely butted in. "I mean Maggie at the launderette was adamant that there were at least four individuals inside, all female, and that didn't include the one that kept her talking at the doorway. Could they also have been the ones inside the car?"

"Now we're talking," Murray agreed.

"Though that group could easily be 'guns for hire.' Tasked with delivering one body out from the car and the other one placed into the machine," Furlong added. "It would be good money for the right kind of person."

"The right kind of person being?" Allan Boyd asked.

"Hookers!" Came the low, unhurried, slightly breathy voice of one, 'tell-it-like-it-is,' Ian Black.

"Interesting terminology, Sergeant."

At the back of the room, perched carefully with her heel against the wall, Afro MacDonald smiled subtly at the inspector's mild rebuke to his latest team member.

"I had also thought along those lines and initially a Reid connection of some sort," Steven Murray rallied. "But with the exception of Lennon using escorts and Ziola looking after them, I can't see how the others fit into that scenario. And what about your man, Joe?"

"Like DC Boyd said earlier, sir, we'll find out all about our 'Charlie boy' later today. Even then that would still give us only half of them with an 'Escort' connection."

"How would 'Bunny' Reid benefit out of any of them dying?" Lorna Harris dared to ask. Keen to feel more a part of things.

"I agree," Furlong said. Offering some much needed female solidarity and beginning a rant. "He's already down thousands of pounds per year with the death of Dr Lennon, plus he called me back last night…"

Heads and several eyes rolled at that surprising piece of info being shared. Even Steven Murray looked heavenward as his romantic partner continued…

"As for Kevin Smith, he told me in no uncertain terms that no one by that name has been involved in anything dodgy or drug related on his patch, and I believe him." She finished off by stating... "So it would appear more than likely that Mr Smith is one of the good guys. Which leaves us with only an employee and a punter - and that's really no link at all."

"Well was his death mistaken identity?" Black asked. "Had they simply gotten the wrong man? Unlikely, I know, and who was it meant to have been? Though who could make any sense of how they were chosen?"

"The other thing with our Mr Reid is..." DCI Furlong concluded. "He's still got his hands full making sure no more of his precious girls disappear and start working in competing districts by all accounts. He's painfully desperate to draw a line under the exodus and if I'm not mistaken, I believe he's already taken such steps."

Barbra couldn't help but smile as she mentioned that fact. Because the very thought of James Baxter Reid suffering, would make those gathered extremely happy.

"Yes, interesting Ma'am," Murray said. As his head gleefully bounced from side to side in uncertainty. "Because, need I remind you that Brooks here, seems to have a view that runs contrary to that train of thought. And I can't say that I'm not inclined to agree with her."

Furlong raised a threaded eyebrow at that remark...

"I've recently heard from a contact in Dundee, that unsurprisingly, they've still gotten no witnesses to the murder of Barry Fitzsimmon, who was recently found in his sprawling Broughty Ferry mansion. However it transpires that several bodyguards had been taken out of commission during that course of events. Now Detective Inspector Murray, am I right in thinking that you're about to confirm for me that you think the Reidmeister actually had nothing to fear from the 'Two Ugly Ducklings' over in Angus?"

"DC Brooks is, Ma'am. Yes." Murray grinned. "Remember it was Reid that planted that seed in our minds. It was his own crazy, idiotic idea. He was adamant that the Dundonians were initially behind it."

Furlong's tongue played thoughtfully with her front teeth for a second or two before beating a retreat.

"We did tell him to leave it with us, while we got to the bottom of things. Yet off he went," Murray vented. "He was oblivious to reality and just wanted as always to steamroll ahead and seek revenge. Though based on Janice's belief, it's 'Bunny' who has either instigated a war or another bitter, far-reaching takeover."

"And the theory is?" Furlong eventually asked.

The group instantly turned toward Constable Brooks. Each one keen to hear her gifted words of wisdom.

"Ma'am, it's a straightforward rational proposal that I'm putting forward. Nothing unique. Nothing mind blowing. Nothing that…"

"Well let's hear it, Constable," the chief inspector urged. Her tone and cadence calm but sceptical.

"I believe the working girls came up with a very level-headed way to break free from the man's clutches and his slave-like hold over them. I don't think for a minute that anyone captured them or took them by force."

There was a small audible gasp from those gathered. A couple of the group even expressed a quiet… "What!"

"My gut says," Brooks continued. "That they wisely and cleverly left all their belongings behind and went somewhere safe to start over. Possibly to do something else entirely or at the very least to work for themselves independently, in better conditions and for higher pay."

"No bodies of the hookers… eh, female escorts that went missing," Black corrected himself. "Have actually turned up. Have they?"

A variety of heads all shook in unity. He was correct.

"But the audio clips we heard?" Furlong questioned.

"I was going to make mention of them later this morning, Ma'am," Joe Hanlon piped up.

"Why, what can you tell us, Sergeant?"

"Well I listened carefully to every minute of those so-called 'torture' recordings once again," 'Sherlock' said.

This time heads nodded in unison. That was a positive.

"Remember, it's not as if they wouldn't have had plenty of professional contacts help them out on that score," Joe reminded everyone. "They'd each have plenty of connections in all fields of technology. But in one specific area, they definitely made an error. A mistake."

Silence. No one dared speak or ask what it may be. Even Steven Murray was happy for 'Sherlock' to remain in the spotlight. Allan Boyd kept his lips sealed, because it appeared from his body language that he'd already been privy to his partner's discovery.

"What we had taken as Gospel was exactly where they went wrong." Joe Hanlon went on to explain. "We had all assumed, as you would, that the various attacks and assaults had taken place at different times, in various locations and on numerous girls."

Now, even Afro MacDonald had emerged from the back wall and moved closer. Sergeant Hanlon was reeling them all in slowly, one by one. His low, quiet voice, the whispering trick that he'd watched Murray use on a multitude of occasions, was working a treat.

"Through some basic software on my own computer, I discovered that the various assaults had in fact all been recorded within the same fifteen minute window."

"Surely you can't possibly tell when things are recorded exactly though?" Murray questioned with uncertainty.

"Not normally without the ultra-expensive gadgetry that our very own Vault Master has at her disposal, sir." 'Sherlock' told him.

Lizzie nodded in agreement and smiled. She was quite taken with her new nom de plume… The Vault Master!

Twenty Four

"All I want is 20-20 vision. A total portrait with no omissions. All I want is a vision of you. If you can picture this - a day in December. Picture this - freezing cold weather."

- Blondie

In recent pillow talk amongst 'Bunny' Reid's escorts, it was being reported that Robert Nielsen was the mastermind behind a child sex-ring. The rumours had gotten stronger in recent days as the Romanian gangs had become incensed at the disappearance of many of the Reidmeister's regular earners, for they too would be entitled to a healthy slice of the profits. Although, business continued to be brisk, with many newly trafficked females required to start work immediately. Be mindful that at his Portobello offices, 'Bunny' Reid continued to proudly display his 'Investor in People' certificate. Exactly like Kenny Dixon did before him.

Was Nielsen's luck finally running out? He'd already been fortunate a couple of years back, on the day that a city centre casino got raided by Steven Murray and a team of officers. Deaths had occurred during that raid as desperate individuals tried to flee the scene and evade capture. Top officers, lawyers and key members of the Scottish legal system lost their careers, and some their lives that evening. Others like DI Nielsen managed to slip through the net unscathed. That night the stakes were high, the buy-in expensive and the winning player was to receive a real-life, scantily clad young woman. It was played on a huge roulette table, specially marked out on the floor. While an oversized roulette wheel appeared from below the ground as if by magic.

In the weeks running up to the exclusive, *'invite only,'* event, numerous girls had also gone missing. One of the croupiers was called Jayne Golden. She had been one of Inspector Murray's love interests back then. Interestingly, she mysteriously disappeared immediately after the raid. However, months later she re-surfaced to help out once again. Only this time, only days after her return, she was stabbed to death in Maurice Hynd's cafe. The popular coffee shop is located only a few hundred yards from Queen Charlotte Street station. The very same station in which, Sergeant Joseph Hanlon was about to share some very interesting and enlightening news with the others...

"However," Joe said. "If the recording has merely been paused and not fully stopped - You can tell."

Once again, Lizzie nodded. That was encouraging.

"And those specific recordings hadn't been stopped, Joe?" It was Furlong that asked. "Only paused?"

"Spot on, Ma'am. It was a very avoidable blunder."

"In reality, Sergeant," Barbra persisted. "What you're telling us is that it was all recorded and acted out like a radio play. It was no more than a very well made theatrical audio book?" With a heightened sense of relief his DCI then appeared to sing her very next line... "So in fact, no one had been tortured, beaten, maimed, raped or killed?"

"Absolutely correct, Ma'am. I'm one hundred percent certain that it was all staged. It was a complete hoax."

"Thinking about it like that," Lorna Harris added. "The fact that none of the women Reid reported as missing or being taken have turned up, should convince us even more of that possibility."

With that confirmation from 'Sherlock,' Steven Murray looked across at Detective Constable Brooks and raised his arms and in an animated fashion he began...

"Based on that and what you said earlier, Janice. It would appear clear that a number of Reid's girls were desperately and definitely looking for a way out and that we have a whole investigation that we can disregard and kick into touch."

Once again numerous heads nodded in agreement.

"However," Furlong added with a slight note of caution. "They wanted an escape that didn't involve them getting beaten to a pulp or severely disfigured if they tried to walk away or even mentioned the possibility of it. So when Reid discovers this, as he most certainly will. We'll need to be on our guard, because he'll make a further point of kicking even more people into touch. Just ask our colleagues in Dundee!"

Having heard those remarks, Steven Murray nodded thoughtfully and concluded…

"If someone was really trying to make 'Bunny' pay, they'd kill the girls. Not hide them and play host to them. Competing thugs don't do hospitality. They have a *'let's put them to work immediately,'* mentality."

Janice Brooks eventually finished her theory, stating…

"Whoever's behind it, they're keen for this to impact on Reid financially. I believe that's what their real motive is. It's personal. And by the way, Ian here has information regarding that horse tattoo on the hand of the individual inside the BMW. Isn't that right, Sarge?"

The man was taken aback by his young colleague's willingness to pass the baton on to him, but he gladly took on board her invitation.

"Yes, quite. Some of you still might not be aware that 'Chestnut,' Dr Lennon's friendly filly and his wife, Charlene, both sport similar tattoos at the exact same position on the back of their hands."

"So it would be good to identify if our BMW is a different horse," Brooks added. "Though it does at least confirm another Reidmeister connection," she smiled.

"We've digressed," Furlong acknowledged. "None of this currently has anything to do with our dead bodies on the board, has it?" Barbra sought clarification.

This time all the heads seemed to shake.

"Yes, it would appear that litter strewn canals, silver BMW's and dimly lit launderettes don't correlate in any way shape or form with doctors, teachers or late night part-time delivery drivers!" Allan Boyd voiced. Exhausted at the thought of trying to figure it all out.

"I'll speak again with our feisty, Maggie," 'Sherlock' confirmed. "She may have spotted if any of the other women that entered the launderette that night, also had a similar tattoo. Because that being the case, we'd have yet another 'Bunny' Reid link to the actual killings.

"So would that be a number of random murders just to cover up one specific target? And which one?" DC Harris threw in. "Like we said previously, that just doesn't seem to add up."

The rookie female detective was beginning to enjoy being part of the squad. Though everyone's game was less than perfect right now. Each individual in their own way struggling to understand and come to terms with DI Kerr's untimely death.

"We've certainly experienced that theory in recent times," Murray advised her. "But worth keeping it in mind everyone. Thanks for that, Lorna."

Then as the inspector was deliberating with the others, his phone sounded. He read the screen for caller ID and an obvious excitement suddenly came over him.

"It's important," he said, raising his voice. "Hopefully this will be beneficial for us all."

Furlong offered a quizzical look. The others paused. Who else had recently become part of their task force?

"Morning Simon," DI Murray began. "I've got you on speaker. We're all listening. What have you got for us?"

Ah, Simon Gore. I hope he has news on Kevin Smith was the first thing that came into Furlong's mind.

"Well I can definitely confirm that there are no official CCTV cameras in or around those streets, Inspector."

"Okaaaay," Murray sighed in a lengthy deflated tone.

"I would guess that's a deliberate act," the man proffered in a professional professorial manner.

"Go on." The inspector urged. Captivated by Gore's eloquent, yet somewhat baffling delivery.

"Well I got some really interesting footage from a few private webcams attached to resident's doors," he said.

"Was that legally obtained?" Furlong blurted out.

'Radical' Lizzie looked to the floor and DI Murray skyward, whilst Afro MacDonald scoured the room and watched - as all of those gathered remained silent.

With no immediate reply from Blood'n Gore's head honcho. That told Barbra all that she needed to know.

"We'll deal with that later," she said, through gritted teeth. "But for now, how does this help us, Simon?"

A massive collective sigh of relief from the others nearly took the room door off its hinges. Heads, legs and shoulders all moved freely once again and relaxed.

"I've uncovered three key things that I think could be very relevant to your enquiries, chief inspector."

"And they are?" Steven Murray interrupted impatiently.

"The first one is a photo taken directly from across the street at the launderette. It shows quite clearly the bold Mrs Morrison receiving numerous bundles of cash."

"What!" Exclaimed Joe Hanlon. "Surely not?"

"And she did such a grand job with the Pantomime Dame routine," Brooks added. Feeling sucker-punched.

Murray's reply was certainly less surprised. It was more measured and thought through, and it later included a sneaky little question for their guest on the telephone...

"She never once removed her hands from the front pocket of her apron. Not even to shake hands."

"And now you know why," Furlong added.

"No, I'm not convinced," Murray replied. "But yes, I do think that she has more to offer. Simon can you tell from that photo if our friendly Mrs Morrison has any distinguishing marks on her hands at all?"

"Give me a second," the man answered.

The others hadn't even shaken their heads, when Simon Gore responded in the affirmative…

"She certainly does, Steven. She has what looks like a tattoo, Inspector. It appears to be of a small horse."

Yet another round of quick gasps, heavy expletives and confused countenances circulated the room. Lorna Harris jokingly thrust her hands into the air for the others to confirm that she was tattoo free. This had turned into the mother of all brainstorming sessions.

"Well if that's whetted your appetite folks. I have two more pieces of information fresh off the press for you all to feast upon over breakfast."

Before Murray or any of the others could shout out: 'Scrambled eggs,' the man's enthusiastic nature took over and he was once again off and running…

"Another shot fascinated me greatly. It was a video image captured just before the female group turned up at the launderette. It was taken from a flat, one storey up. They obviously have a motion sensor device that starts recording when something crosses its path."

Everyone in the room was still getting their heads around the herd of untamed, wild horses that were currently roaming free within Edinburgh city centre.

"When the light went on I couldn't make anything out. There wasn't anyone outside the door or any figures lurking nearby. I watched it several times. Something was obviously setting off the sensor. But what?"

This time it was an experienced private detective doing a great job at captivating his audience and slowly reeling each of them in, one by one.

"On the fourth play I eventually spotted the culprit."

"Was it a bird?" Harris yelled. "My friend has the same problem in her tenement flat," she cried out.

Gore heard her sudden interruption and responded…

"Whoever that was? You were close. It was a similar sized item, but not a live animal," he declared. You could hear the smirk in his voice. His tone was half-daring and half-expecting someone else to interrupt and predict what it was. He wasn't to be disappointed.

"I bet is was a modern UAV," Boyd reluctantly volunteered. "A drone? An unmanned aerial vehicle?" He'd been used to them during his hectic and often traumatic time in the military. They were bigger and more basic back then, but still extremely effective in carrying out their ruthless tasks, he reminded himself.

"Drugs," Furlong reacted with frustration. "Of course. We should have known. We'd just missed some local deliveries taking place. That being the case, there's no way Reid would assign the dropping off of Kevin Smith's washing with his regular cash flow."

"We have pretty good surveillance equipment," Gore reminded her. From what I've witnessed previously, it's the same brand of drone that Andrew Scott used."

"That 'Bunny' Reid has now taken control of," Murray nodded. "Like you said, Ma'am, drugs were being dropped off. His drugs. His dealers. His users. His profits. There were important deliveries being made at the time. Definitely before and or shortly after. You need to speak to your family-friendly Reidmeister once again, Barbra, and quickly."

The others were surprised that the inspector used Furlong's forename. They normally were extremely professional in and around the workplace, but on this occasion there was definite alarm in Murray's voice. An uneasiness and fear even. He continued to address the detective chief inspector…

"Maybe if you're in time, you can swop theories with your buddy and we might avoid further bloodshed."

"You are speaking in riddles, Inspector Murray." Furlong opted for professional rather than personal. "Speak plainly, man. Spit it out."

But it was Joseph Hanlon that chose to interrupt on this occasion…

"I think what the inspector is trying to say, Ma'am, is that if 'Bunny' Reid already has his own drone footage, then he'll want to find out fully for himself what took place between Morrison and those women. And if he hadn't supplied the cash, then by whom and for what exactly had Maggie been paid a substantial sum for?"

"Excuse me folks, but I'm still here you know," Simon Gore reminded them. "And I think you'll find that I've left the best 'til last. I believe DCI Furlong, this one is especially for you. It's all about Kevin Smith."

Barbra smiled confidently. The team didn't need to know that she'd asked for Gore's help independently, especially as it was off the books.

"Good news I hope, Simon?"

"It may not impress you much to begin with chief inspector. However, the ending I suspect will delight even the most ardent pessimist amongst you."

You could hear the quiet, child-like satisfaction in the diligent detective's businesslike delivery.

"We need to get out and about and start chasing up some up these leads," Murray encouraged the man. "So what have you uncovered about Kevin? And tell us firstly is Mr Smith a goodie or a baddie?"

Allan Boyd, still in mischievous mode offered…

"Given the horrendous 'cycle' that the man went through, I'm going to make a 'bold,' 'two-in-one' prediction that Kevin Smith is a super clean goodie!"

Janice Brooks grinned. Murray shook his head to discourage her from - but it was too late…

"I saw what you did there. *Daz* very funny. You must *'Surf'* the net a lot to find all those *'non-bio'* witticisms."

Boyd wasn't at all sure if she was joining with him in the banter or pulling him down a peg or two. He assumed the latter, so decided wisely to remain silent.

"I found out quite a bit about Kevin Smith and yes, he was a genuine goodie." Simon Gore's voice was calm, unhurried and authentic, as he began to offer up a brief résumé of the man's dramatically shortened life…

"Brought up in a Church of Scotland family, he was a prize-winning boy scout with two older sisters. On leaving school, where he'd been a model pupil. He trained to become welder. That was to be his trade right up until his death a few days ago. No police cautions. No newspaper scandals. No wife. No children and no longer sadly with us. Oh and no links to Mr Reid either, or to any local dating sites or escorts for that matter."

The room remained silent, including the playful Boyd. Janice's curt interaction with him had obviously worked wonders. But if a sweepstake were to be run, who would you put your hard earned cash on? Who would break and speak up first? Place your bets!

Good habits from childhood are worth so much in adulthood. To those that lack them they are a wondrous thing, almost magical. They can be learned through small changes done incrementally and are worth keeping once mastered. They are more akin to climbing stairs than being teleported to the peak of a mountain. It's hard work. It's challenging. It takes ongoing perseverance. But eventually you get to pass on those positive habits by being a good role model. People learn more easily by such observation. Then you teleport them to your mountain top and watch them climb even higher. That's the way it is. That's what people do for their children and that's exactly what Mr and Mrs Smith senior, obviously did for their beloved son, Kevin.

It was MacDonald that spoke up. No winners - Not one person had chosen her in the sweepstake.

"When you leave a sentence hanging with the quote - 'For that matter.' What that says is, if you change the terminology, you'll usually find an actual link."

Furlong and the others stared at her in bewilderment. The telephone line had also suddenly went quiet.

"We haven't actually met, Mr Gore, but my name is…"

"Aphrodite MacDonald," Simon answered. His words bellowing out knowingly from the speaker system. "Yes I've heard a lot about you, Ms MacDonald. Would you care to hazard a guess?"

"Oh well, I'm afraid I couldn't even disguise it as a guess, Mr Gore. Because my choice would much more likely be a highly educated thought or deduction."

What is she going on about the others questioned. Whereas, Inspector Murray having travelled with her and seen her operate up close and personal was waiting patiently on her working her magic. He knew already that she would prove to be an invaluable member of the team. He just wasn't too keen on openly repeating that fact! Wait for it though, he thought.

"So for that matter - no dating sites or escorts would make me deduce that he definitely had interaction with a prostitute of sorts then. Someone that can be directly linked up to our current investigation. How did I do?"

Another stunned silence. But Steven Murray knew that she'd most likely nailed it. Which left Barbra Furlong having to check for sure…

"Simon, has that theory any merit to it whatsoever?"

"Several years ago," Gore began in amazement. "Kevin Smith hit a Maxine Binnie with his car. Maxine was a working girl and killed instantly, after being repeatedly beaten by a punter and left for dead on the bend of a busy road. The poor man stood no chance of avoiding her. He was completely innocent and never charged.

In the confines of the room, a knowing glance passed between Steven Murray and the newly added criminal psychologist. The others would've been oblivious, but both the DCI and Brooks saw the snatched exchange and before either could question it...

"Binnie would be her married name," Afro proffered.

"And her maiden name, Inspector?" Furlong enquired.

The tall, expressive figure of Steven Murray could currently be described as pondering. To ponder, one must let the facts roll around the rim of the mind's roulette wheel before coming to settle in whichever slot they feel drawn to. This morning, Murray's creative definition captured that moment perfectly as the truth struck home and eventually, slowly, fell into place.

"She would have been Maxine Richardson," the man slowly whispered. As he sat back on a nearby desk, his head slumped into his hands. How had he missed it?

Puzzled looks were raised by most of the others.

"The younger of the two sisters that had been abused by George Matthew, two decades ago," MacDonald confirmed. "Our Bilton Lane, blue bin man."

"Do we think it symbolic then that Kevin Smith was similarly dismembered?" Lorna Harris questioned.

"I very much doubt it's coincidental," Murray replied. Adding, "He'd been found 'guilty' and held to account for an unfortunate accident all those years ago."

"And his killer, plus others, also held court and passed judgement for a second time on George Matthew, as well as Mark Ziola," Hanlon opined. "Deciding that they'd both also abused individuals under their care."

"And the very same could be said for Doctor Ian Lennon. For he undoubtedly abused those in his care," Brooks remonstrated. "Namely his supposed loved ones. His long-suffering wife and family."

"That would now account for four out of the six," Ian Black said bluntly, though with a renewed enthusiasm.

Barbra Furlong seemed to gain some much needed zest and vigour from that remark. Black was right. Two-thirds of their puzzle immediately fell into place.

"Sgt Hanlon, you and Boyd get out there and find out who or what our 'Proclaimer,' Charlie Reid looked after or cared for in his time working for the council. And I don't want to hear back from you until you do."

At that point, several assignments were given out for the day by both DCI Furlong and her DI. One of which was an interesting task assigned by Steven Murray to his 'radical' friend. She who had remained relatively anonymous during the brief meeting.

"Lizzie can you please check and double check the CCTV footage leading to Bilton Lane the evening before our corpse in the bin was found. Try just before midnight or a few minutes after. Thanks. It's just a hunch I have," the inspector added.

No matter how they tried to avoid it, Reid and the deaths were all inexplicably linked. Care, lack of care, escorting and vulnerability were all in the mix. It still remained a puzzle. A conundrum of the highest order.

"Constable Brooks you stay with Sgt Black for today also," Furlong instructed. "We need to uncover what a humble takeaway delivery guy has to do with all this."

Finally, the DCI rallied her troops by announcing…

"One last thing before you go. We've taken a lot on board during the previous thirty minutes or so, but I need you all to keep your eyes and ears peeled for any interaction or news you may come across with regards to someone going by the name of… The Duchess."

Heads nodded and shook. Shoulders shrugged in the affirmative. But the name never leapt out at anyone. At least no one in the room that was. However, a faint whisper from a forgotten Simon Gore offered up…

"I think I know that name, Chief Inspector. Let me double check and get back to you." The line went dead.

Twenty Five

"There's a man I meet, walks up our street. He's a worker for the council, has been twenty years. And he takes no lip of nobody."

- Deacon Blue

Before Joseph Hanlon and Allan Boyd made further enquiries about their 'Proclaimer,' Charlie Reid, 'Sherlock' felt inspired to take the super lengthy three minute drive toward North Leith and go check if any laundry had been left out to dry - just like the angry police sergeant felt that he had been.

In the UK the yellow-and-black variant of crime scene tape isn't used. Instead the police use a blue-and-white one, as well as a few other colours to signify different parts of a crime scene. Often red-and-white tape marks the inner cordon, to signify its importance to the crime.

This morning however, all tape of any description had gone from around the 'Pound of Fresh' launderette and the business was back up and running. Funnily enough, running was exactly what the enterprising female boss of the establishment wanted to do when she spotted the two officers entering the premises. *Video Killed the Radio Star* played in the background as they approached the faltering figure of Maggie Morrison.

"Found any HUGE body parts in the wash lately?" Boyd joked.

She looked a little guilty about something, as her face gradually flushed beetroot.

"It would appear that you took us for fools, Maggie." Joe Hanlon added. "And that's not good, not good at all. Have you got the cuffs, DC Boyd?"

243

A pair of black, rigid handcuffs were immediately produced by Detective Constable Allan Boyd.

"Whoa, whoa, whoa. Stop the bus a minute, lads." Maggie cried. "Whit's a' this aboot?" She quickly crossed her arms over her not inconsiderable breasts. "That's no happening. Am no goin' anywheur. Whit hiv a supposed tae hiv done?"

Both 'Sherlock' and his colleague nodded toward one another. Firstly to acknowledge that they'd both spotted the horse tattoo on the back of her hand and secondly, to see if their respective partner was any the wiser in understanding what exactly she'd just said to them!

"Any Duty-Free to declare in that custom made apron of yours?" Boyd asked. Once again feeling the need for levity. His companion and superior officer, Sergeant Joseph Hanlon, simply informed her that...

"We have video footage and photographic evidence of you receiving a substantial amount of money the other evening, Maggie. It looked like you had been well paid to turn a blind eye to the depositing of Kevin Smith's body parts and then to call us with some cock and bull story."

"Maybe not so much the bull part." Boyd winked, whilst opening the cuffs and preparing to shackle the woman's wrists. Though before he could do so, Mrs Morrison perched her weary and aged backside on the end of the customer bench that ran up one side of the interior. She held her head in her hands and genuine tears began to cascade down her cheeks.

The tall, skinny, detective sergeant immediately felt inclined to park himself alongside her.

"This is the part where you tell us the truth, Maggie. Otherwise we offer you a choice of bracelets and allow these premises to be locked up and remain closed for the foreseeable future."

The woman tried desperately to compose herself. As she spoke her voice had changed dramatically. The pantomime dame and star-studded comedian had become more sombre. Her tone was noticeably richer and more polite. There may even have been a little touch of Morningside in the lilt. Plus her interaction was far more cultured and affable.

"You gave your address to us as above these premises last time, Mrs Morrison," Sergeant Hanlon interrupted.

"Yet you never arrived here that evening from any nearby tenement building," Boyd added.

"So would you like to start off firstly by clearing that up for us?" Though it was mainly to satisfy Joe Hanlon's curiosity. It was yet another invaluable trait learned from his ageing mentor, Steven Murray.

"I've been here a number of years officers, and I've travelled a long, hard road to get to where I'm at now."

The gags and laughter had stopped. It was now an undeniably polite, upper-class, Scottish accent that addressed the detectives on this occasion.

"I believe you," Joe Hanlon voiced. He looked down toward her clasped hands and added... "We are now fully familiar with your branding also, Mrs M."

Maggie shrugged. "We all come from somewhere. And no matter where, we each experience trials and hardships. Some more than others, Sergeant Hanlon."

'Sherlock' pursed his lips and thought on his late wife.

"I can see from your face young man, that you have came through the other side of something. And I bet it wasn't easy. Was it?" She dared to ask.

Their eyes met and Joseph Hanlon saw a hard-working, honest woman. A female determined to succeed despite the difficult odds that she'd faced in life. The canny sergeant also recognised someone that worked daily in an area a few levels below her current standing in society. Her theatrical character was all an act.

"And the true story regarding our dead body and your stash of money is what?"

After a large satisfactory intake of breath, she began...

"Once upon a time there was a young lady of the night who wanted to better herself, Sergeant. She worked hard and she saved hard. Back in the day you could buy yourself out of your residency, if you could stump up a year's wage. I did just that with Kenny Dixon many years ago and true to his word, he let me go."

Boyd and Hanlon exchanged glances. That seemed like a promising start, so they looked to her to continue...

"I got my foot in the door here. Again I worked hard, saved and eventually secured it for myself."

"So you own it?" Boyd asked, by way of confirmation.

Morrison nodded and continued...

"However when 'Bunny' Reid took over a while back, things changed. He came around lots of the smaller, local businesses in the area, looking to assist us with our insurance policies and the challenges that we may face."

"Old style protection money?"

"Correct. It was old school, but with modern terms, conditions and extortionate rates. I had no option but to pay. The business is a good little earner, a goldmine in fact. One that has allowed me the financial security to live in Colinton village for the past fifteen years."

She playfully winked once again at 'Sherlock.'

"And the money?" He asked her. "That was you paying your weekly dues? Because it looked very much like you were receiving it. Then afterward you made sure not to let your hands stray too far from the cash deposit."

"No, you misunderstand entirely. Let me explain..."

"We'd be grateful, yet again," DC Boyd chirped in.

"Nowadays they don't want any paper trail. So no direct debits or bank transfers are allowed and they only pick up once a month and that cash uplift had occurred only the week before."

Both detectives were now confused.

"These were working girls that were desperately trying to get away from Reid's grip and control over their lives, I knew that part. They also knew that I paid, like most people around here, some form of protection money. They'd informed me that they'd hoped to do a specialised wash and that they wanted me to do the right thing. In return they had clubbed together to give me this month's protection money back. If only they knew exactly how much it actually was. Though to be fair they probably gave me back about a third of it."

"But you'd no idea what their washing consisted of?"

"None in the slightest, Constable Boyd."

"And they specifically said to you - *to do the right thing?*"

"Yep. That was their exact words."

"Because they knew you would," Hanlon confirmed. "In fact they were relying upon it. They needed you to get us involved. They knew that there would be drones operating at that time of night. That someone's camera would capture them. I bet they even persuaded a neighbour or two to focus specifically on your shop front. Reid would get entangled and he'd get hassle that he could do without. Deaths that all connected to him. My goodness, this had all been very well orchestrated."

The sergeant's rant was over.

Maggie Morrison decided to stand… "Are we finished here, officers? Or would you still like to use the cuffs?"

"We're finished, Maggie. Thank you for sharing that version of events with us this time. Why didn't you just tell us all that previously?"

"Because I didn't know if I could depend upon you. Afterward, I remembered your DI from years ago. He was trusted by the girls back then, though Dixon hated him. He was never able to pull a fast one over on him. He'd always try to avoid tangling with Steven Murray."

Both smiled at her accurate recollections of their boss.

"By the way, I knew you were never going to handcuff me, Sergeant. But it was a good bluff nonetheless."

Suddenly her accent changed dramatically. She smiled at them both and told them in no uncertain terms to...

"Get yer hairy ***** oot o' ma shoap, an bugger aff!"

It appeared that her and DCI Barbra Furlong would get along great. The two 'Chuckle Brothers' waved appreciatively toward Maggie Morrison and departed.

'Sherlock' could be heard singing as they made their way to uncover further the life and times of a forgotten 'Proclaimer.' Hanlon's song of choice, accompanied by his colleague on the 'Ah-hahs' was an absolute classic...

"I'm on my way from misery to happiness today. Ah-hah (ah-hah) ah-hah (ah-hah). I'm on my way from misery to happiness today. Ah-hah (ah-hah) ah-hah (ah-hah)."

Both men again creased into fits of laughter. There seemed no doubt after those particular shenanigans that Joe Hanlon was clearly Steven Murray's illegitimate love child.

With uncertainty surrounding exactly how many children DI Murray had sired, the man himself was to be currently found sitting in Edinburgh's Saughton Prison. He was oblivious to all ongoing parental issues.

No, his past hadn't yet caught up with him for the multitude of misdemeanours that he might be found guilty of over the years. But he'd in fact arrived early to meet up with the man that had done such a good job of counselling with him at the start of the year.

That was of course before Malcolm Pope found himself in prison due to aiding and abetting others. Pope had recently helped boost the morale in several wings of the prison, so was in the Governor's good books. Which strongly helped enable this visit to take place outwith the regular visiting hours.

As they discussed things, Malcolm Pope spoke about his overwhelming desire to be released. For the opportunity to be out and about amongst his peer group once again and his simple, yet overwhelming longing for FREEDOM.

Steven Murray pondered on those words. He looked at the bald headed man in front of him. He was certainly no William Wallace, but at the very least he possessed a brave and exceptionally forgiving heart, and today, his choice of words had an added inner-strength.

Murray had felt relieved at sharing and confiding his delusional dreams and spaced-out specifics with someone other than Barbra Furlong. He'd no real idea what could be gained by it, but he certainly hoped that involving another creative soul would reap benefits. His unlikely pairing with this particularly intelligent and agreeable individual had worked well previously, and the DI wasn't one for trusting easily. So having spent fifty minutes at the prison visiting with Malcolm Pope in person, Inspector Murray was hopeful of hearing back very soon from the highly privileged inmate.

The inspector had also been delighted to witness that his friend of old had regained his penchant for wearing brightly coloured socks. Today's nonconformist pair - had been starburst yellow in classic nylon!

Twenty Six

"My possessions will be gone, back to where they came from. Blame, no one is to blame, as natural as the rain that falls - Here comes the flood again."

- Katie Melua

In the offices of the Blood'n Gore Detective Agency, Simon Gore was concerned. The name, *'The Duchess,'* did indeed ring bells for him - worrying alarm bells.

The moniker had come up numerous times recently, especially when he and 'Kid' Curry were following the unscrupulous trail of DI Robert Nielsen. Through various contacts they had discovered that over the past few days, the corrupt and highly dangerous 'Rab' had been regularly asking after someone called *'The Duchess.'*

By all accounts his methods for getting information on the supposed woman were highly unorthodox. Threats, physical violence and intimidation seemed to be the norm. Gore had been able to track down at least two local newspaper adverts that referenced the supposed alias. Numerous flyers had also been posted across the city. Mainly in and around the Leith area of town.

Barbra and the others would need to act quickly if they wanted to find this individual before their psychopath of a bent colleague did, and sadly he was days ahead of them. The newspaper ad that Simon Gore found stated:

Are you a local working girl suffering from trauma? Have you been abused either mentally or physically? Then 'Reid' this because I can definitely help. Call 'The Duchess' direct on...

Gore had made the call two minutes earlier. The line though, went unanswered. His next was to DCI Furlong. Wasn't she just having the best of days? Not!

Brooks and Black meanwhile were getting nowhere with the background of Kieran Flood. He'd been a definite loner and had stayed in the same block of undesirable flats most of his life. Unless you'd been in trouble with the law, served time inside or were in absolute dire straits, you didn't get to live in one of the exclusive properties within his forgotten, rundown, 1960's complex. Oh how the other half lived.

The joys and the sheer sadness, Janice thought. For the past half hour she'd already regaled Sgt Black with her *crime and rehabilitation* theory. The man was noticeably dying on the vine and they were no further forward. They were currently carrying out the best of three for Rock; Paper; Scissors to see who got the honour of calling DCI Barbra Furlong with the news. Black lost.

That was when Janice kindly reminded her colleague that it was actually Hanlon and Allan Boyd that the chief inspector had told in no uncertain terms, 'not to contact her,' if they found nothing new on Reid. Duly noted, Ian Black put his mobile away and gave a magical smile of relief. Brooks shook her head and grinned.

In more recent times, 'Radical' Lizzie has seemed much less radical. As well as working diligently behind many scenes, she'd also been trying hard to hold it together emotionally. Over the past six months her feelings toward Andrew Curry had steadily grown, and over the past six weeks they had peaked. Where does she go from here? As a couple they hadn't even kissed.

But are they a couple? They hang out. They see each other every day. But was he really so unaware of her excitement and pleasure when she was around him? Did he continue to feel like it was just a pity thing after his shooting and his recuperation? Had he even thought about her in a similar way or reciprocated his own personal feelings toward her? That would have to be an overwhelming... No!

Currently beavering away below ground in her den of iniquity known as 'The Vault,' Lizzie was unofficially tracking someone down for DI Murray - of course it was unofficial. During this time she was monitoring the comings and goings at Bilton Lane. Whilst in the background her computers were running ongoing checks to raise any further 'red flags' as regards to Detective Inspector Robert Nielsen.

The woman presently displaying cosmic green hair with a straight fringe, certainly liked to keep herself busy. Today, if she surfaced, it would be impossible not to notice her. Her fashion choice for the past two days had been anything and everything tartan. Right now it was a hand-stitched three-piece suit, complete with waistcoat. Red being the main colour in the bold eye-catching plaid. Our Lizzie wasn't poor, and she wore shiny black Doc Martens to fully compliment the outfit.

By close of day, lots had been achieved and they were definitely closing in on culprit or culprits plural. Collectively they were drained and tired and tomorrow would prove to be even harder for them on many levels.

However in the Murray/Furlong/Curry household enquiries were always ongoing into some strange case or other. The Ten O' Clock News had just begun on TV when the inspector's mobile rang. He saw that the number came up as private. He hesitated briefly. Often he chose not to pick-up unsolicited calls. However on this occasion as he headed into the kitchen, he felt strongly prompted to answer it.

"Hello. Detective Inspector Steven Murray speaking. How can I help you?"

His tone was authoritative. Yet his gut was wary. That soon relaxed when the voice at the other end spoke...

"Hello, Inspector. It's Gordon Green. The governor at HMP Edinburgh."

"Where?" Murray quickly joked. Still not used to the jail's proper title.

"You do know it was never officially named Saughton Prison?" The man replied. "That that's just the area that it's located in. Or at least what it used to be called."

"I do," Murray apologised. "I was just being my usual facetious self. Do you have news for me, Governor?"

"Well it's not quite in keeping with our usual protocol to contact someone at this time of night, Inspector. But my interactions with you in recent times make me think that you're not really a protocol kind of guy. Would I be right, detective?"

"Whatever makes you think that, Mr Green?"

Murray's World Cup winning smile could be felt right all the way directly into the governor's office.

"Anyway, I thought you'd like to hear what Mr Pope had to say in person, Inspector, and as soon as…"

"Really?" Murray interrupted with feverish excitement. "You have him there? He's with you right now? Yes, sure, put the man on. You're a star by the way."

The next voice he heard was that of Malcolm Pope.

"Inspector, thank you for the visit earlier today. It was unexpected, but I enjoyed it nonetheless."

"Yep, I think I'm going to put you on a retainer, Doc."

"You do know I no longer have my license, right?"

"Maybe not, but you still have the knowledge, the wisdom and the insights and remedies I'd hoped for."

Pope laughed, hearing Murray's apparent desperation.

"You don't do too badly with each of those particular traits yourself, Inspector."

The compliment was noted. Then Murray asked…

"So my crazy dream sequence. Is it of any relevance or just the mixed-up paranoia of an overworked, long-in-the-tooth, police officer? Though, I'm guessing you've stumbled onto something or you wouldn't have been so keen to call me at this time of night. Am I correct?"

"Well firstly, I think I'll let you figure it out for yourself, Steven. However, let me repeat back to you as best I can recall some of your key moments. And remember the field of psychology stresses - Clear, concise prose."

"Okay. Go for it," DI Murray instantly encouraged.

He put down his phone and listened intently on speaker to Pope's scary, yet no doubt relevant feedback.

"Well you began with X-ray images biting one another and a body that had been bleached and rinsed."

Pope's voice was slow and deliberate, giving the man time to absorb exactly what he was saying. Gordon Green listened on with intrigue as the recently struck off therapist upped the pace and continued...

"A drill was left behind. The holes filled with cavity wall foam. Your mind ached and Lizzie wore a white tunic. There was a cap on Ziola's head. A set of scales left nearby to polish," he enthused. "Are you up to speed yet? Has the theme or penny dropped?"

Murray's eyes narrowed with concentration as Lizzie, 'Drew' and Furlong all listened with him in the kitchen.

"Here's a final selection," Pope continued. "Your DCI smiled at a local canal and by its roots was a decaying body. Females had been extracted after experiencing a brush with death. And you were driven around like a King with his crown, on an enamel coated wheelchair, chasing a masked corrupt cop - or as good as!" Pope finally let out a sigh of relief. "You spoke about wisdom earlier, Inspector, and that goes with everything that I've just said. So I'm assuming you now have the overall connection running through each of the cruel deaths?"

Lizzie, Barbra and Andrew Curry never uttered a sound. They had no idea what they had stumbled into, but each of them had gotten the link based solely on the last set of statements offered up. Gordon Green also had the detective on speakerphone, and he had recognised that the line had went completely silent.

"Has he gone?" The governor asked Pope.

Malcolm cautiously held up his hand. "Give him time."

A stuttering cackle came on the line. Faint but audible. The words rose phoenix like from the ashes. As they were spoken each one gave further clarity to the situation. The detective inspector felt like an amateur photographer of old, slowly processing his aged prints. Previously, Murray had been stuck in the darkroom. Now having listened to Malcolm Pope he was able to move forward and develop the pictures clearly.

The words came with an exaggerated sound of disappointment and defeat. Not something that Steven had grown accustomed to over the years. His trio of houseguests all witnessed how much of a blow this had been to the man. His body language oozed dejection. He saw this as a major error on his part. The clues, an abundance of them. Had been there for all to see. Now they began gradually and then rapidly, to roll off his tongue with a speedy, constant, disgust and disdain.

"X-ray. Biting. Bleached. Rinsed. Drill. Hole. Cavity. Ache. Tunic. Cap. Scales. Polish. Smile. Canal. Roots. Decay. Extracted. Brush. Crown. Enamel. Masked," and then for good measure, he even added… "WISDOM!"

The listening governor got the gist, but didn't fully appreciate how it tied in with the inspector's case.

"The BMW incident was that very night, Malcolm. So that hadn't been included in my troubled thoughts."

"And does it significantly align with everything else?"

"Yes. The body was thrown out onto Bridge Street."

Another bout of silence did the rounds. Before…

"I honestly wouldn't say troubled, Steven. I would say brilliant. Your subconscious was able to correlate all of those fascinating links, even if you personally hadn't quite gotten around to it. With that said, you came to me. So somewhere deep down you also knew or at least hoped, that there was a relevance, a connectivity."

"I think I was simply grasping at straws, Malcolm."

"Well, I don't believe that for a minute."

Steven Murray was angry with himself. "We've had a demon dentist in town all along."

Furlong, rubbing at her own painful, throbbing jawline was already on her mobile sharing the incredible news.

"It would certainly appear so," Pope exclaimed. "A dentist surrounded and supported by a host of willing villainous technicians, given the evidence, Inspector."

"Absolutely, Malcolm. Thank you so much for that," Murray said again appreciatively. "I need to go and check-up on some people and make further appointments, but I'll definitely visit again soon."

'Kid' Curry and Lizzie both cringed at his awful puns.

"Please do. And yes, I see what you did there." Pope laughed supportively. His unofficial client was hurting after all.

"Governor, that went well beyond what was required. I'm exceptionally grateful and it's been duly noted. Thank you. You may well have saved some lives there."

"You're more than welcome, Inspector. I'm glad I could help. Take care and sweet dreams from Saughton."

"Was that you being facetious?" Steven Murray asked with a lingering smile.

"No. In fact that was me attempting genuine sincerity," Gordon Green admitted bluntly.

Twenty Seven

"Boy, you were right. You said, 'only them good ones die young.' Never in my life did I look this good. Everyone - welcome to my funeral."

- Lukas Graham

Police officers pledge to serve the public good and to put their lives on the line daily. When they pass away, whether from circumstances in the line of duty or otherwise, their funerals should always reflect honour and respect for their service and dedication.

DI Murray and many others will have witnessed those sad, often extravagant events. Days where an entire city comes to a complete standstill, as a lengthy procession with a full police escort winds its way to the nearby cemetery. Such a funeral for a line of duty death would draw hundreds of uniformed officers from across the country. Their demonstration of unity and brotherhood would be a sight never to be forgotten.

Sadly, Detective Inspector Sandra Kerr didn't have one of those memorable occasions. Her grieving family had asked for a small, humble and relatively private affair. No fuss and no excess. Quick and efficient. Today, they had certainly gotten their wish. No more than two dozen or so people had made their way into the pews of the local crematorium in Kirkcaldy, Fife. The aged building with its flaming furnace was a short twelve minute drive from the Kerr family home in Lochgelly.

The intimate gathering consisted of parents and in-laws, three orphaned youngsters, some close family friends and a small smattering of work colleagues from her team. Murray knew she deserved so much more.

The midwife and nurse that had helped to successfully deliver her baby boy were also in attendance. They stood passively at the back. Each desperately trying to hold back their silent, muffled, heart-broken tears.

No minister, priest or humanist celebrant had been called upon to conduct the short service. No, in fact, accepting the family's invitation to host proceedings was none other than Steven Murray himself. Having previously served as a lay-minister (Bishop) in the Mormon church years earlier, the inspector was more than familiar with what was required.

Given the mixed group in attendance and the fact that neither Sandy nor her late husband had ever been churchgoers, Murray opted for a service that included an opening hymn, a brief prayer and no scripture references whatsoever. Instead, they'd begin with a few brief remarks from himself, then Andrew Curry would follow him and they'd finish off with a closing prayer offered up by her former partner, DC Boyd.

Allan Boyd had been extremely touched and honoured when the inspector had extended the invitation for him to do so the night before. The ex-soldier had told Steven Murray that the only prayers he'd previously offered up in his life were when he and his men were under fire during active service. However, in memory of his late colleague, Sandy, he would happily try his best. On hanging up the phone, Boyd instantly thought back a couple of years to when they were first introduced. It was safe to say that the then Detective Sergeant Sandra Kerr, wasn't initially taken by the cocky and seemingly arrogant Glaswegian. His only redeeming feature at that early stage was his ginger hair. And although it was a much lighter shade than hers, the two ginger-tops soon got on famously and over the past eighteen months they'd became the very best of friends.

In Edinburgh at that very moment a young working girl by the name of Sasha Kornsic, lay seriously injured in a hospital bed. She'd been badly assaulted around midnight on the night before. Paramedics had been called and she'd eventually been brought in at 1am.

Presently, medical staff could only glimpse patches of skin through the various bandages and dressings that had been applied to the female's badly beaten body.

This had either been a warning to keep her mouth shut or someone torturing her for information. Either way, her beautiful face remained untouched for obvious reasons. Though the attending doctor recognised that trauma was etched all over it.

Whoever attacked her, knew exactly what she did for a living. But did they know that she was one of Reid's escorts? Was that the reason that they knew better than to permanently mark or disfigure the woman's face?

Currently, every body movement resulted in a whimper and a tender wince. Despite the medication, Sasha was in real pain. Something awful had most certainly occurred, but it would take tests and time to be certain.

Police Scotland had been informed that the security cameras at the plant hire company were broken. It was outside their gates that she'd been discovered lying on the ground. So no footage to her brutal attack existed.

How convenient was that, Murray thought, when he'd been notified at five minutes to eight. Officers would visit the premises directly after the funeral. Though the inspector called Lizzie at 8am asking her to discreetly check out the yard for him when she returned after the service. It was yet another job to add to her ever growing list of favours. 'Discreetly' had been the only word that Barbra had heard as she deliberately turned over in bed out of earshot. She felt it wise to move, just in case there was ever to be any repercussions. No knowledge - no lies - no jail time, she smiled to herself.

In the very non state-of-the-art crematorium the opening hymn, *'Nearer My God to Thee'* had just finished and Steven Murray indicated to the small congregation to be seated. The short, portly figure of Graham Kerr, Sandy's father-in-law, stepped forward to the carved wooden pulpit and offered up some comforting words of prayer. The man was a Presbyterian stalwart and immaculately attired in a smart dark suit, long-sleeved white shirt, plain black tie and polished shoes.

During his remarks the inspector felt his pocket vibrate and he checked his phone. At long last it was Lauren Naulls. Her text read: *Been a silly girl. Help required. NOW.*

Hadn't she realised it was Sandy's funeral? What had she gotten herself involved in? She'd been off the radar for days. Surely she'd sent Lawrie the same message or something similar? It was Al that had been worried sick about her. Well at least she's surfaced, Murray thought. Though it would be at least a couple of hours before he could get to her personally. He sent a reply before the lengthy prayer was over. It said: *I'll send a car, ASAP.*

Straight after Graham Kerr's words invoking God's presence, Murray refocused quickly and spoke of the love, support and friendship that 'Sandy' had given to him and each of her fellow officers over the years. Telling them of how in the decade that they'd worked closely together, she'd been 'his rock.' Then another few humorous, yet poignant anecdotes led brilliantly into a further round of suitable testimonials about her character and her unbounded love for her family.

The inspector's well chosen remarks ended with a paragraph from DI Kerr's favourite poem. It was penned by a young, relatively unknown Scottish poet by the name of Cameron Ewing. Sandy had met the man at a literary book signing several years ago and she would often quote extracts of his work.

Today, Steven Murray chose the following lines to finish with as a fitting tribute to his friend…

"The angel of death is a spirit of nurture. She is the one all souls will trust to carry them to the good place. She will cocoon your soul until your heavenly metamorphosis is complete."

Drew had listened carefully to DI Murray's words. He'd always considered the man to be a gifted public speaker. The 'Kid' was always extremely impressed by him. How could he possibly follow that?

Firstly, he put both hands on his large outside wheels. He was determined not to be pushed anywhere today. This was something he had to do under his own steam.

"Afternoon, everyone." Drew announced and blushed. It was 11am. "Apologies. Good morning, everyone."

From there, he was like a duck to water. His DI had encouraged him to make it personal and speak from the heart. By the time he'd finished, smiles, tears and a thousand and one other emotions filled the room. He not only did himself proud, but Sandra Kerr would have been deeply touched by his moving tribute. He took delight in telling those present how she would often stop during their conversations and instantly thank individuals and colleagues that had shaped her career thus far. Wise people that had allowed her the opportunity to *'give voice, lend an ear and shine a light.'*

"Lucky me to have this great job that has never ever felt like a real job," she would often state.

Curry rounded off by reminding those present of an invaluable lesson that he'd learned from serving alongside this wonderful woman.

"She would alway tell me that the best way to pay tribute to others and to honour their legacy - was by the way that you continued to live your own life."

On hearing those remarks, several tear-stained hankies were again put to good use, and it took Andrew Curry a full second to regain his composure. He continued…

"As they grow up, Sandy would hope that Carly, Stephanie and Andrew are told about their mother being an honest, fun loving and diligent individual. A woman that always strived to do the right thing. One that set a good example. I know that their 'loving mum' certainly inspired me. She made me a better person by watching her actions on a daily basis. In turn, I hope that by leading my life in such a manner, I may also be able to honour our late inspector's outstanding legacy. Today, I may not be in a pub or have an actual drink in front of me ladies and gents, but I absolutely feel the proper thing to do right now is to raise a glass to the outstanding life and contribution of Sandra Kerr."

Curry gripped the side of his wheelchair firmly with his left palm, whilst raising his right hand high up toward the ceiling. It didn't take much persuasion after that. As he passionately cried out…

"To Sandy!"

The emotionally charged room all responded with similarly raised arms and imaginary glasses…

"Sandy!" they all happily proclaimed.

Curry never realised how physically draining public speaking could be as he immediately lost all power in his arms. Lizzie, noticing his dilemma, instantly appeared at his side and wheeled him back to the front pew. Drew nodded, grateful for her timely intervention.

Steven Murray stood to thank all those in attendance. He wanted to acknowledge all the family members and others that had helped to facilitate proceedings so far. He informed everyone that the final piece of music they'd hear as the body was lowered for committal, had indeed been chosen by Sandra herself, in her will.

As the draped coffin gradually made its way downward, the music's volume increased. This female would be smiling. Laughing down even on her family and friends as they listened. People already had anticipatory grins.

They came prepared to hear - 'Stayin' Alive' or 'Another One Bites the Dust.' But no, the sensitive, proud mother in Sandra Kerr took everyone by surprise and they listened to a beautiful tune entitled: *See You Again.*

As tears rolled down the cheeks of DI Murray, of her parents and her in-laws, from beyond the grave, Sandy ensured that people would be mindful that although loss was never easy, this song by Carrie Underwood expressed clearly that there was still always hope. All you need to do is believe that one day you'll be reunited with your loved ones once more. By this point Stephanie and Carly were ideally positioned either side of their *Uncle* Andrew's wheelchair, each holding a hand. No capes were required today, as their real, full-time, inspirational hero was laid to rest.

Outside in the car park as the group of police colleagues made their way back to their respective vehicles, the curious Janice Brooks, who'd only known DI Kerr for a short time asked innocently…

"I wonder if the term coffin comes from origins such as 'coughing?' I know that once the plagues and influenzas took so many, that a cough frequently signified the end. I wonder too if that is why 'fin,' as in the French for 'finish,' is part of the word?"

The others knew only one of them was qualified to answer that question. But 'Babbling' had more…

"Perhaps we need to end the word altogether and simply let the body pass back into nature without causing harm to trees or taking up tracts of land with the dead, with cut stones and engraving. It seems so bizarre to try to bring a sense of permanence, when what we are coming to terms with is the concept of change and renewal, of rebirth and passing on."

"Interesting ideology and thoughts, Constable Brooks. I can see why Inspector Murray rates you so highly," her DCI remarked.

"He does?" Brooks questioned, blushing profusely.

Barbra Furlong continued swiftly with her response…

"Coffin comes from the Old French word 'cofin', meaning a little basket, and in Middle English it could refer to a chest, casket or even a pie. A coffin at this point in 1700 was predominantly hexagonal with its traditional six sides tapered at the shoulders and feet."

As Brooks listened intently, the others shook their heads and smiled. They all knew this response was coming as soon as Janice Brooks asked the question.

"The shape was a cost-saving feature," Furlong went on. "Initially the bottom of the coffin was tapered in order to use less wood." For good measure the detective chief inspector threw in, "Casket was originally a euphemistic term adopted by funeral directors to speak more gently to the grieving family members of the deceased."

Hoping to lighten the mood, Glaswegian born, Allan Boyd decided to enter the fray. Joseph Hanlon tugged at his coat sleeves, unsuccessfully trying to hold him back. Murray smiled at Sherlock's feeble attempt to discourage his partner. At least on this occasion he wasn't attempting to do handstands toward suspects!

"Crows," Boyd said flippantly. "Crows have been documented as holding 'funerals' for many years."

His Police Scotland colleagues were taken aback. Where had this come from? More importantly where was he going with it?

"However," he continued. "Research suggests that they may not be mourning when they gather together."

The others now flummoxed by his random comments, although Sergeant Hanlon was confident it would end in some west-coast humour of sorts.

Boyd's grin grew extra wide. Like a fisherman's hands showing you the size of the one that got away.

"Evidence indicates that the birds may well be examining the body and the surrounding area for potential threats to the rest of the flock."

The others felt a punchline was due any minute now…

"So it's not a funeral," Boyd enlightened them. "In fact it's probably a full scale autopsy. We may even go so far as to call it a *murder* investigation!"

And there you have it. Hanlon winced. Others groaned and shook their heads whilst opening car doors. He had ultimately made them smile with his cheesy observation regarding a gathering of crows. Though his colleagues smiles broadened even further when Barbra Furlong, not to be outdone, politely offered up…

"You do know, Allan, that the term '*a murder of crows,*' reflects a time when 'group' names of animals were colourful and poetic names. Other fun examples were: an ostentation of peacocks, a parliament of owls, a knot of frogs and the crazy - a skulk of foxes!"

The detectives were all due back on shift for two o'clock and the jovial banter was to distract their collective minds from the solemn occasion and the loss of their dear friend. As Murray and Brooks departed, on their return journey, the inspector filled Janice in on the text he'd received at the start of the service.

"Police!" Barked a voice as the intercom was answered.

A warrant card had been thrust firmly against the camera and Lauren was relieved that the inspector had followed up on his word to send help. She immediately buzzed the officer upstairs to her luxury flat and undid chains, drew back bolts and swiftly opened the door.

Unfortunately the first thing Lauren Naulls heard was a loud aggressive cackle accompanied by a mighty flash of excruciating pain.

That's when the woman found herself flat on her back. Blood mixed with strawberry lip gloss had a surprisingly strange texture and the most unpleasant taste.

Bewildered and dizzied, she looked up at the man stood panting wildly above her. His hand still curled in the almighty fist that had struck her clean in the face moments earlier. Anger wasn't a good look. He spat and screamed at her whilst continually delivering a shiny, size nine boot to her unprotected midriff. The woman yelled in distress and instinctively assumed the fetal position. Even scrunched up, bringing her legs tightly toward her abdomen, the man continued to lash out with brutal, sickening kicks. One-Two-Three. She struggled to breathe. Four-Five. The pain was agonising. She'd definitely broken a rib or two. Then - he stopped.

"Wait, don't I know you?" He questioned.

Taken by complete surprise, he stood upright. He needed a moment to ponder on who she was. This woman that he'd been desperately seeking. The individual that had caused them all a great deal of time, stress and most importantly - money, was actually known to him. You could see in his fiery eyes that he was racking his brain, carefully searching his ageing, internal filofax for the answer and also wondering - Would it change what he was planning to do to her?

His pained opponent thought it best to play dumb and stay silent. Her hands continued to obscure her pretty face because she knew only too well where this man recognised her from. And she felt no need or desire to prompt him. At that precise moment in time, she was still keen to stay alive for a little while longer.

Nielsen's voice had been slow, rigid and hard. Though before offering up another abusive diatribe, he delivered a sixth, sadistic kick to the woman's stomach. That was then followed up with repeated powerful blows from his fists to her shoulder, neck and forehead.

He was angry and had a clear liking for this now. It dawned on him exactly where he knew her from and a perverse grin widened across his features. With that in mind, the sadist had decided that his last vicious strike should render his host fully unconscious.

Taking aim with his foot, he paused, while Naulls closed her eyes in anticipation. With the precise accuracy of a man that had done this often over the years, his final decisive follow-through did exactly that.

As Lauren lay lifeless, the desperately red-faced man carefully lifted her mobile from the kitchen worktop, held her fingerprint to the button and immediately sent off two messages. Buying himself a little more time.

The inspector and Brooks had driven at speed to arrive at Lauren's fancy flat in good time. On arrival his gut told him to firstly check the bin area outside.

"How many blue bins do you see, Constable Brooks?"

"I count seven, sir."

"Agreed," Murray nodded.

"Why?"

"There should be eight."

"I don't get it. What are you saying, sir?"

"I'm saying we need to get upstairs sharpish, Janice. That's what I'm saying."

Several buzzers were pushed and at least two 'couldn't care less' residents buzzed them entry without any verbal correspondence whatsoever. Their journey up to the penthouse took all of thirty seconds.

On their final approach toward the door they could see that it was clearly off the latch and slightly ajar. Murray nodded and Brooks immediately called for back-up as her risk-taking boss moved forward regardless. What he saw concerned him, but there was no body. So based on Kerr's funeral song… there was still hope.

Blood found on the laminate flooring, rug and settee certainly indicated a struggle. More likely a one-sided beating, Steven Murray quickly acknowledged.

Janice checked out each of the two bedrooms in awe at the designer labels spread throughout her open-plan surroundings. That was when she heard her inspector let out the most anguished roar. Thinking that he'd discovered the dead body of Lauren Naulls, DC Brooks ran determinedly back through to the kitchen area, only to find Steven Murray on his mobile.

The man was frantically throwing his head backwards and forwards, this way and that. He'd went to make a call to Al Lawrie and that's when he first realised that he hadn't actually sent the earlier text requesting that a car get out immediately to Lauren's apartment. Hence his alarmed scream.

The experienced police officer had been sure that he'd pushed send before standing up to speak at the funeral, but he obviously hadn't. After which he'd turned his phone off for the rest of the service and the 'pleading text for assistance' had just sat patiently waiting to be sent. Meanwhile his local colleagues remained blissfully unaware of any concerns that the inspector had for the safety of Lauren Naulls and ultimately no car was sent.

DI Murray blamed himself. He never accepted for one minute that perhaps the actual blame should lie fairly and squarely with the mentally challenged fiend that had set out to inflict pain and hurt on the homeowner - that particular thought was simply too gracious and never even entered into his mindset. He knew that his officers would've been there well before her attacker if he'd only sent the message, the vital cry for help. Just then, right on cue, the man's phone rang.

It was Al.

Twenty Eight

"Well, I'd left home just a week before and I'd never ever kissed a woman. But Lola smiled and took me by the hand. She said - Little boy, gonna make you a man."

- The Kinks

Al Lawrie was normally always in command. She was generally sure of herself. Nothing ever fazed her. In a crisis you'd want her by your side. Today however, during their call all Murray could hear was desperation, fear and alarm. She still hadn't heard from Lauren.

"Drop everything," she'd yelled at the inspector. "I need to see you at the Queen's residence as soon as."

No Mary Queen of Scots or Lord Darnley had ever attended this regal abode and as Janice and her self-appointed mentor made haste, it would be safe to say that they'd not be received by any Knights of the Realm on arrival. This enchanted Palace was where Murray and Al met for their late afternoon or moonlight trysts.

The Traveller's Inn had character. It was built in the late 1800's and from that day to this, it provided cheap and cheerful accommodation, food and drink. Located in nearby Penicuik, it came complete with rustic stone walls and a large cosy hearth. This was ideal as fire has a magnetic pull. Its hypnotic dance lures you in. It catches unsuspecting souls in its flame and makes them wish that they could dazzle and shine equally as brightly.

Lawrie had none of that welcoming vibrancy about her today as she sat by its fiery embers. The vast ribbons of flame were oblivious to her serious countenance as they offered warmth and safety, alongside the crackling sparks that jumped and flickered merrily.

As the officers arrived and sat around the low level coffee table opposite the award-winning news reporter, the journalist gazed curiously toward the female constable and then immediately at Steven Murray. Her look clearly stating; 'What's going on here? Who's this?'

"She's my partner, Al. Take it or leave it. And I'm guessing going by your earlier telephone manner, you'll take it. Because I reckon two heads will be much better than one today, no matter what you're about to tell us."

They let the air lie silent for all of three seconds before the Gazette's employee eventually broke cover…

"I've not heard from Lauren for over two days and I'm worried for her safety."

"Lauren Naulls?" Brooks felt the need to clarify.

Murray nodded.

"But 48 hours isn't that long. Officially that's not even long enough for us to get involved."

Lawrie gave the officer another critical look. Whilst Murray raised his hand before commenting softly…

"Janice, trust me. Ms Lawrie would never have asked us here if she didn't feel that Lauren was in genuine danger. This is between colleagues and close contacts. Do you understand what I'm saying, detective?"

"I do, sir. It's FAMILY, and I'm onboard, one hundred percent. Do you think we should let her know that…"

Detective Inspector Murray firmly held up his hand.

"The only thing that's required now, Janice, is to get this fine upstanding journalist to tell us the truth and not hold ANYTHING back. Isn't that right, Ashley?"

Lawrie's foot hadn't stopped tapping since the two officers arrived and she'd regularly glanced warily over her shoulder. A combination of adrenalin and real fear had clearly taken over and Steven Murray needed to make that work to their advantage.

"We need to hear it from you, Al." The inspector said.

An almighty intake of breath was taken and she began.

"Operating on the same cold, dirty, graffiti strewn streets was how she and I first met and eventually became close friends all those years ago, Steven."

"By operating on the streets?" Janice asked.

"We were prostitutes, Lawrie confirmed.

Steven Murray was taken aback and sat motionless at this point. He certainly hadn't been expecting that.

"Lauren was only sixteen when she started," Al continued. "We never spoke about our years on the game. They were hard times. It was a period that shaped and moulded not only us, but our futures."

Murray's focus remained on the stained tartan carpet.

"We lived together for three years," Ash continued. "We got to know each other extremely well and we fought and protected one another during those early years. However, and don't ask me how, we eventually emerged from our scruffy, bleak council flat and progressed to superior accommodation and to wealthy, often eccentric clients. Life became good. The money started to roll in and we began to make investments."

"Like the impressive loft apartment?" Murray guessed.

Now he knew where Naulls had gotten the money from. She'd told him that it was from her previous life as a hooker, but he'd always assumed that she'd been joking. Though a little part of him did always wonder. He shook his head in disbelief. He hadn't twigged, but the pieces were rapidly falling into place and he was now starting to put two and two together.

Ash Lawrie always had unfinished business. Her desire to write, coupled with her time on the streets, gave her the perfect CV and cover to be a fully fledged award winning investigative journalist. Without naming her, Al had done a piece on Lauren's life a couple of years previously. She'd even remembered Steven Murray commenting upon it. About how vivid and accurate the portrayal of that girl's time on the streets had been.

He'd been impressed. It was hard not to be by the sheer quality and intensity of Lawrie's writing. Of how often it could impact upon your own personal life. She had a gift. A way of resonating with her readership.

The moving article which never revealed Lauren's true identity, spoke in depth about how this vulnerable woman had left a single parent home at an early age, fell into the intimidating and frightening world of teenage prostitution, yet had eventually fought back to ultimately turn her life around for the better.

"These last few weeks, she'd confided in me. She'd told me that she'd taken on the biggest challenge of her life. It was to be her very own personal redemption. I tried to persuade her otherwise. I begged her to speak with you, Steven."

"Why? What do you mean? What had she gotten involved in? What constitutes a personal redemption?"

Tears began to fall from the hardened journalist's eyes.

"She didn't want to get you in trouble. She said she'd tried to give you clues because they had taken it to extremes. They'd gone too far, but that there was no turning back for her now, though that had never been her intention. She'd wanted closure. To give those individuals a taste of their own medicine. She…"

"She, she's the elusive Duchess," Murray interrupted.

Lawrie wiped the moisture from her face and looked him straight in the eye. Brooks turned to him in shock.

"Don't get the wrong idea," Ash cried. "She wasn't the killer. She never harmed anyone."

"Really?" Brooks couldn't help question that statement.

Lawrie gave her another intense, hostile glare.

"Janice has a point, because Lauren was the contact, yes? She got the working girls to trust and confide in her. Then she'd pass on their details for someone else to carry out the retribution, closure and justice part? Could you really have lived with that, Al?"

Lawrie immediately got the seriousness of the offence and offered up even more valuable information…

"When Lauren had went to place the ad, it was HER phone number that the girls were supposed to call. But the owner of the shop was intrigued by her words and began to speak to her more in-depth about it. She told her of her own personal abuse during childhood and of the mutual bond that they shared. She informed her about her professional qualifications and from there a daring and dangerous scheme was concocted. It quickly took shape, but by all accounts, the friendly newsagent immediately went way over the top and way beyond any of the boundaries that they'd initially agreed upon."

The two detectives were blown away by this revelation.

"Murder and killing hadn't been the plan," Lawrie continued. "Vengeance, retribution and reprisal, maybe. But no one, at no point, was supposed to die. The thing is the consensus of escorts and working girls were happy to go along with it. The vast majority were here illegally. They had nothing to lose. No status, no rights, no home or family here for the best part. They paid no taxes and weren't even known to anyone officially. So to escape from 'Bunny' Reid and set up elsewhere, plus give a painful parting gift to their worst client, their number one abuser - that would be so satisfying. And if the poor specimen of a man never survived his cruel, terrifying ordeal? They could live with that."

All three now shook their heads at that actual thought.

"I know, I know," Lawrie yelled. "Like I say, I tried to dissuade her. But she was determined - like a dog with a bone. When you asked me to make enquiries into 'Rab' Nielsen, it all came flooding back stronger than ever for us both. And she became even more determined."

"I wondered why you'd no memory of him." Murray stated. "I knew he'd have been on your radar from some point before. You were always good with names."

"Oh, he most definitely had been, Steven. He was one of our regular clients back in the day. Though I think he was still, Sergeant Nielsen back then?"

"That would sound about right," Murray agreed.

"Neither of us liked to meet him. He always got very physical. Though I never experienced it too often, because he always had a penchant for Lauren, or 'Lola' as he knew her back then.

Steven Murray's gaze fell back to the floor as he spoke.

"Lola! Lola you say, Al? She had that song playing when I visited with her recently."

Both pairs of female eyes stared at him quizzically.

One set asked… *Did DCI Furlong know about that visit?*

Whereas, Al Lawrie's questioned… *Without me?*

He knew that it would be seen as wholly inappropriate, yet the inspector couldn't help himself…

"Did you know that there's another layer to that classic hit? That the Lola in the song isn't an actual person?"

He was having a Barbra Furlong 'origin' moment. She was obviously rubbing off on him at home. The inspector wondered for a second if that had actually been meant as a subliminal clue to him? A desperate cry from Lauren for help? One that he'd sadly overlooked.

"The song supposedly represented the music business," he told them. "How it was all sexy and enticing, before getting you drunk on champagne and the promise to 'make you a man!' However that was all an illusion. In reality it was a devious powerbroker pulling strings, pushing you around and forcing you to your knees. Do what he says and he'll make you a star."

Al Lawrie, thankful for the respite added …

"It sounds like it was written all about the sex industry. Conniving individuals out for what they can get. Reeling you in with false promises galore, then sucking the heart and soul out of you. Whilst at the same time, regularly beating you to a pulp."

Murray couldn't disagree with that experienced review. Janice remained silent. The diligent DC had monitored her inspector's body language and she could see the change in his demeanour. A light bulb had switched on and Murray's normally placid, Bruce Banner persona was quickly transforming into his alter-ego, 'Hulk.' No alarmist green skin tone, no superhuman strength or furious rage, but a quiet anger and disappointment were clearly etched across his unhappy face.

"Aagh," he exclaimed. "It was her. The stupid woman. Why, oh why?" he screamed, before throwing his arms up in frustration. "I could've helped bring her closure and justice without any killings, without any deaths and without any innocent families being put through hell."

Though he also suspected that the so-called victim's families would be secretly grateful for how things had turned out. Those killed and brutally murdered hadn't been named by Police Scotland as upstanding members of their local communities. Because with the exception of Kevin Smith, they were NOT role-model citizens or loving guardian angels. In fact they were the so-called dregs of society that he and Brooks had spoken about previously. Or were they? What had they each gone through that allowed them to turn out that way? Who or what had shaped them? Had they been helped or hindered in their desire to progress in this mortal life? Those questions were for others to ask, to alter and to change, he'd instantly decided. Murray was once again happy to head for his familiar default setting of burying his head in the sand. Just like so many others had done in the past and would continue to do in the future.

The poignant eureka moment though, had only just impacted on DC Brooks…

"You mean she was the one that had taken on 'Bunny' Reid? No wonder none of his girls had turned up. Like we suspected, they weren't missing at all, were they?"

Both Lawrie and the inspector shook their heads. Steven Murray even threw in an occasional chin rub and a 'James Bond' eyebrow lift for good measure.

"They were never in danger," Janice continued. "It was all just a ruse, a clever deception to get the frightened women away from Reid without arousing suspicion?"

This time - Betty and Al both nodded affirmatively.

"I assume that they're still all safe and well and working regularly? That they no longer have to hand over the majority of their pay to anyone else?"

Ash Lawrie dropped her head to confirm as much.

"You knew this all along, Al?"

Steven Murray's voice was filled with hurt and regret. He'd felt badly letdown. A mutual trust that had taken them years to forge and continually nurture had been savagely broken. Murray knew there would be no way back for them from this. Though he understood the problematic and difficult position that Lauren's actions had placed Al in. And he wasn't sure that he wouldn't have done exactly the same thing. But he was also certain that no more updates could take place between them as a couple and that their relationship had peaked.

"The stubborn foolishness of her actions," Murray reiterated. "She'd chosen to take on and go toe to toe with the madman that ran the biggest 'escort' agency in Scotland." And that was his rant only just beginning...

"It operated throughout all of the Lothians. Though since Andrew Scott's death it incorporated the flourishing and highly profitable networks of Fife and Perthshire also. The areas, it turns out, that no one from Dundee was ever trying to steal. 'Bunny' had that all wrong. But so did we. Our Polish friend in the hospital bed wasn't put their by anyone trying to force her to come and work for them. Though nor was it Reid sending a warning. It was an interrogation. It was because she knew someone's identity," he concluded.

"Which meant Mr Reid no longer thought it was The Brothers Grimm from Tayside. He knew it was someone else entirely. Someone deliberately trying to crush his operation," Brooks said in genuine alarm.

"How come I feel like you're holding something back? What were you about to tell me earlier, Constable, before your inspector here stopped you? Did you think I hadn't noticed that?" Ash Lawrie asked candidly.

Neither individual knew where to look, but any hope they had of finding Naulls, aka 'the Duchess' alive, seemed to be extinguished when DI Murray added…

"You already know that he's Scotland's most ruthless and unforgiving crime boss, Al."

Lawrie's intense scowl did the heavy lifting… "And?"

"And right now our best guess is that he has Lauren."

They all knew that 'the Duchess' had concentrated on girls in and around Scotland's capital city. Mainly because Naulls was intent on enticing the girls away from James Baxter Reid. Her incentive being safety, improved working conditions, better pay and perks. Plus the genuine satisfaction of having your worst client given an appropriate leaving gift. That last one seemed to be the ultimate clincher in having her and many of the others sign up. Though in this elaborate web of murder, revenge and deceit, it seemed that 'Lola' was always destined to come out second best.

Over the past few weeks the private consultant had heard from a host of vulnerable clients with disturbing stories relating to their past. Those sessions had been mulled over free of charge, with a range of extensive treatments being decided upon. Each high-octane conclusion chosen, enabled those individual females to come to terms and gain closure on each of their past traumatic experiences.

As there appeared to be only one specialist in the city addressing the issue, word spread like wildfire. Within days 'the Duchess' soon had a waiting list just to get an appraisal. That was the initial meeting where the potential customer would open up and relate their own worst and most violent stories. After which, the mystery consultant worked in conjunction with each individual woman and together they'd resolve to create a winning solution to eradicate the existing problem.

Today before leaving the the 'royal residence,' Murray checked in with 'Radical' Lizzie.

"Any news on Sasha Kornsic," he inquired.

Lawrie and Brooks stared across the table at one another. Al offered up an opened-palm gesture with her hands. One which was universally understood to mean... *what's going on there?*

Janice quietly informed her of the late night incident that involved the brutal attack on the Polish woman.

"Based on everything that has transpired, I'd guess that she succumbed to her attackers and told them what they wanted to hear. Primarily who the interfering Duchess was. She'd been severely tortured by all accounts and people can only withstand so much."

"I'd no idea what the fallout from this was going to look like. Tell me honestly, Constable Brooks. Is Lauren going to get out of this with her life intact?"

"Steven Murray's exceptional at his job." Janice replied.

"And what does that mean?" Lawrie was confused.

Currently the man was getting an update from Lizzie...

"There definitely wasn't any footage shot on the CCTV outside the yard where Sasha was attacked..."

"Aargh..." Murray sighed. "So the owners were telling the truth after all?"

"Well, not quite, sir."

"What do you mean, Lizzie?" He asked. His curiosity aroused and piqued.

"Well, although the cameras hadn't captured anything. They certainly weren't broken like they told you. In fact, I would hazard an educated guess that they'd been deliberately switched off. Because ten minutes after the last emergency vehicle departed the scene, they started operating normally again. Strange that, eh?"

Inspector Murray abruptly hung up on his colleague with that question left hanging. Because unexpectedly a video message had suddenly arrived anonymously onto his phone. He quickly returned to the table where Janice and Al Lawrie were still deep in conversation. All three scrunched up close together to view it. The attachment was entitled: **Farewell from Rab!**

The females were intrigued, whilst the inspector was exceptionally wary. Nonetheless, he pushed play and the trio couldn't quite believe what they were witnessing. The clip lasted only a minute. At the end both females turned away in stunned horror. Steven Murray remained sceptical. Because he knew in that moment that they had all been backed into a corner with this damning evidence. Though at least they had their man... didn't they?

Twenty Nine

"I am your dentist and I enjoy the career that I picked. I am your dentist and I get off on the pain I inflict."

- Little Shop of Horrors

The premises were unforgivingly dark and set back a few feet from the street. Access was gained through an unmarked door on the left-hand side. You went down a few steps onto a black and white tiled floor. In turn that led to an aged wooden table facing the bar. This was definitely a pub for grown-ups and you were expected to drink like a grown-up in Glasgow. Keeping your voice low; avoiding eye contact with strangers and generally being circumspect and deferential to the staff.

The Admiral was unpretentious, yet louche and you could imagine a tense exchange unfolding there. Exactly like a flickering scene from an aged black and white gangster movie.

Twenty-four hours before Sandra Kerr's intimate funeral, it had been the neutral territory that DI Robert Nielsen had arranged to meet his female nemesis at.

The recently elusive man was all set to hand her over to 'Bunny' Reid and cash in. However the University educated brains behind all the recent deaths and by default, the 'missing' escorts, had a totally different itinerary scheduled altogether. Indeed, it was she that had reached out to the bold 'Rab.' Keen to add a novel twist and a finishing touch to her bold master plan.

"You know I'll be taking you back to Edinburgh and leaving you in the capable hands of Mr Reid," the voice of the disgraced inspector said. Tired, yet determined.

"I very much doubt that, Mr Nielsen. Because you would then lose so much more than the financially rewarding future that I'm actually here to offer you."

His eyes twitched. Sure enough, the mere mention of extra cash being put on the table instantly changed the avaricious Nielsen's demeanour and tone entirely. Had DCI Furlong been present, she would have kindly informed everyone of its origin - *The Latin verb avére meaning 'to crave' provides the groundwork for the word avaricious, and its definition as 'greedy or covetous.'*

"I'm listening," the man hastily added. With obvious excitement draped over every word he uttered. "But this is 'Bunny' Reid we're talking about and you don't cross the man. That is unless the reward is substantial enough and I'm no longer around to feel his wrath."

"Oh, those were my thoughts exactly. And I can assure you, Robert, that you won't be around at all. Because you'll be well and truly dead!"

The woman's endearing wink may have been lost on Nielsen in the darkened booth where they sat, but his gentle nod indicating for her to continue, spoke volumes. So she began to slowly reveal her proposal.

After ten minutes listening in silence, watching video clips and experiencing first hand the contents of the shiny case that sat at the lady's feet, 'Rab' Nielsen was desperate to speak. He was anxious to confirm a few of the finer details before signing off, figuratively speaking, on the lucrative and cleverly thought through deal.

He had witnessed photographs and movie footage of his wife and son. Both were safe and well and being held in a secret location. Although if Nielsen declined the more than generous offer, he'd also been told that they would be killed within the hour. Based on the number of individuals that the woman had already avenged in recent weeks, he knew exactly that she was more than capable of carrying out that particular threat.

The sweetener promised, part of which was already in her briefcase - was two hundred thousand pounds. With his career over and his thirty year pension up in smoke. Could this morally corrupt fugitive from justice, really refuse one last incredible pay day?

It was a no-brainer...

Polaroids of the money had been shown to the man, and the mercenary-minded individual would get to walk away with the ten grand in the case immediately. On his part however, there were a few conditions required to be signed off on. One of which required his death.

"So let me get this straight..."

The man's voice was a cry of defiance, not fear. It was crisp and sombre. He'd experienced much throughout his many years as a detective on the force, but this was by much more personal and highly dangerous. You simply don't go up against James Baxter Reid. Numerous individuals over the years had tried and they were no longer around to speak of their fate. But then again, if he and his family were already dead? Then that was an entirely different story altogether! That's where the need for further clarity and reassurance came in.

The female across the bench ordered another drink and calmly sat back as 'Rab' Nielsen spoke...

"Firstly, you want me to admit on camera to all of the killings? Explaining that I was angry and disillusioned that all those predators and child molesters were allowed to enjoy their freedom and walk the streets. That I was at my wits end and hated society and all that it stood for. Basically that I'd lost my marbles?"

"That's the gist of it," said the well mannered female.

"We then stage the death of my wife and child?"

A nod from his opposite number was offered up.

"Finally we fake a shot of me taking my own life and leave the camera running. Previous to all of this, I'll have contacted Murray to reveal my whereabouts?"

Another nod was given as well as vocal confirmation…

"Now you've taken that all onboard easily enough, Mr Nielsen. So after filming, I'll leave the money and within the hour your loved ones wife will join you. Bank the cash. Transfer it next day and enjoy your new life."

He certainly intended on taking the cash, but had no intention of taking a wife or child with him anywhere. A typed up statement confessing to each of the violent deaths was duly signed by the corrupt officer. It made no mention of the murder of his wife and son.

"There's no reason to specifically highlight that," his current paymaster said.

Dressed appropriately in black, the man offered the briefest of facial gestures. He guessed she was right. In the written statement it spoke of how the deranged officer could no longer sit back and see vulnerable women be abused any longer. He wanted justice, real justice. He hoped that people would understand and that others in power would sit up and take notice.

Next day when the actual scenes were being filmed, between takes the determined female covertly added a live bullet to the chamber of the gun since the desperate and greedy Robert Nielsen had last checked it. He'd made that a priority upon his arrival at the hotel on the outskirts of Edinburgh city centre. After which his mind was too full of secretive, secluded paradises that he could venture off to, to be worried about anything else at all. It was only as an afterthought that he even remembered others were meant to be in tow. So much for one big happy family! With the large, bulging suitcase full of cash also carefully scrutinised by Nielsen early on, the man was now keen to get the filming done, take the money and be on his way. His family's gruesome death scenes had already been recorded, he'd been told. However, not rechecking the gun had been an oversight. A simple schoolboy error.

A small insignificant click was followed up by the dentist instructing him to shoot the scene over again.

"The light wasn't good enough. You're in the shadows. I need you to do it one more time," she cried.

That second attempt was the raw, unedited and shocking footage that Brooks, Lawrie and Murray ultimately witnessed. The one where the man's head was blown clean off with live ammunition.

Ash Lawrie and Janice sat stunned. The consequences of these actions hadn't really sunk in yet.

Was it all over? Did that mean no more deaths? How would 'Bunny' Reid react to this killer outcome? And what part had Lauren Naulls played in it all? Could she be in hiding and now free to reappear?

Both women who had slumped down into their seats hoping that the last few minutes had simply been a bad dream, eventually looked up at the concerned and exceptionally unconvinced, detective inspector.

Please, Steven Murray thought. That Swedish born psychopathic cop was one of the biggest perpetrators of violence and abuse toward women that he knew. This whole thing was a massive fallacy and cover-up. To become an agent of corruption, empathy is a disadvantage and thus seen as a weakness. The part of us that loves, the part God wants and needs us to develop, is silenced for the acquisition of gold.

'Good riddance to bad news' was the bog standard quote that came most readily to the inspector's mind. Though going with a more elevated and educated train of thought, another little gem swirled around briefly seeking to compete for headspace... *The philosophy of money atomised society. Making cold indifference a survival advantage. Thus the most emotionally cold have the greatest advantage and the most corrupted hearts and souls are the winners. Corruption had became a sport and Robert Nielsen had indeed been a gold medal winning athlete...... but only briefly!*

The first words shared by the man before he read his confession and shared it on camera were…

"Yes, finally you got me, Steven. Did you really think I never knew about all your various failed attempts to secretly bring me down throughout the years? No matter. No need to feel blue about it now, but ultimately I think you've been had first. And that's all I've got to say on the matter. All the proof needed is here. I've signed it all willingly. It'll be legal and binding. Furlong will be happy and 'Bunny' Reid will be raging. So here goes." The man began a countdown… "3-2-1."

It was then that both females turned away and the fatal shot was fired. Now the fundamental question was being asked by Al Lawrie…

"So who helped him film that clip and then forward it on to you, Inspector? Isn't that some sort of crime right there?

Janice Brooks shook her head. Even in her short time in the force, she knew that the prosecutor will not be too bothered by little immaterial facts like that. It was probably one of the escorts that he'd blackmailed, coerced, encouraged or simply paid to assist him with all the other killings. So nothing untoward or even worth pursuing. Because they had the killer banged to rights, with half a dozen murders solved in seconds and no expensive costly trial into the bargain. This was a slam dunk and both she and Steven Murray knew it.

"Will Reid give up Lauren now that Nielsen's killed himself?" Lawrie asked with renewed enthusiasm, though clutching at hope-drenched straws.

Brooks looked puzzled. Was that a possibility?

"Let's go find out."

Murray announced this and invited Ash Lawrie to travel with them officially. Within seconds they were on their way to Portobello and Barbra Furlong had been updated by phone about all the latest developments.

As the inspector drove at speed, the words - '*No matter, no need to feel blue about it now, but ultimately I think you've been had first,*' kept repeating in Steven Murray's mind. What had Nielsen meant by them? He was having a go at him. He knew that he was teasing him somehow. But it just wouldn't fall into place. What was he missing?

In what seemed like no time at all, they'd driven through the gates to Reid's vast empire. Not that you'd know it by looking at the rundown yard filled with portakabins. But from his scrap metal dealership and breakers yard to his massage and tanning parlours, the man was worth a small fortune. Those vast official businesses excluded the illegal, unofficial side - his drug dealing, prostitution and trading in human trafficking.

So why even bother with Lauren Naulls? Well unfortunately in his game, respect was everything. He couldn't be seen to be weak. There was no way that someone could poach his girls, get them off the streets or set up elsewhere and there not be severe consequences and repercussions. No favours would be granted by Reid, Murray was certain of that. But he was also certain that the man would give them a frank, if not fully truthful update.

The three anxious figures stood nervously in the larger portakabin of the two main ones at the entrance. A burly, expressionless henchman had hastily gone to round up 'Mr Reid' as he had termed him. Steven Murray had used all his police protocol to ensure that the well dressed man tracked down his boss and told him that it was extremely urgent.

On his return the now breathless minder gestured by hand for each of them to take a seat.

"Well, well, well," the deep husky recognisable voice croaked. "It's Mary, Mungo and Midge. Alvin and his chipmunks or maybe you even go by the Three Stooges these days. What's it to be children? How can I help?"

Murray made a decision. One which surprised Brooks and Lawrie, though they both understood why and Al in particular was exceptionally grateful to him.

"Dismiss your man, 'Bunny.' You'll want to see this," Murray announced as he pulled out his mobile.

Reid considered the order. "Give us five minutes, Phil."

The bold, Philip, wasn't impressed at being dismissed. His unhappiness was plain for all to see and hear by the petty scowl and frumpy sounds emanating from below his flared nostrils.

The inspector displayed the graphic video of Nielsen losing at Russian roulette with a handgun. Reid never flinched. Though disappointment, regret or possibly sheer dismay were all written clearly across his face. Murray played it again and asked 'Bunny' to pay heed to his words more carefully, but the inspector knew that he was speaking to the converted. That James Baxter Reid was a master at taking things onboard, at hearing what wasn't actually said and so on and so forth. He didn't run the biggest drug cartel in the country without picking up a thing or two over the years.

Soon the DI explained to 'Bunny,' Lauren's specific role in everything and about how she wanted to get back at him personally. Steven thought complete honesty the best policy at this stage. Just to see if the Reidmeister had any form of compassion in him whatsoever, but he was stopped in his tracks...

"Slow down right there, Mr Murray," Reid smirked. "I know all about your pretty little 'Duchess' and her personal vendetta against me, and also about her quest to save the souls of many of my girls."

Murray, Brooks and Lawrie were taken aback by that.

"I've known for a while now in fact. You guys were so far off the pace." He paused. "Well with the notable exception of your bent colleague that is. He tracked her down. But that's not likely to help you any now, is it?"

"So you're not holding her somewhere?" Ash asked.

"Ah, my dear Miss Lawrie. For a diligent reporter like yourself, I wonder what your precise connection to all this might be exactly? Is there a lucrative or award-winning story here somewhere that I'm missing?"

"He wasn't saying 'been.' He was mumbling 'bin,'" Murray cried. It had suddenly all fallen into place. He had it. "No need to feel blue - I think you've bin had. Not been had. Then the little finger trick. His 3-2-1…"

"Ah, like the old 80's TV show, Mr Murray," Reid barked. "Ted Rogers and his faithful sidekick, Dusty Bin."

The inspector's knees almost gave way as he exclaimed.

"It was 'Rab' that went to her flat. It was Nielsen that had taken Lauren."

"This isn't good, is it?" Al asked quietly.

"Her blue bin was missing when we arrived at her apartment. Remember you asked me to check?" Brooks confirmed with him.

"I know, Janice. I knew because I realised that hers was the extra bin that we found George Matthew in at Bilton Lane. I had a horrible, suspicious feeling as things developed that Lauren was involved somehow."

"And now?" Al Lawrie asked with a quivering lip.

'Bunny' Reid shook his head confidently and certainly never gave any indication that he'd be seeking further proof on Nielsen's disappearance or supposed death. He was only concerned that no more girls would be going missing and that profits quickly returned to normal. Though who in the force would he replace DI Nielsen with? There's something to keep an eye out for.

Andrew Curry had been saved previously from Reid's clutches by some careful and private interventions from Steven Murray at the time. It has remained confidential between them and never spoken about these days at all.

"Call, Sergeant Hanlon," Murray instructed Brooks.

"You're old partner, Mr Murray. Good idea. Have him discover anything untoward or disturbing."

"Get him and Boyd to head over straightaway to Bilton Lane. We'll be heading there also, Janice."

"And they've to check out all the bins, sir?"

A hoarse cough was offered up. "I suspect just the blue ones, Detective Constable Brooks," Reid grinned.

Ashley Louise Lawrie was all for stepping forward and smacking the arrogant old gangster straight in the face.

Murray stepped in and whispered… "Not today, Al. Let's go."

Boyd and Joseph Hanlon had been first on the scene. Al Lawrie raced from the car, only to be stopped and grabbed intensely around the shoulders by Allan Boyd. Both he and 'Sherlock' shook their heads firmly. There was no way they would let her see her friend like this.

No one had stopped Janice Brooks, however, and the sound of her throwing up could be heard back at both squad cars. She thought she'd just witnessed a double take on George Matthew's body. By the time Steven Murray reached the blue bin, he felt he was as well prepared as he could be. But on reflection, nothing could quite prepare you to see an old flame, a lover, someone that you knew intimately, be sliced, diced and finally deposited in a refuse bin.

In that single moment the man knew that no real justice was going to be meted out in this case. Sure Nielsen had been killed, so that had been a small plus. But there'd be no actual justice for all those minors that he'd abused over the years and now someone else would simply take over his pornographic sites and set up the business anew.

The inspector ventured back to hug Al. The embrace was long and sincere. Both parties were hurting.

He turned and curtly told 'Sherlock' that he'd some outstanding business to attend to and for him to make sure that both Brooks and Al Lawrie got home safely.

Detective Sergeant Joseph Hanlon understood perfectly and nodded in the affirmative. He knew better than to ask any questions whatsoever. Steven Murray drove off at speed. His heart broken, his stomach churning and his mind as twisted and warped as ever.

He still had one last roll of his imaginary dice to roll, otherwise his 'black dog' was destined to be his companion for life. He had an idea. A continual gut feeling that Lauren Naulls was much cleverer than this. She was a woman that would have been prepared for this very outcome. So once again he acted on instinct.

He had somewhere to be and an itch to scratch. As a back-up, the inspector was keen to cross his fingers. But that really did mess with his driving ability, so declined.

Celebrations back at the station were on hold. It all seemed so surreal. Names were about to be rubbed from the board. The chief constable had called to confirm the rumours and vultures, otherwise known as the press corp, were busy forming on the steps in Leith.

Like DI Murray, Barbra Furlong knew it had all been staged. Though the blood spattered body of Robert Nielsen was real enough, and was already being recovered from the city centre Marriott hotel. Rab's hospitality card and room number had been deliberately displayed in the footage, so that Steven Murray knew exactly where to go. The killings had stopped and a long-term, corrupt cop would be blamed and found guilty. In theory everyone should be delighted. But vigilante style justice never seemed right and Police Scotland would now receive the full media spotlight. Who'd even want to look for answers elsewhere?

Thirty

"Today I saw an angel, she was smaller than I'd hoped for. I would have recognised her sooner had there been a shining light."

- Yvonne Lyon

At the time Murray couldn't help but wonder with the exception of 'Lola' being played, why Lauren had chosen to play a relatively obscure Stranglers album that evening as backing for their brief updating session?

Now he realised its full significance given her 'Duchess' credentials. Forensics hadn't arrived yet, so he showed his warrant card to the PC at the door and re-entered her loft apartment. He'd done so with the specific intention of searching her old vinyl music collection.

Sure enough, about midway through, a black raven appeared to deliberately wink at him. It was as if he'd been keeping watch. Standing guard until the inspector returned. As the grinning officer pulled out the inner sleeve which was festooned with the album's song lyrics. He spotted that a red pen had been used to position a beaming smiley face next to the song title: Duchess.

Lauren Naulls seemingly had every confidence that her 'sometime friend with benefits' would figure it all out. The Duchess name was obviously always meant as a clue. Enclosed alongside the actual vinyl itself was a sealed envelope. It contained a four page letter. A short essay intended to offer up more clues and revelations. It would surely make for some very interesting reading.

On the outside her scribbled penmanship read: *No matter what you think you know or what you can actually prove, Inspector. What I'm about to tell you is the truth…*

Inside her words continued: *Dear Steven, I'm sure that you have already had the lowdown from my dear friend, Ashley. She'll no doubt have been worried sick about me and in fairness, the fact that you're reading this letter says that she'd every right to be. Sadly, I guess I'm now dead and gone, and that I'll now become a small footnote within the bigger story. It's an intriguing tale. One that I will happily UPDATE you with. Seeing as you kindly kept me satisfied with regular updates throughout the past year.*

Lauren had even drawn a little mischievous smiley face directly after that remark. A comment that might well be hard to explain to Barbra Furlong when she eventually reads these findings. However given Murray's current thinking, apart from himself, this confessional will not make an appearance elsewhere. Neither with Ash Lawrie for any journalistic reasons or with DCI Furlong for police procedural reasons.

Most of the following will be brand new information to you, Steven. And if not, it will simply build upon what Ash has already told you. I hope you can forgive me or at least understand my initial good-hearted intentions. Anyway, here goes - It started off as a means to help other working girls break away and escape from their current circumstances. I figured that I was able to do it with help and support, so surely with the right environment, I could enable others to do the same and enjoy a fresh start. Though part of the deal I extended, included a previously unwanted client getting his comeuppance. Giving him or her a parting gift that they wouldn't forget. That part turned out to be a fatal mistake. I got in tow with the wrong partner, Steven. If only I'd used a different newsagent things could've been so different and you might well have been giving me yet another happy, enjoyable update?

As the inspector continued to read, his curiosity made him wonder if this had all been written as a first draft? Or had it been like a lump of clay ready to be created, adjusted and formed over several sessions? He suspected the latter and that there had already been several previous attempts discarded.

He had guessed that because this particular edit didn't appear to have one word scored out or gone through with ink. There had been no arrowed corrections, addendums or small forgotten, yet important words being shoehorned in a later stage. It was tidy, neat, clear, presentable and enlightening. It was also very important. He'd already figured out large parts of what had gone down, but the curious detective in him still had theories and unexplained events that he hoped she'd no doubt confirm and clarify for him along the way. He hadn't been there for her when she needed him most and Steven Murray would need to live with that. But not unlike his last major case involving radio and TV personality Colette Ford, Lauren Naulls was about to be his lifesaver and 'guardian angel' once again. She would always be a star in his eyes. She'd had the best of intentions in helping these girls, yet she'd paid the ultimate price. With a tear in his eye, the maverick inspector continued to catch up on her brief bio…

I was taken into care at age 10, literally weeks after being raped by my 21 year-old degenerate neighbour. He'd been left alone to babysit me. Over the years I never got to grips with the fact that such depravity could actually exist straight through the wall from you. He was a waste of space back then and hadn't changed over the years. It was easy to track him down, as he'd never moved. He was still in the same squalid flat and still delivering food for a living. I soon found others that confirmed to me that he'd molested them also. They had never reported him at the time either.

Well that at least solved the mystery of Kieran Flood, Murray thought. A longtime local miscreant and from the sound of things a sexual deviant, who was worthy of having P.O.W added to his name on the whiteboard.

After six years in the hellhole that was supposedly 'caring support' from the council, I escaped. No beating around the bush, Steven, I only survived through prostitution and meeting Ash Lawrie. I bet that part about Al's early life surprised you?

That quip certainly made the inspector smile and he found himself nodding in agreement with it.

She was nearly a decade older and much more experienced than me in all walks of life. But she was my kindred spirit and my sole lifeline. By that point I was no more than a schoolgirl hooker and a predatory thief. More recently, I told Heather Mathieson all about my first ever in-house 'punter' at sixteen years of age. At the time the man looked like a well-to-do solicitor, accountant or doctor. At the very least, a professional of sorts. How wrong I had been, Inspector. To my dismay the client turned out to be no more than a thug. That particular part of his make-up was disguised on a daily basis as he made a living from being a housing officer for the local council.

Our 'proclaimer,' Charles Alexander Reid, Murray realised. So two of the dead could be linked directly to individuals in Lauren's past life. This was possibly worse than he had first imagined for her. If she'd still been alive, he was pretty sure that she'd now be looking at a good few years in prison. Although with a sympathetic jury and a strong defence lawyer, she may well have been lucky. Though she still hadn't actually said who in fact killed her two historical abusers?

This council officer eventually blackmailed both of us into having sex with him. He had a tooth fetish - as in he liked to knock them from your mouth. That was how when I got talking to Mathieson, she quickly decided on the specific fate for each individual. Given that she had qualified as a dental surgeon, but gave it up after a few years, it just made sense. Like myself, she had long sought revenge, some form of appropriate justice meted out to her childhood aggressor. A man that had taken the innocence of both her and her younger sister, Maxine.

So how had George Matthew ended up in that bin? It had certainly been brutal, callous and very personal. At that moment that question and hundreds of others pulsated furiously throughout the detective inspector's troubled mind. Yet still no black dog, at that he smiled.

However this is where I have to plead with you, Steven. I swear that she told me that it was only supposed to be vicious, painful assaults. I still hadn't realised at that point that she was a fully accredited, seriously disturbed psychopath. And here, I thought you suffered from severe mood swings!

Murray shook his head that she could even joke about that whilst writing up her comments. Unbelievable.

I was in the BMW that night. The bold Charlie Reid had been lured to it by two younger escorts in the process of leaving 'Bunny' Reid. Once he'd been taken onboard at the pre-arranged pick-up point, drugs were quickly added to his alcoholic beverage and he immediately became drowsy. I think it would be fair to say that he was already 'out for the count' by the time that we arrived on Bridge Street. None of the rest of us had any idea what his fate was to be. We thought that the tablets he'd been slipped would leave him forgetful for a few days. But no, someone else had other ideas and they casually, yet effectively leaned across from the back seat and 'CRACK!' Snapped the man's neck. There had been no second thoughts, no hesitation at all - just a twist'n go. By then, the second last attack, I knew that I was in way over my head, Inspector. I can only apologise once again. I'm so sorry.

There was no proof though. Could Murray get one of the others in the car to verify Lauren's version of events? Possibly 'Chestnut' was in the vehicle? The tattoo certainly looked like hers. And was there any real point in asking her? They already had Nielsen on tape confessing to all the murders only seconds before blowing his own brains out. He hadn't been forced!

Steven Murray was delighted that the man was dead, but was disappointed that he'd 'bin' had with regards to Naulls. He now realised that the corrupt, crooked and often canny police officer had already killed 'Lola' earlier in the day. For that alone the inspector was glad that the man was no longer in the land of the living. But taking his own life? That never happened. He may have been a mercenary, but he was also a coward.

He would have jumped at the chance to escape, to make off into the sunset and live to fight another day. Someone had gotten to him and tied everything up in a pretty red bow. Would Crown Office go along with it? Would they be happy to accept that series of events and take the win? Six murders solved and the main suspect confessing on film. After which, he then took his own life. It would ultimately mean no expensive, drawn out court case. So a major result.

It certainly seemed like a no-brainer to the rest of his team. They were confident that no more investigations would be required into 'The Spit and Rinse Murders,' as they'd recently titled them. But then, what else might Murray find in this private four page dossier? Because he knew that the real culprits would be getting to walk away scot-free. Though he also knew that initially each of those individuals had been victims of atrocious abuse themselves. But wasn't that vigilante justice? And he could never be alright with that, or could he?

Kevin Smith was an innocent party altogether and that is where the 'Death Wish' paladin of people power strays way off-course. The detective continued to read.

Like I said earlier, the classified ad that I wanted to place caught the attention of the shopkeeper and we got talking. Having explained to me the traumatic events that led to her school closing and George Matthew's part in it all, we instantly made a pact to take things further. That turned out to be a bad combination - I wanted first and foremost to help the vulnerable girls. I wanted to bring down Reid's empire or to at least damage it substantially. The same way that his predecessor, Kenny Dixon, allowed his prestigious clients to damage both Ashley and myself back in the day. He offered no justice for his working girls, no real protection. Exactly like Mark Ziola, thirty years later, failed to protect the current crop of females. If anything, Ziola was worse. Because he actively threatened and took advantage of numerous girls that were supposed to have been in his care.

Thirty One

"Efficient, logical, effective and practical. Using all resources to the best of our ability. Changing, designing, adapting our mentalities. Improving our abilities for a better way of life."

- OMD

Everyone at the station was expecting a busy punctuation day. The t's and i's were needing crossed and dotted. You name it, reports these days required it. Barbra and the DI were tidying away their breakfast dishes at home and about to head out for Leith when the inspector's mobile sounded. Who was ringing him at 7.12am? The caller's ID instantly displayed on his screen.

"Steven," the friendly female voice greeted him.

"Good morning doctor. What do I owe the pleasure?"

"Well I know it will be of no real importance now, but I believe we've got a 95% accuracy match for the weapon that struck the man on the footpath at the canal." Her chirpy demeanour and optimism was strangely reassuring and very, very American.

"You mean, Kieran Flood?"

"That would be the very one," Danni Poll confirmed.

"And?" The man asked quietly. Ensuring that he was well out of range from DCI Furlong.

"It would appear to be a MDP-9.10. It's a unique fixing bolt used specifically in…"

"Prosthetics," Steven Murray quickly interrupted. "The point where the manmade limb is connected up to the real thing per chance?"

"You never cease to amaze me occasionally, Inspector."

"Is that so?" Murray remarked. "Well thank you for the sloppy, back-handed compliment. I think."

The man's mind was now in full flow lapping up this fresh, yet to him, unsurprising information.

"So he or she most likely detached their artificial limb," the Doc continued.

"And gave our Mr Flood several severe, hefty whacks," Murray proffered. "One of which proved fatal?"

"Absolutely correct in every way," Poll confirmed.

Murray whispered, "Thanks" and hung up.

Sandra Kerr's ashes had been scattered in recent days at one of her favourite parks. Her twin girls, Carly and Stephanie did it in the company of their 'unofficial,' Uncle Drew. Andrew Curry had draped a Superman cape over his wheelchair for the whole day. Meanwhile their baby brother was alongside them in his pram. He was being looked after by one very special 'Supergirl,' in the shape of 'Radical' Lizzie.

In contrast, back in Edinburgh two bodies lay in the city morgue at opposite ends of the thirty foot long 'accommodation block.' Robert Nielsen's cadaver was generally intact, only missing his face. Whilst Lauren Naulls' slim features and body parts were being gradually pieced together through the gracious patience and expertise of pathologists Poll and Andrew Gordon.

Events had calmed down dramatically in the last few days. Inside number two Belmont Crescent the lady of the house was happy that going forward, she would be known as Charlotte Murphy. It was only eight o'clock in the evening, but she was already dressed and ready for bed. In her pink pyjama style t-shirt and shorts she sat on the edge of her welcoming and no doubt comfy, king-sized mattress. Tonight she was grateful that she seemed to have a new lease of life.

The woman was also thankful that her problems of the past seemed to be behind her. Relieved and looking to settle down for the night, 'Charlie' had removed her watch and three rings. They'd been placed into her jewellery box on top of the five high chest of drawers. Next, the single parent removed a black scrunchy from her hair and threw it on top of a laundry basket. Finally, came the last stage of her regular nightly routine.

In recent times, technical innovations had combined to make this part much more comfortable and efficient than previous years gone by. It was the part that involved her routinely unclipping and removing her prosthetic limb and placing it by her bedside. However, tonight as she was about to remove it, the doorbell rang. The woman had been expecting it over the last few days. She nodded to herself as she looked outside and saw the now familiar sight of Detective Inspector Murray's vehicle. From her position above, she could only make out the top of two heads. That was until one of them stepped back and looked up. It was Steven Murray that gave her a slow knowing look. A look that said, *'I know everything.'* Charlotte nodded, waved and began to make her way downstairs.

Both Eric and Emily were stood on the landing waiting for their mother to answer the door. The woman hadn't even bothered to cover up. There was no point, she told herself. Let the truth come out. Her pyjama shorts would suffice and she'd happily embrace the consequences of her previous actions. It was time for her to literally step out from the shadows of the woman that she had been forced to become. The abused, downtrodden Charlene Lennon was no more.

"Charlene - Charlie," Murray corrected himself, as she opened the door to him and his colleague. He looked down briefly at the grey, gun metal limb protruding noticeably from her shorts and passed no comment.

Though he did raise his gaze to meet her eyes. She in turn, extended her palms out wide for the man's handcuffs to be instantly fastened securely around them. However, what happened next took the woman by complete surprise. For that was when Steven Murray moved cautiously toward her and clasped her outstretched hands in his. The man gently placed them back by her side and shifted away, thus allowing his female partner access to 'Charlotte Murphy.' The homeowner could only stand in amazement and shock.

An emotional reunion is often told in the sole connection of the eyes, in the sweet touch, in the strength of the long anticipated hug. For in that precious moment comes the sweet release, the relief, the chance for joy to take centre stage and to dance merrily off into the distance. And so it was, that a gaunt-faced woman gently raised her hands and softly placed her daughter's flowing hair behind her ears. Mary Murphy's long, slender fingers eventually came to rest on the pyjama clad shoulders of her only child.

Charlie's voice faltered into unintelligible croaks. She was stunned. It was her mum. Why would anyone do this for her? She then recalled Steven Murray's recently privately whispered words to her at the station. His words had been... *"We all deserve second chances."*

Wow! He had known all this time. Words failed her. Her ailing mother knew that the story of her own life, her original, yet wholly unremarkable book was almost at an end. The most optimistic of doctors had given Mary's cancer six months and that was eight weeks ago. The intervening lost years had not been kind to her.

Lizzie, undertaking one of her numerous discreet tasks for DI Murray had discovered Eric and Emily's grandmother living in a woman's refuge in West Lothian. For two decades, she had literally been a bus ride away from her own family and loved ones.

In the brief weeks that she had left, she could now be happily reconciled with her loving daughter and learn all about her two wonderful grandchildren. Having secured this legacy, it would give her great peace upon her eventual passing.

That evening, Steven Murray uttered one last profound line to the couple before he graciously walked away…

"Healing doesn't mean the damage never existed. It simply means that it no longer controls your life."

Mary Murphy continued to weep as two teenagers joined her in a group hug. At the same time their own mother lifted her head and offered an appreciative nod in the direction of the departing detective inspector. From the edge of his car he turned back one last time to witness the long overdue embrace exchanged generously between mother and daughter.

His current ethos reminded him of how ageing women were such an immense blessing to society. That nothing on this earth could beat the loving arms of a mother with the wisdom of experience and the temperance of time. He turned on his ignition, smiled at that golden nugget of a thought and drove off through the soft, flurry of snowflakes that had filtered down from above.

Next day the lawyers, prosecutors and officers involved in the investigation were still delirious at getting a result. Let's not forget, members of the general public would have their faith in Police Scotland restored momentarily as well. At least until the next major politically driven bump in the road came along, Furlong thought.

At this rate would there even be another case for Steven Murray to handle? Had he had enough? Was the bureaucracy too much for him? Agendas seemed to hide around every senior officer's door? His resignation letter was in his pocket. Was it the time to hand it in?

Barbra would still have Joseph Hanlon, Janice Brooks and Lizzie on the sidelines to offer superb support and back-up. Then there was Boyd, Harris and Sgt. Black safeguarding the rear. So there was really no need to worry about the strength within the team at all. It was in safe capable hands. Most were young and did things differently. They even spoke, thought and acted differently. Often way outside the box, especially given the aid and assistance of modern-day technology.

This time around, Murray definitely felt that the line had been crossed. Though with probable justification - because it was, after all, the so-called *head heid yin's* that wanted it put to bed swiftly and ideally with no extra expenditure or costs. It was to be a brilliant win/win!

Sure - Robert Nielsen was an official 'wrong un.' And yes, five out of the six brutal murders were of seemingly 'no good,' abusers. But Kevin Smith wasn't!

And that's the key. It's inevitable that with all forms of vigilante justice you'll always get an innocent victim caught up in the crossfire at some point along the way. Was that collateral damage really a price worth paying?

As an LDS bishop in what seemed like a previous life, Steven Murray on numerous occasions worked closely with people given second chances in life.

He'd witnessed up close and personal what powerful transformations could come about in many homes when they embraced a fresh start. He hoped that several key players in this recent deadly game could do just that.

For example, you had the handful of Reid girls that had helped hoist up Ziola. That had pinned down Doctor Lennon and that had happily drugged and dispatched Charles Reid from a moving BMW. They were in fairness, bit part players, but others not so much...

The deaths had in the main been carried out by females and all DI Murray was left with was unsubstantiated theories. It was to be their way of retribution, redress or even a reckoning. The Duchess was extremely careful in her notes not to identify who killed who, and the inspector was fully conscious of that as he'd read them. It made him wonder at the time if Lauren had known in advance that Robert Nielsen was earmarked to take the fall for everything?

He was confident that she did. It was maybe her idea?

However, 'Rab' had caught her off-guard sooner than expected. She had contacted Steven in a panic. So she'd certainly suspected that someone was out to get her. The inspector never ever shared her written pages, her dossier with anyone. It was now safely hidden away.

Regarding the actual death of each individual, Murray was intent on keeping his speculative conjecture to himself also. It would serve no good now. Though he did admit that, yes, sure, in a few month's time sitting around the dinner table with Brooks, Hanlon, Barbra and the others, his crazy unfounded theories may well be discussed at greater length and in finer detail, before eventually being dismissed and finally laid to rest.

Discussions that night may revolve around how:

Although far from innocent on so many counts...

Robert Nielsen - was definitely 'Not Guilty' of the murders that took place. He was a convenient 'fall guy' that was about to be charged on a range of child sex offences and human trafficking. No doubt the public would be delighted. He wasn't granted a second chance.

George Matthew - had been hacked to bits at Lauren's trendy penthouse apartment. Forensics had confirmed that to be the case. Steven Murray was now convinced that Lauren had lied to him in her letter and that she in fact had lured Matthew to the flat and cold-heartedly executed him. He wasn't given a second chance.

Charles Reid - by implication in Lauren's letter, had his neck broken by the mysterious dentist/turned newsagent. The inspector was convinced that was the deal that clinched it for Naulls to sign up to the crazy plan in the first place. That Richardson would kill Reid in exchange for Lauren taking out Matthew. The sick pedophile that ruined the lives of two young sisters. He wasn't granted a second chance.

Kevin Smith - drove around a corner and couldn't possibly avoid the body of Maxine Bennie as it lay unconscious on the road. 'Bunny' Reid's girls may have taken him for a 'spin,' but again Murray was convinced that it was the vindictive and nasty Heather who had sliced and diced the poor man. He deserved better.

Mark Ziola - was the chosen target for the escaping escorts to get back at, so half a dozen of them helped lift him onto the wall. Murray was certain it was the dentist's work. Her accuracy with the nail gun gave her away. Remember this was all playful speculation for brightening up a future dinner party. Though in Janice's book, for wearing those gaudy Hawaiian shirts alone - that man was never getting a second chance.

Kieran Flood - *'I have no idea who killed my child rapist,'* Lauren said in her dialogue. Another lie, Steven Murray reckoned. She definitely knew, but didn't want to get the individual in trouble. That was because the Duchess had recognised that the woman and her two children had suffered enough over the years. Maybe that was the conclusion that an emotional Steven Murray had reached also - because he'd given her a second chance.

Ian Lennon - no one had a good word to say about the man. Surely no matter how, when, where or by whom, it was just a relief for everybody in this man's circle of influence that he was gone? The twist or 'tryst' in this killing was that Eric Lennon was with 'Chestnut' earlier that day. He knew she'd be visiting with his father later.

Murray was convinced that all three were involved, and that Charlene and Kirsten Beale became close after the doctor's death. On the night she had an alibi. She was with Emily at a friend's house, but 'Chestnut' had been working out with Ian Lennon. Murray suspected that it was Eric that let in the harem required to hold his father down after he'd become intoxicated. And this was also the only murder that the inspector guessed hadn't been committed by a female!

Sick as it may seem, Steven Murray's speculation on this one was that it was his own son that did the drilling and killing. With Kirsten Beale (Chestnut) and others supporting with the cavity wall insulation. Eric had witnessed first-hand, his father's cruelty and abuse to his mother over the years. Possibly even witnessing the rape and molestation of his younger sister, who knows. There would definitely be a jealousy angle also - they had both slept with Kirsten after all. That had made this Murray's hardest decision of them all. He had anguished over it the most, but ultimately decided that - Eric had sneaked in, deserving of a second chance.

It was a disappointing case and investigation on so many levels. Too many unanswered questions and no proof, just educated guesses taken to fill in the blanks. Lauren Naulls certainly didn't deserve to die like that. She was a good woman. She'd triumphed and overcame some very serious adversity in her life.

On the other hand - Robert Nielsen - You're welcome!

Life was evolving. Another season, another changing of the guard. As night fell and a brief shower of rain descended upon East Lothian, a voice could be heard...

"Are you seriously thinking of packing this all in?"

Barbra's question threw Steven Murray entirely. She was stood naked at the bottom of the bed - smiling!

Epilogue:

"It's been a long December and there's reason to believe maybe this year will be better than the last."

\- Counting Crows

That weekend a busy workman had a touch of deja vu as he and a friend put up a new gate and did some much needed fence repairs on an old cottage in the back streets of Haddington over the past five hours.

The homeowner had watched them carefully from her empty bay window, but never once opened the door to express thanks to them. She was however, humbled by two random stranger's generosity of heart. In a rare day off, Detective Constable Allan Boyd and DS Hanlon had both wondered how the wily, Steven Murray had managed to sweet talk them into carrying out the work.

Elsewhere, hundreds of miles away in the south of England. A mother and son were about to embark upon a new life together. One were violence and verbal abuse played no part and the Nielsen name would ring no alarm bells. Sat between them was a well travelled briefcase. The ten thousand pounds it contained, would be a great help to them in getting settled.

It was that very same evening that April Walker met up with Sgt. Black outside one of the fancy restaurants that Janice had spoken to him about on their last drive into Musselburgh. To Ian Black his date looked great. She wore very little in the way of make-up, had chosen flat sensible shoes and was the fitting epitome of a down-to-earth, middle-aged woman. The seasoned officer loved the look. Especially her fleecy, olive green parka-like jacket.

The older couple stared with curiosity through the decorative smoked glass of Pablo's Bar and Grill. There they saw younger, much more affluent couples being wined and dined in their trendy modern outfits. They witnessed glasses being chinked and many private, cheery conversations and celebrations taking place.

April winked cheekily at her new beau, pulled up her hooded top and confidently moved toward Ian Black for a warm embrace. Clinging tightly, arm and arm, they duly departed and walked away at pace from the overly congested and no doubt overly priced establishment.

Ten minutes later on that chilly December evening the unlikely pairing were spotted once again. This time they were huddled close together on a nearby wooden bench sat along the Portobello coastline. They happily shared hearty laughter and awesome smiles. As well as an extra-large fish supper, complete with mushy peas!

"Well how was I supposed to know that the Assistant Chief Constable's sexy adventurous wife would be on Tinder?" Ian Black questioned with only the merest hint of mischief in his voice.

"And when he found out that you'd dated her, he placed you on the Bad Boy list? I think that's absolutely hysterical," April giggled.

"I think it's friggin' hypocritical myself. But I'm just glad to have brightened up your evening," he smiled.

They both chuckled and reached for another chip.

Next day an early call was made. When the receptionist answered, a voice said… "Hi, it's Barbra Furlong, I'd like to cancel my dentist appointment, please!"

Later that same morning in a busy, bustling east London street free from snow, a rundown empty shopfront had been revamped and given a recent makeover. The simple blue and white signage above the door read: Heather's Newsagents. In the window - an interesting classified ad had just been put up…

THE END

Dedicated to the memory of:
John Crerar Robertson

A devoted follower of
Detective Inspector Steven Murray
and a dear friend.
(6th April 1937 - 7th May 2023)

Other books in the DI Murray series:

In order…

The Winter Wind

Departing Footprints

Third Degree Burns

Forthcoming Vengeance

It's Five O'clock Somewhere

Six-Geese-A-Laying

Seven Deadly Inches

Intimate Secrets

And due early 2024… **Perfect Ten**

www.detectivestevemurray.co.uk

Twitter: @DI_Murraynovels

Instagram: detectivestevemurray

Printed in Great Britain
by Amazon

24243855R00179